Fishing for Trouble

A Cassidy Adventure Novel

by

Kelly Rysten

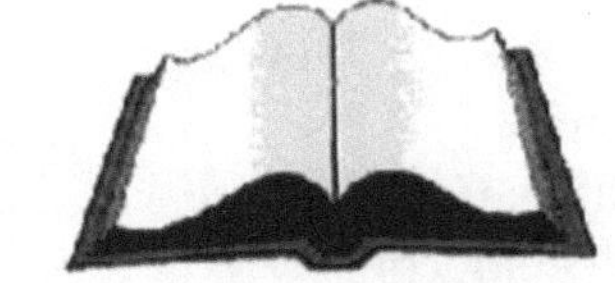

CCB Publishing
British Columbia, Canada

Fishing for Trouble: A Cassidy Adventure Novel

ISBN-13 978-1-77143-527-7
First Edition

Library and Archives Canada Cataloguing in Publication
Title: Fishing for trouble : a Cassidy adventure novel / by Kelly Rysten.
Names: Rysten, Kelly, 1960-, author.
Identifiers: Canadiana (print) 20220199531 | Canadiana (ebook) 2022019954X | ISBN 9781771435277 (softcover) | ISBN 9781771435284 (PDF)
Classification: LCC PS3618.Y78 F57 2022 | DDC 813/.6—dc23

Cover artwork credit: by Kelly Rysten: www.kellyrysten.com

Author photo on back cover by Erica Stephens Photography:
https://www.ericastephensphoto.com

This is a work of fiction. Names, places, and characters are a product of the author's imagination or are used fictitiously and are not to be considered as real. Resemblance to any events or persons, living or dead, past or present, is purely coincidental.

Extreme care has been taken by the author to ensure that all information presented in this book is accurate and up to date at the time of publishing. Neither the author nor the publisher can be held responsible for any errors or omissions. Additionally, neither is any liability assumed for damages resulting from the use of the information contained herein.

Publisher: CCB Publishing
British Columbia, Canada
www.ccbpublishing.com

Dedicated to those who need a safe dose of adventure and danger.

And to Gary, my love, who makes these books possible.

Other books by Kelly Rysten

Kelly Rysten is the author of the Cassidy Callahan Adventure Novels. Cassidy Callahan is a young woman who grew up on a quarter horse ranch. Given free run of the local hills she developed an eye for tracking, and with the help of Detective Rusty Michaels, she joined the local search and rescue team to track lost hikers. Unfortunately she is also a terrible trouble magnet, and her job brings her into contact with more trouble than the police can keep her out of. One adventure follows another as Cassidy tracks her way from one mishap to the next.

The books are:

Triple Trouble - Published 2009 – ISBN 978-1-926585-41-3

Car Trouble - Published 2010 – ISBN 978-1-926918-03-7

A Cache of Trouble - Published 2011 – ISBN 978-1-926918-87-7

A Double Dose of Trouble - Published 2012 – ISBN 978-1-77143-025-8

A Shot of Trouble - Published 2013 – ISBN 978-1-77143-107-1

Looking for Trouble - Published 2015 – ISBN 978-1-77143-249-8

Trouble in Hollywood - Published 2016 – ISBN 978-1-77143-294-8

A Little Trouble - Published 2017 – ISBN 978-1-77143-337-2

Trouble Grande - Published 2018 – ISBN 978-1-77143-366-2

Trouble's Last Call - Published 2020 – ISBN 978-1-77143-421-8

Kelly is also the author of two novels that incorporate the hobby of geocaching.

Geogirl - Published 2014 – ISBN 978-1-77143-150-7

On Beyond Paris - Published 2020 – ISBN 978-1-77143-435-5

Chapter 1

My phone rang and I picked it up. If you work Search and Rescue you always pick up.

"Hello?"

"Hey kid," Chase Downing said in his snake-in-the-grass voice. Was it sounding friendlier or was it just my imagination?

"Hi! What's up?"

"Did you find your man?"

"Of course I did."

"Atta girl. I've got a job for you."

"*You* do. You have a job for *me*?"

This sounded backwards, not that I had called on Chase many times. It's just that he's the more experienced tracker and he didn't need my help. Was Chase finally admitting his age was catching up to him? Nah, that couldn't be it.

"Yeah. You need help up there. Find someone to mentor and teach them to track."

Ha! I knew he wasn't slowing down. Chase just couldn't. He was a legend and legends don't slow down.

"Chase, it took me twenty years to learn how to track. I'm still learning. I can't train a tracker in a short period of time. It's impossible. Both of us grew up tracking because it's in our blood. It's not something you can just pick up any time you want to. You can either track well, or you can track lousy. Most people only learn to track lousy."

"I agree. That's why I want you to choose somebody you think has the right understanding for it."

"Those people are so rare. I doubt that another person like that lives in the area, and even if he does he probably doesn't know he has it."

"Strict, Schroeder, and I have been brainstorming. He's got three officers interested in trying."

"Do you think any of them have what it takes?"

"No, but they're some guys you want on your side. If they don't work out I'd like you to come down to Academy. I want you to teach tracking this term."

"Me? No. I mean, I don't mind teaching tracking. I can teach tracking. I just can't teach copping."

He laughed at me, "Copping? Don't you mean coping? If there's one thing you've always done it's cope."

"No, I mean copping. Chase, you and I both know I'll never be officer material. Just like they don't have the right kind of brain to track, I don't have the brain for being an officer. You should see me. The few times I've tried to stop a suspect I stand there, armed, and yell out, 'Police! Freeze! Stop and put your hands over your head!' and they either keep going or they laugh at me."

"I'm not asking you to make officers out of them. That's what the rest of Academy is for. I'm asking you to teach them how to follow tracks. You know it doesn't take much time to run through the tracking they do at academy. Three classes."

"Follow tracks? If I'm teaching tracking, I am not teaching people to follow tracks. I'm teaching them to read tracks. And there's one more thing. I haven't done urban tracking. Tracking Andario was the closest I've come to doing urban tracking. He was a high school kid who decided to walk off into the desert and disappear. Cops scoured the city looking for him. I studied the facts, found a missing piece of Andario's life, and questioned the businesses near his house. I lucked out and found a guy in a coffee shop who pointed me in the right direction. After that it was a typical search. I don't know much of anything about the urban part of it. I just followed my instincts, and it paid off."

"Sergeant Stafford and I will teach urban tracking. I'll let you off the hook on that one. You can *attend* the urban tracking classes. Maybe you will learn a thing or two. But I want you to come teach these cadets and keep an eye out for someone you can put to work in Joshua Hills."

"How long did you watch the cadets until you came up with me?"

"I have a feeling cadets will be more inclined to learn for you than they do for me. When I teach tracking I'm like a drill instructor. When you teach, you lead. Guys will follow you anywhere. You don't stand there and tell them to look; you show them how to look. You lead them to a new way of seeing things."

"That's what tracking is."

He paused a moment. "Maybe it is. I never thought of it like that."

"That's funny. I thought that was what made me odd. I didn't see things like normal people do. I thought it was why I could track and most people had trouble even learning how."

"Now, you see, you're even teaching me something about tracking. Can I count on you?"

"I'll call Strict."

"Schroeder."

"Okay, I'll go see Schroeder."

"Why can you call Strict but you have to go see Schroeder?"

"Because I can read Strict over the phone. I have to see Schroeder to know what he's really thinking."

"And why do you have to know what he's really thinking?"

"Because… he's Schroeder."

"Let me know what happens."

"Okay."

I hung up and thought about what Chase had said. He felt very strongly about this issue. I could tell, because he was on the phone for more than thirty seconds. I was the only professional tracker search and rescue had on hand in Joshua Hills district. All of the officers had been through basic tracking classes but basic tracking classes didn't cover much. Those that had reason to use tracking kept what they had learned. They could follow a basic trail. Those who didn't lost the ability, quickly becoming like most of society, able to see tracks on loose dirt but unable to really gain any knowledge from them. The district really needed another tracker. And they needed that tracker to be a trained officer. The fact that I made it through academy simply meant I jumped through all the hoops successfully. I knew the only reason they kept me on board was because I could do something the other officers had a hard time with. I could read the ground.

When I started tracking for Search and Rescue and the Joshua Hills Police Department I had every intention of making it my life. Then Rusty pulled a fast one on me and proposed. I didn't know what to think! I didn't know what to do. If I said yes I saddled him with a trouble magnet. If I said no both of us would have been miserable. So I became a wife. Since then I had become a mother. A mother! And the more trouble I ran into the more it affected my family. Katie was going to be two soon. She was going to start understanding and when understanding set in I was determined that I had to break the pattern I was in, and find a way to stay out of trouble. The only reason Rusty could deal with my kind of trouble was because it was his job, and even he had a hard time with it. Katie wasn't hardened. Katie was very malleable and I didn't want to see her hurt by the things that happened to me. Even if I had to lock myself in the house, I was going to prevent trouble from touching Katie. Maybe I *should* train up another tracker. But, who?

Chapter 2

I knocked on Schroeder's office door. I brought Katie and a bag of cookies as a peace offering. Schroeder opened the door, saw who was standing there and thought twice before stepping aside so I could enter.

"Chase sent me to see you," I said.

"Are you sure you want to do this?" he asked.

"I thought it over. I think you need more than one tracker to call on."

"I've got three guys who are ready to try. I've got to hand it to you, Cassidy. If the guys want to learn tracking bad enough to deal with the trouble you bring they must value what you can teach them."

"Maybe they are thinking of all the tax dollars they will save the county if they can get me off the force."

"I don't think so. Sit down."

He took Katie from me and walked over to his desk. He looked over at the bag of cookies and I slid it across the desk to him. He took one out and broke off a piece for Katie.

"The guys want to learn tracking because they know how many times we've wanted to call you but refused to involve you. I'd like you to take these three guys, sight unseen, for a week and see how much you can drill into them."

"No."

His eyebrows went up a notch.

"Tracking isn't something you can drill into somebody. That would be like taking them to an art gallery and then trying to make artists out of them. You could teach them how to mix colors, all the rules for sketching and perspective. You can give them all the right supplies. But you can't make them see the world like an artist does. You can't make a tracker out of a cop unless he can see the world like a tracker does."

"You taught your nephew how to track."

"No, I didn't. Patrick learned how to track on his own, just like I did, because he was born with a tracker's eye. He just has this wacky aunt who keeps having wild adventures and he's young enough to think that adventure is a good thing. He thinks that tracking will take him out into the mountains and he will get a chance to have adventure, too. He has a teacher at the ranch, a young Indian man. They go out tracking together. I haven't had much of a chance to teach Patrick, but he'll make a good tracker when he's old enough to be called upon."

"I still want you to take these three guys out and teach them what you can. Chase says that you can teach them more in a week than he could in a lifetime."

Sigh, "Okay, get with the guys and set up a time."

"How much time do you need?"

"Give me a few days to arrange babysitting. They would benefit from any daylight hours you can spare them. Who am I working with?"

"Kent Jacobsen, Reilly Tucker and Thez Brockman."

Thez Brockman? Oh, please no. "Thez isn't even an officer," I said.

"Thez is an experienced officer. He was a cop for a few years, tried his hand at firefighting. His interest in acting took him on a different tack, but law enforcement is in his blood. He went back to academy, not to earn his badge but to come up to speed technologically and physically. He's got experience on the streets. He's a good man."

"And he's scared to death of rattlesnakes and things that go bump in the night."

"Maybe he has a healthy respect for rattlesnakes."

"Jumping five feet straight up into the air and yelping like a kicked dog isn't a healthy respect. It's just plain fear."

"Have you met Reilly Tucker?"

"Young guy, first year, short, black, proud of his uniform, a little too fond of the siren?"

"Yeah."

"No, I haven't met him."

We both knew I'd met Jacobsen. It surprised me that he wanted to learn tracking. He was a good, all around police officer. If there was a poster cop it would be Jacobsen. Close cropped hair, cool sunglasses, flashy smile, tanned from being outside on the job a lot. He kept in shape. He wasn't afraid to be my senior officer. It took a real cop to be my senior officer. And occasionally it took a sharp man to figure out how to justify the crazy things I did when he wrote out his police reports. Being my senior officer was serious business. I wasn't sure he had the mindset for tracking, but I was sure he was willing and able to do what it took to try. On the other hand if Thez was his usual talkative self and Reilly was his usual overzealous self, maybe Jacobsen would help stabilize the group.

I walked over to Rusty's office. I knocked and peeked in through his little window, then entered the room.

"Rusty help. Schroeder wants me to teach some of the guys to track."

"I know. I think it's a good idea. We need a guy to track apprehensions and crime scenes."

"Yeah, the idea is a good one. I am just questioning the guys that got chosen for me to work with."

"Oh yeah? Who's that?"

"Kent Jacobsen, Reilly Tucker, and Thez Brockman."

His smile was not encouraging. He took Katie. She reached for his desk drawer and he opened it. Rusty kept Matchbox and Hot Wheel cars in there and he gave them to bored kids who had to sit in his office waiting for their parents to finish whatever business they were there for. Katie chose a toy car for each hand.

"Wha's dat?" she said holding up a car.

Rusty looked at it. "1976 Trans Am," he said.

She held up the other one, "Wha's dat?"

"Umm, 1968 Charger."

She held up the Trans Am, "Car!" she said.

"What does a car say?" Rusty asked her.

"Vroom, vroom," she said.

"Good girl! Cass, just put aside who these guys are and start from scratch."

"I saw that smile. You thought it was an odd choice, too."

"Give them a chance. You owe it to the guys. A week tracking with the officers in the desert sounds like something you will enjoy. Jump into it like I see you jump into everything else, with both feet."

"Fee-feet!" said Katie enthusiastically holding up a foot.

"I'll try. I'm just not sure where to start."

"Start anywhere you like. This is your ball game. You can call the shots."

"I don't want to go at this the way the other training classes are taught. I can't just stand in front of them and be an instructor. They all outrank me."

"Cass, they know you, even Reilly. He's heard the stories, so he knows what he's getting into. So what if your method is a little different? They know anything that involves you is going to be a little different."

I went back to Schroeder's office and knocked once more. He came to the door and opened it.

"Yes?"

"Do you mind if I call in some help?"

"What kind of help?"

"There's a couple of guys at my parent's ranch who are tracking pretty good. If my dad can spare them we'd be one on one. Chase has met these guys. If you're hesitant to say yes, talk to Chase."

In the morning I got another call from Chase.

"That was brilliant. A couple of guys. You didn't tell Schroeder that one of the guys is nine years old."

"Did you?"

"No."

"I thought we'd get further if we could work one on one."

I called my dad.

"Gordon's Quarter Horses," Martha answered automatically.

"Hi Martha! It's Cassidy."

"Cassidy! How are you dear?"

"I'm fine. I was wondering if I could talk to Dad."

"Oh dear. Are you sure everything is okay? You never ask for your dad unless you've met with some trouble."

"No trouble. I just have a question for him." I could hear her walking around looking for my dad. "Mister Gordon? Sir, it's Cassidy. She says she has a question for you."

"What did she do this time?" Dad asked.

"I don't know. She didn't say."

"Cassidy?" Dad said. "How are you?"

"I'm fine, Dad. How is everybody doing at the ranch?"

"Wyatt's got the flu. Other than that everybody's fine. I know you didn't call to pass the time of day. What can I do for you?"

"I was calling to see if you could part with Elan and Patrick for a week."

"I assume this has something to do with tracking?"

"I'm going to teach a class. There are going to be three officers in the class and I thought if Elan and Patrick could help me we'd be able to work one on one. Rusty really wants me to teach this class because if the police have more officers who can track they will be less inclined to call me."

I knew my dad would support any efforts to keep me out of trouble. I could feel the wheels turning in his head.

"The police department is not going to let a nine year old kid teach tracking to trained police officers."

"I already talked to Schroeder. Schroeder talked to Chase. Chase backed me up. Maybe they don't know Patrick is nine but they did like the fact that the officers would each have a teacher. Patrick does know more about it than they do."

"I'll talk to Jesse and Elan."

"Don't let Patrick overhear."

"I know."

Another advantage to having the three of us teach the class was that we now had sample tracks for a woman, a man, and a child. All of us were used to long hikes in the hills. At first Patrick thought I was crazy.

"I want you to hike around the back of this hill and then hike back over it. Don't hide your tracks, they aren't ready for that yet. Patrick, what do you do if you meet a rattlesnake?"

"Back off and stay at least half the snake's body length away from it."

"Is that the rule?"

"Yeah, I looked it up."

"How do you know how long it is?"

"I always just assume about six feet away is far enough. I picture a person laying down and stay that far away."

"How often do you see snakes?"

"Every day that I go out in the hills. I know what their tracks look like now. There's this one place they like to lay in the sun."

"Okay, one more rule about snakes. If you're working with Officer Brockman and he sees a snake. Don't make fun of his reaction."

Both of them snickered. They were hoping Thez met a snake so they could see it.

"A couple of times a day we are going to lay out a long trail and then you will help one of the officers figure it out. We'll switch off so you will always be working with a different man. We don't want to just teach them how to follow a trail. We want to teach them how to find it, how to look at it to see it clearly, how to read it. So you're not just following along saying, 'good job Mister Officer.' Help them see the nuances that tell you what the trail is saying. Mounds of dirt signify something to a tracker. Tell them what the mounds mean, how they indicate a direction of travel. Then after they understand it make them work to see those things for themselves. Give them time to figure it out and when they get stuck give them hints. Don't just read it for them. Help them see what you see. Any questions?"

"If I see a snake track can I follow it just in case Mister Brockman *does* get to see a snake?" Patrick asked.

"Rattlesnakes are dangerous. I expect you to make sure he doesn't get bit."

"But if he just gets scared that's okay?" he asked innocently.

"If you do it too many times he's going to be scared to follow your trails. If you see any animal tracks at all you might follow them a little just so they can study animal tracks, too. You're likely to run across coyote, rabbit, ground squirrel, mouse, lizard, and snake tracks. Take advantage of them but don't be vindictive."

When we gathered back at the Jeep after laying our first set of trails

Patrick was disappointed.

“I didn’t even see one snake. I looked in the rocks and everything and there wasn’t a snake to be found.”

“We have lots of trails to walk. You’ll find one eventually.”

“How often do we have to do this?”

“Twice a day for a week.”

“Then we have to walk it again when they track it?”

“Yup.”

“I’m going to get my exercise, that’s for sure.”

Chapter 3

We met at the police station in an empty meeting room. Schroeder was busy in another part of the station, but it was just as well. I was trying to sneak Patrick in without him noticing.

"Gentlemen, this class is going to be a little bit different from other training classes you've taken. There's going to be no barking of orders."

"Thank God that's past!" Thez said with an air of relief.

"You're going to think twice when you see your instructors."

"Instructors? I thought you were going to teach us," said Jacobsen.

"I will, but I wanted you to work one on one with a tracker so I imported a couple more."

I waved Elan and Patrick in and they entered the room.

"This is Elan. His family taught Chase Downing how to track. He's been working on my father's quarter horse ranch. He trains racehorses and work horses and teaches Patrick tracking. Patrick is my nephew. He seems to have picked up both my tracking and trouble tendencies. You'll find he knows more than he looks like he does.

"The only way to learn tracking is to do it. So we are going to go out to the desert and find some tracks. I happen to know where there are three trails we can use. For future classes I suggest wearing old clothes that you can move around in and get dirty in. When you progress to tougher trails you're going to be down on your hands and knees in the dirt.

"Now for formal introductions. Patrick, Elan, this is Officer Jacobsen, Officer Tucker and Officer Brockman. And I am Cassidy, or if you want to be technical, Reserve Deputy Cassidy Michaels. But I suggest just calling me Cassidy."

"Do they have to call me Mister Marshal?" Patrick asked.

"I don't think you'd like that. Let's load up."

I quickly realized we wouldn't fit into my Jeep, so Jacobsen was issued a Suburban for our trip out to the hills.

"Where to?" he asked.

"A hill in the desert. Want me to drive?"

He parted with the keys reluctantly. Patrick was excited because he got to ride in a real Sheriff's truck.

"Why is the seat so hard?" Pat asked.

"So prisoners can't tear it up," Jacobsen answered. "They don't like getting hauled in. They get destructive at times."

"Why is there a metal grate between the front and back?"

"Because prisoners get mean, too. It's to protect the officers up front from the prisoners in back."

"Am I a prisoner?"

"Of course not. How old are you Patrick?" Jacobsen asked.

"Nine."

"And you can track?"

"Yeah, Elan and I track each other almost every day."

"How much experience do you have?"

"About three years more than you."

"Kent," I reminded him, "you met Patrick for the first time back when he was six. He was tracking a little then. I had promised him I would take him stalking deer when he could sneak up on a wild rabbit and touch it. He did that when he was six. I was laid up and had to stay close to home so he came down here and we stalked deer in my back yard. I think you were one of the officers who responded to a 911 call to my neighbor's house? Patrick had tracked a man from my house to my neighbor's house and called 911 because he thought the guy was after me."

"Can I take Katie stalking the deer?" Patrick asked.

"She'll just scare them away."

"Not if I carry her. I can stalk with her riding piggy back."

"If you can carry her piggy back, you can try it."

"I feel like I'm going on a family outing," said Thez.

I pulled off the pavement and headed down a dirt road.

"Cassidy, are you sure you don't want me to drive?" Jacobsen asked.

"This thing has four wheel drive," I said.

"Yes, but…"

"This part is what I do best."

"That's what I was afraid of."

"Don't worry, Officer Jacobsen," Patrick said. "We already drove out here once. It's not so bad compared to some other roads Aunt Cassidy goes on."

"That makes me feel *so* much better," said Thez.

"Get used to it," I told them. "You signed up for a week of this."

"Why do we have to go way out here when we all have dirt in our own backyards?" Jacobsen asked.

"I guess we could use my backyard," I observed. "I just think this is more fun."

Fifteen miles of desert dirt and arroyos and I pulled up to the spot we had started at earlier in the day. The men all looked at the tracks in dismay.

"They all look alike!" Thez lamented.

Golly, I hadn't even thought about what shoes we'd been wearing. Sure enough, we were all in tracking mode, so we all wore moccasins.

"Rule number one," I told them. "Don't cover the tracks. If you step on tracks, you erase them. If you are tracking and you see tracks, any tracks at all, avoid them. You need to be able to see your clues. The tracks of people other than your missing person can still tell you something. Secondly," I fibbed, "this is part of the lesson. It's up to you to figure out which set is which. Think. What differentiates a track made by a man or a woman? How do you tell a kid's footprint from a woman's footprint? Look carefully and then decide."

I looked. I know. I should have looked a long time ago. It should have come naturally, but when I did look…golly. Patrick and I wore almost the same size shoe! I looked…and I looked some more. Our mannerisms revealed the difference.

"Don't worry," I told the guys. "The tracks take totally different routes to the same place. You won't have to distinguish them as you go. This is the easy stuff. We'll get to the hard stuff in a few days."

Jacobsen looked at the tracks with a critical eye. He was calculating.

Tucker was looking at the tracks and shaking his head, "Damn!" he said. "If I didn't know better I'd say the same person made all three trails."

I gave them a hint. "Which track was made by the heaviest person? The heavier the person the deeper their tracks will be. Look at the width across the ball of the foot. A man's track should be a little wider."

Elan was about thirty pounds heavier than me, Patrick about thirty pounds lighter. Hmmm, this was tough. Thirty pounds was a very small amount to distinguish when it came to tracks. I usually went by the width of the tracks to determine whether a man or woman made a track.

"Choose a set of tracks and follow them back to the truck. If you have questions just ask. This class isn't to teach you to follow a trail; it's to teach you how to read a trail. There's a huge difference between reading a trail and following it. When you read a trail you build a history and a profile as you go. The difference won't be clear at first but as you gain experience you will read more and more into the tracks. To learn how to read tracks you need to think about the reason for each movement that went into making the tracks. So…Reilly, pick a trail."

His white teeth gleamed as he thought about his choices. "I want to track the kid. I think this kid's going to give me a good workout."

"Thez?"

"I'll track Elan. I've never tracked a real Indian before. Did you know I played an Indian on stage once? I didn't make a very good one. I'm too outgoing to play an Indian."

"There are outgoing Indians, too," Elan said.

"I haven't met many Indians," Thez admitted.

Jacobsen looked at me. "Guess I'll track you," he said.

Reilly said, "Okay, so which trail is really which?"

"You chose Patrick's trail. So…find it. Think. Patrick is the smallest and lightest. He's going to have a shorter stride. He tends to come down on his heel a little harder than the rest of us."

"I do?" said Patrick.

"You do."

Patrick looked at the three sets of tracks.

"Huh! I guess I do!"

Reilly said to Patrick, "You mean you can tell which tracks have a deeper heel print than the others?"

"Sure."

"Dang!"

"You'll find that tracking requires a different view of things. You have to train yourself to notice very subtle signs. Things you would pass over normally might be a vital clue. The depth of a track is not measured in inches or centimeters, and it changes with every soil type. Okay, let's get down to business. Find your trails. As you go, figure out what tools will help you. Use your hand to measure the width or length of tracks. You might want a measuring tape for measuring stride until you develop a feel for it. In the mean time you can measure the stride by comparing it to your own. Reilly, you wanted to track Patrick. Compare your stride to the tracks on the ground. That'll show you Patrick's trail."

"It's just a guess," said Jacobsen, "but I think this one's yours."

"What makes you say that?"

"I can't really say."

"I bet if you describe your thinking it'll all make sense to me. I know you guys aren't used to sharing your thoughts but you're going to have to occasionally in these exercises. I think you will find intuition pays off, you just need to voice it so I know it's paying off."

"I don't mind telling my thoughts," said Thez. I knew that all too well.

"Okay, Thez, did you choose which set of tracks was Elan's?"

"I did."

"And what makes you think they are Elan's?"

"The tracks remind me of Mingo."

"Mingo?"

Elan scoffed. "A TV show Indian," he said.

"Elan, TV show Indians are the only picture of Indians that many white men have seen. You have to admit he picked the right trail. What makes you think the tracks look like Mingo's, Thez?"

"They look… purposeful."

"What do you mean by that?"

"They look like he was thinking about each step as he made it. They are all even. There is a full imprint of each one. Well, so far."

I looked at Elan and Elan looked at me. He shrugged. Guess he wasn't going to argue with that.

"Jacobsen? You see what we're driving at here?"

"Uh…yeah, these tracks just feel familiar."

"Okay, that's a valid clue. That's one way I have of ruling out the officers from the missing person when I go out on a search. Familiarity is very useful in tracking. You can't trust it one hundred percent, but you will generally know when it is okay to rely on it and when you should look for something more solid. Okay, everybody's got their trail? Get to work. Ask lots of questions. Patrick, Elan, I want you to ask lots of questions, too. We'll meet back here as soon as we can. All the trails are about the same length unless a certain young man went on a long search for rattlesnakes on the way."

"Rattlesnakes?" said Thez and Reilly simultaneously.

"I didn't find one," Patrick said dejectedly.

"Whew!" said Thez.

"This is an easy trail. You should be able to track it in time for lunch. Let's go."

The three officers stood over their respective trails and proceeded step by slow step, from track to track. Gradually they began fanning out as the three trails separated.

"You made this easy," Jacobsen commented.

"It'll get harder."

"I expected it to be hard from the beginning. You had to really think to lay this trail. One reason I wanted to take this class was so I could learn to track you. When you get in trouble we can't wait for Chase to drive up from San Diego, though you're one of the few people he'd make the trip for."

"People think Chase is so rough and hard to read. I don't find him that way at all. He might look rough but he's a big old softy."

"That's because he's got a soft spot for you. I bet you say that about a lot of the guys."

By *the guys* he meant the officers at the station, firemen I had worked with… all those guys that needed a tough front to do their jobs properly. It was true; once I got to know them their tough exterior melted away and I found out that they liked playing merry go round with Katie in the exercise room at the station. They talked baby talk to Katie and they searched out bowls of cookies whenever they saw me at the station.

"That's true," I admitted. "But even when you guys are out there doing something because it touches your heart, your tracks read like tough guys. Maybe more so. I think, if you were to go out on a search, you'd find my tracks read the same."

He reached a section of trail where I zigzagged several times so I began asking him questions concerning the trail.

"What made you decide to go that direction?"

"I could see the next track."

"Assume there isn't a next track. Go back. Look at the track before the turn. Examine that one track and decide which direction to look just based on that one track. Talk to me as things come to you."

He squatted beside the track and looked at it carefully.

"Just this one track?"

"Dissect it. Imagine it being made. Picture what a body does to turn. Then translate that to the track before you."

"If the track was going to go forward the weight would be square on the ball of the foot."

"But it turns and there's a way you can tell which direction it is turning. The pressure pushes a mound of dirt and the direction of motion is directly opposite it."

"So this… right here. That's not much to go on."

"This is about as obvious as it gets. See the slight rise in the soil on the outside of the track? The rise is to the left so look to the right for the next track."

"You read all that into one footprint?"

"Yeah. I told you, I'm teaching you to read. Reading is a track by track activity. Sometimes you can revert to following tracks but when the going gets tough you have to take time to read and read carefully. What would you do if you only had one quarter of that track and nothing after that? You have to stop and read. Analyze the little bit you can see."

When the trail turned the other way I told him, "This time look at the track and imagine the motion that went into making it. You can use the track to formulate a motion and you can imagine a motion to form a track. Both are useful. If you can picture what made the part of the track you can see, you can imagine where the rest of the track is. If you can imagine it, sometimes it shows up just a bit more."

"Have you ever failed to find the person you were looking for?" he asked me.

"Of course, but not since it mattered. The times I lost the person I was tracking was when I was just practicing. Either I had to stop because I ran out of time, or I was young and the tracks got all mixed up with other tracks. I've found everybody Strict has sent me out to find. Twice I got there too late."

"You've had some rough ones."

"Yeah, well, I don't track because it's easy. Actually I enjoy it more when it's a challenge, but I prefer the challenging ones to be the less serious ones. Does that make sense?"

"Of course."

"It's very frustrating when you know someone needs to be found quickly and suddenly you're faced with a huge rocky area that yields no clues. We'll study that, too."

"You really think we'll get that far?"

"You'll go where I take you. You'll try everything. You aren't asking many questions."

"I'm finding it pays to listen."

The trail dropped down into an arroyo. Jacobsen looked at it with dismay because I had walked up and down the arroyo six times. It looked like a group of people had passed through there. The sand was loose so no one set was very clear. He was just about to jump off the edge into the arroyo when I stopped him.

"Not there!" I warned him. "Take a good three or four steps away from the known tracks before you jump in. You don't want to scatter sand into already hard to read tracks. If the tracks look like they will head up the arroyo then walk down to get away from them. If they look like they will head down the arroyo then walk up the arroyo. You always want to approach the tracks from behind so they appear as normal as possible to you."

He watched the tracks approaching the arroyo, saw a turn, a side step and another side step before the tracks reached the bottom of the arroyo. He identified the first sandy footprint before walking down the rim and hopping in.

Even though the tracks were easy to spot he still had to go track to track because he had to be sure he was seeing the tracks that were on top.

"How do you know you're reading the right tracks?" I asked.

"They're all your tracks," he said.

"That's true, how do you know you're reading the right ones?"

"They are the most recent ones."

"Actually they aren't but they are supposed to look like they are. You're doing good. Keep going. How do you tell the most recent ones from the older ones?"

"The most recent ones will be on top. What if you were tracking a missing person who walked up this arroyo and somebody else walked over their tracks?"

"Then keep a sharp eye on the tracks and make sure you don't confuse them. And in that situation keep the tread pattern memorized. I know it doesn't show up much in this loose sand but it can show up enough. We'll do more of that later, too. And we'll do it with tread. Sorry about all the moccasins. I never see three people in one place, all in moccasins so I didn't think about that. I'll buy Patrick some tennis shoes if he didn't bring his boots. I may buy him tennis shoes anyway. He needs to wear typical kid shoes for this."

"He doesn't wear tennis shoes?"

"I doubt it. He wears boots to do chores and moccasins for play, well, you wouldn't consider it play, but to him it is. He stalks rabbits if he isn't allowed to leave the ranch and he tracks and stalks deer in the hills when he is. Elan and Patrick go out and track each other a lot. If you hear a loud yelp you'll know Patrick was successful in leading Thez to a rattlesnake."

"You let him do stuff like that?"

"I told him to keep Thez from getting bit."

"And how's a kid supposed to do that?"

"He'll know where the snake is. He'll see its tracks."

"You let him track snakes?"

"He's careful. I asked him what to do if he saw a snake and he had looked up snakes and researched just how far they can strike. He's got it all figured out."

"Are you sure he's a kid?"

"No, not always. Anyway, I'll make sure we have regular shoes tomorrow. That'll make things more realistic."

We climbed up out of the arroyo. There was some normal tracking and then we hit a patch of hard pack. I waited to see how he would tackle it. It wasn't large so he circled it and picked up my tracks on the other side.

"Go back and track the hard pack," I instructed him. "If you're tracking and hit a large patch of this stuff you'll want to know what to watch for. Grab a stick, it'll help you see things better."

"A stick?"

"Yeah."

He broke off a stick and came back.

"Find the track leading in. Now look for the next one. Don't see it?"

"I don't know. Do you?"

"I don't see it from here but I know how to see it. That's why I led you here. So you could learn how to see tracks on hard pack. Get closer. Closer. Really close." I sat down waiting for him to get the idea that really close meant down in the dirt close.

"Cassidy, I don't see it."

"I can see it from here." Hint hint.

"Why can you see it from eight feet away but I can't see it one foot away?"

"Because you're looking from the wrong angle. The way the light plays on the dirt can hinder… or help you. Make use of it."

He walked around and around it.

"Kent, I can see it from here. Get to where you can see it from this angle."

He crouched down, "I think I see it, and the next one. What if I'm not sure?"

"Take your stick and draw a line next to the line you see. Try to make your line follow the contours of the track, but don't actually draw on the track."

I waited as he drew two lines.

"Now stand up. Look at the track leading into the hard pack, then the two lines you drew. Do they make sense?"

He looked down at the three tracks and nodded.

"Good, now get down and find the next three."

When he'd been down on hands and knees for a minute he said, "There's an extra track over the third one. It's got tread. So it's not yours."

"Whose do you think it could be?" I asked.

"I don't know."

"Maybe you should follow it."

"I'm supposed to be tracking you."

"It might tell you something if you follow it."

"We don't have time. This is slow going."

"Tracking is slow going. We always have time to learn something new. Track the tread. See where it goes."

He took an impatient breath and tracked himself in a circle around the first puzzling track.

"Oh." he said, simply.

"Don't step on the tracks, rule number one."

"Yeah, got it."

"Rule number two. Never lose your last known track."

"Got it."

He continued across the hard pack until we were back in upright mode again.

"What secondary sign did you find back there?" I asked.

"I was too focused on primary sign."

"Sometimes the secondary sign is more helpful," I commented.

"All right," he said dragging me back. "Show me."

"You still have to be pretty close, but see these little scratch marks? Those don't happen by accident. They usually point the same direction a foot was moving in. And this broken branch could have told you to look at that side of the hard pack. It would have narrowed down your options."

"Those tiny scratches are from your tracks?"

"This time they are. If I am trying to hide my tracks I try not to leave any sign."

"Hmm"

As we approached the back side of the hill I told him, "The next part of the trail is a lesson in different gaits. I want you to tell me what kind of gait you are reading."

The ground was very readable here. I specifically chose it because the differences would show up easily.

"This appears to be your normal walk," he said.

"Actually it's my abnormal walk, but that's okay. If I used my normal walk this trail would be ten times harder. Even Patrick and Elan would have trouble with it."

"Great, so I'm learning to track Cassidy's careless twin."

We came to a part of the trail where the heel and toe both bit very deep.

"You were running here," Jacobsen observed.

"Good, what made you decide that?"

"You came down on your heel and you usually come down gently on your heel but mostly on one side of your foot. The toe print is deep indicating you pushed off hard."

"Good, it's important to recognize a run. Keep going."

I was wondering what he was going to do when he got to my little mishap.

"Cassidy, you didn't really run all the way up this hill, did you?" he asked huffing and puffing.

"You'll see," I replied.

Pretty soon my tracks slowed to a jog and turned. He paused, unsure if he really saw a change or not.

"Your stride shortened. What does that mean?"

"You can figure that out. Picture a run. You knew I was running. Now shorten the stride in your mind. What do you see?"

I could see the wheels turning and he nodded understanding.

"You've slowed to more of a jog," he reported.

The tracks pointed downhill again. I picked up speed. I leaped. I misjudged. I almost landed on a cactus. A quick leap to the side and a somersault through a mesquite tree and I lay flat on my back, winded. Jacobsen followed my tracks to the leap and the tracks stopped. He stopped. He looked at the last track. It bit deeper than the others had.

"Is this some trick?" he asked.

"No. If you're chasing fleeing suspects you have to expect the unexpected. This looks like a trick but actually I think you'll get a kick out of what really happened."

He looked and looked at the last track but there wasn't another one.

"Which way does it point?" I asked.

He examined the track. The direction was obvious. He walked downhill, watching the ground. He stopped where he thought the next sign was. It was there. It just didn't look like tracks. It was a single toe print.

"All the leaves on the ground are a big hint," I told him.

"What the hell were you trying to do?' he asked.

"I was just trying to put a few extra feet in between tracks. I didn't think I'd land that close to the cactus. When I did I was worried about running into it. I've pulled out cactus spines with pliers before. Believe me, you never want to have to do that. If you can avoid cacti, by all means, do it."

"So, where did you end up?"

"You're the tracker here. You tell me."

He looked at the toe print, noted the twist, looked at the mesquite tree and the scattering of leaves beneath it, and confirmed the twist would send me in that direction. He walked around the tree. It wasn't enough of a tree that he could walk under it. It was more of a bush with a little trunk. He found the flat spot in the dirt, then he followed my footprints as I walked around getting everything back in place.

"You sure you're okay?" he asked.

"The tracks will tell."

He followed the tracks a little way.

"I don't see it. I mean, I see the tracks but I don't see how to tell how you were feeling after the crash with the tree."

"It'll take some practice to see it. You have to have a feel for the tracks already so you can spot abnormalities. If you remember my old tracks, you'll admit that my left footprint now leans further outward than it did before. You know how a twisted ankle makes you twinge when you step down. Now imagine the motion that twinge causes to the foot. Just a slight outward push."

"I don't see it."

"Like I said, it takes practice. I don't expect you to see it your first day out. I didn't notice things like that in tracks until I was sixteen. Even then I didn't know I was seeing it. I'd just get this niggling feeling in my brain that something had changed, and when I finally put a name to it, it was pain. Slight pain that affected the walk. It always accompanied a motion that involved falling or twisting. But pain is a good thing to be able to recognize in your job. If you can see that your suspect is in pain, you will know if he was wounded, or clumsy, or overly tired. All those things are handy to know in a cop's job. Pain in any part of the body will transfer to the tracks if it affects body movement. If an arm is painful enough to cause a person to cradle it, you will see it in the tracks. Even an arm that gives an occasional twinge will transfer to the tracks, but we won't worry about that yet and we're not going to break anybody's arm to find out."

"You're walking now," he said, eyes still to my trail, "trying to get your ankle to settle down."

We tracked along until he noticed a change again. He slowed down, studying it.

"You tried jogging for a bit but you went back to walking."

He noticed when my pace picked up again and he followed my running tracks over the hill until they looked like they ran smack dab into a rock.

"Cassidy…"

"You chose this trail."

"No I didn't, it was the default trail."

"You of all people should recognize this. You did it a hundred times in academy. So did the other two."

He walked around the rock and found my footprints about five feet away from the rock on the other side.

"Guess the ankle didn't bother you too much," he commented.

"Take note of the depth of the tracks. A hundred fifteen pounds coming from five feet up in the air. All these little facts stay in your brain. Someday you'll be tracking a man and he'll jump off a platform or a ledge and you won't remember this moment but it'll help you judge the tracks when you see it again."

"You really think they will use me for tracking?"

"You will have to keep in practice. If you don't use it, you'll lose it. At least until it becomes a part of you. Once the attitude sets in you don't have to worry as much about losing it."

"The attitude?"

"You'll know when tracking is a part of you when you apply it to everyday life. I even track people at the mall, at the grocery store. I watch people who are sitting with their feet up. I take note of the tread, the wear spots on their shoes, everywhere I go I am tracking in some form. I don't watch tennis on TV. You want to know why?"

"Why?"

"Because every move the players make has to get analyzed. Every stop, every lunge. I can't keep up with it, so it drives me nuts. If I only focus on the guy with the ball I can watch football. I like baseball. Golf is boring. I picture all that grass being flattened and hacked up."

He grinned at me. "What teams do you root for?"

"The Dodgers. When it comes to football I ask Rusty who he or his brother is rooting for and I adopt that team. If nobody cares I just pick a color. I know, I'm a typical blond when it comes to sports."

He was watching the ground as we talked but he stopped and bent closer over the tracks. It was my turn to grin.

"Okay, I give up. What are you doing here?"

I didn't answer.

"I'm starving. The truck isn't far. Come on, just tell me."

"Do you see anybody at the truck?"

"No," he admitted.

"Then they are still tracking. What does it look like? Just talk through it and I bet you come up with the answer on your own."

"If it weren't for these little extra scratch marks I'd say you were jogging fast. But the scratch marks scratch that idea."

"Is there a scratch mark on every one of them?"

He made sure before he said, "Yeah."

"So what goes step, scratch, step, scratch?"

He scratched his head.

"You have kids."

"Three."

"Any girls?"

"One."

"How old?"

"Twelve."

"Maybe you should ask her. I'm sure she'd recognize it."

"You're not going to tell me, are you?"

"See if your daughter recognizes it first. Then remember the pattern. When you are tracking a fleeing person they might use this to get their rhythm back. We did in the Marines, if we got out of step."

He went back to the steps, looked again, matched the motion with the tracks.

"Okay, I got it now. You were skipping. Let's finish this thing."

"Have you had enough tracking for one day?"

"Is there more?"

"You've already done a lot more than you did at Academy."

"We didn't cover everything. At academy we did a little tracking in grass and through water."

"Don't worry, we'll get to that. Today we figure out where everybody stands. You did well, although I think any adult set on finishing this trail could follow it. You will get more out of the tracking the more you talk. I've got all kinds of facts in my brain about different tracks and different terrains and sometimes it takes some talking to trigger it. Just like it takes an odd search to bring the knowledge to mind where I can use it. Things long filed away quickly surface if given the right trigger."

"Could Patrick follow that trail?"

"Patrick can not only follow it he can read it to you. He can track well enough to substitute for me in an emergency. It's too bad he lives so far away. He'd like to be put to work but he's not old enough."

"Would you really want him to go through what you've gone through on searches?"

"Yes and no. If I could pick and choose them, there are a few I'd definitely send him on, and a few I definitely wouldn't. The ranch is such a sheltered life. I guess I just wish he really could get out and have some adventures. He's got the talent. He's a good tracker, and he can handle a rope like nobody else I know."

"What do you mean he can handle a rope?"

"Well, don't call it trick roping in front of him. He doesn't think of it as tricks. He just carried normal roping to an extreme level. But any normal person would call it trick roping. I'll have to see if there is a lariat in the ranch truck."

"Does he help out on the ranch?"

"Oh, sure. He grooms horses and exercises horses that need to be worked. He mucks out his share of the stables, feeds the horses. I bet the hands take him hunting this year. I've never seen him shoot but if he hasn't learned it's about time. His mom is a little protective. When I got a new rifle the Christmas he was down here he knew to ask his dad for permission to shoot it. James let him shoot one of Chase's old 22s. My 45 was too powerful for him back then."

"You have a rifle?"

"Sure, though I prefer my 9mm for normal purposes. But if I get a risky call I pack my 45. It packs real well. Rusty bought it with that in mind."

"Here comes Thez."

"I hope he didn't insult Elan too much. Elan is very patient but even I have trouble with Thez."

"How so?"

"He's just so…theatrical."

"I wonder why," he said sarcastically.

"I've gone on searches with him. An elk was poking around our campsite at night one time and he screamed like a little girl. It scared the elk half to death. It took off running and trampled my tent. I was lucky it didn't trample me, too. It snapped two tent poles. My tent was useless."

The two men got within hearing distance so we turned to the matters at hand.

"How did it go?" I called out.

"Him heap good tracker man!" Thez said.

"I'll talk to him," Jacobsen muttered.

I didn't wait for Jacobsen. "Thez, we need to talk."

I stalked off into the mesquite and Thez followed. When we were out of earshot I turned on him.

"Did you talk to him like that the whole time you were out?" I accused.

"No, of course not!"

"That is just plain degrading. Heap good tracker man? Where in the world did you get the idea Indians talk like that? TV?"

"Well, yeah."

"Elan graduated from high school. He may have gone to college. I don't know. But I do know his English is better than mine. He is always polite and articulate. He is talented and hardworking. He deserves respect and respect doesn't include jokes about his upbringing. Now, in plain old English, how did it go?"

He cleared his throat, uncertain how to start after my tirade.

"I'm glad I chose his trail. He was a big help. He lives up to his name. Did you know his name means friendly?"

"Yeah, did he ask what your name means?"

"I didn't tell him my real first name but I told him he could call me Thez, like the other officers do, and that it meant actor. He said that was appropriate because I was a natural born actor. He isn't a dumb Indian. I know that. He knows his tracking, too."

"Good, did you learn something today?"

"Yeah, me learn heap big much."

"Treat him like one of the guys."

"Okay. Cassidy? Are you mad at me?"

"No, not if you listened to me and will treat Elan right. My anger never lasts very long. You don't need to worry about that."

"That's good, because I couldn't stand to see you mad."

"What are we doing for lunch during these classes?" Kent asked.

"What do you usually do for lunch when you take classes? All the classes I've taken, they just break up and tell us when to be back."

"That's a little hard to do with one car and ten miles to town."

"We'll drop anybody off at the station who wants to be dropped off and the rest of us will go to... Trujillo's to compare notes. Does that sound reasonable?"

When Reilly and Patrick got back Reilly was grinning ear to ear.

"Oh man!" Reilly said. "That kid must have looked under every rock on the hill for a rattlesnake! We didn't see one either, although we did our share of looking."

"Did you get any tracking done?"

"Oh! Yeah! We tracked, too, didn't we kid?"

"Yeah. We tracked the whole trail," Patrick said.

"We figured we'd go to Trujillo's, dropping anybody off at the station that didn't want to go," I told Reilly.

"Sounds good to me," Reilly said.

"Isn't that the place where the policemen hang out?" Patrick asked.

"Yeah, it's Mexican food. Do you like Mexican food?"

"I like almost anything, especially if it isn't venison."

"I don't think I've ever seen venison on Benny's menu," I said.

Chapter 4

Nobody wanted to go be dropped off, and everybody was hungry, so we just went straight to Trujillo's.

When we were all seated and our orders were placed I went through a mental checklist.

"Okay, did everybody cover the basics? Right turn, left turn, with and without a twist in it, a walk, a run, a jog, through sand, soft sand and hard pack."

"That's all we were supposed to do?" Patrick asked.

"Well, I wasn't specific when I told you what to do, but you and Elan have been laying trails for each other for a long time now. I thought you'd think of your own lessons and make a simple trail involving a little bit of the basics."

Patrick and Reilly looked at each other. No wonder they took so much longer than the others, between hunting for rattlesnakes and tracking Patrick's obstacle course.

"What did you do to him?"

"Nothing! Plus you said to help him and ask questions. I thought I could do fun stuff if I was supposed to help him."

"What exactly is fun stuff?"

Reilly answered first, "This kid is crazy. His trail just ended and I couldn't find anything to go on. It finally turned out that he had stepped backwards over his tracks until he could hop up on a rock. Then he climbed the rock and took off on some back way."

"Patrick. Think beginner trail. Okay? We're just teaching. We're not trying to trick them."

"But what if they are chasing bad guys? Bad guys can get tricky!"

"I've never seen one get that tricky," I said.

"Thanks!" said Patrick and the guys laughed.

"Actually, Patrick, bad guys are usually in too big a hurry to get very tricky," Jacobsen said. "They just run like hell."

"Well…if you ever have to track Aunt Cassidy you have to be ready for anything. She *is* sneaky."

"Okay, we'll agree with you on that one," Jacobsen said.

"When Elan and I track each other we try all kinds of tricks. It's fun."

"We'll have more fun when they have more practice in," I told Pat.

"But…practice *is* fun!" he insisted. "I think the tricks are the best part of tracking Elan. One time he walked half a mile without touching the ground."

"How did you do that?" Thez asked.

"Where we live it is easy," Elan said. "There are many large, old trees and the roots protrude from the earth. We can walk along them until we come to a broken branch or a rock. We sometimes see how far we can go without touching the ground. If we park the tractor beside the stables outside the barn we can walk from one end of the ranch to the other without touching the ground."

"Aunt Cassidy was the first one to do it. She did it when she was a kid. You start at the back corner, walk the back fence until you get to the gate out the back of the ranch. Then you unlatch the gate and it swings open until it hits the side of the barn. Climb the meters on the barn until you get to the roof. You walk across the roof to the fence at the front of the barn. Walk the fence, hop onto the tractor and then climb from the tractor to the paddock fence. Then you can walk the fence all the way to the front of the ranch by my house."

"How old were you when you discovered that?" I asked.

"I don't know. I tried it a couple of days after you told me it could be done, except I fell off the fence until I grew enough to stretch from the fence to the tractor."

"Well, this week let's keep our feet on the ground. Okay?"

"Aw shucks."

"And tomorrow, no moccasins. We need to look like normal people do when they get lost."

"But I only brought moccasins. You said we were tracking."

"Me, too," said Elan.

"We'll go buy some running shoes tonight. Most people who get lost are wearing running shoes."

"But they are so recognizable," Patrick complained.

"Not to a beginner."

As Patrick ate his eyes began to water and he drank more soda than I thought was good for him. His nose began running. Finally he left the table and went to the bar.

"You're too young, Patrick," Benny said.

"Can I see a menu?"

Benny put a menu down in front of Pat.

"What do rellano and caliente mean?"

"A rellano is a chile pepper stuffed with cheese, dipped in a batter and fried. Caliente means hot. So, did you find it hot enough for you?"

"Yesir. I thought Caliente was a place in Mexico."

"No sir, it is all of Mexico. Is it too hot for you?"

"No, but next time I'll get the translation first."

"Good idea. Would you like some fried ice cream?"

"Even the ice cream is caliente?"

"It's not hot. You'll like it."

"I'll ask my Aunt Cassidy."

Patrick came back to the table. "This is a weird restaurant. How do they fry ice cream? Doesn't it melt into a big mess? It sounds yucky!"

"It's good," I told him. "It's got a coating on it and they put caramel sauce on top. I'll split one with you."

When he saw the round ball on his plate he was still skeptical.

"You have to break it open to get at the ice cream," I told him.

He poked at it with his spoon until it broke with a crispy *crack* and he looked inside like he was expecting it to bite him.

"Get a little ice cream and some of the coating on your spoon, make sure it has a little caramel sauce on it, then try it," I said demonstrating.

I think I got three bites. Patrick took one tentative bite and devoured the rest as I took a couple of quick bites in between his.

"I'm going to ask Martha if she can fry ice cream!" he said.

Martha is the cook and housekeeper at my parent's ranch. Patrick lives in a smaller house on the outskirts of the ranch property. It is a short walk from his house to the ranch house. He makes the walk every day to do chores. If he is home at dinnertime he eats at his house. If he is at the big house then he eats with the ranch hands. About once a week his family eats dinner with the rest of the family in the big house, so he knows Martha very well. Martha will try to cook anything.

"What are we doing this afternoon?" Patrick asked.

"Does everybody want to try another trail?" I asked.

There were affirmative shrugs all around.

"Okay then I need two volunteer suspects."

"Ooh, me!" Patrick said raising his hand.

"Patrick, what does a fleeing suspect do?" I asked.

"Run like hell."

"Anybody else?"

"Sure," said Thez. "I can play a suspect. I've seen enough of them."

"Laying tracks is a good way to learn how they are made. When you run just give us a variety of things to work on. Turns, jumps. Think about what you are leaving behind on the ground as you go. You can even cross each other's trails."

"All right! I like laying tracks. It's fun," said Patrick. "Are we going to be eating here a lot?"

"I don't know," I admitted.

"Can I have fried ice cream again?"

“I bet your mom wouldn’t like you to have that much sugar,” Thez commented.

“I say he’ll earn it and he’s going to exercise it off anyway. A little dessert won’t hurt him as hard as he’s going to be working,” I said.

Everybody chipped in when the check came and I paid the balance. Then we drove out to the desert again.

I took them to a place where I knew there was an abandoned shack about a mile away. It would make a good landmark.

“Remember you’re a fleeing suspect. If the police catch up to you you’re going to jail for the rest of your life. You can pull any tricks you can think of at a dead run. You can slow down and rest if you need to, just like a real suspect would, but keep going. There’s a shack due east of here. Run to the shack and back, taking any route you think a suspect would take. Don’t go into the shack without a thorough inspection. I’ve met critters in there before. Critters you don’t want to surprise. Got it?”

Patrick nodded enthusiastically.

Thez said, “Got it.”

“We’ll give you a fifteen minute head start. Go!”

Patrick took off running. Thez jogged off into the desert complaining, “I just ate a big lunch!”

Jacobsen asked, “You let him run over those rocks in flimsy moccasins?”

“He knows how to move in them. He’ll be fine.”

“How’s he going to know where the shack is?”

“I told him it was due east.”

“How does he know which way due east is?”

“He knows where north is. So he knows where east is.”

“How does he know where north is?”

“His shadow will tell him.”

“You have a lot of faith in him.”

“No, I know what he has learned because I know what it’s like growing up on that ranch. He knows his directions. You don’t need to worry about that. And if you track his trail and it doesn’t seem to go east, don’t worry. He’s just trying to make things interesting for us, that’s all.”

“Interesting?” Reilly said, “Better hope that kid stays on the right side of the law! If he doesn’t he’ll give police a hell of a time.”

“He’s a good kid. He’ll only give us fits trying to outdo me in the trouble department. It’s a little harder to do these days. When I was a kid we were free to go just about anywhere we wanted. Patrick is somewhat limited in that regard. He can’t jump on a dirt bike and head for town. He can’t learn to drive until he’s sixteen. So in the meantime he learns ranch work. He tracks, stalks deer. He’s lucky there are still deer back in the hills. The more people build back there the fewer deer there will be."

Elan said, "Steve told Patrick he could go on the hunt this year. Patrick doesn't want to."

"That doesn't surprise me. Has he been learning to shoot?"

"He has his own twenty-two now. He's a decent shot. He likes target practice with the guys. He just doesn't want to shoot at living things. The deer are his friends."

"I expected as much. Is Dad disappointed?"

"He doesn't care as long as the ranch gets a deer or two for meat. He doesn't care who brings it in."

"He sure did when I was a kid. It was one of the few times I got any praise out of him."

"Patrick is also tired of venison. He'd rather not help bring more of it into the house."

It didn't take Patrick and Thez long to get out of sight.

"Are you ready? Elan and Jacobsen take Patrick's trail. Tucker and I will take Thez's trail."

As we hit the trail Tucker turned to me. "You can call me Reilly. It's shitty being a cop named Tucker. Can't ease up in a foot pursuit or they ask me if I'm tuckered out. I've heard that old joke so many times I quit using my last name. So you can call me Reilly." He pronounced it *rally*, though.

"So is it Reilly or Rally?"

"Oh, I don't care, just so I don't get tuckered out."

"Running tracks are not hard to follow in the desert. I want you to get running tracks ingrained in your mind. If you are tracking an apprehension the suspect is not going to be ambling along. Give it a try."

He began following Thez's tracks but he kept talking. "That nephew of yours is really something. He can out talk me. He knows his tracking. It was like having an informative shadow when I was tracking this morning. I thought this morning was very valuable. I never thought I'd learn so much from a kid."

"You don't have kids, do you?"

"Me? No, I'm not even married."

"Kids teach you something every day from the moment they're born."

"How old's yours?"

"You know Katie. She's a fixture at the station. When I go to the station sometimes I don't even see her the whole time I'm there because everybody passes her from one person to another. She's almost two."

"Oh! The little blonde girl, curly. Always has a Hot Wheel car in her hand."

"Her dad keeps a drawer full of toy cars to give to kids when they get bored in his office."

"Uh, oh, Michaels. You're Michael's wife?"

"Yeah."

"Aw shiiiit. I thought you were younger than me!"

"Are you paying attention to the trail?"

"Yeah, sure, it's right here."

"Are you reading it or just following?"

"Oh, yeah, I guess I'm supposed to be reading, ain't I?"

"Following this trail should be simple. It's the reading that we're interested in... I don't know about Thez. Looking at his tracks, he runs like he's in a Nike ad. I wonder what he does when he really has a crook to catch."

"They don't grade you on style in academy. Guess he got the job done."

"I guess."

Every time I saw Thez's tracks change I made Reilly stop and tell me what the change was. One thing about Thez's picture perfect tracks was that changes were obvious. Well, to me they were. Reilly had to study them to find anything different about them. Reilly needed to develop an eye for the minute. One part of the trail in particular got both groups puzzled. Elan and I stood back as Reilly and Jacobsen argued over the trail. Elan and I smiled and let them hash it out.

"Those are Thez's tracks," Jacobsen said. "They're way too big to be Patrick's."

"Well, then, where'd Patrick's tracks go to?" Reilly countered.

"You've tracked Patrick before. You'd recognize them before I would."

"You're the ones reading Patrick's trail. We're after Thez. If these are Thez's tracks, we're in good shape. It's you who's stuck," Reilly said.

"Cassidy said they could cross each other's paths. That must be what we are seeing but where did he go once he crossed Thez's track?"

"How long should we let them puzzle this out?" Elan asked me.

"There's Thez. Let's let him catch up and see what he makes of this," I answered.

"How's it going?" Thez said as he approached the group.

"Maybe you can help Jacobsen and Reilly. They seem to be a little bit stuck."

Thez walked over and glanced at the tracks.

"Am I supposed to help them?" Thez asked.

"Help with Patrick's trail," I told him.

"Patrick's? These are my tracks."

"The two trails intersected. They're trying to pick them back apart."

I whispered to Elan, "Find the spot where the trails separate again."

It only took him a moment of inconspicuous observation to find it.

"He stayed on Thez's tracks for maybe sixty feet," he informed me quietly.

"How'd he do that? He doesn't have Thez's stride."

"If you look closely he only used Thez's left foot tracks. Patricks' right foot tracks are still there, if you know what to look for. It's just that Thez's tracks are so much more obvious that they aren't seeing the less visible tracks of Patrick."

I nodded. It sounded like something Patrick would do.

"I could see Pat's track inside Thez's," I said. "I didn't get close enough to figure out more than that. Did you teach Patrick to do that?"

"We try all kinds of things. We wonder what it looks like if we try this or that. So we go out to the corral where the dirt is loose, knowing it'll be much harder to read in the hills. Patrick remembers everything. Anything sneaky, he remembers. I think he's looking forward to the day he can stump you."

"Does he know Chase already tried that?"

"Yeah. He knows he has big shoes to fill. It's just a personal challenge to him."

"Good."

"Cassidy?" Thez said.

"Should I bail them out?" I asked Elan.

"No, it's a classic trick."

"Then you help them."

He sighed and walked over.

"I'll show you one set. It's up to you to see the next." He went over to the tracks. "This line right here is the outside of Patrick's left foot."

"Damn!" Said Thez, "It's my own track and I didn't see anything different about it!"

"The right foot print is between Thez's tracks." He pointed to it. All the men bent over the set of tracks. They tried to see what we saw. I wandered over. They would never see that right footprint. It was so faint.

It was Reilly who surprised me. I thought he was more interested in getting out into the hills and exercising his jaws but he saw it without help.

"Look," he said. "See this little rock? It's turned and beside it, if you get down low enough, you can just see the ball of his foot."

Everybody became so intent on finding Patrick's tracks that they forgot they were supposed to track Thez, too. Even Thez got into it, but it was the comments of the group that did most of the teaching that day. As they bounced ideas off each other they started looking at tracking in different ways until, finally, something worked. In a way I wished I was tracking Patrick's trail. If Patrick wanted to challenge me I might need to familiarize myself with his tricks.

I learned a lot that day. I thought to get the guys to learn tracking I needed to get footprints embedded in their minds. But I found out they already knew what footprints looked like. They learned a lot faster when they were just presented with a problem and had to figure it out. After they were shown how to read Patrick's tracks within Thez's they managed to find each one until the tracks departed from each other again. They tracked all the way to the shed and back. Patrick's trail took twice as long as the other trail to track. When he caught up with us I had him join a group and help.

Chapter 5

"How did the tracking go today?" Rusty asked when we got home.

"It was too easy," I replied. "We need to go on to more challenging things tomorrow."

"That's good. So… the guys did know a thing or two about tracking," Rusty said.

"Oh, they didn't have to," Patrick said. "This was waaaaay easy. Even you could have done it."

"Gee, thanks, Pat," Rusty said.

"After dinner we need to go to town. Patrick and Elan need different shoes to lay trails in. It was a little confusing having three trails of almost identical moccasin tracks."

"The stores will be closed by the time we eat dinner."

"Oh darn," said Patrick with mock disappointment, "I guess we'll have to skip the shoe shopping, or go get a big fat pizza pie to save time."

"Pizza!" said Katie.

"Elan?" Rusty asked.

"Sounds good to me. I agree, we need to distinguish the trails more than we did today."

I took Patrick to the shoe section of a large department store. We found a pair of running shoes that he could walk in. We compared the tread to the shoes Elan had chosen, then chose another pair because the tread was too similar. I made him walk up and down the aisle to be sure they fit correctly.

When we were sure we had a successful shoe hunt he asked, "Aunt Cassidy? Can I go look in the toy department?"

"You don't even like toys," I said.

"I know, but I want to bring something back for Wyatt," he answered.

"Okay, don't be rowdy. And don't talk to strangers."

Later, he walked up with a bag, ready to go.

"What did you find for Wyatt?" I asked.

"I found some action figures. He collects them and plays pretend games with them."

I should have questioned him further. He was awfully anxious to get to the pizza place and then to get home and he was antsy to get going the next morning.

"Where are we tracking from today?" Pat asked.

"I like the idea of tracking right out of our backyard today. We will be starting out in dirt but as we go south we'll hit trees and forest. The guys can transition into harder tracking quickly this way. Since the tracking will be tougher make the trail shorter. And don't try to trick them. It's hard enough to see footprints in the woods without you hiding your tracks."

"All right! Can I go now?"

"You haven't even had breakfast yet."

"That's okay. I'll work up an appetite."

"Do you remember where the deer meadow is?"

"I think so."

"Just follow all the deer tracks. Leave some obvious sign in the meadow before you come back." I looked at his feet. "And wear your new shoes. Your tread needs to be readable."

"Oh yeah! I forgot."

He went to the bedroom and switched shoes.

"Can I sleep in the gazebo like Chase tonight?"

"If Uncle Rusty can find the hammock."

He went out the back door with Katie toddling after him saying, "Me too! Me too!"

"No baby, you're not big enough for this. It's time to eat. Are you hungry?"

"Eat!"

Katie was always ready to eat.

When Patrick came back in we were just finishing up breakfast. Rusty was ready to head for the office. Katie offered Patrick a sample from her highchair tray.

I was in mom mode.

"When you get to the station can you have Jacobsen round up the guys and bring them here? Bertie is supposed to meet me at the station. They can bring her too."

"Bertie hates riding in the squad cars. She says it gives homeless people a bad reputation."

"Tell her I got new shower gel."

"What?"

"One of the things she likes about our house is the sexy shower. If she has fancy shower gel she'll come no matter who's bringing her. Tell her she can make snicker doodles. She loves to do that."

"I'm supposed to go out to a busy downtown street and bribe a homeless woman into a squad car with shower gel and snicker doodles?"

"Oh come on. You act like I sent you to the grocery store for necessities."

"You want me to do this in front of the guys?"

"No, in fact you can just have Jacobsen do it. You can blame me. They'll believe anything, if you blame it on me."

"You expect Jacobsen to bribe Bertie into the car? He's more likely to pretend to arrest her and then bring her here instead. He's not going to bribe her with shower gel."

"Rusty, this is a simple thing. She's a babysitter. All I need is a babysitter."

"I'll watch Katie. You go get her."

"Will you fix breakfast for Patrick? He's been out laying a trail."

"Yes, I can even fix breakfast for Pat."

"Okay, I'll try and hurry. Even if I hurry you'll be late for work."

"I'll work late."

"Men!" I muttered to myself as I took off for town.

I got in the Jeep and backed out of the driveway, pointed the Jeep west and followed Lost Hills Road to Sunset Drive. I turned right and headed toward town. I was hurrying, thinking about the day and how much needed to get done, wishing things could be simple for once. And then trouble sent me a curve ball. Around a curve, of course, so I couldn't see it coming. A little Mazda convertible rounded the corner too wide, saw me ahead and headed for the shoulder. I screeched to a stop and the little sports car swerved in front of me and went bouncing through the desert in a cloud of dust. It stopped with a crunch of dry desert sagebrush and the teenage driver got out cursing up a storm. He was bleeding from facial wounds. I looked the car over briefly thinking it would be a fun car to drive, and walked over to make sure the kid was all right, but before I could get close to him he sprinted as fast as he could into the desert.

Oh shit. I didn't have time for this. Suddenly I went from pissed off wife to cop mode.

"Stop! Freeze!" I yelled. "You don't just run away from an accident. You might be hurt."

I wasn't in uniform and I didn't want to take my gun. He was only a kid, and probably worried about getting in trouble with his dad. But he was hurt and I couldn't just leave. I sprinted after him. The class would have to wait. In fact, maybe we should track this trail. It's the kind of thing they'd have to track for work, anyway. I was just saving time by laying a trail and picking up Bertie at the same time. Right?

Wrong.

This kid was fast and he was scared. Why would he run? Was the car stolen? I was just enough of an officer to look for a motive behind his actions.

I couldn't imagine any parent being that mad at a kid for banging up a car, not even *my* dad and my dad was plenty scary. I wanted to yell after the kid,

"Hey! My dad is scarier than your dad!" but I knew it was just silly. As I ran along the kid's tracks I got out my cell phone and called 911 even though I didn't think it was an emergency.

"Nine one one emergency response," a woman said.

"This is reserve deputy Cassidy Michaels. I'd like to report a traffic accident on Sunset Road. There is no address. There is a tan Jeep on the side of the road and a white Mazda convertible sports car off the side of the road. The kid who was driving the Mazda ran away. I'm following him through the desert. He's bleeding but I don't think the injuries are serious. Send an officer to the scene."

"Is this a medical emergency?"

"I don't think so. Look, I need to go or I'm going to lose him. This kid must be on the cross country team or something!"

"Please stay on the line until emergency personnel arrive on the scene."

I knew this was standard procedure but under the circumstances it was a bit impractical to think the police were going to arrive on the scene. On the scene was changing by the minute.

Talking and running at the same time caused me to become winded faster.

"Jacobsen. Tell Joshua Hills station to send Jacobsen. He'll find me. I've got to go."

"Please stay on the line…"

I held onto the phone and ran. Okay, I'd stay on the line.

"Stop!" I yelled, "Halt!"

He didn't stop. He didn't halt.

"Police! Freeze!" I yelled though it didn't carry far because I was trying to catch my breath. "I'm just trying to help you!" I called out, but the kid kept running.

I was trained for this. Admittedly, a bout of trouble had left me on a long, slow recovery but I thought I was nearly back to my normal self. I jogged at the gym and improved every day. I finally felt like I was getting in shape. Then something like this happened.

I slowed to a walk to help slow my breathing. While I was walking I decided it was a good time to check in with the 911 operator.

"Hello?" I asked, "Just letting you know I am still here. Did you get ahold of the police?"

"Cassidy?"

"Yeah, Cassidy, who were you expecting?"

"Sorry."

"I'm still trying to locate the other driver but I couldn't run any more. Did you get hold of Joshua Hills Station?"

"An officer had been dispatched."

"Did you find Jacobsen?"

"Not yet."

"Okay, let me hang up. He's not expecting to be on duty today. He is taking a tracking class. I'm supposed to be teaching it but I got sidelined by this accident."

She hung up and I looked up Jacobsen's phone number in my cell phone. I hit *call* and waited.

"What is it Cassidy?" he asked.

"I'm going to be late. I had a little traffic incident with a kid in a sports car and he took off into the desert. He's only slightly injured but he isn't slowing down one bit. You can kill two birds with one stone if you can gather up the guys and track me down."

"Cassidy, why didn't you just call it in?"

"I did, but I can't just let the kid go. He might be hurt."

"And he might be wanted for grand theft auto. You never know."

"Well, he's not getting away. I'll tell you that much."

"I'll be there soon."

"Can you bring Bertie?"

"Bertie Bag Lady? No way!"

"Come on, Jacobsen. I need her. She's my babysitter. I was going into town to get Bertie and tell you to come to my house for class today."

"I'm not taking any civilian to a potential crime scene."

Sigh, "Okay, we'll figure out Bertie later. I'll probably have to hunt her down on the boulevard if I don't show up at the station pretty soon. Are you bringing Reilly and Thez, too? This is a good example for you guys to track. A classic case."

"Cass…this is not a game. Just drop it."

"I can't."

"What's the plate number on the car?"

"I was more worried about the kid. Are you guys looking for any white convertible Mazda roadsters?"

"A plate number would be helpful."

"Sorry."

"I tell you what, I'll give you a refresher course in procedure if you'll stop chasing this kid and go back to your car. Meet the responding officer and we'll take it from there."

"I'm too far away from the Jeep to turn back now. Damn, where's this kid going? Do you think you can find me?"

"Yeah, we're on our way. We'll see the Jeep from the road?"

"You should, I need to go. I better pick up my pace again."

I hung up and started jogging along the kid's tracks, glancing down, trying to profile a bit as I went. I started running through the possibilities of why this kid was so determined to distance himself from me and the car. Maybe the car *was* stolen. Maybe the kid was a runaway. Maybe he just feared what his parents would do when they found out about the car. Knowing the status of the car would tell me a lot about what I was getting into.

I found a spot where the kid had stopped to rest. He was winded. He stood, bent over, probably hands on knees trying to catch his breath. I could tell because his weight was all forward on his toes and the balls of his feet.

I caught up to him at a house. I could see him off in the distance approaching the house cautiously. He watched the house briefly from a short distance away and went on to another house farther down the road. Some of these rural houses could be seen from quite a ways away. I tried to guess which street the house was on. It had to be within a mile or two of my house but I had never driven the roads in this direction.

At the next house a woman was getting ready to leave for work. She walked to her car, all dressed up for a day at the office, crisp slacks, high heels, a colorful scarf fluttered on the breeze. She loaded a few things in her car and went back into the house.

No! Don't do that. Not now, I thought.

The kid was watching, too.

When the woman went back into the house the kid jumped in her car and looked around. I ran forward. Even if I couldn't catch the kid I needed whatever information I could draw out of the situation. I pulled out my cell phone as I ran. I hit redial.

"What is it?" Jacobsen asked tersely.

"I'm leaning towards the grand theft auto. He's looking for another car and he might just have found one."

"Where are you?"

"I don't know. About a mile east of my Jeep."

I ran out of the desert just as the kid slammed the car door shut. He looked around for some keys and I slammed up against the car door, knocking on it as hard as I could.

"Open this door!" I yelled.

"Get off my case, lady!" the kid yelled back.

"You take this car and you're going to be in even bigger trouble."

He locked the door.

The woman stepped out of her house.

"What are you doing to my car?" she wailed. "I'm going to call the police!"

"Be my guest," I said. "Make sure to give them your address."

I could hear Jacobsen yell, "Cassidy! Get back here," as I handed the woman my phone. I stepped around to the back of the car, trying to prevent it from leaving.

"Don't start this car!" I yelled at the kid, "Come out! Let's take a look at your injuries."

"I'm going to injure *you* if you don't quit!" he yelled back.

Aw hell, stubborn kid. He started the car and threw it into reverse. He stomped on the gas and the car lurched backwards. All I had time to do was jump. I landed half on and half off the trunk as it backed out of the driveway. I grabbed hold of the spoiler and knelt on the bumper. How in the world did I get myself into these things? Easy, I told myself, Jacobsen tells you to stop and you don't do it. You're just as stubborn as this kid and just as dumb, too. I told myself to just let the kid go, that the police would find him, but I couldn't let go without a tumble on the asphalt. I hung onto the silver Trans Am with a white knuckled grip as it sped toward town. The car tore off down Sunrise Terrace and turned right on Sunset Drive. I was getting closer to home and my Jeep. Too bad I couldn't let go. The car was traveling way too fast for that. I knew what it felt like to jump out of a moving vehicle and it hurt. I wasn't ready to take that chance yet. Sixty mile an hour wind whipped my hair around. The kid saw me on his bumper and started weaving around, trying to shake me off. Suddenly I saw the lights of a police car in the distance. I wanted to call them but the woman still had my cell phone.

Slowly the officers closed the gap. Jayce Thompson gawked at me through the windshield of his squad car. He debated what to do. He didn't want to drive too close in case I fell off, but he needed to put the pressure on the kid. There were some radio transmissions. I assumed he was getting some help. When the radio transmissions stopped he sent a question my way. What it was I didn't know but I sent an answer back. I was ready, whatever happened. He crept up on the Trans Am. Only a foot separated the two cars and I prayed the kid didn't try anything sudden as I lowered myself back onto the bumper and got ready to hop onto the front of the squad car. I took a look at Jayce, making sure this was really what he had in mind. If there was one thing I didn't need right now it was our unspoken plans to not match up. I'd be a goner. The jump had to be controlled. I had to be ready. I had to be alert. Hell, alert was no problem. I held up my fingers counting down one, two, pause, pause, oh man, was I ready for this? Three. I pushed off, jumped slightly and landed on the hood of the police car. There was nothing to hold onto! Jayce started slowing down and the Trans Am sped off. I braced myself but almost slid right off the hood of the car. I caught a quick glimpse of Jayce's shocked expression coming through the windshield at me. When the car stopped I slid off the hood and ran around to the back of the car. Jayce unlocked the car and I hopped in the back seat.

"Go get him!" I said.

"Cassidy! Are you all right?"

"Right enough. I'm supposed to be teaching a tracking class and instead I'm running through the desert and doing movie stunts jumping off moving cars."

"Any idea what's really going on here?"

"Only vaguely. This kid ran off the road in a little Mazda convertible. I got out to see if he was injured and he took off running. I chased him down until he stole the Trans Am."

"How'd you get stuck on his back bumper?"

"I tried to stop him from leaving with the car. He didn't listen."

"Is he armed?"

"Not that I could tell."

My Grandma Gordon would have had the time of her life. The one time she got to ride along with an officer he only handed out a speeding ticket. She was disappointed. This was almost everything she had hoped for, speeding through the streets of the city, the staccato radio transmissions of the pursuing officers, the challenge of trying to get the kid to stop without injuring him further. It wasn't my idea of a fun time. I kept picturing Jacobsen, Reilly and Thez camped out at my Jeep waiting for me to get free and call for a ride. I couldn't even call for a ride, though. I'd lost my cell phone in the commotion. Rusty was waiting to get to work. Bertie was waiting for a ride to my house. And I was kind of tied up, along for the rest of the ride. Was it possible to get kidnapped by the police, I asked myself jokingly.

More cars joined the chase. Shots were fired. Tires were blown out. The kid jumped out of the Grand Am and fled on foot, but this time he was met with four armed officers.

I waited in the squad car, ready if they needed a tracker, but leaving them to their police business. I thought I'd met with trouble again when Ben Tomlin stuffed the kid in the squad car I was sitting in.

"You!" the kid said as he struggled angrily.

I fumbled with the lock and realized there was a reason you couldn't unlock the back doors of a police car from the inside. The car rocked and Ben stuck his head in barking orders for the kid to settle down.

"Cassidy, what are you doing here?" Ben asked hauling the kid back out.

"It's a long story. This whole chase started with me and I ended up along for the ride."

"That figures. Thompson wanted to haul the guy in. He said to use his car."

By the time I got to the station Bertie had come and gone. I tracked her down to the park near the downtown area. She was sharing an old sandwich with a flock of birds and a stray dog.

"I've got something better to eat at my house," I said. "I ran into a bit of trouble on the way here. I ended up tracking a kid across the desert and then I got involved in a car chase. Sorry I'm late."

"Leave it to you. Most people would say they overslept or they ran out of gas. Or they missed the train."

"Well, I missed the train, too. My Jeep is on the side of the road. I got a ride to the station in a squad car."

"You're going to give housewives a bad name if you're seen riding around in those squad cars."

"I'm not too worried. There are plenty of normal housewives out there to balance out our reputation."

"So you still need my babysittin' today?"

"Yeah, I hope so. I think I still have a class waiting to start. We just have to figure out how to get there."

"Well, it better not involve a squad car."

"Okay, I'll see what I can do."

I cringed as I called home.

"Hello?" Rusty said.

"Hi, sorry I got tied up."

"Cassidy, where have you been? I had a ten o'clock meeting."

"You hate meetings. I'm with Bertie now but I don't have a car. Can you come to work and I'll take the Explorer home? I'll come back and pick you up after we track."

"What happened to your Jeep?"

"Nothing. You'll see it on the way."

"You're not telling me everything."

"We don't have time for me to tell you everything. If I told you everything we'd be on the phone for another hour."

"Are you okay?"

"Yeah, surprisingly, I'm fine. Can I meet you at the station?"

"I want the whole story."

"You'll get it. You can start with Jayce Thompson, then Kent Jacobsen and finish up with Ben Tomlin. I'll fill in the gaps after dinner. Maybe you can fill in some gaps for me, too."

When Rusty arrived he had Elan and Patrick along. He had seen the Jeep on the side of the road. Jacobsen, Reilly and Thez were slowly working their way down the trail of tracks from when I'd chased the kid. Katie was asleep in her car seat. Okay, I thought, we can start the day. I took Bertie and Katie home and rushed out to the site.

"Hey," I said as Elan, Patrick and I caught up with the group, "It looks like you're doing pretty good following. Are you reading the tracks, too? Who's reading which trail?"

"There's more than one trail?" Thez asked.

"Yeah. Tell me what you found. What can you tell me about the people you've been tracking?"

"Well," Jacobsen started out, "He's in good shape. He's been running."

"How did you decide it was a guy?"

"Because you said he was," Jacobsen said.

"Patrick, what do you think of these tracks?"

Pat looked over the tennis shoe tracks sprinting through the desert. "I think it looks like a guy, too. It's either a man or a teenager boy."

"I don't know how old he was. He was old enough to steal a car," I said.

"We ran the plates on the Mazda. It was stolen. A tow truck took it in. We figured we could get your Jeep home."

"Thanks."

"So you recognize the fact that you're following a young man or a teenage boy. You've figured out that he's running. What about my tracks? Who's following my tracks?"

"Your tracks?" Jacobsen said.

"We haven't seen any trace of your tracks," said Thez.

"Oh, come on guys, I wasn't even hiding them. I was just chasing the kid. Have you been covering them up all this time?"

"At least we didn't get very far," Reilly put in.

"Jacobsen, you knew I was chasing the kid. I was talking to you on the phone as I did it."

"I thought we were going to track my trail," Patrick said, disappointed.

"We will. We'll do that after this. We're just doing this because my little fiasco this morning caused this trail and everybody ended up at it. Jacobsen, you said you wanted to learn how to track me. Find my tracks."

"Do you see them?" Jacobsen asked.

"Of course I see them."

"But you made them."

"I made a whole slew of them. This is just one small part. Remember I was running after the kid. So you are looking for more running tracks. I was wearing tennis shoes, because I was ready to start our class."

He looked and looked. The others waited, all except Patrick. Patrick couldn't wait. He looked around, too.

"I don't suppose you found them," Jacobsen said to Patrick after a short search of the nearby ground.

Patrick just looked smug.

"How about if you show me enough to get me started here," Jacobsen asked Patrick.

Patrick looked to me for permission. I nodded an okay. Patrick drew a circle around two tracks. Jacobsen squinted at the ground.

"That's what your running tracks look like when you're chasing a kid? You weren't even thinking about your tracks."

"I'm always thinking about my tracks, but I wasn't hiding them."

"I hate to think how hard they would be to read under normal conditions."

"Okay. We have two starting points. Patrick and Jacobsen read my trail. Elan, Reilly and Thez read the kid's trail. They stay pretty close together. I'll monitor both groups."

Elan's group went a lot faster than Patrick's did. Pat was letting Jacobsen do as much reading as he could by himself and it was tough going. Even my running tracks were light and quick. When I slowed to a walk to talk to Jacobsen on the phone it got even harder to read. Even Patrick struggled with my walking tracks.

Elan, Reilly and Thez had more to work with. They dissected the trail as they went. Despite wasting most of a morning on a minor incident, then unexpectedly being given two trails to work I thought the class was doing pretty good. At least these trails were not contrived. They were a real chase, like the guys might get in their real work. When we got closer to the house I had Elan's group slow down and tell what happened.

"He stopped." Reilly said.

"And what do you think he's doing?"

"He's just standing there."

"People rarely just stand there, especially if they are being pursued. What is he doing while he's standing and I am closing in?"

They looked closer. I could see Elan glance at the tracks, glance toward the house. Elan knew.

"Stuff like this is important when you're pursuing a suspect. He didn't stop for no reason. He had a purpose behind it. You have to decide based on the evidence before you what this guy was thinking. Which way do the tracks face? What can the guy see?"

"He's checking out the house," Jacobsen said.

"Why would he check out the house?"

"Lots of reasons. He might be looking for a place to lose you. He could be looking for transportation. He might want a place to hole up. He might even be looking for an easy buck. You have to consider all the possibilities when you're in pursuit."

"Right," I said. "Now see what he did next."

They tracked him to the second house until he stopped again.

"Look at these tracks. He's not just standing there this time. How is the weight distributed?"

"How should we know?" Thez asked.

"Look. Just look at it. Remember the previous standing tracks? What is different about these standing tracks?"

It was asking a lot to expect them to figure it out. The difference was so small and they weren't in the practice of remembering previous tracks yet.

"Compare the different parts of the track. You can see which part of the track is deeper."

I thought it was funny that they all leaned forward just like the kid to examine the tracks. All of them put their weight on the front of their feet. All their tracks would match the kid's.

"He's checking out this house more carefully. He's more serious about this one."

They followed his tracks to the driveway and saw that he got in a car.

"Now what?"

"So, while the kid was doing all this what was I doing?"

They went back and decided I had chased the kid to the driveway. They saw that I had talked to the woman. They noted her irritated walk back into the house. They saw that I stood behind the car and… that's it.

"Where did your tracks go?" Jacobsen asked.

"The next track can be found in the park in Joshua Hills."

"Wait. How did you get all the way into town without going back to your Jeep?"

"It's kind of complicated. I'll tell you about it on the way back."

Oh, man, if I'd remembered that Patrick was there I sure wouldn't have told the guys the whole story.

"That is so cool!" exclaimed Patrick. "It's just like in the movies and a real police car chase! I wish I could have gone. Next time you go pick up a babysitter can I go, too?"

"Patrick, it was all an accident. I was just reacting to the things that happened to me. If you'd been at the house when the car backed up you would have been left behind."

"No I wouldn't! I'd jump on, too!"

"Then, no, you can't go next time I pick up Bertie from town. Just because I do something doesn't mean it was a good thing to do."

"Then why did you do it?"

"I had to jump or get run over. And when I jumped I landed on the car. The car took off before I could let go. I was stuck. Then I jumped to the other car because I trusted Officer Thompson. It was dangerous, but it wasn't as dangerous as hanging onto a fleeing car. And Grandma and Grandpa aren't going to hear any of this… right?"

"Aw, that's no fair! I have a good story to tell and I can't tell any of it?"

"You have to remember, they are parents. If they knew everything that happened to me they would do nothing but worry."

"You mean we don't know everything?"

"Of course not!"

"Golly! You're lucky you're still alive!"

Jacobsen added, "She nearly wasn't a time or two."

When we got back to the cars it was well past lunchtime and everybody was hungry.

"Let's just go to my house. I've got enough of *something* to go around. Even if it's just sandwiches. Patrick's trail takes off from there. He's anxious to have you track it. It'll take you up into the forest. You need some experience with varying terrains and vegetation, too."

"Now there's three trails," Patrick said. "When you went to town I knew I had time to do another one, so me and Elan both did another trail."

Bertie ran to the guest room when we all trooped into the house. When she came out she was dressed, but her hair was still all wet from a shower.

"You could give a woman a little warning before you bring in a whole passel of men!" she said.

"Our trail for the afternoon takes off from the back yard," I said.

I laid out sandwich fixings and all the guys built up sandwiches however they liked them.

"Do you have any tomato?" Reilly asked.

"Yeah, I just need to cut it up."

I added lettuce leaves, tomato slices and onions to the table. The guys helped themselves to drinks.

Thez started poking around in the freezer.

"What are you looking for?" I asked.

"Cookies," he replied.

"Try the cookie jar," I suggested.

"It's empty," he said.

"And there's none in the freezer?"

"No."

"Then you're out of luck. Take out the cheesecake."

"You should have warned us about dessert before we made three sandwiches apiece," Jacobsen said.

"I didn't think about dessert until Thez brought it up."

"You were right. This is a different training class than we usually go to," Jacobsen commented.

"Sorry about the cookies," Bertie said. "They was chocolate chip."

"It's okay. We can always make more. Just don't let Katie have as many as she wants."

"But she's so cute when she says 'cookie'," Bertie said.

"One cookie. That's all. I usually give her a few little pieces several times a day."

"Oh." said Bertie.

"How many has she conned you out of today?"

"Three, but that's because we ran out."

"How many did you have?"

"I don't know. Your house is the only place I get chocolate chip cookies."

"Katie only gets one. Okay?"

"Okay."

I checked on Katie before we took off. She was down for her early afternoon nap, sleeping peacefully in her crib. I wondered how long she would fit into it.

We went out back and I sent out the groups on their assigned trails.

"Patrick, take Officer Jacobsen down Elan's trail."

"Aw, why?"

"We all need a little practice. You can practice on Elan's trail."

He looked disappointed.

"Elan, take Officer Brockman down Patrick's second trail."

"Reilly and I will take Patrick's first trail, since it is older."

Patrick looked worried. That made me worry. What had he been up to?

"Pat? Can I talk to you for just a second?"

"Umm, yeah…" he said.

I took him aside.

"What are you hiding from me? What did you do on your trails?"

"Nothing!"

"Did you see any snakes?"

"No!"

Hmm, that *no* was way too quick and sure. If he hadn't seen a snake it would have been a disappointed *no*.

"You didn't see any snakes? What did you do?"

"Well, maybe I was a little bit sneaky."

"A little bit sneaky as in what?"

"You're a sneaky tracker. You can help Reilly."

"Officer Tucker."

I wasn't convinced but we set out on our respective trails. I'd told Patrick not to hide his tracks and he hadn't but I got a mischievous feel off the trail. Reilly couldn't tell. He didn't see the tracks lean this way and that as Patrick looked this way and that for opportunities. Opportunities for what? Reilly followed the trail doing the basic reading of it until the tracks went up into the pines. This was where the guys would run into trouble. They weren't used to dealing with vegetation. This was where the instruction would really count.

"If you don't see the tracks take your first clues off the plants. What looks disturbed? It looks hard at first but after a while broken plants will stand out to you, and soil that plants grow in is more likely to be soft enough to leave a good impression."

Reilly struggled along.

"I wonder what a kid like Patrick will grow up into. A brain like his needs to be put to good use. He's got enough spirit in him it's too bad there's no place to explore. If he grew up in the sixteen hundreds he'd have been an explorer. He wouldn't be content to stay home on a farm. He'd be off on some ship somewhere. What's a kid like him got to look forward to these days?"

"Well, he'll always have a job. He can always work horses on my dad's ranch."

"That'd be a shame. He's got more talent than that."

"I know, but it's always an option. You notice I'm not on the ranch training horses. Because there's more to life than that. I think Patrick takes after me enough to branch out. My sister might not like it, but I highly doubt Pat stays on the ranch."

We were watching plants, brushing them aside and looking underneath, examining beds of pine needles, when I spotted what Patrick was disappointed about. Four inches from a very interesting track that would take some reading was a nice, big, rubber snake. Reilly didn't even notice it.

"I wonder how much time we have," I said to Reilly.

"Don't know. We can't see the others. Why?"

"I want to take some time to teach Patrick a lesson."

"Patrick? Why?"

"Stay within a few yards of this spot and look at the tracks. Patrick didn't just walk through here. It might look like he did, but he didn't. I'm going to teach him a lesson."

I looked around for a forked branch and broke one off. I got out my pocketknife and whittled the fork so it had a hook on one end and a stub of branch sticking out of the handle. I poked the fork into the ground near the snake's body. I tied my shoelace into a loop and then tied the ends to the sapling and the snake's tail. I hooked the loop onto the stick. When Patrick picked up the snake it would pull the string loose from the trip stick and the sapling would pull the snake out of his hand and up into the tree. Reilly watched my actions with interest. I tossed some forest litter over the shoe laces to hide my work.

"Next time Patrick hides a rubber snake on the trail I expect you to see it," I told him. "And keep Patrick's secret. It might prove to be entertaining."

"How did you see that? I tracked right over that spot and I didn't see it."

"I saw the fact that Patrick was trying to hide his tracks. The snake is in plain sight. You should have seen it. Don't focus on the trail to the exclusion of other things. You'll miss secondary sign if you do that. In your job secondary sign might be as important as primary sign. Secondary sign frequently takes the form of evidence, so watch for it."

"So, can I come back with Patrick when he retrieves his snake?"

"I'm not sure when that will be."

"Can I play it up?"

"What are you going to do?"

"Oh, nothing much, just tell Thez we saw a snake *this big* and how we were lucky to come out without so much as a scratch, how we jumped clean out of the county when it rattled at us…"

"How did you know this was a set up for Thez?"

"Because Jacobsen would just shoot it."

"Who says it wasn't left here for you?"

"Umm, 'cause I wouldn't have seen it?"

"Have you ever seen Thez see a snake?"

"No."

"Neither has Patrick, but he'd like to."

"So it *was* set up there for Thez."

"Yeah, it was. I knew Patrick was up to something."

After finding the snake we relaxed a bit. Reilly was impressed with both sides of the practical joke. We were quietly tracking along reading sign when Reilly jumped with a shriek.

"Ahh! What's this doing up here! It's supposed to like deserts! Cassidy! Look!"

"Now do you know what Thez looks like when he sees a snake?" I asked calmly.

Reilly was about as black as they come but he blushed anyway. I wondered how a black person blushed. I decided it was body language. I picked up the rubber tarantula. Reilly jumped back.

"It's fake too?"

"He said he was buying something to bring back for his brother. I should have suspected something then."

"What do you think? Now that you've fallen for one of his pranks, what should we do with it?"

"Aw, put it back. You say Thez jumps like that, too?"

"Yeah."

"Then put it back. I want to see what happens when Thez sees it, too."

"You're sadistic."

"Okay, I'll admit that."

The tracks left the pines and dropped down into junipers again and Reilly had easy tracking again.

"We need to track in the forest more. That was tough."

"We will. We still have a lot to learn. We'll take the Suburban up into the mountains and track the creeks and rocks."

"Oh goodie."

When we met back at the house I didn't mention the snake or the tarantula to the guys and, as far as I knew, neither did Reilly. Later, while I was cooking dinner Patrick quietly disappeared. Rusty came home. Right before dinner was done Patrick came in the back door.

"Where have you been?" Rusty asked him.

"Aw, ummm, well, I guess you could say I've been taking notes."

"You went back for the snake, didn't you?" I asked.

"That was a good trick you played. Do you want your shoe laces back?"

"Yeah, that might be helpful. Do you want to tell Uncle Rusty about it?"

"Will I get in trouble?"

"Did you get in trouble from me?"

He smiled. "Is that all the trouble I'm going to get?"

"From me."

"Thanks," he said. "It gave me a better idea. Do you have any fishing line?"

Over dinner he told Rusty about the snake and the tarantula.

"Reilly didn't see the snake but he sure saw the tarantula," I told him. "He jumped almost as high as Thez does. He didn't dance around like a girl though."

"I wish I could have seen it. He won't tell Thez will he?"

"No, he can't wait for Thez to jump like he did."

"Good," Pat giggled. "Do you think I can make the snake move if I tie fishing line to its head? I can thread the line around a tree so I can reach it from behind Thez. He should be in the lead anyway."

"So…you want to be paired up with Thez next time?"

"Can I?"

"Stay out of the way when he jumps. He's a good jumper."

"Okay."

Chapter 6

The next day we were working out of Elk Meadows. The camp Rusty declared jinxed. I didn't tell him what we were doing. The first time I'd been there I'd been chased by drug dealers. I didn't spend much time there because I was riding a stolen dirt bike as fast as I could to get away from them.

The second time I went there Chase and I had a tracking contest. I got very ill on that hike and ended up holed up, barely aware of the things going on around me. Even Chase couldn't find me.

The third time I was there I was looking for a missing teacher and after that an unpleasant bout of trouble sent me on increasingly dangerous searches.

Rusty would rather I avoid Elk Meadows. But Elk Meadows was handy from a tracking standpoint. It had the meadows. In another direction we could easily reach a creek. And a little way down a trail was a big shale mountain. The guys needed to learn how to deal with rock. Rock is the bane of trackers everywhere. So the big shale mountain made a good learning place.

Patrick's pockets bulged. I assumed they bulged with rubber snake and tarantula.

As the guys made their way up into the mountains from the station Elan, Patrick and I laid a trail across the meadow and up into the pines behind it. Since this was show time for Patrick I had all of us lay trails fairly close together. When Thez made his big jump everybody wanted to see it. I felt a little sorry for Thez. If I was going to make a fool out of myself I wouldn't want it to be in front of my coworkers, but by now everybody knew about the ploy except Thez and Jacobsen. Jacobsen would keep quiet. Reilly couldn't really say anything because he knew he had jumped, too. So I only felt mildly guilty for setting up Thez.

"You can do what you want in the meadow. The bent grass will give you away. That's the reason for even walking through the meadow, so they can read the grass. In the pines just give them a variety. We'll take a short rest so they can see what a resting spot reads like."

We walked across the meadow and up into the pines. We sat in the shade of some pine trees and Patrick went to work rigging up his snake. He put the head an inch from where he had sat and he ran the fishing line around some sturdy weeds so that when Thez bent down to read the spot Patrick could make the snake's head move. Patrick gave it a few experimental tugs and seemed satisfied that there would be no way for Thez to miss seeing the snake like Reilly had. We continued up the mountainside throwing in a couple of tracking tricks, then turned around and made our way back to the Jeep.

"This one is too easy," Patrick said.

"They just need experience. Besides, the afternoon will be more challenging."

"Do we have time to lay those trails, too?"

"We won't need to lay a trail. I want the guys to watch me lay just a small section of it. It'll be tough for them even if they watch me do it."

"I don't get it."

"You will when you see it."

When the officers drove up in the big, black and white Suburban, Patrick was ready to roll. They might have looked like campers but their weapons and their demeanor still said cop all over it. Thez walked tall and official like. Reilly was quick and cocky. His attitude was contagious. Jacobsen was calm authority.

"Hey guys!" I greeted them as they walked up, "I have a surprise for you. We're not going back to town for lunch. We're cooking it here at the campground so we can work grasslands, rocks and streams all in one day."

"Oh great," Thez said, "Backpacker food."

"This is different backpacker food. It's a specialty of mine. But first we have to track the meadow."

"Let's do it then!" Reilly said. "I know when a woman says something's a specialty of theirs it's worth workin' for."

"This is Cassidy," Thez reminded him.

"If it's half as good as her cookies it'll be worth it."

"I don't claim to be the world's best cook but I also haven't gotten into trouble in the kitchen so far."

"That just goes to show trouble's got to be male. And he knows better than to get in the way in a woman's kitchen," said Reilly.

"Uncle Rusty sure doesn't look puny," said Patrick.

"Okay, tracking first. The sooner we finish the first trail the sooner we can start on lunch. The meadow shouldn't be too tough. I want you to look at the vegetation. It will tell you most of what you need to know. Without even seeing a track you can see what direction the person traveled in. You just need to be careful not to trust the grasses too much. You still have to verify you are on the right tracks. It's too easy to lose a trail in this stuff. One deer walking through the meadow can lead you in the wrong direction if you don't verify the tracks. Choose a trail. By the time you cross the meadow I want you to be able to tell me who you were tracking. Then the trails will go up into the trees for a while before circling back."

Jacobsen chose the middle trail without hesitation. Reilly chose Elan's and I saw Patrick do a silent "Yes!" as Thez was left with his trail.

We had just started out when Jacobsen confessed, "I cheated."

"How so?"

"I knew this was your trail before we started. It just made sense that you'd walk in the middle so you could talk to Elan and Patrick as you went along. If there's one thing you are, it's practical."

"Tell me how you can tell by the tracks."

"You…you have a procedure to your walk. There's a purpose behind it. Can you tell me what it is?"

"Sure, but describe it and you might explain it to yourself."

"I uh… I guess I noticed mostly from watching you walk, not from the tracks. You come down lightly on your heel and you transfer your weight gradually. Eventually the weight is smoothly distributed over the length of the track but most of the weight seems to be on the outside of your foot. Why walk like that? There's got to be something to it."

"There is. I feel the ground as I walk. When I am in the woods I am either watching for animals or I am tracking. Either way I don't want to worry about what my feet are doing. So I let my feet take care of themselves. They feel their way while I do more interesting things. Through a meadow or almost any open ground I can walk confidently because I can feel things as I come to them. If I feel a sharp rock or a stick I just adjust my footing so I don't step on it."

"Interesting. You must look at your feet some. I haven't spotted a place where you started to put your foot down and changed your mind."

"You probably have but you didn't notice it because I didn't put my weight down until I was sure. You would see the more readable one and ignore something that barely showed up."

"Still, that's a good thing to know. If I was looking for you, and noticed that, it would be a sure sign I was on the right track."

"No matter who you track, try to pick up on their mannerisms. If you can do that it'll help you as you go. If you pin down their normal behaviors, changes from it will be easier to spot. That makes profiling easier, too."

"What do you do when you profile?"

"Just like criminal profiling. You build up a whole bunch of little facts in your head as you go along. Start out with things like: size ten shoe, heavy guy, long stride means he's tall. How tall? If the stride is longer than yours he's probably taller than you. You get the idea. Then add in habits they have on the trail. Some people break off branches that get in the way. Some people bully their way through crushing everything in their path. There are lots of examples but you have to be observant to spot them at first. "

"I think I get what you are saying. How long does it take to get a feel for a person's mannerisms on a trail?"

"The obvious ones are easy to spot. As you gain experience you'll spot more and more of them. At first you will only see the fact that the track is there. Then you will begin realizing that the tracks are clues to more detailed things. That's when you begin to *read* the tracks. When you read tracks long enough you will realize the little facts present a picture of a person. A calm person will have calm tracks. A tense person will have tense tracks."

"You think I could do that now?"

"I think you could see a definite difference if you did it on good tracking ground. Haste and injuries create more sign. That's easy to spot. People's trail habits help you tell one person from another, too. Take Thez and Reilly. Thez is always concerned with image. It shows in his tracks. Reilly doesn't care what people think. He prances through life heedless of what other people think. He's a bit of a show off and it comes out in his tracks."

"What about me?"

"You're a typical cop. Your tracks say you have a job to do and your feet are a very minor part of that. Your tracks are all business."

"Hmm."

"Hmm what?"

"Nothing."

"What?"

"I guess you couldn't know me other than from the job."

I laughed quietly, "You're disappointed that your tracks don't stand out in some special way? Everybody's tracks are different. Just because you're a cop doesn't mean they are identical. If it helps at all, Rusty's tracks are very much the same, yet I could pick up his tracks anywhere. It's kind of handy being able to find him anywhere there's dirt."

We waded through the grass, Jacobsen checking the tracks occasionally.

"You can often tell the mood of the trail by how thrashed the plants are. A run will really tear them up. A lost person will stumble a lot in a place like this. That gives you important clues about their condition. A person who stumbles a lot is wearing out. It's time to step up the search if you see the steps fumbling and stumbling. Even just a walk leaves a good trail, although the grasses will spring back up eventually. It can be a real pain to have to track a person through a meadow if the trail is a few days old. You have to check under the grass because it doesn't bend like it did when the trail was fresh."

"I feel like I'm taking a walk with a tracking encyclopedia."

"Does it bother you?"

"No, it's just like drinking out of a fire hose. But I figure I'll retain some of it. Maybe if I hear it enough I'll know enough to make a difference."

"The knowledge is always helpful, even if you never use it. Just having it will change your thinking. Changing your thinking to include the minute will make you more observant in everything you do."

I looked around to see how the others were coming along on their trails. I was kind of hoping to be nearby when Thez saw the snake.

The walk across the meadow wasn't much of a challenge but the climb up the mountain on the far side had most of us winded. Elan and Reilly arrived first. They sat on a fallen log to catch their breath. Jacobsen and I joined them. Patrick always seemed to take the longest. I thought his trail through the meadow had been fairly straightforward but there was no telling what his feet had been up to without going back and tracking it. Pat was also more of a talker. He was probably talking Thez through every step and bugging him for police and firefighting stories. I wondered if he tried anything tricky or puzzling that Thez might be stuck on.

"I'm hungry," said Reilly. "You got something good down there?"

"Rusty always likes it."

"What is it?"

"Mayo Jar Steak."

"Huh?"

"It gets its name because I pack it in an old mayonnaise jar and carry it around in the mountains before I cook it. It also has to be cooked over a campfire. Every time I follow that recipe people love it."

"Weird recipe. No teaspoon of that, or a cup of this?"

"Well, yeah, there's that, too."

"It's steak. We'll like it," said Jacobsen.

Thez came huffing and puffing up the mountain and Patrick jogged up. It was amazing how much a simple practical joke could energize a kid. He didn't want to rest here. He knew a much better place than this.

"We'll get back on the trail in a minute," I told him. "Let Thez rest."

"How'd you pack so many tracking tricks into one kid?" Thez asked.

"What do you mean?"

"You weren't watching him while he laid that trail?"

"Some of the time. We were never far apart so I pretty much just let him go. We were just going up the side of the mountain and then back to the car. He wasn't going to get lost."

"You track him next time," Thez said.

"Patrick? What did you do?"

"It's confusing when the grass goes one way but the tracks go another," complained Thez.

"Pat, lost people don't stop to mess up their trail. We're trying to teach these guys to find lost people and fugitives."

"Aw, you said I could have a little fun."

"He climbed up into a tree and dropped down from a branch so his tracks were ten feet apart. How was I supposed to know the tracks didn't continue forward?"

"Patrick, if you're going to pull a trick on somebody you shouldn't frustrate them first." I was referring to the snake but Thez thought I was referring to the tree trick.

I was a little worried about sic'ing the snake on Thez so soon after coming off a frustrating trail. I hoped the steak would make it up to him a little bit.

"I'm starving," said Thez. "Let's finish this thing."

I looked at Patrick and he looked at me. Neither one of us knew what to do. Thez settled it by finding his set of tracks and setting off by himself.

Reilly and Elan had been sitting longer than the rest of us so they were ready to go. I think Thez was the only one really tracking. No one was thinking about the trail anymore.

"It's important for you to be able to recognize a resting spot. A resting spot will tell you a lot about the person you are tracking. Make a note of the amount of time you think they stayed there. Every minute they rest gives you time to catch up. You can judge the time by the amount of movement there is. People are rarely still, even when resting. If they sit cross-legged their feet fall asleep and they have to straighten out. They might take the time to eat or drink. Any hints you can pick up will be helpful. All three of us stopped here to rest. See if you can find all three spots and guess how long we were here. Try to figure out what we might have been doing."

"It just looks like a spot in the forest to me," said Thez.

"Look for flattened plants, smoothed earth, broken branch tips, plucked leaves, scuffmarks from feet moving around. At times Patrick was walking around while Elan and I rested. Just see what you can see."

Jacobsen, Reilly and Thez put their heads together moving around the clearing while trying not to step on any sign.

"Is that a flat spot?" Thez said. "It's hard to tell a flat spot from a not flat spot."

"Maybe the dirt looks the same as when you test out a new chair at a furniture store," Reilly said.

"What?" asked Jacobsen, not catching the link between tracking and furniture shopping.

"You know how you sit on a new chair and when you get up you can see your butt print in the seat? I bet the dirt would look like that, except…dirt colored."

"So we're looking for butt prints in the forest. Great," said Thez.

Patrick was sitting inconspicuously at the end of his fishing line, waiting patiently, trying not to snicker.

It was Reilly who found the first resting spot.

"A butt! A butt! I found a butt print! Were you three sitting close together?"

"Not buddy buddy close, but within talking distance," I answered.

"All right! We can do this! And then we eat!" Reilly said. "Butt print number one! Two! And Three!" he added triumphantly.

"That's just the first part. How long were we here? What did we do?"

Patrick gave me a thankful look and snickered silently to himself, hunched over his invisible fishing line.

"Couldn't've been long," Jacobsen mumbled. "Cassidy never stays still for long."

"Here's a scuff mark."

"Hey, yeah," said Thez, "let's check the others."

The group moved from butt print to butt print pointing out little tell tale signs. Patrick waited until they were poised over the snake and gave the fishing line an experimental tug. He went for a smoother puuuullll, just an inch.

All the color drained out of Thez's face. He screamed, "Aiiiiiiiiii!" and jumped four feet straight up in the air. He came down and stomped the snake into the ground. *Stomp! Stomp! Stomp!*

"Damn it Thez! Just shoot the thing!" Jacobsen said pulling his forty-five. He pointed it at the snake. *Bam*!

The rubber snake was dead.

Elan stood back, in his own quiet way enjoying the scene unfold. Patrick was rolling on the ground laughing. Reilly was slapping his leg and guffawing along with Patrick. I thought I better run for camp and have those steaks done to perfection when everybody came to strangle me. Jacobsen eyed his handiwork.

"Did you kill it?" asked Thez from several feet away.

"Yeah, it's definitely dead," Jacobsen said, picking up the rubber snake. Thez backed up several more feet. Jacobsen took the snake over to Patrick.

"You wouldn't happen to know anything about this, would you Patrick?" Jacobsen asked.

Patrick's eyes got real big. He swallowed big, looking up into Jacobsen's face. Jacobsen was not happy. Cops are real good at not looking happy. Patrick got the full force of *the look*.

"Uh, yes sir," Patrick said.

"You think this was funny?"

"Uh, yes sir."

There was a flicker of a smile.

"At least he tells the truth. *No more*. You got that? You could have gotten someone hurt."

"But it was still funny," Reilly said.

"Uh, Officer Jacobsen, sir?" Patrick said uncertainly.

"Yes."

"Can I have my snake back?"

"Why? It's headless. Nobody's going to fall for a headless snake."

"I know, sir, but it'll make a good story back home. If there's one thing the ranch can use it's a good story."

He handed Patrick the rubber snake.

"If anyone asks questions, it *was* a snake. *A big snake*. Eight foot long rattler!" Reilly said. "It would've killed Thez if it weren't for Jacobsen."

"Okay!" I said brightly, "Lunchtime!"

We forgot about tracking and walked back to Elk Meadows. I jogged back and got the fire going in the fire pit. I knew firewood was scarce so I bought a bundle of wood at the grocery store. When the guys approached I dug out chips, dips and fruit. I scraped the grill and put the steaks on.

"You're right," Jacobsen said. "This is most definitely not like other training classes I've been to." He pulled a cold soda out of the ice chest. I was wondering if he was referring to the food or the snake incident. I chose to think it was the food.

As I was flipping over the steaks a ranger truck pulled into the campground. It was Kelly and Tate. Kelly smiled broadly as they walked up to our group.

"I was hoping it was just you," he said. "We had a call-in about shots being fired."

"One, only one, and it wasn't me," I answered.

"Hey Mister Green!" Patrick said.

"Hey Pat!"

"Sit down. Lunch will be ready soon," I said.

"I've still got this call I've got to check out."

"Then consider it checked," Reilly said. "It was a rattler! Eight feet long! It would've bit Thez except Jacobsen shot it."

"Reilly, I've half a mind to write you up," Jacobsen said.

"Kelly will think it's funny," I told Kent. "Pat, show Kelly the snake."

Patrick pulled the headless snake out of his pocket.

"Isn't it cool? I always wondered what a gun would do to a snake. Officer Jacobsen's a good shot! He took its head off with one shot!"

Kelly tried not to laugh. "You shot a rubber snake?"

Jacobsen shrugged.

"This is a rubber *corn snake*. They're even more harmless than real corn snakes," Kelly said.

"A snake's a snake!" said Thez.

"I couldn't see it very good after Thez stomped it into the ground," Jacobsen said in self-defense.

"Okay, I think we checked out the shots fired report," Kelly said.

"Can you stay for lunch?" I asked. "We're taking a break from a tracking class."

"That isn't Mayo Jar Steak, is it?" Kelly asked.

"Yeah."

"Oh man! Tate, have you ever had Mayo Jar Steak?"

"No," said Tate.

"Okay, I'm staying," Kelly said.

"We have work to do," Tate said.

"Sit down. It'll be worth it. We're investigating a shooting. Remember? It can take hours to investigate a shooting."

Ten minutes later I had seven guys making five jars of Mayo Jar Steak disappear.

"How do you do this?" Reilly asked, stuffing another bite into his mouth.

"Soy sauce, brown sugar and ginger. Put it in a mayonnaise jar. Stuff in a steak. Take it up in the mountains. You have to eat it off a campfire up in the mountains. That's a rule."

"Aw, why?"

"It just makes it better."

"It's better if you backpack and eat it the first night out," Kelly said. "The farther you pack it the better it gets."

"That makes no sense," Reilly said.

"Maybe the farther you pack it the hungrier you get," I offered.

"Now *that* makes sense," Reilly admitted.

After lunch Kelly and Tate went back to work. I led the guys to the creek.

"This is going to be your toughest track yet," I told them. "We're only going to be working this little section of it that you can see here, but it's still going to be the toughest track yet. I'm going to walk from here to that tree over there. When I get back you're going to find the path I took."

"But it's all rocks," Thez said.

"Yup, and I've had to track somebody over these rocks, too. I won't be hiding my tracks. I'm going to tromp through them like a typical hiker. When I get back you can start deciphering it."

I set off just walking, being sure to scrape the rocks, finding little sandy spots to leave a partial track, wading through the creek and coming out the other side. Then I walked back by a different route.

"Okay, there you go. A fifty yards of trail. Good luck."

They grouped around where they saw me take off from.

"Dang!" said Reilly.

"Okay, what do we look for first?" asked Thez.

"Not footprints," said Jacobsen.

"Then what?" asked Reilly.

Always the analytical one Jacobsen suggested they only look at the first two rocks they had seen me step on.

"Is that it?" Reilly asked pointing to a possible scratch.

"I don't know. It's not enough to go on."

"If you're waiting for something to go on, you can't read track to track," Patrick said.

"You can track through these rocks?" Jacobsen asked.

"I don't know, I just know I wouldn't try to see all the tracks here. I'd look for something unusual. Did the rocks shift when she stepped on them? I'd look for rocks that had moved. I'd look for tracks in between the rocks. If I found a footprint in sand, I'd look for sand on top of the next few rocks."

Reilly shrugged, "Wow. That actually makes sense!"

"Lichen!" Thez said.

"Liken it to what?" Reilly asked.

"No, we can examine the lichen on the rocks."

"We can try but there isn't much," said Jacobsen

"Then we can't liken it to much of anything," Reilly said.

"Who did you track over these rocks?" Patrick asked me.

"Chase."

"Oh, wow, how'd you do that?" Pat asked.

"The same way you are doing it."

"But you didn't see him make the tracks. How did you find *anything* in all these rocks?" Patrick asked.

"It wasn't easy. After you track my known route you'll do it without seeing me do it. If you are tracking a lost camper you won't see them pass over rocky places. You'll only have tracks to work with. Patrick had some good suggestions, though."

"So, do we see any rocks that moved? How can you tell if a rock has moved?" Jacobsen said.

"It's near a creek so maybe the underside would be moist," Patrick suggested. "Maybe you can find a moist part of the rock showing. Or a ridge of sand where the rock pushed."

This was new to Patrick, too. There were no rocky creeks near the ranch to practice on. I liked his thinking.

"Try using a little psychology," I suggested. "Look at the tracks leading up to the rocks and look to see where you would step. If you're a lot taller than me then think shorter stride."

"Okay, okay," Jacobsen said pressing his fingertips to his eyes. "We can only do so much. We've got some things to work with. Let's uncross our eyes and try this again. With just what we know now. No more suggestions. We're getting bogged down in suggestions."

By the time they had followed my trail for ten feet they forgot the route I'd taken. Join the club, guys, that's the way tracking goes. After spending an hour looking at the same ten feet of rocks I called them off.

"Okay, let's try something else. Here's what I want you to do: see the creek bed between that tree and that other tree?"

They all looked at the boundaries and nodded.

"Walk around on these rocks. When you feel a rock shift get down and see what the result was. Did it do anything that you can make a mental note of? Walk around and see if any ideas come to you. Basically… track yourself for a little bit."

They spent the rest of the afternoon walking fifty feet of creek bed, getting down on hands and knees and examining rocks. We left Elk Meadows feeling rather defeated, but at least they had forgotten about the snake.

"Meet back at Elk Meadows tomorrow. We have some other rocks to practice on."

"Oh goodie," said Thez.

Chapter 7

"How was tracking class today?" Rusty asked as we entered the house.

"Half of it was easy and half of it was impossible," I said.

"And funny and yummy," said Patrick. "Are we going to tackle those same rocks tomorrow?"

"Those and some other kind."

"Oh man, that was hard."

"Hard is good for you. It forces you to think."

"My thinker has thunk enough for one day. Even my eyes are tired from staring at rocks all day. It's hard to spend a day thinking about scratches on rocks. I'm used to more of a variety."

"I think the snake prank would have provided a little variety."

"He, he, yeah, too bad I couldn't pull it again in the rocks."

"Thez would have broken a leg if you had done it in the rocks. As it is you're lucky Jacobsen is a good steady shot. He could have shot Thez in the foot!"

"I thought he was going to arrest me," Patrick admitted.

"I don't know what he would have charged you with… assault on an officer?"

"Only on his pride," added Elan.

"I better be real careful where I spring the spider," Patrick said.

"No. No tarantulas."

"Aw, why?"

"Because if you do Jacobsen is going to kick you out of class."

"A student can't kick out a teacher."

"You know he can."

"He wouldn't do that. He's nice."

"He has a responsibility to maintain law and order. Thez's reaction to the tarantula wouldn't even come close to being orderly. You had your fun. Now drop it."

"Can I show it to him?"

"If you can do it in an orderly manner," I said.

I started cooking dinner not even thinking about the tarantula. Patrick stuffed it in his pocket and went to feed the birds. As I cooked our dinner I made up little foil packets that would cook easily on the grill after our frustrating morning at the creek. I didn't think I was supposed to teach these guys and feed them, too, but I also didn't want us to be stuck eating backpacker food or having to run to town and waste a couple of hours at a café. It was easier to just pack a picnic and bring it all along. It wasn't hard. I just cooked way too much chicken and cut it up into fajita pouches along with some onions and bell peppers. We still had chips and fruit left. The guys had gone strictly for the steak once it was available.

Over dinner I gave Elan an assignment.

"I want you to hike a circle out of Elk Meadows. You saw where we were at the creek. Follow the creek, making the rocks a minor part of it. In about half a mile you will see a canyon branching off to the south. Cut into the canyon and follow it around. It will bring you close to a trail leading out of Elk Meadows. Take the trail until you see a deep cleft in a rocky mountain. Chimney climb to a ledge and then follow the ledge. It'll lead you around back of the mountain and you'll be near the meadows. Spend a little time wandering the hills behind the meadows and then come back. We'll track that this weekend and see how much the guys learned."

"How far is it?" Elan asked.

"Three or four miles."

"Is it rough?"

"The creek is the toughest part."

"Can I go with him?" Patrick asked.

"That would make it too easy."

"Then can I lay the trail?"

"No, it's too far for you to go by yourself."

"It stinks being a kid."

"You're doing more than most kids."

"Yeah, I guess."

"I know something the guys would like," I said. "It'll kind of make up for the scene today. Look in the ranch truck for a lariat. The guys would like to see you turn a rope."

"They would? Why?"

"Because, it's something they could never do. They can appreciate the skill involved in it. Do it at lunch time tomorrow."

"It's just roping."

"It isn't to them. Will you do it?"

"Aw, I guess."

"Good!"

"I better practice a little after dinner."

He brought in an old, dirty lasso from the ranch truck. It had horsehairs embedded in it. It made me homesick.

He pushed the living room couch over a little to give himself room to work and then he began turning the rope smoothly by his side. He tried sticking a foot in the turning loop but it got caught.

"I haven't done this in months," he confessed. "Between homework and ranch chores I don't have much time to goof around with a dirty old rope. If I can just get the rhythm back…"

"Even if you just lasso a tree stump it'll impress them."

"I think I can manage more'n that."

He spent the evening turning the rope, relearning how to jump into and out of it as it turned. Katie struggled to go play, too. Patrick handed her the rope and she wiggled it around giggling. We had to take it away when she tried to eat it.

The phone rang later in the evening. Rusty picked it up in his office and then brought the phone to me. It was Schroeder.

"Cassidy? How is the tracking class working out?"

"Why? What have you heard?" I asked picturing Jacobsen in Schroeder's office ranting about rubber snakes and kids.

"Nothing. That's why I'm checking in."

Whew!

"It's going about as good as I would expect. The guys are learning. This isn't something that can be learned fast, though. It's going to take time. Years."

"Okay, so look three years down the line. Will any of them be able to pull off a search on their own?"

"It depends. If they tag along with me for those three years and pay attention and learn something every time they go out…maybe."

"You don't sound very sure."

"Reilly needs to get serious about it. I'm not saying he isn't learning and I'm not saying he isn't doing well, but he needs to focus. He won't learn to really read until he changes his attitude. Same with Thez, in a different way. I'm not sure why Thez is here. He is picking it up, but he also seems detached from it all. Jacobsen is focused, he might have what it takes, but I think he'd be better used on the streets. He's a cop. He doesn't really want to spend his time tromping through the woods. I'm not putting any of these guys down. I'll keep working with them. The knowledge is always good to have. I just think tracking is not what these guys were put on the force to do. Their niche is in some other area. Saturday we're going to test what they know. I'll have a loop laid out for them that covers everything. We may be out overnight, but we'll finish the loop. By the end of that drill we'll know more."

"Saturday?"

"If the guys are willing."

"And that's the end of the week."

"Yeah, I'll take on whoever wants to learn more but I think this weekend will convince them one way the other on that count."

"Let me know how it goes."

"Okay."

Chapter 8

The next day our tracking was frustrating, as all tracking on rocks tends to be. We ended up just testing different surfaces. What does it take to scratch a river rock? What does a shifted rock really look like? How long does it take that little line of moisture to dry up and make the rock look normal again? We asked ourselves question after question and tried to answer as many as we could. Some questions just didn't have answers. I led them back to Elk Meadows and we heated up our foil pouches over the fire pit.

"So what it boils down to is you hope your missing person avoids creeks and rocks."

"Well, no, you hope they will find a creek, so they have access to water. You just hope they got to the creek by a route you can follow."

"What do you do if you lose a person's trail?"

"As a beginner? You mark the last sign and call Strict. After you've gained some experience there are other things you can try. You can zigzag the direction you think the person went, hoping to pick up a new part of the trail. I don't recommend that to beginners because if the trail is hard to spot in the first place just think how hard it will be to see some random footprint in the forest. You'd have to be in the right place, at the right time, looking at the right spot, the right way. So until you develop an eye that can catch things like that you stick to the last known track."

"What makes you do this?" Reilly asked and I knew when he asked it that he didn't belong in this role.

"Why do I track? Or why do I work for Strict?"

"Both. If it's so tedious and frustrating, why do it?"

"I like the challenge. I like to see the small things, how one plant can point the way, or one line in the dirt can bring a conclusion to an hour's searching. To me it might get tedious at times, but that just makes beating the challenge all the more rewarding. It's what makes people think I can read the ground like a newspaper, when I can see something nobody else could. Why do I work for Strict? Because it helps people. You've seen people who need help. When it comes, it's like a lifeline. They grab onto it and they have hope again. I like restoring people's hope. I like erasing little kids' fears. I like the phrase *ten sixty-five found, ten forty-five A*. I like hard trails and cold nights, lousy food and hot chocolate on cold mornings, and hearing the guys complain because they have to get up at first light."

"What?"

"You heard me."

"Only time I'm up at first light is when I work a night shift."

"Not if you're on a search with me."

"Believe me, she's serious," Jacobsen said. "She shakes all the tents as soon as the sun appears over the horizon."

"Which reminds me, tomorrow we are going on a search drill, so bring your camping gear."

"Camping?" Reilly said.

"Yeah, bring a tent, sleeping bag, two days worth of food and water, a change of clothes, and any weapons you would carry on a real search. Pack it up into a pack you can carry for two days and meet me here first thing in the morning."

"Camping?" he asked again.

"Yes, camping," Thez told him. "As in pitch a tent under the stars and sleep on rocks. You'll need a camp stove and eating utensils, too."

"I don't have none of that stuff. I never been camping in my life!"

"Well, bring what you do have. Borrow a pack, tent and sleeping bag," I told him. "We can share my stove. Go to Gear Up! for backpacker food."

"Camping! My mama ain't never going to believe this!"

This weekend was going to be interesting.

"I asked Patrick to show you guys something. It has nothing to do with tracking. It's just something he thought up when he was bored. His dad told him to practice roping and Patrick got tired of lassoing fence posts, so he started experimenting. Pat, go get the rope and show the guys what you can do."

"Aw, do I really have to?"

"Just a little bit. You're good at it. I bet they've never seen a kid turn a rope like you can."

Patrick went to the Jeep and pulled out the lariat. It took him a few minutes to get warmed up, but even getting a steady loop moving impressed the guys.

"Hey! Just like on old west TV!" said Reilly.

Pat turned the loop sideways and opened it up wider. He jumped through the loop and back and all the guys smiled broadly. They were too macho to clap.

"The more I grow the harder that gets," said Pat. "It's easier to do it this way." He closed the loop in to a smaller circle and turned it beside his feet. He stepped into and out of the loop as it turned.

"Can I try that?" Thez asked eager to learn anything he could apply to his acting.

"You can try, but I tried to teach Uncle Cody how to do it and he gave up. You have be smooth and consistent and it takes a while to get the right feel for how the rope works."

"Stand on my feet," Thez said. "I can feel the motion while you do it."

Patrick stood on Thez's feet and got the rope to turning Thez put his hand on Patrick's arm as it went around and around but as soon as Thez tried to do it on his own the loop wiggled around and collapsed.

"Smooth and steady," Patrick instructed.

Thez never did get the hang of it before we had to go on to other activities.

After lunch we hiked the trail out of Elk Meadows until we got to the cleft in the side of the mountain. I stepped into the crack and chimney climbed up a few feet.

"Cassidy, what are you doing?" Thez asked.

"I'm leading you to our next lesson. You need to learn to track over different types of rock."

I continued the ten or twelve feet to the ledge and pulled myself onto it. Thez came up next, then Elan. Reilly balked.

"You really think I can climb that thing?" he asked.

"Sure, just push out with your hands and feet. They will support you. Push up with your hands, then push up with your feet, all the way up."

"I ain't never done anything like this either. The most I ever climbed was a bunk bed. When you have four kids in one room you learn bunk bed climbing early on."

"I'll show you!" Patrick said. "See? It's easy!"

"Easy for you! You're a kid. I bet you climb walls."

"Just the barn wall. I spy on the ranch from up on the roof."

"I rest my case."

I gave Patrick a hand up onto the ledge and Jacobsen waited for Reilly to talk himself into it.

"Come on!" Patrick said. "It's a lot easier going up than it is coming down."

"Now that's real encouraging, boy. You just keep on and I might just go back to the car and wait."

"You can't be a real tracker unless you are willing to follow the tracks," Patrick said. "Pretend the tracks led up here. If the tracks go up you have to go up!"

"Okay, the tracks go up, the tracks go up," Reilly said as he stepped into the crack. "Just push out. She-it, I…am…going…to break my neck!"

Patrick led him through the sequence until he was most of the way up. Elan gave him a hand and pulled him over onto the ledge.

"Weeell, will you lookee this! I made it! They need to teach rock climbing in academy. How can they expect us to climb rocks if they don't teach us how?"

Jacobsen ascended the rock and stood with the group giving a nod in the direction we needed to go. The way was obvious, at least Reilly hoped it was. We followed the ledge as it curved around the side of the mountain. Reilly looked down as the ledge wound higher. When it ended we were a short climb down from the backside of the mountain. A plane of loose rock lay before us.

"Awwww no!" Reilly exclaimed. "Not more rock!"

"This is the other kind you are likely to run into," I explained. "It poses different problems. You'll see."

"I got enough problems without adding to 'em," Reilly said.

"Tracking is nothing but problems," I told him. "You have to learn to deal with all of them."

"Why?"

"Because the problems you are dealing with might be minimal compared to the problems your missing person is dealing with."

"Ah, okay, so let's get to it."

We dropped down onto the bare rock. It was an area about forty feet wide by about a hundred feet long. Dirt surrounded it so we could lay a short trail across it.

"How do you find these places?" Jacobsen asked.

"This place? I found it while I was running from some marijuana farmers. I climbed the cleft to get away from them and followed the ledge to see if it was a way out."

"And what if it wasn't?"

"Then I was armed, in a defendable position."

"Reilly, I tell you what. You don't like rocks. Give us a nice, readable trail across these rocks. All you have to do is walk from the dirt onto the rocks and leave us some sign."

"All right!" he said enthusiastically. He found a starting point with plenty of readable dirt. He strode out onto the rocks and checked his tracks. Hmm, a few steps onto the rock and his footprints disappeared. He watched for small rocks and ground at them with his feet. He dragged his feet when he walked. He looked decidedly unlike any hiker I'd seen. Ten feet onto the rocks and he was looking embarrassed.

"Damn rock, don't take a print no how," he said.

"Keep going," I instructed.

As Reilly ground and scraped his way across the rock Thez began looking at the tracks leading in.

"What do you see, Thez," I asked.

"At first it isn't too tough. I can see the tracks leading in. There's sand where the first tracks are on the rocks. Then it gets impossible."

"Not impossible, just more difficult. What's the last readable track?"

We all gathered around a sandy spot on the rock. It wasn't even very sandy, but it could barely be discerned that the sand held a track.

"Okay, Thez, find the next sign."

He looked and looked. I took a magnifying glass out of my pack and handed it to him.

"You got to be kidding," he said.

"No, I've been known to use it. You're the actor. Play Sherlock Holmes."

He adjusted his cap and bent over the track Sherlock Holmes style. Patrick laughed quietly. Thez quickly found out that you can't see a thing looking at the ground through a magnifying glass standing up. He had to get down on his hands and knees before the magnifying glass did any good.

"Sherlock Holmes needed glasses," Thez said. "I wonder what his optometrist said when he asked for glasses with a focal point of four feet."

Patrick reasoned out, "They didn't make glasses that good in Sherlock Holmes's day. If they did, they could have made a magnifying glass that worked from that distance, too."

"There wasn't much call for a magnifying glass you could see the ground with," I told him. "Sherlock Holmes wasn't even real. So all the pictures you see of him are artist's depictions. It's the artists who were shortsighted."

Thez crawled around on the rock very unHolmes like and then said, very Holmes-like, "Ahaaaa, I think I see something. Watson! What do you make of this?"

He pointed to a white smudge that only showed up because Reilly had ground his foot into the rock and a tiny pebble had been mashed in the process.

"Good find!" I said. "Though you can drop the Sherlock Holmes act. It's going to get old really fast. Okay, so you found sign, Jacobsen, try for the next one."

When Elan had gotten the idea of what we were doing I nodded to him that he could hike the loop and meet us back at the campground. He quietly disappeared.

Jacobsen got down on hands and knees and continued the search for the next sign. I was glad to see him try for a side view. He looked through the magnifying glass. He found a spot where Reilly had dragged his foot. There were little scratches in the shale.

"Okay, everybody take a look through the magnifying glass so you recognize these things when you see them again. If you look closely at the scratches they tell you the direction as well as the force behind it. Someone running will put deeper and more forceful scratches in the rock than a walking person. Even though they are hard to see, scratches carry information that is very handy to have. After you look at it with the magnifying glass look at it without it. It's better if you can learn to spot the scratches while standing."

Reilly and Patrick looked through the magnifying glass, too.

"Okay, Reilly, you've got the magnifying glass, find the next sign."

And so it went, all afternoon, all the way across the rocks. We hit the other side with a sigh of relief.

"Okay, Jacobsen, show Reilly how a hiker would cross this rock," I said.

Jacobsen got up wearily and went back to the other side of the rock. He laid a trail that was more typical of what we'd find on a real search.

Reilly shook his head. "Ain't no way," he said.

"Yes there is. It's slow and it's hard but it is possible." I reached into my pocket and pulled out a bunch of loose change. "I'm going to track this. When I see sign I will place a coin near it, within a foot. I want you guys to find the sign I found. First one to spot it gets the coin. Let's see who comes out of this the richest."

I dropped pennies in the first two tracks leading in. The more difficult the sign was to spot the larger the coin I left beside it. They learned real quick if they saw a quarter they would need a magnifying glass.

"If you find the sign, explain to the others what you found."

They had their hands full, between watching me track and figuring out the part of the trail they were on.

"Wait a second!" Reilly said. "There's only a penny here. What makes this as easy to read as a regular track?"

"Jacobsen stepped up onto this rock. The ledge broke off. There's pieces of freshly broken rock all over underneath his track," Thez said.

"Oh, is that what it is?"

"Okay, Reilly, for a dime, how do I know it is freshly broken off rocks?"

"Ooh, ooh, I know!" said Patrick.

"Give Reilly a chance," I said.

Reilly bent over the rock. "The edges are sharper. Umm, not really sharper, they are rougher."

"Okay, I'll give you a nickel for that. Anybody else?"

"I'll go with Reilly's answer," Thez said.

Jacobsen didn't care about the money involved. He stood back observing.

"Okay, Patrick, let's hear your answer."

"Reilly's right," Patrick started out, "but there's other signs, too. See, if you pick up the broken off rock the inside is a different color than the outside. The outside has been rained on and blown on and it's dusty and dull. The inside is rougher and darker and sparklier. Then if you look at the big rock you can see that it shifted a little bit. There's a gap between the rock and some dirt that got blown in beside it. That means that rock moved and the weather hasn't had a chance to break down the dirt again. So the rock moved within the past few days. The gap would tell you how Jacobsen's foot pushed off from the rock. It moved to my left so Jacobsen was moving slightly to the right. Then there's this plant. It might grow like that but, if you look at it, I think the rock pushed it over so it's at a weird angle. These little dry leaves could have fallen off when it got jarred."

"Humph," said Reilly. "Are you sure that's all?"

"Yeah, I think so. I want to see if there's critters under the rock. If the rock wiggles when you step on it, it's able to be moved. Can I see if there's critters underneath it?"

"Sure, but we're moving on."

"I wish I had a jar!" Patrick said.

"Imagine that, getting all that information out of one rock," Reilly said as they once again bent over the rock. The next track had a quarter on it. They got down on hands and knees.

I was studying the shale for clues when all of a sudden all three men jumped to their feet in a miniature version of the wave. A little brown blur ran by.

"Oh, that was so cool!" Patrick said, "A scorpion! Did you see the scorpion! It was really ugly! And fast! Where did it go?"

"Don't catch it!" I called to him. "They sting really bad. Let it go."

"Aw, I want to see it up close."

"You're lucky you didn't *feel* it up close."

"Do you think there's others up here?" Patrick asked.

"Patrick? I'll give you a quarter to go back to the Jeep and read a book," Thez said.

We never did finish reading the tracks in the rocks. We all got bogged down on a particularly hard stretch. We kept at it until Elan rejoined the group and then called it a day.

"Can I ride back in the police truck?" Patrick asked me.

"That would be up to the Officer Jacobsen," I told him.

Jacobsen towered over him. He put his hands on his hips. He tapped his fingers on his big, thick, leather belt. "No snakes?"

"No sir!"

"No scorpions?"

"No."

"I'll drop you off at Cassidy's house on the way in."

"Yes!"

"Remember," I told them. "Tomorrow you have to be ready for a real search. We're tracking a loop and we won't go home until we make the circuit. Bring a tent, sleeping bag, backpacker food, a change of clothes, water. Remember when you're backpacking you need water for drinking, cooking and washing up. Each meal takes a cup of water. So plan accordingly. Don't short yourself. Reilly, I can understand if you can't come up with a camp stove. I don't expect you to buy one unless you plan on doing search and rescue work. If you have my job you need to be able to hit the trail immediately and you need to be prepared to spend days and nights on the trail. You have to be self-contained. Food, clothing, shelter, weapons, gadgets, everything."

"Gadgets?" Reilly asked, "We get gadgets?"

"Radio, GPS, climbing gear, whatever Strict thinks you will need, you have to carry."

This was no problem for Thez and Jacobsen. They had worked search and rescue before. They just had never tracked before. Reilly was still a rookie.

Jacobsen climbed into the driver's seat of the big Sheriff's Suburban. Reilly climbed into the front passenger seat.

"Can we do the siren for the kid?" Reilly asked.

"No." Jacobsen answered "not in the campground."

"On the road?" he asked.

"Depends on traffic," Jacobsen said.

Thez and Patrick got in the back seat and buckled up.

Elan and I packed up the ice chest and loaded the Jeep then climbed in and followed the Suburban out of the campground. It was a steep, windy road that led into Elk Meadows, then a steep windy highway leading down into town. When they reached an open stretch of road Jacobsen turned on the siren.

"I bet Reilly likes the siren more than Patrick does," I said to Elan.

The siren switched off and the Suburban continued down the road. We were half way to town when the black and white began rocking violently. It weaved around a little bit and quickly pulled off the side of the road. Thez jumped out and dashed up the steep hillside. I pulled over and parked behind the Suburban.

Jacobsen looked for oncoming traffic before he exited the truck and made his way around. The other doors opened and Reilly and Patrick got out. Reilly gazed back inside the Suburban. Thez was angrily pacing the hillside, shivering, brushing off his clothes. He wasn't shivering from the cold.

I got out and walked over to the group. Cars zoomed by.

"What's up?" I asked.

"You told me I could show the tarantula to Mister Brockman if I did it in an orderly manner. I only…just…asked him if he wanted to see something.

He said, 'okay'. So I showed it to him."

"How can you touch those things?" Thez exclaimed. "It's ugly and…it's gross."

"And it's rubber," Jacobsen added, "Thez…get a grip." Then he turned to Patrick. "I asked you if you had any snakes or scorpions."

"Yes, sir."

"You said you didn't."

"Yes, sir, I didn't."

"Tomorrow I'm going to frisk you before we hit the trail. Got that?"

Patrick nodded. Jacobsen picked up the tarantula and squeezed the abdomen. It squeaked like a dog toy. Patrick giggled, "That's what Mister Brockman sounded like when he saw it."

Chapter 9

"Mommy!" Katie said excitedly as she ran for the front door.

Patrick ran past and put away his things then came out to play with Katie.

"Katie! Let's go look for deer! You want to stalk the deer?"

"I doubt if they are out there," I told him. "The cars probably scared them away."

"We can go see. We can check for tracks."

He grabbed Katie by the hand and they went out the back door. Katie was saying, "Ga-go da-deer." I wondered at what point adding syllables became stuttering. She seemed to just like adding the extra syllable to the front her words. I thought she was proud of her big words, whether they were wrong or not. I kept hoping she'd outgrow it.

"Katie had a lot of energy today," Bertie said. "She almost jumped off the couch and the breakfast bar. I didn't know she could climb up the drawers in the kitchen."

"She didn't get out the knives again, did she?" I asked.

"No, she can't open that drawer enough to get them out. I think you baby proofed that one good enough."

"Finally!"

"But she can open it enough to get a toe hold in it to climb to the counter."

"Okay, we'll try gluing them closed," I joked. "What's for dinner?"

"Shepherd's Pie."

"Did you write down the recipe?"

"Ain't one. It's stuff with mashed potatoes on top and baked in the oven."

"What kind of stuff?"

"Depends on what tried to get the sheep that night. If the shepherd shot himself a wolf, there's wolf in it."

"What tried to get your sheep last night?"

"A cow."

"Oh really? A cow tried to get the sheep?"

"Yeah, just ask Shadow. And there was beef in the freezer. There wouldn't be beef in the freezer but what somebody got them a cow."

"Thanks for cooking. Are you ready for a vacation?"

"Yeah, I never run so much in my life. You sure Rusty has this weekend off?"

"Pretty sure, we'll ask him when he gets home."

"It feels strange living in a nice warm house, then going back to the street.

I like both in their own way. Just seems the streets feel less and less like a place people are supposed to like. You think I ought to get myself a little apartment somewhere?"

"Could you?"

"Don't know. There's funds I could take advantage of that I'm not. I just kind of built up this life of mine and it was fitting for me for a while, but now I'm wondering if maybe I ought to be moving on. I'm not getting any younger. But in a way I like the streets because…well, because I ain't getting any younger. Someday I cain't live like this with nary a care. I'd like to do it while I can. It just don't seem as right as it once did."

"I know exactly how you feel," I told her.

"Nah, you couldn't. You ain't lived long enough to understand why a woman would choose the streets."

"Yes, I have, because at one time I basically did the same thing, only I didn't hit the streets, I hit the mountains. I'd backpack up into the mountains and live off the land, just living on the trail. I made snares and hunted my food with only a knife and fire making tools. In a way I enjoyed it. I was proud of my resourcefulness. But when I met Rusty I began seeing that there was more to life than surviving."

"Nah, you wouldn't do a thing like that. Look at you. You're everything I'm not. You're…"

"Bertie…don't put yourself down. I'm only me and once I was just as homeless as you. I had a home, but I was homeless inside. That's worse than being homeless only on the outside. I see the real Bertie in there. I see a wonderful person or I wouldn't let you watch Katie. And I see a person who knows how to live in any situation. I don't judge you by your house. So, don't judge me by mine."

"Fair enough," she said.

"Hey, you can make Shepherd's Pie. I'm looking forward to that. I've enjoyed your cooking this week. You've got me spoiled. After this class is over I'm going to have to eat my own cooking again."

"Rusty…"

"Rusty what?"

"It's hard to figure out what I'm a tryin' to ask. How did Rusty change your thinking on living in the mountains?"

"I don't really know. I still like living up there, but I like his world, too. He gave me a glimpse of his life. He gave me a chance to join him in that. Then he invited me to stay. And once I did I couldn't leave him by himself in it."

"Why?"

"Because…then we'd both be homeless…so I stayed."

Bertie seemed unusually quiet the rest of the evening. Rusty came home oblivious to the fact that he was being watched. Bertie had something on her mind, but I left her to it. Her life was her choice. Homelessness wasn't the end of the world. I had faith that she'd make do whatever she chose, just like I had.

Patrick came in just before dinner and Katie was beaming.

"Katie can walk and sneak at the same time!" Patrick announced proudly. "I taught her to sneak by playing Red Light Green Light except we use different words. When I'm not looking I tell her to sneak and when I look at her I tell her to freeze. She won't freeze for long but she's learning. She's smart for a baby!"

"Oh lordy!" said Bertie, "just what I need."

Rusty was late coming home that night. He had things to finish up before his weekend home. He came home tired so I took Bertie to town after dinner. I felt guilty dropping her off at the homeless shelter after our talk. She looked at it differently. She had babysitting money in her pocket and a different outlook on life. But it was her life and her decision.

Chapter 10

"You're going to be gone all weekend?" Rusty asked forlornly.

"We're going to be gone until the guys finish the trail. It would be good for them to be out all night, especially Reilly. He's never even been camping before. He needs to see what he'd be getting into if he sticks with rescue work. Thez needs to stay acclimated. He still jumps whenever he sees something crawl. He almost jumped out of a moving vehicle because of a rubber tarantula."

"Is that what Jacobsen was talking about?"

"What did he say?"

"He didn't appreciate Patrick's pranks."

"Patrick only pulled one prank. He scared Thez with a rubber snake. The second time was just kid curiosity. He wanted to see what lived under a rock. He couldn't help it if a scorpion decided to run straight to where the guys were tracking."

"And the rubber tarantula?"

"He was following orders. He asked if he could just show the tarantula to Thez and I told him he could, if he could do it in an orderly manner. He asked Thez if he wanted to see something. Thez said yes. Patrick took it out of his pocket and Thez freaked."

"How is Thez doing in the tracking department?"

"I'll know better tomorrow. Right now I'd say he could follow an easy trail. He's got more tools than he did before. But he isn't developing the focus and determination it takes to track a difficult trail."

"Reilly?"

"Reilly is doing better but it's hard to tell because he seems to be out there for the fun of it. He can't wait to see what Patrick comes up with next, whether it's tracking or rubber snakes. He's learning. He could get good at it, but I think he needs some time to mature as an officer. I don't think tracking is going to be his forte. Jacobsen is in this for the wrong reason. He could get good at it but the force needs him on the streets. He likes to take on my trails but it's because he thinks somebody needs to be able to track me. He doesn't want to have to wait on Chase whenever I get into trouble."

"That's good."

"It sure can't hurt for him to develop that far but I think it would take him away from what he's really good at. He needs to be teaching Reilly how to be an officer, not following a bunch of tracks up in the hills."

"How many people discouraged you from pursuing tracking? Are you doing the same thing to these guys?"

"Maybe, but you can't keep a real tracker from tracking. I can take these guys out into the mountains. We can follow a trail, but the real test of a tracker is to follow them at the mall, or at the beach, where the last thing on their mind should be tracking. If they go to the mall but they still follow people's tracks, if their eyes are glued to the sand at the beach instead of the girls, then maybe they are a tracker."

"You'll take care of my girl out there?"

"You know I will."

In the morning I outfitted Patrick and Elan with the gear they needed. When you work Search and Rescue you tend to accumulate a lot of gear. If something new came out I bought it to test it.

My pack and I had been through a lot. Once I was on the trail a short time the pack felt like part of me. Even the weight of it felt right. My body knew what three days felt like. It felt like thirty-six nice, compact pounds strapped to my back.

"I'll see you tomorrow," Rusty said with a big hug.

This was about the safest camping trip I could ever choose to go on. No actual missing person. Three armed officers. Just a track in the woods, one night out. Since this trip had the potential to limit my calls a little, he was more inclined to look at it in a positive light.

"Me too!" said Katie.

"Sorry, baby, maybe next time. This isn't play. This is work."

"Me too!"

I gave her a kiss and a hug and handed her up to Rusty.

Elan and Patrick got into the Jeep and Rusty pulled me into a long kiss. "Track fast," he said.

"I'm not going to be doing the tracking. I'm just getting them past the tough spots. The number and type of tough spots will tell me what they've learned."

"Bail them out fast."

"I'll see you tomorrow."

"Love you."

"Love you, too."

We did a quick gear check before heading out.

"Jacobsen, Thez, you have your typical three day pack?"

"Yeah."

"Reilly, what have you got. I see you found a tent and a sleeping bag. Did you buy backpacker food? Let me see what you've got here."

He opened the pack and it contained one change of clothes and backpacker food. The main compartment was full of foil wrapped backpacker meals.

"What are you going to do with all this food? Each packet takes a cup of water. Are you carrying water for all these food packets, too?"

"They looked small. I don't know how you expect a man to live off one little pouch of food. Look…it doesn't even fill a third of the pouch."

"It's not supposed to. You need space in there for water and the food expands as it cooks. Reilly, you don't need all this. Only pack what you need. You weren't planning on cooking all your meals, were you?"

"You told me to bring backpacker food. I brought backpacker food."

I took out the packets. Chicken Parmesan, lasagna, green beans, mashed potatoes. It looked like he was planning on cooking a three-course meal three times a day. I hefted his pack. It weighed a ton.

"Have you put this on your back? How are you going to pack all this stuff?"

I opened the top of the bag his tent was in and felt the material. Canvas. Oh man…

"Where'd you get this tent? You'd have to go back in time to find a tent this heavy."

"It was my dad's, or maybe my grandpa's. The sleeping bag belongs to my niece. Don't laugh. It's purple and it has Bratz on it."

"I'm not sure whether to laugh or not. If you decide to stick with tracking you're going to have to buy your own gear. Don't go shopping alone. And don't take your niece."

I stuffed all the food back in Reilly's pack. He had to learn. And I decided he would learn the most by living with his decisions. If worse came to worse we'd be set for a week, all six of us. If it went like I thought it would, he'd be ready to ditch the tent and half the food before lunch. He was going to freeze at night. But he wouldn't freeze to death, just enough to see he needed real gear.

Jacobsen turned to Patrick. "Turn out your pockets," he said.

Patrick took out a couple of shiny rocks, a pocketknife, a magnesium stick, his wallet. I noticed he had cash sticking out the top of it.

"What are you doing with this?" Jacobsen asked, taking the magnesium stick out of his hand.

"Aunt Cassidy carries one. They're useful. I can start a fire with it."

"I know what it is. What does a kid need a fire starter for?"

"If I'm away from the ranch and I get throwed off my horse…I might need it. To keep warm. I don't use it. I've only used it to learn how. Just like the pocketknife. I only have it in case I need it. On a ranch you need a pocketknife for lots of stuff. But I don't expect to need the stick. I just like to be prepared, that's all. On the ranch we learn lots of things city kids shouldn't learn. I can shoot a twenty-two. I can rope a horse or a calf."

"I'm sure you can," Jacobsen said.

Patrick pulled out a white lump and Jacobsen took it from him.

"What's this?"

"It's a coyote track. When I track a new animal I make a plaster cast of the track. I just think they're interesting."

"There's no telling what you're going to find in a boy's pockets," I said. "What did you carry around when you were nine years old?"

Jacobsen looked embarrassed and handed the track back to Patrick. "Are we ready to go?" he asked.

"No," said Reilly. "This pack weighs a ton. How far do we have to backpack?"

"It's not how far, it's how long," I told him. "We backpack until dark. If we haven't gotten to the end of the trail then we spend the night on the trail and continue the next day. The faster you track the faster you get to go home."

"Then this pack is going to turn me into a tracking machine!" Reilly said.

"How much does it weigh?" I asked.

"I don't know. I brought what you said to bring."

"Well, this will certainly be a learning experience for you even if you don't do any tracking," I said. "Next time, weigh your pack. A guy your size should have no trouble with a forty-five pound pack."

"Forty-five pounds? I bet this weighs more than my Aunt Ladonna. She's one big mama!"

"It doesn't weigh that much, but it'll feel like it by the end of the day. You can leave some food behind but the real weight is in the tent and you have to pack that."

"Aw sheee-it."

"Let's go before Reilly keels over," I said. "Elan, give us a starting point. If you are on a real search Strict, or an officer in charge, will usually give you a starting point. A camp or a vehicle…something. Strict will have talked to the family. He knows where the missing person at least started out. So you will usually be given a set of tracks to get you going. The trail you will be tracking today is one day old. That's easy compared to trails you will have to track in search and rescue. If you are tracking apprehensions or crime scenes the tracks are usually newer. So… Reilly, get us going here. You'll feel the weight less if you are thinking about other things."

Reilly bent over the tracks and almost fell over forward.

"How do you move! I cain't move!"

"Another thing you need to learn," I said.

"Aw, you're kidding. You got to see things that are barely there, in places you never seen before, under a ton of weight…"

"Do you want to trade packs?" I offered.

It's kind of hard for a black guy to turn white but he almost did it. He did it in thought, if not in color. There's an unspoken backpacker rule. Reilly didn't know the backpacker code, but he knew the macho guy rule. The macho guy rule was the same as the backpacker rule. It said, written in stone since the dawn of time, the man has to carry the heavier pack. Or at least appear to be.

"Uh, no, that's okay," he said lamely.

"If anybody has trouble seeing what our lead tracker is seeing just speak up. I need to know where you are having trouble."

And so we were underway.

Reilly struck a balance and located the tracks beginning our search.

The trail leading out of the campground had typical hiking tracks. The tracks were intentionally laid to be visible to beginning trackers, though the traffic from other campers had obscured them. A typical search. The officers picked apart the layers of tracks until we got away from the campground; then, as the number of tracks thinned, Elan's trail became easier to follow. As the grass thinned out the trees took over, dropping leaves and pine needles to obscure the trail. When Reilly got stuck the others would get involved, there was pointing and discussion as they puzzled it out. When they all stood again I knew we were back in business. They did pretty well for about half an hour, but then they stopped over the trail and the pointing began. Comments flew. Speculation set in. Finally they called me over.

"What do you know?" I asked.

"The last known track is here. It points to the next track being right about here. There's nothing to hide the track, so why isn't it there?" Reilly asked.

"How hard is the ground here?"

"It's the same as the last track."

"Are you sure? Test it."

Reilly stuck a finger into the dirt and it left a good print in the dirt beside the track. When he poked the ground where they thought the track should be it was harder but it still left a print.

"Hmmm," he mused. "Do you see it?"

"I didn't see you try everything."

"But do you see it?"

I looked at the track. It wasn't exactly where they thought it would be.

"Yeah, I see it."

This is how the whole morning went until we hit the rocks beside the creek. Then things got tougher.

Patrick got very bored. He would have done better if he was doing the tracking but the most he could do was explore nearby while the officers bent over the footprints. If a question came up he jogged over, daypack bouncing against his rump, only to find out that I wasn't giving any answers. Then he would look at whatever had stumped the guys. Sometimes he figured it out and went on with his exploring. Other times the guys thought they could get help from Patrick, if not from me.

We ate lunch at the creek. We'd gone a quarter of a mile. Maybe I should have told Rusty we'd be back in a week. Reilly opened his pack and took out a backpacker meal.

"What do we do with these things?" he asked.

"Read the instructions," I told him.

"I need boiled water," he reported.

"Okay, so boil some," I said.

I took out my camp stove and tossed it to him. He opened it up and looked it over.

"This?"

"Yup, that. Pump it up, turn on the gas and light it carefully."

We all watched Reilly as he tried to light a camp stove for the first time. *Pump, pump, pump.*

"Nope, keep pumping until it gets tough to push it down again. It'll take ten pumps or more."

He started again, then started looking for matches.

"You're losing pressure. You need to have everything ready."

"Do you have a match?"

Sigh, I tossed him my lighter. He had to pump it up some more. *Foom!*

"Woohoo! We have liftoff!" Reilly said.

"Every time you make a meal you use up gas. If we run out of gas before we run out of trail we eat cold food."

"How do you measure the water?" he asked, "Oh well, I'll just guess."

We were all ready to hit the trail and Reilly was still trying to get water to boil. When he had hot water he poured the contents of the backpacker meal into the pot.

"No!" I said, trying to stop him. Too late.

"How are you going to wash that?" I asked him. "Next time pour the water into the pouch. Then you won't have to wash dishes."

"It'll melt it!"

"No it won't. It's made for that," I said.

He stirred the contents of the pot.

"I think I'm having lasagna soup," he observed.

"Lasagna soup doesn't sound bad. A little messy," Thez said.

"Speaking of which, how to do eat it?" Reilly asked.

"How about with a fork? Spoon? Whittled down stick?" I suggested.

"Aw forget it. Let's go."

"Nope, you have to do something with it. Eat it or trash it but if you pack it in you pack it out."

He sat down with a huff and looked beat. I handed him my fork.

"Sometimes we don't even stop to eat," I told him. "We just eat while we walk."

"No wonder you're so skinny. Lugging packs over miles of mountains. Hardly eating," Reilly said.

"We haven't gone a mile yet. We've got a long way to go and we have to track it all. Thez, it's your turn to take over. We're going to be stuck here a little while. Reilly, eat up, wash the pot and nest all the pieces, and stash it in a pack. Then you'll be set for the trail again."

It took Thez an hour to puzzle out the rocks, with me along to point out hints to him. Fifty feet in an hour. Elan had purposely made those rocks trackable. I wondered as we continued on if the guys would be able to track a missing person over them at all.

We continued up the creek away from the rocky creek bed. I backed off and let Thez track it himself. Things slowed to a crawl again.

"I'm going bug-eyed," Thez said. "How can you spend so much time looking at grains of dirt? After a while they all start looking alike."

"I'm not looking at dirt. I'm looking at links… to a person… in an unknown situation. Wait'll it counts and it won't be dirt anymore."

He thought about it a moment and nodded that he understood.

"How fast could you figure out this trail if there was someone on the other end who had been without water for a day or more, who didn't know where they were or how to find their way out? What if they had fallen off a ledge and lay somewhere with a broken leg? What if there was a kid out there who had gone a day without food? You've got food in your pack. You might not just see it as a bunch of dirt if it led you to where they are."

"How about if you hike back to camp," Thez suggested, "and we'll try to get there before trouble hits you?"

"Nice try, you're not getting rid of me that easily."

We arrived at the canyon and I was looking forward to some quick tracking in its sandy bottom but we were running out of light.

"How much farther do we have to go?" Reilly asked.

"We're almost a third of the way done," Elan reported.

"You mean we got to go twice as far as we went today?" Reilly asked.

"Twice times one third, makes two thirds, yup, sounds right to me," said Jacobsen.

"Can we at least finish this canyon?" Thez asked. "It finally looks easy."

"We'll have to see how far we can get. I really don't want to camp here," I told him.

"Why?" Thez asked.

"See that tree crosswise in the narrow part of the canyon?" I said pointing up.

They all looked to a spot where the canyon was perhaps fifteen feet wide. A tree was wedged in the rocks about two thirds up the side of the canyon wall. It was a big tree. It took a lot of force to put it in its final resting place.

"Yeah," said Thez.

"It landed there in a flash flood. If it landed there in a flash flood how deep was the water in this canyon?"

The guys all stared up at the tree.

"I say we track faster," Thez said, always the cautious one.

"Aw, this is southern California. It don't rain that much here. Heck, it hardly rains at all!" Reilly said.

"Go ask the tree how much it rains," Jacobsen said.

"Can I climb up to it?" Patrick asked. "It looks like fun."

"No, we're trying to get up this canyon before dark. Jacobsen, you want to take a turn at lead?"

After a short time there was no denying it was too dark to go on. I didn't like the location. There was very little flat ground and we ended up pitching tents up and down the sandy wash. Reilly's old, canvas tent was so moth eaten there were gaping holes in the roof. I was glad we weren't expecting rain. It was an old pup tent. I think his grandfather had used it in World War One. His sleeping bag was made for an eight year old kid and would only come up to his armpits. It was also rated for indoor use. Kids' slumber parties. He was going to freeze. Nobody laughed at the Bratz designs on the sleeping bag but we all wondered if we were going to get any sleep at all with Reilly freezing in the next tent.

We started up the stoves and heated water for dinner. Reilly opened up pouches for cheeseburger casserole, green beans and astronaut ice cream. He really was having a three-course meal. I added more water to the pot. Patrick chose macaroni and cheese.

"Aunt Cassidy? Can I have trail mix?"

"Do you want trail mix or do you want to pick out the M&Ms from the trail mix?"

"Aw, you know me too good. I can trick Mom that way."

"You're a kid. A kid is always going to pick out the M&Ms. You can pick out the M&Ms after you eat the main course."

When the water was boiling Patrick brought his pouch so I could pour enough water into it to rehydrate the food inside.

"Zip it closed and let it sit for fifteen minutes," I told him.

I added water to my pouch and handed the pan over to Reilly. He poured water into the Cheeseburger casserole, the green beans… and the ice cream.

"Reilly, the ice cream is meant to be eaten dry. You just made ice cream soup," said Jacobsen.

"What do you mean dry? How can it be ice cream if it's dry?"

"How can it be ice cream if it is floating around in hot water?" I asked.

"Umm," he said uncertainly.

"You can try it," I said. "Who knows, you might have invented a new backpacker dessert."

He didn't though. He sealed his main course closed and then the green beans, then he frowned at the contents of the astronaut ice cream packet. He set it aside. Fifteen minutes later he ate the casserole. He was too full for the green beans. He opened up the ice cream.

"Um…anybody for Neapolitan soup?" Reilly asked.

I looked in and there were little blobs of pink, white and brown floating in mud colored water.

"I don't think you're going to have any takers," I told him.

Before I could even think about what he was doing he poured out the contents about four feet from the corner of his tent.

"Reilly! What are you doing?" I asked, surprised at his ignorance.

"I wasn't going to eat it…none of you wanted it! What was I supposed to do?"

"You never, never, ever leave food out at night when you camp!" I admonished him.

"Why not?"

"Because animals love people food. Leaving food out is an open invitation for any animals within a couple of miles."

"Oh. Anybody want green beans?" he asked.

There were no takers.

"Now what do I do?" he asked.

"You eat it, or pack it out," I stated flatly. "And… think ahead. Only rehydrate what you know you will eat."

"Remember we're up at first light!" I announced as I headed for my sleeping bag.

"Aw, shee-it," said Reilly.

"Let's just hope we can finish this tomorrow," said Jacobsen.

"Now I lay me down to sleep…" said Thez.

"Good night," said Elan.

"Aw, can't I stay up!" said Patrick.

"Sure, you can scare off the critters that come after Reilly's ice cream," I told him.

"What kind of animals?" Reilly asked.

"I don't know. Whatever is in the vicinity," I said.

"Will you tell me a story?" Patrick asked as we headed for bed.

"You've heard them all."

"Come on, I know there's something I haven't heard yet."

"You tell me a story."

"Okay, once upon a time there were three bears, a papa bear, a mama bear and a baby bear. One day the papa bear said, 'Sniff, sniff, I smell some camper's ice cream. I wonder what ice cream tastes like.' And the mama bear said, 'I don't know, are you sure it's ice cream you smell?' and the baby bear said, 'I don't care what it is, now you've made me hungry. Let's go see.' So the three bears went for a walk through the woods to find the elusive *ice cream smell*. Papa bear followed his nose past the campground, over a creek and up into a narrow canyon."

"Alright already!" said Reilly. "I can take a hint."

"Where did you learn the word *elusive*?" I asked Pat.

"That's what deer are. They keep to themselves and hide when people come. That makes them elusive."

"I know what it means. I was just wondering how *you* knew what it meant."

"Oh, I don't know. Maybe I read it in a book somewhere. Maybe that's how Elan described the deer to me when we went out stalking."

"How are you doing on the stalking?" I asked.

"Okay. I just like visiting with the deer. To visit with the deer you have to think like one. That's why I go stalking. If I don't get very close I don't worry about it. They are just feeling more elusive than normal. Can't blame a deer for acting like a deer. But sometimes I get real close into the herd."

As we warmed up in our sleeping bags we got drowsy and eventually we both fell asleep.

Chapter 11

The camp was quiet. It was still dark. What time was it? If it was almost dawn there was no point in going back to sleep.

A shivering sound came from Reilly's tent. "B-b-b-b-burrrrrr, damn it, I'll never get to sleep."

A snuffling sound.

"Shit, not s-s-snoring, t-t-too," Reilly mumbled.

More snuffling sounds. A nosing around a tent. A riiiiiiiiip! A high pitched scream. A startled "Whungh," from a large, black bear.

"Ahhhh!" cried Reilly, "A bear! A bear! Somebody get the bear spray! Ahhhhh! Get away from me! Go… you….bear! I'm trapped!"

"Oh boy!" said Patrick excitedly, "A bear!"

"Reilly, calm down!" I said.

"Easy for you to say! You're not smelling bear breath in your tent!"

"Patrick, avoid the bear and go see Jacobsen."

"Aw, I want to see it."

I got up and shined a flashlight at the bear. I could see Reilly through a big hole in his tent, cowering in fear.

"Reilly, quit acting like food," I said. "Where's your pack?"

"It's right here!"

"Oh. Unzip your tent and back out the doorway. Then stand up and look big a threatening."

He started dragging his pack out with him.

"No! Leave the pack. He's more likely after the pack, not you. Just get out, get away, act big. Do you have your weapon?"

"Y-y-yeah," Reilly stammered.

"Aunt Cassidy! Maybe trouble is on vacation! The bear didn't go for you this time!" Patrick said.

"That's because I didn't leave bait out for him. Reilly did."

All the guys were up now standing around the edges of the camp. Reilly was the only one worried about the situation. Patrick was excited. Jacobsen was patiently optimistic and slightly ticked off. Thez was backed up against the nearest tree looking like he could climb it, even though it lacked branches for at least ten feet of it's length.

"Leave the bear a way out. Don't block the exits up and down the canyon," I instructed.

The bear nosed his way deeper into Reilly's tent. We waited as the bear devoured everything inside. When he was done the bear forced his way through another hole in the tent and ambled my direction.

"Yah! Bear!" I yelled looking as threatening as a little blond woman can in the pitch black night. He squinted at me and walked closer. He wasn't angry or threatening, but he was big. The wall of the canyon was behind me. We'd left the ends of the canyon open so he could leave easily so that put our backs to the wall.

The bear stood up on his hind legs, squinting and sniffing. He lowered his front paws and took another couple of steps.

"Uh, guys? Anybody got a gun?" I asked knowing all the officers were armed with 45 Glocks.

"Where's yours?" Jacobsen asked.

"This was a tracking class! I wasn't going to shoot anything in a tracking class. And it's only a 9mm. It would only make him mad."

Thez tossed me his sidearm and I barely managed to catch it in the dark. The motion piqued the bear's interest and he stepped closer. I checked the gun over, thankful it was Thez's. If it came right down to it I wanted Jacobsen armed. I knew he'd keep his cool. The bear stood before me. If I'd have taken three steps I could have touched him. The guys were getting nervous. Another step.

"Uh, Cassidy…"

"He hasn't threatened me yet. He's still friendly."

Another step. I really didn't want to shoot him. So far all he'd been doing is acting like a curious bear.

"I wish he'd do that to me!" Patrick said.

I yelled at the bear again, "Yah! Get gone bear! Get out of here!"

After a while the bear sniffed the air. He stood up on his hind legs again and sniffed deeply. We stared at each other eye to eye. I brought the gun up, ready, just in case. He looked around, like he didn't like what was on the wind, then he dropped down to all fours and loped away up the canyon.

"Awww," Patrick lamented, "my first bear track and I don't have anything to take a print with. Lookit the tracks! That's so cool! Look, it's bigger than my hand! Wow, it's even bigger than my foot!"

"Reilly, what have you learned on this trip?" I asked.

"The mountains are damn cold! Don't leave food out. Don't leave food in. What made him take off?"

"I don't know. Maybe he just didn't like so many people around. Maybe he smelled a bigger bear coming and he thought he ought to clear out."

"A bigger bear?" Thez asked.

"I was just kidding. Look, it's late. We'll take stock of everything in the morning. Grab what's left of your sleeping bag and find a tent to room in."

"My dad is going to kill me. Look at this tent!"

"I doubt if he's mad," I told him. "It was in pretty sorry shape to start out."

"I can't sleep with a bear in the canyon," Thez said.

"Looked like he was hightailing it out of here," I said.

"How can you be so calm?" Thez asked.

"The bear is just a neighbor. Just like neighbors in the city, you be nice to them and they'll be nice to you. And just like neighbors in the city, if you leave your garage door open they might just borrow your lawnmower. I'm not worried about the bear and I suggest you get some sleep. We have a long day tomorrow, beginning at first light."

They all went to bed. Thez gave Reilly a spot in his tent and in short order everything got quiet again.

"Do you think the bear will come back?" Patrick whispered.

"No, he looked like he had places to go."

"Can we come back and make a cast of his tracks?"

"We'll see. If the weather is calm his tracks might still be around. Uncle Rusty is expecting us home tomorrow."

"Katie might like a hike."

"We'll see. Go to sleep."

I fell into a light sleep, keeping my ears tuned. In a few hours I was drawn from sleep by coughing. I opened my eyes and the tent seemed lighter than it had before. Then the smell hit me. Smoke! I sat up in bed and sniffed the air like the bear had. I wondered if the bear had smelled smoke hours ago and decided he had better places to be. I unzipped the tent. The light was not coming from the sun. The sun wasn't up yet. The light was coming from a wall of flames on the west side of the canyon!

Chapter 12

"Guys! Wake up! Come on, we've got trouble. You need to get up and you need to be alert. Class today is officially canceled."

"What? Cassidy, you're not making sense. It's only three AM," Thez said.

Jacobsen came out of his tent in a rush. He took one look at the canyon wall and went back in for his shoes and his gear.

"Get!" he commanded. "We're clearing out. Pack up your gear and find an article of clothing you can use for a mask. Soak it in water. Keep it handy. Patrick! Where are you?"

"I'm right here," Patrick said wearily. "What's all the commotion?"

"Pack up, we're getting out of here," Jacobsen repeated.

By now we were all standing in the middle of the canyon looking up at the fire. We looked to the other wall. No fire. Yet.

Once the situation was understood we all quickly broke camp. We quickly rolled up or stuffed our sleeping bags and took down our tents. When our camp was on our backs again we discussed our options.

"We don't know where the fire originated," Jacobsen said. "We can assume it's worse to the west. The bear headed up canyon. I trust his judgment. But that takes us away from the campground."

"The campground is west of here," I reminded him. "A camper could have left a campfire burning."

"Cassidy, you know the area."

"Well, we're stuck in the canyon. I suggest we follow the bear up canyon. If we can't exit the canyon that way we hightail it down canyon. We have one thing going for us. There's very little that will burn down here and the smoke should go up."

Jacobsen said, "Thez, you're in charge. You know what could happen."

Thez didn't like our situation one bit. He knew all too well what could happen.

"Everybody get something to cover your nose and mouth with. Dampen it with some of your drinking water. It'll cool the air. Keep it damp, but make sure you can breathe easily through the fabric."

I poured water over an old t-shirt Patrick had packed and slipped it over his head, then pulled it up around his nose. I pulled it back so it was just barely snug around his face.

"Try to keep it like this. Got it?" I said.

"Yeah, my eyes sting."

"I know kiddo, just do your best and if you need help call one of us."

I wet a shirt of my own and pulled it over my head, positioned it and followed the guys up canyon. I made sure Patrick was ahead of me. We walked quickly, but calmly. It seemed every time I found trouble a calm head was what got me out. So… Keep calm. Keep the breathing regulated. Keep walking.

The smoke took on a red haze as dawn colored the sky, but it didn't feel like morning. Even with the sun up it was dim. The sun filtering down through the smoke did little to cheer us. We knew we were in trouble when we caught up to the bear. We all ground to a halt. The bear paced back and forth moaning at a wall of dense smoke. We turned around and headed down canyon again willing that thick wall of smoke to remain stationary.

A plane flew overhead. Thez took note of it and kept going.

Patrick was worried. He kept looking up at the wall of the canyon.

Elan buckled down. He was all business. He knew the danger, but he saw a way out, at least for now.

Reilly went into cop mode. He analyzed the situation. It was good to see that side of him.

Though Thez was placed in charge because he'd been a fireman, Jacobsen remained the leader of the group. Everyone seemed to look to him. He took the responsibility like he took everything else. That's another thing that made him the poster cop. He lived up to it.

As the wind up top increased, ash began snowing down on us. The smoke grew thicker. We tried not to think about it and made our way to the end of the canyon. A burned tree broke off and tumbled into the canyon behind us. Patrick jumped with the sound of it and looked behind him uncertainly.

"You're doing great, Pat. Just keep on," I said.

"I don't like fire," he said.

"You just don't like the situation and I don't blame you. We'll get through this."

The plane flew overhead again.

"Do you think they're looking for us?" I asked.

"If they are it's good news and bad," Thez said.

"How's that?"

"Why would they look for us unless they were really worried?" he pointed out.

"If they saw the truck at the campground they'd know there were people unaccounted for," I said.

"Let's hope the campground is still there. They'll try to save it, but if the fire originated there…"

The fallen tree sent a cloud of smoke and ash down the canyon.

When we could see the other end of the canyon it was bad news, too. The creek flowed peacefully behind the flames. The route to the campground was blocked. So far the east side of the canyon was fire free but the fire could jump the canyon at any time. I had never explored east of the canyon. I only discovered the canyon while I was tracking Chase. I looked around me at the guys. They seemed to be holding up pretty good. We looked at our back trail and the bear was following us, looking lost and trapped. Just what we needed, a moody bruin and a canyon that was gradually turning into a trap. We all gave the bear plenty of room as it made its way to the wall of flames and pawed the earth. He swung back around, clearly agitated.

"Come on, I know one way out," I said.

I led them back up the canyon until we came to a fallen tree that was leaning against the east wall of the canyon. I knew about this tree from tracking Chase. He had used it to try and trick me into continuing up the canyon looking for tracks. The trick didn't work and I was very glad it didn't because it looked like our only way back home. I started up the tree.

"Cassidy, are you sure about this?" Jacobsen asked.

"It's this or the canyon. Maybe we can get around the east side of the fire."

"And what if we can't?" Jacobsen asked. "If the fire jumps the canyon there will be no going back."

The bear was in a panic. When he saw me climbing up the tree he liked the looks of that escape route, too. He charged through all the guys and lunged for the tree.

"Oh shit," I said and started climbing faster. The bear was outclimbing me quickly. He was going to climb right over the top of me, if I didn't do something quick, so I grabbed hold of a branch and dangled there. I was going to drop back down and start over but, before I could, the bear stepped on my hand in his climb to the top.

"Let go!" Jacobsen yelled up to me.

"I can't! He's standing on my hand!" I called down.

The distinctive barnyard smell of wild bear wafted around me as the bear ground my hand into the rough branch. When he got to the top he had trouble navigating onto the cliff and I thought he was going to tumble back down onto me again. He scratched and clawed his way over the ledge, knocking the tree down in the process. I fell to the ground and rolled away from the falling tree as it came crashing to earth beside me.

"Aunt Cassidy! Are you all right?" Patrick said as he ran over.

"Well, you wanted adventure. Are we having fun yet?" I asked.

"Now what are we going to do?" asked Reilly.

I sat on the ground nursing my hand, wondering myself just how we were going to get out of this predicament.

"Now you really can say you touched a bear in the wild!" Patrick said.

"Yeah, but I don't think Grandma wants to hear how it happened."

"Neither does Mom," Patrick added. "Is this what trouble usually feels like?"

"No, Pat, trouble is different every time."

Thez knelt in front of me. "Let me see your hand," he said.

I held it out for his inspection. I'd seen him on rescue calls. He was a decent EMT when it came right down to it. He felt the bones in my hand.

"I've got to hand it to you, Cassidy. I was wondering if all your trouble in this class was going to consist of pranks with rubber animals. When *you* come up with trouble, it's real trouble. Wiggle your fingers…good…now make a fist."

"I think it's just squished," I told him.

He nodded agreement. "I don't think anything is broken. You're lucky you aren't pinned beneath that tree."

"Luck and trouble seem to go hand in hand," I said.

"Enough with the hand puns!" said Reilly.

"What hand puns?" Thez and I said.

Jacobsen and Elan just shook their heads and I tried to replay the conversation to catch the puns.

"You are so blond," said Reilly, "but, really, how are we going to get out of here?"

"I hear a helicopter," said Patrick.

We all stopped to listen.

"They can't see us for all the smoke," Thez said.

We were red eyed from smoke, covered in ash, had t-shirts wound around our heads. We still had bed head. We were a sight. And we didn't care. As long as we got out of this alive we would all go down to Trujillo's and have a party. Nobody would admit they were worried. But I'm sure we all were.

"Aunt Cassidy?"

"What is it Pat?"

"We want to get up there?" he asked pointing to the east wall of the canyon.

"Yeah, I hope. I don't know what we are going to do once we get up there, but it's at least further away from the fire."

I was still amazed that the fire hadn't jumped the canyon.

"I have the lariat," Pat said.

All ears swiveled Patrick's way and I knew the guys were ready to try the eastern wall.

"Why didn't you lasso that bear?" I joked. "He would have pulled us out of here!"

"Lasso a bear! Cool! Yeah! I should have thought of that. I can just see my excuse report. I missed school because I had to rescue a bunch of police officers from a fire by lassoing a bear!" He laughed, "Talk about creative excuses! I bet my teacher would read that one out loud and nobody would believe it."

"Get used to it. If you have the trouble gene…"

"Patrick, do you think you can lasso that bush?" Jacobsen asked.

"I can try. I never had to lasso anything above my head before. Usually when you lasso something you let gravity work for you, not against you."

"Give it a try."

Patrick tried and tried but he couldn't get the loop high enough. Jacobsen tried but he didn't let the rope play out right and the loop closed before it got to the bush. This was no fancy trick roping but it still took a bit of skill in managing a rope. I tried to lasso the bush because I had lassoed a calf or two in my time but I couldn't get it high enough either.

"Kent? Can you stand with me on your shoulders?" I asked.

"If you sit up there you'll hardly be taller than my arm when it's extended."

"What if I stand up there?"

"Can you balance?"

"It can't hurt to try. I've stood on a moving horse before." I got tossed off into a fence when I did it, too.

I took my pack off and climbed onto Jacobsen's shoulders. He straightened up and planted his feet shoulder width apart for balance. I took the lariat. If it had been a long rope we could have tied a weight to the end and just thrown it over the bush, but the lariat wasn't long enough to do that. I stood up slowly and shakily, trying not to cough because of the smoke. When I found my balance I opened up the loop, felt the weight of it in my hand and flung it up and over a little. The movement set me off balance and I grasped at the lariat instinctively. At first I was just falling but then the lariat caught on the bush and I felt the rope snap stiffly in my hand. I rode the rope right into the side of the canyon.

"You did it!" cried Patrick.

I sure did. I body slammed myself. I slid to the end of the rope and invited anybody who wanted to go first to start climbing. Patrick jumped at the chance.

"Whoa, hold up eager beaver," Jacobsen said. "We need an adult up top just in case someone needs help. Thez you take a look at Cass and be here just in case we have more trouble. I'll climb up and help those coming up."

Thez nodded and made his way over to me.

"You okay?" he asked.

"Oh yeah, you can't get me down that easy. This is nothing compared to what trouble usually throws at me."

After Jacobsen climbed up Patrick headed for the rope.

"Patrick? You know how to climb a rope?" Thez asked.

"Yeah! Aunt Cassidy put a rope on my tree house when I was five."

"Okay, go for it. Stay near Officer Jacobsen once you get up there," Thez told him.

Elan followed Patrick up and then Reilly climbed the rope. Thez offered me a hand up and I knew it was my turn. I pulled myself to the top and Jacobsen hauled me over the edge onto firm ground again.

The smoke was worse on top. Everybody stood around blinking and coughing, as Thez made his way up. When he got to the top he pulled up the end of the lariat and my pack was tied to the end. Oh, man, I was really slipping. We needed that pack. Besides the contents and the fact that it contained a map of the area, it was a gift from Rusty. It was more than a pack to me. It was a tool, a link to past searches, a link to Rusty… if I'd left it I would have gone back for it if at all possible.

"Thanks, Thez," I said, "I'd be really sad if I left it behind."

I untied the rope and handed it over to Patrick, then pulled the map out of my pack. Jacobsen, Thez and I bent over it.

"Here's where we are," I said pointing out our location on the map. "The fire's to the west. We have to go east, no choices there. East covers a lot of ground, though. Any suggestions?"

"North is out," Jacobsen said. "Look at the lines. It's too rough. South looks more manageable, if it's free of fire. There's a road that way, too. Due east is a possibility but there's nothing for miles."

"If we go due east we are guaranteed another night on the mountain," I observed, "We've got the food and water. Reilly will have another cold night. I think, except for the lost tent, we are in pretty good shape."

Looking across the canyon all we could do was hope it took the fire a while to jump the canyon. We all geared up again and set off to the south east, hopefully to a highway going through the mountains. We kept a steady pace, though we were all weary and our minds were crowded. The south end of the fire began pushing us more and more east and farther from a road.

It was late in the afternoon and my thoughts strayed home, to my nice, peaceful house. Rusty and Katie waiting for mommy to get home. I wondered if they knew about the fire. I hoped they didn't. I'd rather they have a peaceful day playing, maybe taking a nap on the old brown couch. Days with Katie were rarely peaceful. They were usually spent monitoring her every move. There were too many climbable things in the house. I was glad we'd managed to baby proof the knife drawer. I was hiking along, following

Jacobsen when my subconscious screamed, “Stop!”

“Kent wait,” I said.

“What is it?”

“I don’t know,” I said, tuning my senses to the things around me, “Give me a minute.”

Everybody ground to a halt as I craned my ears. When I couldn’t hear anything distinctive I looked at the ground. Something had caught my attention. What was it? I backed up several yards. It was something I’d seen within the last few minutes, maybe even seconds. It took me a minute to find it. A track. What was a track doing here?

“Thez, take a look at this. Does it look familiar to you?” I asked.

He squatted down to where he could get a better look.

“Fire department boots.”

“Why would the fire department be out here?” I asked.

“Maybe they dropped some guys behind the fire line. We don’t know exactly where the fire line is, but they do,” Thez said.

“You mean it could be closer than we think?” Reilly asked.

“Let’s follow the tracks. All the firemen have radios. If we can find them we’ve got a way out.”

I followed the tracks. They were all business. Heading for work. Hot, sweaty, dirty, dangerous work. The smoke got thicker until it looked like we were walking through a fog.

“Aunt Cassidy, my head hurts,” Patrick said. It was his first word of complaint all weekend.

“It’s probably from the smoke,” I told him. “We can’t get rid of the smoke. Try tracking. Maybe it’ll take your mind off your head.”

The further we went the more tracks we saw. The more tracks I saw the harder I pushed myself. I knew I shouldn’t push but I was worried about Patrick. I didn’t feel well either. My throat was sore and I had a nagging headache, too. My eyes burned and my breathing was getting more labored. I sure hoped these guys were…

“Aunt Cassidy! What’s that?” Patrick asked pointing into the smoke.

There was a flash of reflective strip on the sleeve of a coat. Thez saw it, too. He dashed after it and pretty soon he came back with an astonished firefighter. Jacobsen and Thez identified our party in terms the firemen would understand at which point we were declared ten sixty-five found.

“Ten forty-five?”

“Forty-five unknown.”

A request was made for a pickup and there was some confusion about how to do that. A call was made to the helicopter to find out where a pickup could take place. As the men talked we were ushered to a less smoky area.

When Patrick began stumbling the fireman stopped and gave him oxygen.

"Hey, buddy," the fireman said, "What are you doing with this group?"

"Teaching tracking," Patrick's muffled answer came through the mask.

"How do you feel?"

"Okay, I guess."

"Atta boy, keep the mask on. Breathe nice and even."

"We did it," Pat said. "We beat trouble again."

"What's your name?"

"Patrick. What's yours?"

"Bodie Maverick."

"It sounds like a cowboy name," Patrick said.

"A fireman is about as close as you can get to being a cowboy in southern California."

"I live in California on a ranch. I help my dad and my grandpa with the quarter horses."

"Then you're more of a cowboy than me," Bodie said.

When the helicopter clattered overhead the radio talk started up again. They started to send down the basket.

"No." I told Bodie, "We don't need a basket. These guys have earned the right to be treated like equals."

"And you are?"

"Cassidy Michaels, tracker, Joshua Hills district. Just tell them what to do, they'll be fine on the cable. Ask Jacobsen. He'll tell you."

"Have you ridden the cable before?" Bodie asked.

"Many times."

"The kid's not going to freak out?"

"If I ride the cable, he'll ride the cable."

"Jacobsen, talk some sense into her," Bodie said.

Jacobsen looked at Patrick, then to me, then to Bodie. "Let him ride the cable. He kept his cool when confronted by a bear. He can track as well as any of the officers. He's kept calm through the fire and smoke. He's earned the chance to ride the cable like the rest of us."

The cable came down with six harnesses.

"Put it on like I do," I said to Patrick. "It's kind of like harnessing a horse. You want it to be snug enough to hold you but loose enough to be comfortable. See this clip? That's going to attach you to the cable. When you go up, just hold on. When you get up to the helicopter it will be really noisy. Watch for a metal bar. Grab the metal bar and pull yourself over to it. Keep hold of the bar until you have your balance. A man up there will make sure you're away from the opening, unclip you, and point you to a bench. When he does, just sit down and wait. Don't move around in the helicopter. There's going to be a lot going on and you need to be out of the way. Got it?"

"Got it. Boy when you get in trouble it sure can get complicated getting out of it."

"Tell me about it. Let me check your harness. Not too loose? Not too tight?"

"Thanks for standing up for me. They was just lookin' out for me but I'm glad I get to ride the cable."

"Pay attention to your balance. Stay upright. All right, Thez is up there. Listen to him. I'll be up soon."

I clipped the cable to his harness and watched as he was pulled up into the air. I turned to Elan.

"You ready? You heard what I told Patrick. Are you okay with the cable?"

"Your world is too different. Next time I will try to keep my feet on the ground."

"It's a deal. Next time I will try to let you."

When I got up into the helicopter it wasn't exactly what I expected. They had put Patrick back on the oxygen. EMTs were checking out Elan. Thez had either passed inspection or dodged their ministrations.

"Look, Aunt Cassidy! This machine tells how much oxygen is in your lungs. See? Oxygen, carbon dioxide, this funny line is my heartbeat. If I hold my breath all the lines go weird. Watch."

"Pat, they won't let you off the oxygen until the readings are close to normal. You mess with the readings and you could be there a long time."

"But it's fun."

The EMTs looked amused.

"I don't think we have to worry about this one," one of them said.

Chapter 13

"Pat, this is Doctor Ron. He's my doctor and he just wants to check you out."

"And who do we have here?" Doctor Ron asked.

"This is Patrick. He's my nephew."

"Where are his parents?"

"Out of town."

"You know I need a consent form."

"That's okay Doctor Ron! I don't mind!" Patrick said brightly, "I'd be glad to wait in the waiting room."

"He's as bad as you are," Doctor Ron said to me, "What happened?"

"We spent half a night and most of the day finding our way out of the path of that forest fire."

"Any mishaps?"

"Aunt Cassidy got stepped on by a bear! It was so cool!"

Doctor Ron looked at me, one eyebrow raised.

"If it were anybody else I'd have trouble believing that."

As he was talking he was giving Patrick the once over. Listening to his lungs and looking down his throat.

"How do you feel?" Doctor Ron asked.

"I'm fine!" Patrick said, knowing if he felt badly it was asking for a shot or medicine of some kind.

"Pat, does your head still hurt?" I asked.

"A little."

"Your throat?" I asked.

"What does it mean if my throat hurts?"

"It means we need to buy ice cream on the way home."

"Then it hurts bad."

"I like this kid," said Doctor Ron. "When are his parents due back?"

"He has to go home tomorrow." And I sure wasn't looking forward to it.

"I can't do anything at this point. There's nothing life threatening here. If he still has a headache and a sore throat in a few days have his mom or dad take him to his regular doctor for a checkup."

"All right!" Patrick said hopping down from the table.

"Patrick, you can wait for you aunt in the waiting room," Doctor Ron said. "Now…what about you?"

"I think I'll stop for ice cream on the way home."

"Sore throat?"

"Yeah, everything you'd expect."

"You know the drill. When was your last period?"

"February first. I remember because Katie had an appointment for a checkup that day. Why is it as soon as you have kids you gauge time by what your kids were doing?"

"It's human nature. Do you know how long ago February first was? You're sure."

"No! Yeah. It can't be. I am not… if that's what you're thinking, stop thinking it. Anybody could be late as much as I've had going on."

"We need to find out. As weird as your life is you need to know… Cassidy, what's wrong? You're as white as a sheet. Are you okay?"

"You're the doctor. You tell me."

"Look, what were you expecting? Katie's what… two now?"

"Almost. But…"

"Have you done anything to prevent this?"

"Well, no, but… this was always something that was going to happen some day. But not today!"

"Don't panic yet. We don't know. You know what to do. Go give them a sample and come back here. Then we'll do a thorough exam. Did you really get stepped on by a bear?"

"Yeah, just my hand. Then I got slammed into a cliff trying to lasso a bush."

"I could write one of those unbelievable excuse books just because of you. How did you get slammed into a cliff trying to lasso a bush and why were you lassoing the plants up there, anyway? Never mind. Maybe I don't want to know. Go get the test run and then come back."

I felt like a zombie walking to the lab. I got the little cup and took a while to get their sample. I hadn't been drinking much water while we were thinking about the fire. We were pretty much in survival mode. I had very mixed feelings about this. Doctor Ron was right, it was about time. But I wasn't ready for two kids! I was barely getting the hang of one kid. And how can you pay enough attention to the first kid when another one comes on the scene? I had enough trouble trying to keep up with Katie. How was I supposed to keep up with two? And what if it was a girl? I really wanted to give Rusty a son… eventually. My mind was going like this so fast that I could hardly think.

When I got back to the examination room there was a paper gown on the table. Gulp. Did he already know?

I think time stands still in a doctor's office or at least slows down a bunch. And the more you have on your mind the more it slows, until you can go through every aspect of a situation and scare yourself silly in the time it takes to get a test run, or for the doctor to see a patient with the flu and get back to you. I changed into the little, blue, paper gown and sat on the paper on the examination table and waited, trying to still my thoughts. At least I could tell Rusty in a little more normal manner than last time. I waited and waited and looked around for a magazine and waited some more.

When the nurse wheeled in the cart and I saw the instruments on top, I knew.

"What's the matter, Cassidy? You look like you just saw a rubber snake!" Thez said when I caught up to the guys in the lobby. We always met in the lobby after the excitement was over because we had to figure out how to get home or back to the station. Frequently our wheels were still up on some mountain at a base camp, or at the compound where we picked up search and rescue vehicles to get to base camps.

"Nothing," I said "snakes don't bother me much. Do I really look that bad?"

"We all look that bad," said Jacobsen.

We had washed some of the ash off but there was no way to get it all off without a thorough shower. Even then it was doubtful. I had ash in places I thought impossible. Inside my clothes? Under my bra? How did it work its way in there?

I thought I ought to feel different. I thought I should feel pudgy or bloated, or be hungrier. Hell, I'd hardly eaten all day. I was squinting into the smoke, hiking, looking for a way out. But I didn't feel different, physically.

"Well, guys, we need to finish this class. I recommend not going back up to Elk Meadows next weekend. Call me in the next few days when you know when you can go out again. I'll probably meet with Schroeder tomorrow or the next day."

I called Rusty for a ride home.

"Cassidy? Where are you?"

"Joshua Memorial. We're all okay. What have you heard?"

"I'll try to get there before the news van."

"Oh great. What have they been saying?"

"Schroeder called, asked me to turn on the TV. Then he asked where you were holding class. The news just said four officers and two civilians were unaccounted for. They showed aerial views of the fire. I called Chase to see where you might have taken the guys. He knows that area. He knows what you know of it. He wasn't encouraging. He told me about several places you could be but, when I found them on a map, a couple of them were covered by fire. All we could do was alert the fire department and wait."

"Where did the fire start?"

"Elk Meadows, then it spread east."

"That's what we thought. I wonder if the Jeep survived."

"Babe… don't worry about the Jeep. I'm on my way."

After I hung up I turned to Thez. "You're the actor. You've been a cop. You've been a fireman. The press is coming. I hereby name you spokesperson for the group."

Thez's eyes lit up behind the ash.

"Just don't say anything Schroeder wouldn't say," I advised him. Then I turned to the others and said, "If you don't want to talk to the press, I suggest you scatter."

"What wouldn't Schroeder say?" Thez asked.

"Well, he wouldn't say that the reason we had two civilians out there was because they were teaching the police how to track. And he especially wouldn't admit that one of them was only nine years old."

I could see the wheels turning as he tried to make up a plausible story, then I scattered.

We couldn't sit in the lobby. We were so covered in ash that we hesitated to even walk around inside the hospital. Since Thez was in the lobby as a distraction for the press, Elan, Patrick and I slipped down a hallway and walked around until we saw a glowing green exit sign. When we got outside we found out we were in the staff parking lot. We worked our way around the building to a place where we could see the Explorer when it arrived. I knew it would take Rusty half an hour, at least to bundle up Katie and her diaper bag and then drive all the way into town.

We sat under a bare fruitless mulberry and waited.

"Aw rats, now you're going to finish the class without me," Patrick said.

"Sorry, kiddo, the fire kind of put an end to our search."

"If it had been a real search, would you still have done the same thing?"

"No, if it had been a real search we would have had a radio. Jacobsen or Landon would have radioed Strict and we would have had regular status reports. There would have been a lot less guesswork. If it got right down to it they could find us easily with a helicopter because we have GPS on a search. We can radio in our coordinates. Everything can get as high tech as we want to be."

"Who will lay your trail for the new search?"

"I'll just have to lay it myself."

"Are they ready to track your trail?"

"I'll wear Uncle Rusty's swat team shoes," I joked.

The news vans pulled into the parking lot and we took a stroll in another direction. There was a dialysis center and a building full of doctor's offices nearby so we walked around those buildings still watching the parking lot.

"There he is!" called out Patrick. He pointed to the driveway labeled Emergency. I called Rusty's cell phone to redirect him from walking into the mess of the Emergency ward or the press in the lobby.

"Turn left at the end of the drive, instead of right," I told him.

"Where are you?"

"You'll see us. We're heading your way."

He pulled up to the red fire zone and leaped out. He took my pack and put it in the back of the truck. Patrick and Elan loaded their packs, too.

"Uncle Rusty! I saw a bear!" Patrick said.

"You did? How close was it?" Rusty said trying to sound excited about Patrick's adventure.

"Aunt Cassidy made me stay with Officer Jacobsen. I only got to see it in the flashlight. But Aunt Cassidy got to see it real good! We got to see it three times! First it invaded our camp. And then, when we were trying to find a way out of the canyon we saw it again. We were stuck in the canyon with the bear and he wanted out just as bad as we did. And the third time…"

"I think Uncle Rusty has heard enough," I interrupted.

"Aw, but it was cool and it was daylight so that's when I really got to see it."

Thankfully, Rusty figured he could get the whole story later so we all loaded up. Katie was anxiously waiting in her car seat. As Patrick got into the Explorer she reached for him saying, "Pa-pat-trick, me too!"

"I'll play with you at home," Patrick told her.

"Me, too!"

"After a shower," I told him.

"What have you eaten today?" Rusty asked.

"Just what we could grab on the run."

"We should get some dinner on the way home. Any votes?"

"French fries!" said Patrick.

We drove through and got a mess of greasy burgers and fries and a handful of ketchup packets. Katie held up each French fry and proudly announced, "Fra-fry!" before she chomped it down.

It was late by the time we were all showered and semi-normal again.

"Do I hafta go home tomorrow?" asked Pat.

"You need to get back to school. They were nice to put you on independent study for a week. Have you been keeping up with your work?"

"Sort of. I can do it on the way home. I'll have four hours of sitting to do. I read the chapters when you made me go to bed too early. The math is easy enough, unknown integers. It's all just regular math scrambled up. Once you unscramble it it's easy."

"What do you have trouble with in school?"

"Teachers. They think just because we're kids we have to do things the easy way. They could be teaching kids a lot more. They skim over the bare facts about science. Science could be really interesting if they would get more into it. But then they turn right around and do the opposite for no reason I can see. Like long division! There's an easier way to do it than fill a whole paper with columns of numbers. So why teach long division?"

"Long division is a thinking process. The numbers just give you a way to implement it."

"Then why do twenty of the crazy things? If I can do it for one number I could just as well do it for any number."

"Not if you haven't memorized your math facts. And division checks whether kids have learned their math facts, too."

"One time I had to write a report. It was kind of fun because I decided I was going to include every school subject I could think of in the report. I had to do a report about President Roosevelt and so I wrote out his history and I got into the social studies by explaining how the government worked in those days and about the depression and to get the math in I figured out how old he was at different times in his life. When I did all the subjects I could think of I asked Mom what subjects I was missing and she added home ec, so I looked up a bunch of depression recipes and explained how they had to do without sugar and how some basic things were rationed and so the recipes back then were different than they are now, because we can get anything we want, when we want it. And then Dad said that a lot of inventions came about because of the war and the depression so I looked them up, too. The report had to be two pages long but I got so into it that I wrote ten and then I got marked down for 'not being concise'. And I got called up to the desk and my teacher shows me my report and says, 'this was supposed to be a short report about President Roosevelt and it's practically a whole chapter of your history book. What did you do that for?'"

"Don't worry about teachers like that," I told him, "You go ahead and put your all into it."

"Mom says I ought never to ask for a job from Reader's Digest. But I read lots of cool things in Reader's Digest. Why couldn't I?"

"You can. I bet someday you do."

After Katie fell asleep, Rusty and I turned in, too. He pulled me close with that worried hug I was so used to.

"Do they know how the fire started?" I asked trying to put off the inevitable.

"A camper didn't put his fire all the way out before he went to bed."

"And it spread all the way to the canyon."

"And beyond."

"That was my next question, whether or not it jumped the canyon. We didn't stop to look. Part of our chosen route ended up blocked with fire but we didn't take time to dwell on how far it had spread."

"You did well, leading the guys out of there."

"It was team work. Jacobsen took over as leader and we looked to Thez concerning the fire. Then we stumbled on some tracks and followed them to where the firefighters were working."

"What's this I hear about a bear?"

"It wasn't a mean bear. It went after Reilly's food and when the fire spread it was trapped in the canyon with us. It was frightened but it wasn't frightened of us, just trying to get away from the fire, too. So we crossed paths a few times."

"And Doctor Ron…"

"Said the EMTs did their job right and we appeared to have come through it with minimal side effects. He said if the headaches and sore throat don't go away in a few days to make an appointment, but I already feel a little better."

"So what's next?"

"Tomorrow Patrick and Elan have to go home and I need to go into town to talk to Schroeder."

"Why don't you just call him?"

"Chase asked me the same thing. I need to talk to Schroeder in person. And I think he'd rather talk to me in person, too. I need to be able to see him. I can't read him over the phone."

"Most people would prefer not to be able to read Schroeder."

"Well, I'm not one of them. What he says and what his body language says are not always the same."

Chapter 14

It wasn't easy saying goodbye to Patrick and Elan. Maybe I was ready for another kid if I wanted to keep Patrick. Why do kids have to come without any programming whatsoever? You have to start from scratch with every kid. And they are so little and helpless. I felt helpless myself having a crying baby with no idea *why* it was crying, only knowing I was supposed to figure it out and make it stop.

Patrick and Elan loaded up the next morning and away they drove, Patrick looking forlornly out the back window until the truck went out of sight. Rusty put an arm around my shoulders and led me back into the house.

"When can we get my Jeep back?" I asked Rusty.

"The fire spread east. So the campground may be accessible. We'll have to check at the station," he said. "I'm warning you, though, what I saw on TV of the Suburban doesn't leave much hope for the Jeep."

Katie and I rode into town with Rusty. He had a meeting to get to, so I searched out Schroeder and then, when I found him, I couldn't interrupt him, so I went to his office and waited outside. Katie got heavy so I put her down and she immediately zipped around the corner and pounded on Rusty's office door. Rusty wasn't there so she called out, "Daddy! Up! Daddy!"

Her cries didn't bring Rusty out, but doors opened along the hallway and pretty soon Katie had friends to visit with. Tom took her for the tour so I went back to Schroeder's office. He showed up after a short wait. He came up short when he saw me waiting for him. See? I'd have never caught that if I'd called him on the phone.

"The whole office is breathing easier since you were found," he said.

"Funny you should put it like that. The smoke was pretty thick by the time we ran across that fire crew working the east end of the fire. The guys didn't get a very good test of their tracking abilities but we did work pretty good as a team. How soon do you think we can try again?"

"What's the rush? I say let the guys put some time in on the streets, then see how much they remember."

"Umm, that might not be a good idea."

"Why? You need to know how much they've retained. So give them a break."

"It's not them. It's me. I may have some changes coming up. I need to get this trial search over with."

"So, tell me how the first day went."

"Tracking-wise, they need work. They need experience. Only experience will provide them with enough practice to remain useful. If they really apply themselves to a search, they could pull off simple searches. I doubt they can read a crime scene for you other than telling you what a person's feet did. They do not translate the tracks to whole body movements and they don't profile a trail. All that takes time."

"Would you be willing to take them along when you get a call?"

"Sure, if they came prepared and preferably only one at a time."

"Who do you think would prove more useful?"

"Jacobsen, though when push came to shove Thez buckled down and did a good job. Reilly did well tracking but he doesn't have any of the right gear. He needs to get outfitted first and I wouldn't push it unless he is really sure he wants to pursue that path. He had never been camping before, never had to carry a pack. He is the one who will have to adjust to the job the most. After yesterday he may not want to. Somehow I think having a bear in his tent might have discouraged him a bit."

"And you still want to give it another try as soon as possible."

"Yes."

"What's going on to put you in such a rush?"

I couldn't tell him. I hadn't told Rusty yet. So I fudged and told him something that was plausible.

"Tourist season is coming up. I need these guys to show me what they can really do on a trail before it comes down to a real one. The longer we wait the more likely it is to be put off by one of Strict's calls."

He seemed to catch the hesitation but nodded anyway and I heaved a sigh of relief.

Chapter 15

Katie and I went to the park and I pushed her on the swing. She loved to climb the ladder to the kiddy slide and slide down but she liked the big slide better. The steps on the big ladder were too far apart for her to climb it herself so I climbed up with her and she sat on my lap as we slid down. All the time we were playing I was thinking, how am I going to do this with two kids?

We went grocery shopping and took the groceries home and as I was putting them away I was thinking about my house. My house was shrinking. Katie would need a bedroom and we would need a nursery and then where would Rusty's office be?

And my world was shrinking down to a family of…four. We were going to be four. And it used to include all the outdoors. My world used to be sun and rain and cold nights and long trails and now it was going to be this little house. The same one that I thought was too big and too elaborate. My whole world was going to be trapped in it, and now it seemed too small. I didn't want my world to shrink. There was too much to do, too much to see. Just thinking that way made me feel hemmed in and I wanted to stretch. I needed to get out. So after I put away the things that needed refrigerating I gathered up a few things: diapers and baby wipes and a bottle of juice and, for me, a bottle of water. I took Katie by the hand and we went out into the hills behind the house.

"Mommy go!" Katie said as she pulled me along. I let her go and followed her. I didn't mind her exploring as long as she didn't eat anything. She was outgrowing that stage but in nine months I would start it all again. Nine months.

Shadow kept careful track of Katie as she ran ahead. He kept an eye on me, too, but he seemed to know the little sheep was his responsibility and the big one was to be obeyed. Katie thought the little sheep was to be obeyed, too. She had watched me go through obedience exercises with Shadow and would tell him to, "hee-heel" or "ja-jump" or "tay!" If Shadow didn't obey her she would stomp her foot and repeat, "Dadow, ca-come". Shadow was not going to come, though. Katie would clamp him in a hug until he squirmed loose. He knew better than to let the little sheep catch him.

Katie led me higher through the junipers. As long as we wore jackets it was nice weather for a walk. She crawled under a bush and picked up a little stick and twirled it between her fingers. I enjoyed these walks. I liked watching Katie delight in little things. And I knew I'd love to see the delight in another child's eyes, too. A completely different child. I wondered what kind of personality this new child would have. Would he accept everybody as a friend the same way Katie did? Maybe. Katie only knew friends because she had only met friends. Lots of them. Even people who weren't friends, Katie thought they were. Even the one the police arrested and hauled off to jail.

"Oh, Katie, what are we going to do?" I mused aloud. It was safe musing around Katie. She couldn't repeat any of it yet. She roughly understood most of what was said to her but she didn't take it seriously. "Another baby in house…what are we going to do?"

Katie had led me around to the back of Hazel and Wally Mireau's house. Katie spotted Hazel in her back yard, which, like mine, was open to the hills behind it.

"Hazo!" Katie said as she ran for Hazel's house.

"There's my Katikins!" Hazel said, opening her arms wide. "What are you two doing out and about?"

"We're getting out and about," I said, obviously.

"Look, Wally! It's Katie and Cassidy!" Hazel called into the house.

Wally waddled to the back door and slid it open.

"Wowie!" said Katie excitedly. Katie loved Wally because he would make a fool of himself just to hear her laugh at him.

"All the girls say that when they see me," he bragged. "I've been trying to teach her to say *kazowie* but all I get is *wowowie*. Come to Wally, Katie!"

Katie let Wally pick her up and then she was ready for the tour of Hazel and Wally's house. First she needed a cookie, which at Hazel and Wally's house meant pink sugar wafer cookies. Katie was more interested in listening to the chicken shaped cookie jar cluck and cackle when it was opened.

"What does a chicken say?" Wally asked.

"Buck, buck, buck," Katie answered, knowing she'd be more likely to get a cookie if she talked.

"Hazel, I was just thinking back to how I had to tell Rusty I was pregnant. Do you remember how you told Wally? You've got three kids."

"Oh, my, do I ever! Well, in those days we didn't have these handy little test kits like they do now. You had to go to the doctor and they ran a test but you had to wait a few days for the results to come back. I faked a flu and went to the doctor for 'the flu' and when I came home I told Wally it was a virus and that I'd just have to get over it. Then I waited on pins and needles until the doctor called me back. He called back, but Wally answered the phone. He didn't know my doctor, because we went to different doctors. And Wally says, 'there's a *man* on the phone for you.' He was very suspicious like. Like, what is a *man* doing calling you? I took the phone and said, 'hello?' and of course it was Doctor Leiberstein and he wanted me to make a new appointment, that the test confirmed his suspicions. I was in shock! I didn't know what to do!

And when I hung up Wally was standing there with a *well?* look on his face. And I was so much in shock all I could blurt out was, 'I'm pregnant!' and Wally says, 'by whom?' I was mortified!"

"Well, what was I supposed to think?" Wally said. "This strange man calls you up and then you blurt out that you're pregnant!"

It was an interesting story and very Hazel and Wallyish but not very helpful as far as I was concerned.

"What about the second time?" I asked.

"The second time I didn't even know I was pregnant and my mother told me in front of Wally! We went for a visit and she was watching me in the kitchen and she says, 'Hazel! I swear! You never tell me anything! How far along are you?' and Wally and I just looked at her hornswoggled! We had no idea we might be pregnant and so I said, 'Mother! What a thing to say! I am not pregnant!' and she said, 'you sure enough are. Just look at yourself. You just look… maternal.' I told her that's because I was a mother but she insisted I was pregnant and so I looked at the calendar and holy smokes, she could be right! So I went to get the test and this time Wally was waiting for the news so he was there when the call came."

Sounded like Hazel took after her mom. Interesting, but again, not very helpful. My mom wouldn't notice something like that and she surely wouldn't announce it in front of people. I hoped. No, this was something between just Rusty and I. I had to tell him myself, in private this time. And I had to somehow make myself ready. And I wanted it to be special. I just needed it to be special to me first.

Hazel took Katie, cookie in hand to the next stop on the tour, the Christmas tree. Yes, it was mid-March. Yes, Hazel really did have her Christmas tree up. All year round. She used it to hold her collection. She collected Christmas tree ornaments that looked like neon signs. There was one of a pink flamingo and several that looked like pub signs and more than a few advertising beer companies, a '52 Chevy, a palm tree, the list went on and on and Katie loved to find ornaments on the tree as Hazel asked her to point to them.

"Find the bicycle, Katie!"

It was the one advertising Fat Tire Beer.

"Find the woody car!"

Point.

"Find the Route 66 sign!"

Point.

She had done this so many times it was hardly a game to her anymore. At our house she pointed out animals in storybooks and told us what they all said. Here she identified neon sign ornaments. Katie was adaptable.

After the Christmas tree she tried on Hazel's hats. Hazel had a hat for every occasion and some for occasions that would never come up again, like a big, flowery bonnet that she wore to Easter egg hunts in the 1950's. These days in southern California people rarely wore hats and they were rarely a fashion statement. I only owned one hat. It was a faded and crumpled bucket hat that I only put on if the sun was pealing the paint off the barn. Ordinarily Katie didn't like hats but she'd make an exception for Hazel's hats. They were funny. They made her look like the funny people in her storybooks. And she did look cute in the hats, her blonde, curly hair framing her face; the outlandish hat perched atop her head.

My cell phone rang in my pack. I had to shrug out of it, unzip it and fish around for the phone and by the time I found it the ringing had stopped. It was Rusty. Oh golly, what time was it? I had his Explorer. I walked back to the living room and called Rusty back.

"Is everything okay?" he asked.

"Yeah, the phone was in my day pack and I didn't find it in time," I said.

"Where are you?"

"At Hazel and Wally's. I'll be right there."

I found Hazel and Katie in Hazel's bedroom. Katie was wearing a big, floppy, lime green, hat and a string of pearls. She was shaking a big beaded bracelet on her little wrist. She took it off and stuck it in her mouth.

"Time to go!" I said. "Time to get Daddy!"

"You've got Rusty's car again? What happened to yours?" Hazel asked.

"It's stuck in a fire zone. The fire department won't let us retrieve it yet."

"You don't mean that awful Elk Meadows Fire!"

"Umm, how awful was it? I was kind of distracted at the time."

"It's eaten up half the forest!"

"They all seem like that. Yet the forest is mostly still there. Have you heard any specifics?"

"Yes. They found the officers they were so worried about. One garage was burned down but they managed to save the house. It's eighty percent contained."

"That's good. I'm glad they found the officers. Anybody I know?"

"Of course! You know all of them."

I wondered what Thez had told the press, since Hazel didn't seem to know I was involved in the fire in any way. Oh well, time to go. I took Katie and the daypack and jogged home down Lost Hills Road.

"Cassidy!" Hazel called after me, "Don't you want a ride?"

"I was out for a walk. Why would I want a ride?" I answered.

I put Katie in her car seat and tossed in the pack. She fussed at being strapped in the seat for a whole trip to town. She had gone through two other car seat rebellions, one when she was about eight months when she was starting to get mobile, and one right before she turned a year old when she started walking. Every major advancement in mobility brought with it a distaste for the car seat. It reminded me a bit of my own situation. My mobility was threatened and I was rebelling against the thought. But was it really? Would I go back, if I could? No. I couldn't. I wouldn't. Even if I had the choice. Katie was a joy to me. Some of the worries I had in the beginning were still worries today. I had been worried that I couldn't discipline my kids because I could see their point of view, and understand why they did the things they did. I still worried about that. But I'd also baby proofed the knife drawer and I kept Katie from ingesting everything she was curious about. And when she fought the car seat I turned up the stereo loud and sang along. She could rebel all she wanted. She was safe. I never heard of a baby yet who died from a temper tantrum.

Rusty was waiting outside the station when I drove up. He motioned me into a parking place.

"Switch places with me," he said, wanting to drive. "How was your day?"

"Good," I answered. "Katie and I went to the park and the grocery store and Hazel and Wally's house. Good, but kind of dull."

"Good," he said, which meant *good* as in *no trouble*.

When we left the station he didn't head for a restaurant or for home. He headed for the Jeep dealership. Bad news. My Jeep was toast.

"Rusty, aren't you jumping the gun a little bit?" I asked.

"You need a car. I know you want another Jeep."

"But..." I did want a Jeep. I'd always had a Jeep. But... now I was wondering if I might need a mom mobile. "You've been driving this Explorer for at least five years. Why don't *you* get a new car this time? What kind of a car would *you* like?"

"Then what would you drive?"

"The Explorer. It makes sense. It's warmer and more comfortable for Katie than a Jeep. It hauls groceries and strollers."

Just tell him, Cass. But I didn't want to tell him sitting in a car dealership's parking lot.

"You want to take my Explorer?" The question was so disheartened sounding I backed off.

"Not if you feel strongly about it. But isn't there a car you'd like to have?"

He looked thoughtful. This wasn't an easy question.

"Mommy, g-go," whined Katie.

Rusty started the truck and we drove to Zeke's. We talked over pizza.

Katie smeared pizza all over the table. She even ate some of it.

Later at home he asked, "What's up? I don't get it. Why do you want me to get a new car? It's your car that got burned up."

"It's just about time you had one. How old is the Explorer?"

"Nine years old. But it's still a perfectly good truck."

"You don't want a new car?"

"I don't know. Something just feels off about this."

Just tell him!

I can't!

He'll be thrilled.

I know! But I can't.

You should. You know you really should.

He went quiet on me and I started working in the kitchen and he went to his office. When I peeked in later he was looking at cars on the Internet.

When I was watching Katie take a bath I heard him on the phone. He was really curious about this car issue. He was curious enough about it to do a little detective work.

"Has she told you anything?" he asked. I was guessing he was talking to my sister, Jesse, or my mom. "I know. I know she would but…I don't even know what kind of a car I'd want. There's a dozen cars any guy would like to have, a dozen cars that are sensible…. It just rubs me wrong to take the money for Cassidy's car and buy something for myself…. I'd buy her any car she wanted but she wants my old truck? It doesn't make sense…. I like my old truck…. Yeah I could do that."

He walked into the other room and I lost track of the conversation. The next thing I noticed he was pricing new Explorers.

Next my cell phone rang. It was Jesse. Ha, I knew it. In a way I was glad Rusty was comfortable enough with my family to talk to them. I was also a little irritated that he couldn't just listen to me and find a car.

"Hello?"

"Cass… what's up?"

"What do you mean?"

"Why do you want to take over Rusty's Explorer?"

"It just makes sense. Why can't anybody accept the fact that Katie and I would be better off in the Explorer?"

"I think there's more to it than that. If everything was on an even keel, and you were your normal self, you would just go buy another Jeep Wrangler. I know you. You're a Jeep girl. So… what's up?"

"Why can't a girl change her mind? I remember the first time I voluntarily wore a dress. You asked me if I was all right, like I can't decide to wear a dress. A person can change." They can get big and fat and become a mother of two. Oh golly, why did I have to remind myself?

“So you’re going to become a Ford convert?”

“You act like my car is a religion. A car is just a tool. Maybe I need different kinds of tools to work with.”

“Aha! And why is that?”

“Because… I’m more of a mom than I used to be. I don’t think I want to make Katie hike ten miles through the blazing heat to get a ride into town because of some mishap in the middle of nowhere. I’m… I guess I’m settling down a little.”

I was hemming and hawing and stumbling over the words but I was getting them out.

“I still say something’s up. And Mom thinks so, too, but she said to have patience and we’d find out.”

“Okay, you do that.”

“You’ll tell me then?”

“When and if there is anything to tell.”

She had to be content with that. Sigh, things were getting tenser. Now I had three people guessing.

Chapter 16

The next day an odd thing happened that threw a monkey wrench into everything. A man came to the door. He looked like the kind of person my mother had always warned me about. He had gray scruffy hair, a two day beard, and piercing eyes. He wore a loose, tattered, plaid flannel shirt, paint splattered jeans and boots that looked like they had been bought second hand by the guy's grandfather. He stood there on my doorstep arrogantly, a step back from the spot friendly people stood in. He wasn't smiling. He was assessing. He was checking me out. Not in the sexual sense. He was measuring me up. What kind of measuring stick he was using, I did not yet know.

Shadow stood warily to the side. Usually he greeted visitors, excitedly wagging his tail.

"I'm looking for Cassidy Michaels," he said.

"What can I do for you?" I asked.

"Tell me where I can find Cassidy Michaels."

"Why don't you give me your name and a number and I'll make sure he gets it?" I said.

"Is he still looking for a tracker?"

"Yes and no."

"What's that mean?"

"Go see Sergeant Schroeder at the Joshua Hills Police Station. He'll tell you what he needs."

His eyes narrowed.

"Why are you giving me the run around?"

"I married a cop. Caution is my middle name."

"Not cautious enough. If I wanted to hurt you, I would have done it by now. Sergeant Schroeder?"

"Yeah."

"Where can I find Cassidy Michaels?"

"If you make it past Schroeder, I'll know. And I'll tell you."

He turned on his heel and left. I watched as he got into a hacked up pickup truck. It was primer gray with the top of the cab removed. He must have frozen driving that thing anywhere in the winter. The letters across the tailgate were barely there but spelled Chevrolet. His license plate was from Wyoming. I don't know about the truck. The truck could have been from anywhere.

I checked on Katie and she was still asleep. I thought I better use this short quiet time to give Schroeder a heads up.

"Hello?" he said.

"Schroeder? This is Cassidy. I just sent a guy to see you. He was looking for me but I didn't tell him he'd found me. He knew you were looking for a tracker, but I didn't trust him."

"Cassidy…I'm kind of busy right now."

"When he shows up just screen him. Make sure he's legitimate. If you think I should work with him send him back. If you don't, you can probably arrest him for something. Look over his truck. You'll find something."

"How am I supposed to know who he is?"

"He'll be looking for me. And he looks like Chase's rebellious little brother."

"He looks worse than Chase?"

"Yeah. And I don't think he'll be too pleased to find out he needs to go through police academy to work here."

"Okay, I'll call you tomorrow. I've got to go for now."

"Okay, thanks, bye."

"Bye."

As it turned out the guy never went to see Schroeder. He drove away, parked and walked back. I didn't know. I did the dishes. I thought about a hundred different ways to break the news to Rusty and rejected them all. I sorted a load of laundry. Big, exciting day here. Rusty had taken the Explorer so all I could do was housework or walking. Shadow barked at me to come play and I put him through the agility course once. Katie jumped up and down and clapped her hands to see Shadow race through the obstacles. After Shadow completed the course I was walking around outside with Katie, checking for weeds that might be springing up after the winter rains when I noticed odd tracks. A man. Wearing boots. I pulled Katie close and scanned the brush surrounding the property. It wasn't thick, though it could hide an experienced scout. I took Katie into the house and made sure all the doors and windows were locked.

That evening when Rusty came home I asked him to watch Katie. His eyebrows shot up when I took his shoulder holster and put my 9mm in it. I pulled on a jacket to cover it and headed for the back door.

"Where do you think you're going?" he asked.

"I need to follow some tracks and I need to do it inconspicuously."

"Why the gun?"

"Because I don't trust the guy I think I am tracking."

"Then let me go."

"No. I said I needed to do this inconspicuously. Besides, if you do it he'll think you're me. He was looking for Cassidy Michaels, but he thinks Cassidy is male, so I sent him to Schroeder. Then later in the day I found his tracks in the back yard. I just want to see what makes this guy tick, whether I should trust him or not. If he was out there for a long time and didn't try anything he was probably just information gathering, which is something I would do. I have no problem with that. I want to go out and get the facts so when I talk to Schroeder we can compare notes on the guy."

"Why don't you trust him?"

"He's a tracker."

"Just like you're a tracker."

"Trackers tend to be an odd bunch. This guy heard we were looking for a tracker so I sent him to Schroeder. Do you know if he ever showed?"

"No, I was out of the office a lot today."

"Well, I'm just going to go read the tracks. I'll be back in an hour."

He watched out the window while I returned to the tracks I had seen earlier. I followed them backwards to a truck parked about an eighth of a mile from the house.

He was still here.

I faded into the junipers, caution tripled. I made my way back to the house in stealth mode, a shadow flitting from hiding place to hiding place. I crouched in hiding scanning the landscape. Where was he?

I spotted him, finally, not well hidden but inconspicuous. I watched him as he watched the house. He'd seen me leave and observed me tracking so he knew I was the tracker. I had to assume he knew I was Cassidy. What was he thinking? Why was he here?

I snuck around in back of him. It took me a half hour just to do that because I had to take my time, staying out of sight, moving noiselessly, waiting until his eyes were fixed on the house, making sure my reflection wouldn't show in any of the windows. I stood behind him and pulled the gun, though I had no plans to use it. He heard the gun come out of the holster and stiffened.

"You're in no danger," I told him. "I'll take you to meet Cassidy now."

"Then why the gun?"

"My middle name is Trouble. When you've seen as much trouble as I have you learn to minimize it. Stand up."

He stood up.

"Spread eagle."

"What is this?" he asked as he assumed the position.

"Guess I'm just enough of a cop to not take any chances," I said as I gently frisked him. If he had a gun it wasn't very accessible. I walked around in front of him. "Walk to the house."

He started toward the house and I walked behind him but when things stayed calm I came up beside him.

"I'm Cassidy," I said as we walked toward the house. "Why didn't you go talk to Schroeder?"

"I'm not too keen on talking to the cops."

"Are you sure you want to go in that house then? Your choice. But if you really want to track you'll have to work with the police. You'll have to go through reserve deputy training. Why are you here?"

"Got kicked out of where I was. Saw the news on TV as I was passing through. Looked up the Joshua Hills tracker. Here I am."

"I need to get unlisted somehow."

"You're not exactly listed. It took some poking around, talking to people. People sure know you around here."

"Oh yeah? Who?"

"Guy named Paul. He's got a passel of stories about you, too."

"Ranger Paul?"

"Yup."

"Damn, I need to go have a talk with him."

"I never would have guessed you were the person I was looking for until I saw you track."

"That's what most people say. What kind of tracking do you do that doesn't involve police work?" I asked.

"The cops and me have an understanding. I don't talk. They don't listen. They need somebody found, I find them. Folks need someone found they see if I'll do it. They have enough cash… I go out."

"People pay you to find people?"

"Not enough. People don't go missing enough to make a living. That's why I got kicked out of town. The sheriff accused me of helping them go missing so I'd have work to do."

"Did you?"

"I done some things I shouldn't. If I ever hurt a person it was in plain sight where there were witnesses. Never been arrested. Uh, I take that back. Never been convicted. When I got kicked out of town I started drifting. Only thing is tracking don't pay at all if no one knows there's a tracker they can call on."

"Tracking doesn't pay here because it is all volunteer work. If you're looking to make money here, forget it."

"Think I'll stick around and see what goes down."

"There's no money to be made. If I'll go out for free why would somebody pay you to do the same thing?"

"I'm probably willing to take on some cases you wouldn't."

When we got to the back door I couldn't even make introductions.

"Rusty, this is a tracker whose license plate says he's from Wyoming. Mister…tracker, this is my husband, Rusty Michaels."

"Zeb. You can call me Zeb," he said.

Rusty extended his hand and Zeb hesitated. He shook hands with Rusty reluctantly. He looked like he was walking into a trap as he entered the house.

"Nice place," he said.

"Thanks. Are you hungry? Dinner will be on in just a little while."

"I'd appreciate it," he answered.

"Where's Katie?" I asked.

"In her crib," Rusty answered.

"And she's not mad at you for leaving her there?"

"She was at first but then she settled down."

"Yeah, right. She doesn't like the crib if she's awake. You didn't put her down for a nap did you?"

"No. She'd be up all night."

"Then why isn't she fussing?"

"I'll go get her."

Rusty disappeared into the nursery while I checked dinner.

"She's not in there," he said as he came out glancing around on the floor.

"Jump! Jump!" I heard from the living room. I dashed in there ready to catch a jumping toddler.

Zeb let things happen around him, quietly observing. When I walked into the dining room with Katie in my arms she peered at him for the longest time and when I put her down she hid behind my legs. She followed me around the kitchen watching Zeb with wide eyes. When Rusty sat down at the table she got braver. She crouched down and, keeping her eyes on Zeb the whole way, walked to the table, then peered at Zeb from behind Rusty's chair. I wanted to call Patrick and exclaim, "Katie sneaked and walked at the same time!" On the other hand, Katie usually walked up to anybody. *Everybody* was Katie's friend. Everybody except Zeb. Hmmm. Rusty picked her up and she grabbed a spoon and banged on the table.

"That's spooky," Zeb said.

"What?" I asked.

"How old is that kid?"

"She'll be two next week."

"How'd she learn to do that?"

"My nephew likes to stalk deer. He tries to teach Katie to do it but he hasn't had much luck. This is the first time I've seen her come close to getting it right."

"How's the tracking out here?" he asked.

"Varied. Even in the desert we have different types of desert soil that take tracks differently. Both the desert and mountains can be very rocky. It is slow and frustrating, but I've always found my man. One advantage we have out here is that the distance a person can go is limited. There are lots of roads crisscrossing the mountains and the desert. Sometimes I wonder how they get lost."

"You ever find any rich people?" Zeb asked.

"A couple, but it made no difference to me."

"Who?"

"Well, Sherri Champlain. And I suppose Mark Mireau might have some money. He has a fancy office in a skyscraper. He goes on safaris all over the world. But money isn't what gets me out on the trail. I find people because they need to be found."

"You've never gotten a call from some millionaire asking you to find his lost daughter because she got tired of living the good life and took off with some country boy in a white flatbed pickup truck?"

"No. And if I did, I'd ask how old their daughter was and if she was eighteen I'd wish her all the luck in the world."

"What if they offered you a reward for finding her?"

"Not if she was of age and didn't want to be found."

"How many missing people cases do the cops have ongoing right now?"

"Many, but…"

"And how many parents would buy the services of a tracker if they thought their kid could be found?"

"You're not talking tracking here. You're talking private investigation."

"Okay, so maybe my tracking goes beyond the ground reading type. I've found the cops get discouraged and quit too soon. And they wear the wrong clothes. People don't like opening up to a uniform. People will talk, if you give them reason to."

I got the feeling the reason might be sly manipulations, or threats, or bribery. If this guy really wanted to do tracking, he should move on.

"Mister, we don't mind giving you a meal. But you need to either go talk to Schroeder, or find another town," Rusty said.

Zeb sat back with a "we'll see about that" look to him.

When dinner was on, Zeb looked over the table. "Were you planning on having leftovers?" he asked.

"Go for it," I answered.

He let Rusty and I take what we wanted before he chose things for his plate. Then he piled it high and dug in with a vengeance. Three times. It was a typical meal for us. Marinated chicken, fried rice, steamed vegetables. Nothing fancy. There wasn't even a grain of rice left in the pan by the end of the evening. He pushed his chair back with a satisfied belch.

"So, you think a big California town like this won't support a tracker/people hunter like me?" he asked.

"I'm saying if you want to go through the usual routes you'll have to go to academy and work with the police," I said. "The tracker we're looking for has to have the authority of a level one officer. I'm a level two. They need their tracker to be a level one, and though I could go back to academy and achieve a level one, I don't want to be an officer. I'm not cop material. I've had to do the job before and, being a trouble magnet, it has always been in tough situations. I've done what needed to be done and paid too much for it. So I'm staying a level two and looking for that elusive level one tracker out there somewhere. I'm trying to train up a few level one officers in the art of tracking."

"Is that guy on the news one of them?" Zeb asked.

"Tall, balding guy?" I responded.

"Yeah."

Zeb cracked a spooky little smile when I hesitated and nodded.

"Good luck," he said.

When Zeb left it was a shake of the hand and a, "thanks for dinner", then he walked down the road, hands in pockets, to his truck. Rusty closed the door and turned around.

"Steer clear of that guy," he said.

"What if he goes to talk to Schroeder?"

"He's not going to get within a half mile of the station."

Steering clear of Zeb was easier said than done. For one thing he didn't have any place better to be. For another he was a tracker. On top of that he was curious about me and had a plan in mind. In a way he helped me. And in a way he worried me.

When I went out the next day, to lay a trail for the guys to track, I took my rifle and Katie. I didn't really want to do both but I didn't have much choice. I wasn't going to go out unarmed and I wanted to make a show of it in case Zeb had any ideas. I knew he was following me within the first quarter mile. I kept seeing a movement out of the corner of my eye when I turned to check on Katie. I circled back around until I came to his trail. I knew this was going to puzzle the guys but, hey, they might have to track a person in this very situation. Come to think of it I'd send Thez and Reilly down Zeb's trail and let Jacobsen track my trail. He wanted to learn how to track me. He could just do that. This could actually prove to be interesting. I could do things that affected Zeb's movements and let the guys puzzle out what really happened. The only problem was I needed to search out some rocks. This wouldn't be a real test of their abilities unless it included some tough spots. So I was packing Katie, carrying a rifle out of baby reach, looking for good tracking tricks to play on Jacobsen, and keeping track of Zeb. This would be a very complex trail, if the guys read anything into it. Likely they would just follow the prints…but, if they *did* read something in the tracks, I really wanted to know it.

Katie rode happily. She liked going places. Occasionally she would point to something and ask, “Wha’s dat?”

Trees, clouds, birds… anything that caught her attention was worth an inquiry.

“What does a birdie say?” I’d ask.

“Tweet, tweet,” she said.

“What does a coyote say?”

“Ou ouoooooo!” She liked coyotes. Sometimes we could hear them in the desert at night. The first time she really noticed them she was afraid of the spooky sounds. It was one of Shadow’s rare howls that convinced her the coyotes were like Shadow.

I hiked along sometimes making my trail obvious to see if the guys would catch it, other times looking for ways to make it tough.

Two miles later Zeb couldn’t stand it anymore. Tracker curiosity overcame tracker stealth.

“What are you doing?” he asked.

“Laying a trail.”

He seemed surprised at my calm answer.

“How long have you known I was here?”

“Long time.”

“What are you laying a trail for?”

“The officers to track. I’ve been teaching them tracking for about a week and this will tell me how much they learned.”

“It’s going to take beginners days to get through this trail.”

“It’s supposed to.”

“They’ll never get through the rocks.”

“Sure they will. They won’t go home until they finish the trail. I left sign.”

“I didn’t see you.”

“Well, it’s there nevertheless.”

“I’ll see for myself.”

“Please don’t. You’re laying a trail, too. I was going to have the guys track both trails.”

“I am? Why didn’t you say so earlier? I could have made things interesting.”

"You weren't there earlier, remember?"

"How far are you going?"

"A mile or so farther, then I'll go back by a different route."

We stopped for lunch and I handed over my sandwich and made do with fruit and trail mix. Katie had a half sandwich, which she took apart and ate separately, some of it mixed with dirt.

"Why are you being nice to me?" Zeb asked.

"I try to be nice to everybody."

"You aren't scared of me?"

"Why? Should I be?"

"Most women would freak out if they were followed through the woods by a strange man."

"I'm not most women. And I can understand why you're doing it. As long as your intentions aren't harmful, I'm not scared of you."

"Maybe you should be."

"I'll keep that in mind. For now I need to get back in time to cook dinner. I'd invite you to stay, but I think Rusty would rather you made yourself scarce."

"Smart guy."

"Okay, Katie, up and over?"

"Up! Up!"

"Okay, arg, she's getting way too big for this!" I said as I lifted Katie over my head and into the backpack on my back. Pretty soon I'd have to take it off and put her in it before it was on my back. She found the leg holes and settled in.

"Go!" she said.

"Don't make the trail too hard," I told Zeb. "They are just starting out."

"Go, Mommy, go!"

"Okay, we're going. Go fast?"

"Go fast!"

I set off at a gentle jog, Katie bouncing and laughing in the backpack behind me. Zeb shook his head as we left him behind. He didn't follow us home but he did lay a trail that paralleled mine, then drove off in his hacked up truck. Later I went out and found where it was parked so I would know where to start Reilly and Thez out in the morning.

Chapter 17

Next morning I drove quickly into town to pick up Bertie. Zeb followed me there, too. He must have thought it awfully odd that I would drive to downtown, pick up an old, homeless woman off the street and drive home. Maybe he thought I was desperate for people to feed. Maybe that's why I let him stay for dinner. I laughed at the thought.

"What's so funny?" Bertie asked.

"Nothing. There's a guy following me and I'm wondering what he thought about me picking you up off the street."

"There's a guy following us?"

"Yeah, he's been following me for a few days." Changing the subject, I said, "Katie has learned how to climb out of her crib. So you'll have to be careful how long you shower when she's napping."

"Aren't you worried about being followed?"

"He'll follow me during class, too, so you don't need to worry."

"I wouldn't exactly say that isn't cause for worry." She craned her head around. "He drives a junker truck. He sure looks worrisome to me."

"It's okay. His type likes to put the fear in his victims. When he becomes really worrisome he'll let me know."

"You seem awfully confident. Does Rusty know about this?"

"Yes and no. He's met the guy. His name is Zeb. But he doesn't know I've been tailed for two days."

"You should tell him."

"I'll be out there with three cops. We'll all be armed. There's no use worrying about us."

"You're all going to be staring at the ground. What if the guy's armed, too? It only takes one shot."

"He's just seeing how this tracking thing works around here. And he's curious about me. So far he's harmless."

"Ain't no such thing as a harmless man in my book. No such thing."

"Well, you don't need to worry about you and Katie. This guy will be following me."

When we arrived back at the house Jacobsen, Reilly and Thez were already there.

"Reilly, show me your gear. I hope you're better outfitted this time."

"Whooee! You should have heard my grandpa! 'That tent done made it all the way through World War II and you borrow it for one weekend and bring it back no better'n a shop rag, not even as good as a shop rag! A shop rag's absorbent!' On the other hand my niece was real proud to have a sleeping bag that had been tromped on by a bear."

"But did you manage to find better gear this time?"

"Yup! I went to the store and I found this coolio tent. You just flip it and it pops open and you just hammer in a couple pegs and you're all set."

"What about your sleeping bag. Did you find a warmer one?"

"Rated to minus five! I even bought me a stove."

"Why the sudden interest in camping?"

"My girlfriend thinks I'm some big shot outdoorsman because I faced me a bear. She wants to go camping, too. Only for starters she just wants to camp in a campground, so I got the smallest tent I could find," Reilly said with a wink.

"And you brought two days worth of food and water?"

"Yup."

"And you're armed?"

"Yup."

"Good. Jacobsen? Thez? You're all set?"

"You're expecting trouble." Jacobsen said.

"Not expecting it. Prepared, just in case."

"Why?"

The three officers stood waiting for an answer. Thez and Reilly might not have even thought about it, but now Jacobsen had brought it up. The question piqued Rusty's interest, too. He noted the rifle.

"I've had a shadow lately. A guy's been following me around. Name's Zeb. Everybody look to the hills and say 'Hi! Zeb!'"

Thez turned toward the hills, grinned broadly and called out by himself, "Hi, Zeb!" then looked around sheepishly.

There was no response from the hills and Thez blushed.

"Don't worry. He is out there. He came to us wanting to track. I sent him to Schroeder but he never showed. He thinks he can learn more by watching me. Thez and Reilly, you're going to be tracking Zeb's trail. Jacobsen, since you wanted to learn how to track me, you're following my trail. I'll be checking on both trails. They are never far apart. You can always call me over if you get really stuck."

"I miss Patrick," Reilly said. "That kid kept us on our toes."

"Don't worry, you'll have enough to do," I said.

Rusty took me aside. "You didn't tell me that guy was still around."

"He's just observing. He hasn't threatened me in any way."

"Where is he?"

I scanned the hills. I could pick a spot that I thought he was sitting in but I couldn't be sure.

"If he doesn't want to be seen, we won't see him," I said.

"Take care of my girl out there," Rusty said. "You'll be back tomorrow?"

"If all goes well. This trail is shorter but I won't be helping the guys as much. We'll never be more than three miles from the house."

I got Reilly and Thez started. "This guy is wearing boots. He's about five ten, a hundred eighty pounds, but he's a tracker so there's no telling what his trail will look like. I want you to get as much out of the trail as you can. I know he followed me but I don't know what pains he went through to stay out of sight. It could prove to be a very informative and interesting trail. Get a feel for his stride, the size of his tracks. When you think you will recognize his tracks in more difficult conditions go ahead and start."

I jogged back to Jacobsen.

"I had Katie on my back so my tracks should be pretty easy to read compared to normal. Profile as you go. Tell me what you see. There are several things you should notice as you go, like at what point I knew I was being followed, how that affected my tracks, all that stuff. I'm interested in seeing how it all fits together myself."

I jogged back to Reilly and Thez. I got the feeling I was going to hike ten miles to their three that day.

They had their heads together bent over the trail.

"What have you got?" I asked.

"Butt prints," said Reilly.

"Okay. Good. So, how long do you figure he sat here?"

"Long time. He was watching. He was watching your house."

"He's lucky I actually did something interesting. Go on with the trail. He could have been there for several hours."

"That doesn't bother you?"

"Not yet, it doesn't."

"Hell, it would bother me. It would give me the heebie jeebies to be watched like that," said Reilly.

"Well, get used to it, he's probably watching now."

"Don' choo tell me things like that," Reilly said.

"You're a cop. Deal with it," I told him.

I kept tabs on both trails and Jacobsen gradually pulled ahead of Reilly and Thez because I had made the mistake of putting the two talkers together. They discussed the trail in minute detail, which probably taught them more, but it sure made for a long walk for me. Jacobsen, the steady turtle plugging away at his trail and the two rabbits running off at the mouth. The turtle was winning the race. I was losing.

"Something changed," Jacobsen said when I approached for the tenth time in a quarter mile.

I glanced at the tracks. “Good catch. What is it?”

He squatted over the tracks. “I don’t know and I don’t want to go back and compare. If I was just running off instinct I’d say you put the track down and then changed it somehow, but I don’t know how. It doesn’t really look changed. It just feels changed. Does that make sense?”

“Sure and if I show you how it was changed it’ll make sense to you. It doesn’t happen every track, right?”

“Right.”

I demonstrated walking, pausing, looking at my back trail. It was subtle.

“See, the slight mound caused by a pause and a turn… where was Zeb, based on my actions?”

“Five o’clock.”

“Good that’s where I was looking. I don’t know where he actually was at this point. But it was a good catch.”

When I got back to Reilly and Thez they were talking, as usual.

“This guy is spooky. He keeps a bush or a tree between him and Cass all the time. And these tracks. They aren’t like…people tracks. It’s like he’s some alien or something disguised as a person.”

“It’s perfectly explainable scouting tracks,” I said and both men jumped. “He’s crouched forward, making his profile smaller. He’s keeping brush between us so I won’t know he’s watching. Look at the track and you can see the weight is more on the front of the foot.”

“Oh, yeah…right…the front of the foot,” Reilly said and punched Thez on the shoulder, “I *told* you it was the front of the foot!” he said.

Reilly was quickly working his way straight back into a squad car. I doubted he was ever going to make a serious tracker.

By the time we’d gone a mile I was ready to drop. Between walking at least three times as far as the guys and being pregnant I was flagging, but I couldn’t admit it to the guys. I rested more and zigzagged less.

I was walking once more from Jacobsen to the Reilly/Thez team when Thez said disapprovingly, “Cassidy, I thought we were through with the snake jokes when Patrick went home.”

I looked to the group. Thez stood there hands on hips, irritated, then he walked a few feet away and reached toward the ground. A sand colored snake drew back menacingly. It was dry and crusty and had the distinctive rattler diamonds down its back. It eyed Thez’s hand coming down, groping around…

“Thez! Stop!” I yelled.

The snake pulled back its head. Thez’s head came up when he heard the warning. I pulled up my rifle. The snake’s head came forward. I drew a bead on the snake's head. It was within a foot of Thez's hand. I squeezed off a shot and everybody froze as the snake jerked up into the air and then thrashed around on the ground. Within seconds a shot came back at us from the brush and we all hit the dirt. The snake continued its death dance and Thez grimaced as the headless body whacked him on the side. The guys all reached for their side arms.

"Wait!" I called out. "Zeb! Stop! That shot wasn't meant for you! Put down your gun! It was meant for a rattlesnake! Come out, peaceful like, and I'll show you."

The hills remained quiet.

"I've got a dead snake here to prove it!" I yelled. "Show yourself!"

Slowly he came out of the brush.

"Are you okay?" I asked.

"No thanks to you!" he spat out.

"Thez, next time you pick up a snake, make *sure* it's rubber first."

"What?" asked Thez, though I was sure he heard me.

"I didn't play any trick on you. You nearly picked up a real snake. *Look at it*! Next time… just look at it… from a distance… you were half a second from being bit."

Thez was covered in snake blood. His face went white. He looked at his hand. He shook it. He found the dead snake, now still beside him.

Jacobsen came jogging over right about then. I picked up the dead snake and walked with it toward Zeb.

"It was real?" Thez asked no one in particular.

I held the snake out to Zeb.

"I hit what I aim at." I explained. "If I was shooting at you, you'd be just as dead as this snake, so don't push me."

"You. Shot the snake."

"I was the only one who saw the danger," I answered.

"Can I have it?" Zeb asked. I handed the snake to him and Thez shuddered.

Zeb carried the dead snake over to the place I had been standing. He paced off the distance between me and the snake.

"Nice piece of shooting," he commented, then he knelt down and proceeded to skin the snake.

"Zeb, this is Thez Brockman, Reilly Tucker, and Kent Jacobsen. Guys… Zeb. Zeb is interested in tracking in these parts, but he doesn't choose to do it your way."

Zeb glanced around as I made introductions but he didn't offer to shake hands and I doubt the guys would have anyway. Thez would have been appalled that the guy would shake his hand while skinning a snake. Jacobsen would have been suspicious and backed off. Reilly was just out of his element. He could handle the shooting and the action but this was all a different world to him.

The snake's skin pulled off easily but would have to be cleaned better later. Zeb discarded the meat and rolled up the skin until he got to the rattles. He shook the rattles experimentally. He shook the rattles at Thez.

"Rattlesnakes bite. And it hurts like hell," he told Thez. "Thanks for finding me one, though."

"No problem," Thez answered unconvincingly.

"Okay guys, back to the trail. The action's over. We have a trail to track."

"What about him?" Jacobsen answered.

"Zeb can take care of himself," I said.

"He's armed and he shot into a group of people."

"Out of self-defense," I countered.

"Do you know how many counts we could throw against him just from that one shot?" Jacobsen asked.

"Could. Doesn't mean we have to. Give him a warning. If he doesn't heed it, then you can arrest him. If we arrest him now we have to put off the tracking a day. You'll miss work on Monday. The trail will be a day colder. Do you really want to try to track my two day old trail just to bring a guy in for shooting in self-defense?"

"Assault on a police officer."

Okay, so there were disadvantages to having a poster cop along.

"Jacobsen, just drop it. He might have been a bit quick on the trigger but he didn't do anything you wouldn't have done if pushed."

Jacobsen turned on his heel and grumbled back to his trail.

"Now… make yourself scarce," I said to Zeb. "Reilly, Thez, I think you have work to do."

Gradually they all got back into tracking mode, except that Thez kept finding little bits of rattlesnake on him and picked it off with a shudder. The Reilly/Thez group picked up its pace since the shooting had silenced them for a little while.

A quarter mile later as I approached Reilly and Thez, Reilly shook his head. "Cassidy," he almost whispered. "That guy was stalking you."

"Good catch."

"No, I mean he was *really stalking you.*"

"I know. I knew long ago. He's stalking us now."

"And that doesn't bother you?"

"No. I stalk people. I stalk animals. I have no intention of harming them. He hasn't done anything to make me think he isn't doing the same thing. I do it to get information, to see how invisible I can be. He's just gathering information. He wants to know what the competition is. But I'm glad you figured out that he was stalking me. Now explain why you think that."

"I see where we are in relation to where Jacobsen is. I see there's something to hide us from his view everywhere we go. I see him pausing. He isn't just walking. He's not just going some place. He's got an agenda."

"How is the tracking itself going?"

"Slow. We'd never catch him if we were after him."

"Why is it slow? What's slowing you down?"

"It's these little rocks. We don't get a good impression with all these little rocks."

"And why is that?"

"I don't know. We can see lines but we rarely see tread."

"And why is that?" He thought about it until I decided to explain it to him. "Each of those little rocks lifts the foot just a smidgen off the ground. There's tens of little rocks each supporting a fraction of his weight, so they keep his shoe from touching the soil. If you know he's the only one who could have made that track then you know the lines are his tracks. So you can verify the track and keep going. Stop to read when something changes."

"I don't know… I think I want to know what this guy was up to."

"Well, we want to finish this in two days. Don't stretch it out to three or you might go hungry."

I think Reilly learned more about tracking once he got interested in what Zeb had been up to. He would call me over and read the ground asking if what he saw was what I saw, too. Often he read into the sign more than was there.

"Look, he's kneeling down. He's moved around. Like he was reloading or something."

"Why would he reload? He didn't shoot anything," I said.

"Maybe he was watching you through binoculars."

I thought Reilly's imagination was getting the best of him.

"Maybe. Keep going."

The rocks gave the guys trouble, as I knew they would. I spent more time with Reilly and Thez on the rocks because I knew I had purposely left sign for Jacobsen. I saw Zeb up on the higher rocks observing. I strolled over.

"I told you to make yourself scarce," I told him.

"It's like watching grass grow," he said.

"I never have recommended tracking as a spectator sport," I answered.

"They've had a week of tracking and this is how far they got?"

"You should have seen them when they started out," I said.

"I still think you were shooting at me," he said.

"You kind of have to know the history to know why I was shooting at a rattlesnake. We'd already had a practical joke or two involving rubber snakes and Thez thought it was just another joke. It almost bit him. The shot was a split second decision."

"And these are California cops?"

"Yeah, they do better on the streets than they do in the woods."

"These are the woods?"

"Yup."

"Shit. I don't know whether to stay because I can outwit the cops or go home where they have real woods. Would that cop really have arrested me?"

"Yeah, if I hadn't intervened."

"Thanks for sticking up for me. I hope you don't regret it."

"Me, too. I better get back. Rocks can be frustrating."

"Tell me about it."

Zeb's trail through the rocks was difficult even for me. I went through all the mechanizations. Side views, finding little rock scratches, getting out the magnifying glass. To make it even tougher he hadn't just been laying a trail when he was on the rocks. He'd had plenty of time to climb around and wander while he was watching me. It was a little worrisome for me because he was watching, seeing how I dealt with the trail. And I wanted him to know, if I did need to track him down, I was capable of doing it.

"Cassidy?" Jacobsen called.

I marked the last known track and jogged over. We'd all shed packs on the rocks and settled in for an hour's tracking close by the packs.

"Sorry," I said. "Reilly and Thez have it even rougher than you. At least I left you clues. Zeb had no idea he was laying a trail for someone else to track. What's the problem?"

"Here's the last known track. I wouldn't call it a track. A tipped rock here. A scuff there. I've looked at it every way I can think of."

"Okay, which way does the scuff point and how long is my stride?"

He looked at the spot the track should have been in, probably for the hundredth time.

"Try looking at the bigger picture and gradually narrow your vision down until you get to the part you can use. Tracking is mostly learning to see things in new ways. So if one way doesn't work try a different way. At least I just walked across the rocks. Zeb seems to have gone on a rock climbing trip and he didn't leave much sign."

"I've tried every way I can think of short of standing on my head."

"Maybe you should try that then. But seriously… did you try what I suggested? Start about ten feet out and narrow your vision a little bit at a time. Even if it doesn't work this time it's something to try, one more tool at your disposal."

He stood there seemingly staring at the ground, which is what tracking looks like most of the time, but then, when he had narrowed down the view just enough, a plant caught his eye, and he bent down to inspect it. If only Reilly and Thez could be so lucky. This could take all day even if I tracked it myself. I'd been stuck on a rocky stretch of trail half a day before.

For Reilly and Thez I had to track the trail myself and tell them what I was seeing. I made them get down to whatever level I had to to track it so they could see the trail the way I had seen it. It was tough work. We were all hot and tired by the time we finally made our way off the rocks and into a dry wash. At least the wash was fairly readable and predictable, though Zeb had not ventured down it. He had walked on the firmer ground above and so to alternate between groups I had to climb into and out of the wash. By the time we camped for the night I was ready to turn in without any dinner. I set up my tent, tossed in my sleeping bag and lay down expecting to sleep like the dead. But I lay my head down and remembered that Reilly had a brand new tent and a brand new stove and he probably needed some instructions. Let the guys do it, I told myself, they're capable. But I really did need dinner if I wanted to be of any use the next day. Eating jerky and trail mix on the run wasn't the way to live. And I wasn't just thinking of me now. I had to remember I wasn't just watching out for myself. And that got the old battle raging. How was I going to tell Rusty? To stop that line of thinking I crawled out of the tent and took stock of how the guys were doing.

Reilly's tent did, indeed, pop up. It also staked down but he hadn't bothered.

"Reilly, peg your tent down a little," I told him.

"Why? Lookit it. Isn't it better than the last one?"

"Much better, until it gets blown away. Two pegs ought to do it, though four would be more comfortable and easier on the ears."

"How can a peg or two affect my comfort? I'll be sleeping like a baby."

"Okay, just remember, I told you so."

At least it was a calm night. Maybe it wouldn't matter. When we did get a windy night he'd learn. There's nothing more irritating than a flapping, bucking tent in the middle of the night.

Next he couldn't remember how to start my stove but the one he bought was different anyway.

"This thing don't look like it'll cook anything," he said.

"Attach the can of gas to it. It'll make more sense then," I told him.

"Can of gas? Yours doesn't have a can of gas."

"It has a built in tank that I have to refill. Yours you just attach a can of fuel you can buy at GearUp! You did buy fuel for your stove, didn't you?"

"Aw hell. How was I to know?"

I looked it over. It was a nice stove. Good quality.

"Well, it'll be a good stove for you once you get everything you need. Did you buy pots and pans to go with it? What were you going to heat water in?"

"Leave it to a woman to think of all the kitchen stuff."

"It's not kitchen stuff," said Jacobsen. "It's camping gear. It only makes sense; if you're going to be heating water you need something to put it in. Something that will take some heat."

I heated enough water for both our dinners and we were in business. Then with a sigh I remembered our stalker. I walked to the edge of camp and called out, "Zeb? Do you have dinner out there?"

"All taken care of, thanks," he called back.

What was I going to do about that guy? I thought he'd give up, but maybe he was easily amused.

I went to bed, my mind a tangle of home and trail. I decided I was settled enough on the idea of being a mother of two that I should just tell Rusty in a quiet moment at home. I could do that. And he'd be thrilled. Things were relatively quiet. Trouble had been manageable. I'd just tell him, simple as that.

I woke with a start. I poked my head out of the tent. The guys were still up.

"Reilly? Where's your pack?" I asked.

"Jacobsen strung 'em up. No bears tonight."

"Good. And if a bear does come, don't panic. Just lay quietly in your tent and he'll go away."

"Unless you snuck a Snicker's bar in there," Thez said.

"Nope, no, I learned my lesson, no food, no *nada* in the tent at night."

Jacobsen walked over to my tent and squatted down in front of the door.

"You okay? Usually you're out here telling stories until we're all yawning."

"I'm just tired. I walked twice as far as any of you guys."

"Still…you've done more without even thinking about being tired. Everything's okay?"

"Yeah, I'm fine."

"Just checking."

The next day I woke up to light streaming through the tent fabric. Oh man! I overslept. The guys were talking quietly. I brushed my hair quickly.

"I'd ask Michaels," Thez said to Jacobsen.

There was an affirmative but unintelligible male response.

I stuck my head out of the tent and saw all the guys gathered around steaming pots of water. I pulled on my shoes and joined the group. I'd learned long ago, mostly through the military and Thez, to sleep in my clothes. I never knew when I'd have trouble strike in the middle of the night and running around in the woods (or desert in the case of my military service) without clothes on was a little embarrassing. A thirty-year-old woman brandishing a rifle in the nude was not a pretty sight unless you were into something kinky. Nights in the mountains tended to be cold any time of year so clothes won out.

It was Thez's turn to voice concern but I assured him I was fine.

"Sorry to hold things up," I said.

"Don' be apologizing to me," said Reilly. "I was glad to not have my tent shook at the crack of dawn. Not that I'd have noticed. The dang thing shook all night."

"It would shake less if you'd pegged it down," I told him.

"Are you still feeling the effects of that fire?" Thez asked.

"No, I feel fine. The sore throat cleared up in a few days and the headaches settled down as soon as I got away from the smoke."

"Maybe she's just feeling middle aged," Reilly said.

"Uh oh, you're treading dangerous ground," Thez told him.

Middle aged? Was I? How could I be middle aged? I was just getting around to my second kid. I didn't care about the guys joking about my age. Actually I was quite pleased they didn't think of me as a kid. But... middle aged?

I added water to a packet of oatmeal and a cup of hot chocolate and ate my normal camp breakfast without thinking about it. I washed up the cup and stuck it back in my pack, then took down and rolled up my tent.

"Are you ready?" I asked the guys.

They weren't. They'd stood around talking while they waited for me to catch up. They hopped to it.

It was another long, slow tracking day. I could see Zeb off in the distance bored stiff. Why did he stick around if he wasn't learning anything? The guys stuck it out even when dusk settled over the desert and my house could be seen off in the distance. Rusty walked out when he saw us in the hills. He put his arm around me and watched the guys at work.

"Where's Jacobsen?" Rusty asked.

I pointed to where Jacobsen was working my trail. Rusty walked over to see how he was doing. Jacobsen stood up when he saw Rusty approach. They talked for a minute and then both men bent over my tracks. Rusty let Katie go and she ran back to me. I picked her up. Golly, she was getting heavy. I knew she was small for her age, but it felt like she had grown in the couple of days I was gone. Maybe it was just that I was trying to hold her in a thirty-pound backpack.

"Guys, let's call it quits. You've done enough. We've worked over four miles of ground. You've got to be bug-eyed by now."

They all stood wearily.

"How far is a search?"

"It varies. I've been on searches that were maybe a mile and others that were ten or more."

"Dang, so this was an average search?" Reilly asked.

"Yeah, I guess you could say so."

"What's next?" Reilly asked.

"Well, I'll go talk to Schroeder. When I get a call he'll decide who should go out with me. If it's likely to be a medical call Thez will go, because he knows how to work with the EMTs. If it's just a lost camper call he'll decide between the three of you. Reilly, you're more likely to get a real call if you show me you have all the proper gear. If you want me to go to the store with you and make sure you have everything you need, that can be arranged."

"So we're done?"

"Until we get a call. You can practice if you want to. It's always good to practice when you find yourself on a patch of dirt."

The end of class seemed rather anticlimactic.

"But I got questions," Reilly said.

"Well, come in the house and ask questions, then," I told them.

"I'll take Bertie home while you finish up," Rusty said, but Jacobsen stopped him.

"You might want to stick around for the questions."

When we were settled in the den in a circle around the coffee table I let them know they could begin. Rusty stood off to the side, arms folded over his chest, just listening.

Reilly started the questions. "How long did it take you to notice you were being followed?"

Damn, did he have to start out with that? I looked to Jacobsen, since he had been tracking my trail.

"What do you think, Kent? Did you notice when I figured it out? I know it showed in my tracks. I'm just wondering if you caught it."

"I noticed a change. It was more of a hesitation in your tracks."

"That's because I was looking behind me a lot. But it turned out Zeb wasn't behind me. He was beside me. When did you first notice the hesitation?"

"I don't know, it was pretty early in the trail, though."

"Actually I knew he was following me about a quarter mile from the house," I said answering the question.

"Shee-it," said Reilly. "And it didn't bother you?"

"Kent, did it bother me? Did you get any feel for the change in the trail?"

"No, I wouldn't say it bothered you. If it had you would have changed your mind, gone back or something, but you didn't. You kept track of him. That's what I guess the hesitation can be attributed to. But I wouldn't say it bothered you."

"Good. Reilly, Thez, did you see any indication that Zeb knew he'd been found out? Did he change the way he did things?"

"He was staying out of sight of you until about half way through the track. Then all of a sudden things changed."

"That's because I talked to him. I told him what I was doing and that you guys were going to track both trails. So after he knew he was laying a trail he probably changed his ways quite a bit."

"Wait a minute," interrupted Rusty. "You get followed into the woods by this guy, Zeb, and you take time out to talk to him? He could have killed you."

"He isn't dangerous. He wants to work out here. He's just seeing how things in California work."

"I don't like the idea of you being followed around when you're by yourself," Rusty said.

"I wasn't by myself. Katie was with me," I said and regretted it as soon as it escaped.

"That's supposed to make me feel better?" Rusty asked.

"I had the rifle," I added.

"And the guy knows she can shoot, too!" said Thez.

Oh man, I was getting in deeper and deeper.

"And how does he know that?" Rusty asked.

"Cassidy took off a snake's head at twenty paces," Thez said examining his hand again.

"Does anybody have any *tracking* questions?" I asked, trying to steer the conversation any other direction than the one it was heading in.

"We're just getting started at this tracking thing, aren't we?" asked Reilly.

"Yes, this is just the bare basics. You haven't dealt with multiple layers of tracks, and you still have a lot to learn about things like creeks, and where tracks can be hidden, and you need experience with different soils and weather conditions. It takes years to learn to track well. Right now you could follow an easy trail as long as nothing unexpected comes up. Unfortunately, in my experience, something unexpected always comes up. The most common thing is rocks. People like rocks. They head for rocks to climb on. Low rocks are easy to walk on. People are used to cement so hard pack and rocks are easier walking for them."

Reilly groaned. He really didn't like tracking on rocks and Zeb had not made it easy either.

"I still don't know how you tracked that guy over the rocks, even though you showed us. You showed us invisible things."

"I know. It takes practice. You all need practice. You'll see the next call you go on. You know more than you think and there's more to learn than you could possibly imagine. Tracking is one thing you can never be an expert at. Every trail will teach you more. So… you need a trail. I'll take one of you at a time on calls I get and you can get some practice in."

I chickened out of telling Rusty my news. I didn't want him to think of his pregnant wife being followed around in the woods by a man who had been kicked out of one town and was looking to take over mine. I'd give him a few days to let things settle out. Zeb would get bored and leave. Then I'd tell Rusty.

Chapter 18

I rode into town with Rusty the next morning.

I knocked on Schroeder's door tentatively. I didn't have good news, but neither was it unexpected.

"I talked to Jacobsen this morning," Schroeder said. "Unfortunately, he had something else on his mind than the class. What's this guy doing following everything you do?"

"I told you. He wants to track here."

"Ah, yes, the guy you sent here the other day," he said.

"He never showed."

"I know. But he shows up every time you turn around."

"Only because I'm more observant than he expects out of a woman. If I hadn't told the guys about him I doubt they would have known he was there."

"They did after he fired at you," he pointed out.

"Yes, well, that was Zeb's mistake."

"He has a name now?" Schroeder asked.

"Don't know if it's his real name. Don't know his last name."

"Cassidy… this has the makings of a Cassidy disaster. I want it stopped."

"Okay, so stop him. He's probably parked half a block away from the station. He drives a primer gray Chevy pickup truck with the top of the cab removed. His plates are from Wyoming. Should be fairly recognizable."

"What has he done?"

"According to me? Or according to Jacobsen?" I asked. There was definitely a difference between the two.

"How about if we just deal with this from your point of view for now. We'll worry about the other guys in a minute."

"I don't think he's done anything wrong. He did fire at us, but it was because he thought I was shooting at him."

"And why did he think that?"

"Because I had to shoot a rattlesnake. Zeb was following us and almost took the bullet."

"And the rattlesnake?"

"Is probably a hat band now. I gave the dead snake to Zeb."

"Cassidy… this is just getting stranger and stranger."

"I thought you'd be used to that by now."

"This character follows you. He shot at you. He refuses to have anything to do with the police, but he hasn't done anything wrong?" he asked. He was really puzzled about why I didn't want to jump on Zeb's case.

"No. Not here anyway. His history in the last town he lived in is questionable. Maybe that's why he hasn't given me a last name yet."

"Maybe," he said sarcastically.

We did eventually get around to talking about the class and he agreed that Thez would be the choice medically and that Jacobsen would be the choice until Reilly was properly outfitted. I told him about my plans to teach the tracking class at academy and he nodded his approval. He had talked to Chase about that and he agreed I'd probably get further with the cadets than Chase would.

Then he sat back in his chair, folded his arms in a don't mess with me way, looked me straight in the eye and said, "Now, I want to know what you are hiding from us."

Gulp. "Hiding?" I said.

"The guys say you haven't been yourself."

"Of course I have."

"Should I ask Rusty?"

"No!"

"Why?"

Gulp again. "He doesn't think I'm hiding anything. Why would the guys?"

"They know you better than you think they do. At least Jacobsen does. And you just admitted that you *are* hiding something. What is it?"

"I did?"

"You did."

"How did I?"

This was a cop trick. I knew it. I did not admit I was hiding something. Did I? This had to be a trick. But it was also Schroeder. I knew he meant well, but…

"You said that Rusty doesn't think you are hiding anything. That means that he could. And it means you've been hiding this from Rusty, too."

Sigh. "I've just been waiting for the right time… and the right time has been elusive."

He picked up his telephone, started punching a number…

"Schroeder, no, please don't."

"Go talk to him."

"Not now," I almost whined at him.

"How long have you been saying *not now*. If not now, then when?"

"First Strict, now you, what is it about you guys? Can't a girl find a right time for these things? How did your wife tell you? I bet she didn't have some big shot at the station push her down the hallway and knock on your door and…" I almost blew it… I did blow it. He knew. He backed off. He canceled the call and began a new one. I gave him *the look*. He put the phone to his ear.

"She's been dying to do this. Let her... Nancy? Do we have plans tonight? How would you like a dinner guest? ... It's just Katie. I gave Cassidy an assignment and she needs a last minute babysitter.... good... okay." He hung up. "It's settled. Is that okay?"

"Schroeder... this is unheard of. Your wife should *never* have to baby sit your officer's kids. If everybody did this..."

"I told you, she's been dying to do this. She loves Katie and she never gets to see her, or you and Rusty for that matter. Let her do this. You'll at least tell her how it went."

"If you don't let on that you knew before Rusty," I said.

He got serious again. "This isn't something you should hide from us. It affects the assignments you're given. It affects what you are capable of. We need to keep these things in mind."

"I know. It's still early. I can do anything I'd normally do."

"I know you can. And you'll take on anything, but that doesn't mean you should. When can Nancy expect you?"

"Right before Rusty gets off from work. We're still down to one car."

"Okay."

I went to Rusty's office, knocked even more tentatively. He answered it but he had someone in his office.

"Are you going to need the Explorer today?"

"There are other cars I can use."

"I'll be back before you get off."

"Okay."

"I'll see you then."

"Okay."

Whew! Now what?

Chapter 19

I rushed home and looked through my closet. I pulled out the dress that I knew Rusty liked, found the shoes that would go best with it. When I finally got Katie down for a nap I rushed through the shower and blow-dried my hair. I curled it and applied makeup carefully. I was nervous. I hoped it went better than last time. Last time was… it just was not the way to do it, but I hadn't had much choice. The circumstances were just against me. Strict had ordered me to tell Rusty and when I got to the station things were tense. Rusty was angry about something. But I'd had to tell him anyway. It was just all wrong. I wanted this to be right. I wanted it to be right for both of us. At least Schroeder had been nice enough to give me a little time. I tried to count my blessings and not get cold feet again. I had to do it, so there was no use wondering how to do it. I'd just do it, jump in with both feet, and get it over with. And Rusty would be happy. He was the one who wanted kids. As in plural kids. Not just one kid. He'd be happy with as many as he could get. I wasn't so sure. I thought one was okay. I thought two would have to be okay, too. If this was a boy I'd have a hard time going for three. Who was I kidding, I'd have trouble going for three anyway. I was still struggling with the idea of having two.

I slipped the dress over my head. It was an old dress, but Rusty had liked it from the first time he'd seen me in it. I had worn it for my twenty-fifth birthday party. It felt so long ago. Since then, I hadn't worn it often. When he saw me in this dress he'd be curious from the start. This dress was different. It signified something. He might even guess what was going on before we left the station.

Oh, oh. What about Zeb? I got out the phone book and chose a restaurant that I knew he couldn't get into. I was in a dress. Rusty would be in a suit and tie. I was guessing Zeb didn't even own a tie. We'd go somewhere a suit and tie were required. Let's see… here we go, François. Zeb would never venture in there. Starched white tablecloths, fancy napkin sculptures in the wineglasses. Wineglasses. Oh well, I'd just have to settle for iced tea. That would get Rusty wondering, too. I called and made a reservation.

There was a wolf whistle from the hills when I walked to the Explorer. I put Katie in her car seat. Zeb came waltzing out of the hills.

"Well, well… the little tracker has a different side!" he said.

"I've got a date, and I'd appreciate it if we could go out in peace," I said as I slammed the door shut and started the engine. I drove away and left him smiling in my driveway.

"Katie," I said as we drove along, "Can you say *Schroeder*? You're going to be staying with Mrs. Schroeder. Say *Schroeder*! Come on baby. Say *Schroeder*!"

"Doder," she said.

"Good girl! Can you say *missus*?"

She just looked at me like I was crazy. I had to admit asking her to say *Missus Schroeder* was expecting too much. Nancy knew that.

When I got to the Schroeder's house Nancy looked me up and down.

"And exactly what kind of assignment is this Schroeder has you doing?" she asked.

"Schroeder will tell you when he gets home, but when Rusty comes to pick up Katie you can't let on that you already know. At least I think Schroeder guessed right. I can't think of any other conclusions he could have jumped to."

"If Schroeder can tell me, why can't you?"

"Because I want Rusty to be the first person I tell."

"But if Schroeder knows…"

"I didn't tell him. He guessed. He didn't want it to be like last time so he asked you to baby sit so I could do things right. I feel bad making you baby sit for something that should be so easy. But it hasn't been easy. It's been hard and then inconvenient and then there were reasons not to… But now I have to. Schroeder told me to."

"This is not police business. You don't have to tell Rusty. This is between the two of you. If you don't want to tell him…"

"No, I should take this chance. It's my one chance to do it right. I better do it."

"Can Katie talk yet?"

"Oh yeah! She says lots of things. We were working on *Missus Schroeder* on the way over here. We didn't make much progress. Katie, say *Missus Schroeder*! Can you say *Missus Schroeder*?"

"Doder!" said Katie.

"Well, that's closer than I expected," Nancy said.

"She loves doing animal sounds and she loves story books. Oh and she can climb anything. She climbs up onto my counter all the time. She'll love your stairs. Just don't let her climb up the outside of the railing."

"She'd do that?"

"At the gym she climbs the *outside* of the play place."

"Oh dear, okay."

"And she loves to jump off things."

"How do you keep up with her?"

"Don't worry, she announces when she's going to jump."

Rusty took a step back when I arrived back at his office door. I looked inside. Nobody was there. I stepped in and closed the door behind me.

"What's going on?" he said with a silly grin on his face.

"We have free babysitting for a few hours. I thought we should take advantage of it."

"Are you going to tell me what's going on?"

"Yes, when the time is right. We have reservations for a nice quiet table at a romantic restaurant."

"You hate fancy places."

"I chose it for a reason. You'll just have to deal with that."

He smiled. He did like fancy places. He just didn't understand this sudden change.

"You? Chose a fancy restaurant?"

"For a reason."

"What reason?"

"Ooo, don't spoil it. It was a good reason, but knowing what it is will spoil it."

He was still smiling. I guess that was a good thing.

"Oh, come on, Rusty, would you go out to dinner with me?"

"You know I will. I'm just curious."

"Good. The sooner we get there the sooner you can stop being curious."

"I don't know. I think it's kind of interesting watching you stew. What have you got up your sleeve? Where's Katie?"

"We'll pick her up after dinner."

"So she's not with Bertie."

"Rusty! You're not a detective tonight. You're my husband and I want to have a special evening with you."

"Okay, let's go have a special evening," he said, still with that silly grin on his face. He buttoned the top button on his shirt and tightened his tie. "We didn't have a special dinner like this for Valentine's Day."

"That's because Katie managed to say *Chucky Cheese*. I still think it's funny that she beat you at Skeeball."

"We put all the tickets together, anyway, so it didn't matter who won. We said at the time that we'd do our Valentine's Day later when the restaurants weren't as crowded. Is this that day?"

"No, this is a different day," I said as we both headed for the driver's side of the Explorer. I'd have to fight for the keys or tell him where we were going. I didn't want to fight for the keys so I went around to the passenger's side.

"Cassidy, what's wrong?"

"Nothing, I guess I'm just a little nervous."

"About going out with me? Since when were you ever nervous about going out with me?"

Well, there was the first six months that we knew each other… when I couldn't believe he'd actually asked me out.

"It's okay. I was just on automatic, because I know where we're going."

"So, where are we going?"

"François," I said.

"You're kidding."

"No, why? Is that okay?"

"Um, yeah, it's fine. This evening is just getting stranger by the minute. You make fun of places that have pepper grinder brandishing waiters and then you choose a place where you can't even park your own car or put your napkin on your lap."

"I did? I've never been there before. I just chose it because…"

"Yes?"

"Because I knew we could be alone there."

He drove to François. How he knew where it was, I had no idea. I only knew approximately where it was because I had looked it up online. He got in line at the valet parking and handed the boy a tip. He held the door open and I walked into France. There were murals of the French countryside painted on the walls. I don't know how I knew they were the French countryside. They just said France, without any words whatsoever. I felt like I was gawking. Rusty put an arm around my shoulders and led me to the maître d's podium.

"Reservation for two," Rusty said.

"Name?"

"Michaels."

Almost every word from then on out was in French. Even the American looking waiters and waitresses spoke French. I smiled and nodded, I hoped at the right time. Rusty was enjoying my plight. He didn't understand French either, but it didn't bother him. We were shown to a little table next to the part of the mural that depicted a vineyard. All the tables had lace tablecloths. My little napkin sculpture was of a peacock. The waiter pulled out my chair for me and after I sat down he snapped open the napkin and placed it on my lap, then helped me scoot my chair in. I was wishing I could take the napkin apart myself so I could figure out how to turn a napkin into a peacock.

We were given menus and I opened mine and squinted at the squiggly, little print. All the names of the dishes were in French. Parts of the descriptions were in English but it was more like: French meat in a French sauce, French meat cooked in a French way with French vegetables.

A waiter appeared and asked a French question, which I took to mean that he wanted to take our drink order. That was always the first question, wasn't it? So I said, "Iced tea."

Rusty ordered a red wine.

Rusty smiled, "Ordering iced tea in this place is like going to a gourmet restaurant and ordering a hamburger cooked well done."

"It's okay. What are you ordering?"

"The Beef Bourguignon. What are you ordering?"

"Some French meat in a French sauce."

He laughed at me, "You really didn't know what you were getting into picking this place, did you?"

"No. But we're alone. That's what counts."

"Why?"

"Let's order first. Then I'll know we will have time to talk."

A waiter brought our drinks and disappeared. Then another came to the table and asked a question.

"Yes, everything is fine," I said.

"I think he wants our order," Rusty said.

"You go first," I said.

I hadn't decided but since nothing made sense anyway I was judging by price. Hmm, no prices either. This might not be a good sign. The waiter was pleased with Rusty's order and I held up the menu and pointed. The waiter smiled and I took his words as a positive sign. He scribbled something in his little order book and went away.

"What did you order?" Rusty asked.

"I don't know. But I promise to like it."

Rusty leaned forward with an expectant look. I was waiting for him to say, "Well?" but he didn't do it. I got the hint though. I fidgeted nervously. I stuck my spoon into the tines of my fork and made it rock back and forth on the table, then thought I'd just preformed a major faux pass in a fancy restaurant so I took them apart and just fidgeted with the fork. Rusty was amused.

Just do it, I told myself, jump in with both feet and the conversation will go from there. Just do it!

"I… um… Rusty…" shit, I was stumbling all over my words. He just waited, which made it worse. Okay, Cass, you can do this. The time is right, the setting is right. Just do it. I swallowed hard. "Rusty, when I got done with the camping trip and the fire. Doctor Ron checked me out and I was fine, but we found out something unexpected. I know, I should have told you a week ago, but I was having a hard time with the information and I wanted to tell you when I could feel good about it. I had to wrestle with it for a while. And I'm not really sure I'm through wrestling with it yet. But…" it stuck in my throat. Here I was ready to make the big announcement and I couldn't get it to come out. Then the woman at the next table jumped to her feet. She stared down at the table she just got up from in a furor.

"You jerk! This is the first time in, what, *six months* we've gone out. We've been married *six whole months* and the first time you take me out… to a place like this… to tell me you want a divorce! I can't believe you. I just can't believe you! I could just… Grrrr! I don't know *what* to do!"

Yes she did. She took his drink and threw it at him then she turned around and ran square into our table spilling everything on top of it. She grabbed for something to steady herself and that turned out to be Rusty. She looked at him and blushed darker than his spilled wine. Then she grabbed my iced tea and threw that at the guy as well. She clenched her fists, stomped in frustration, and then stormed out of the restaurant. The three of us left behind looked at each other, then the man got up and spoke to the maître d', who ran over alarmed and started rattling away in French. We had wine and oil and bread spilled all over us. We were taken aback at the sudden turn of events.

The man came back rather sheepishly.

"I'm sorry. I didn't think she'd take it that bad. I thought she wanted out just as much as I did. Look, I'll pay for your dinners."

"I guess it's just a night for news," I said. "You don't need to do that."

"I might as well, it's one thing she can't take from me in the settlement. I hope your news was better than mine." And he walked away.

The waiter came back and settled us at a new table, this one with French curtains overlooking the street. I preferred the quaint corner table but… Rusty looked at me and I looked at him. My birthday dress was ruined. His suit would need dry cleaning. We were a disheveled mess. When new drinks were set before us, I tried again, this time with more success. I figured I better get it out or I never would.

"Rusty, we're expecting again," I said simply.

He sat still.

"Again?" he asked.

I nodded. "Can't do it the first time again. We already did that twice."

"Cass… that's wonderful! I mean, I know it was unexpected. Why didn't you tell me?"

"I told you. I needed to wrestle with the idea for a little while first. At first I didn't even believe Doctor Ron but you can't argue with a test. I still don't know what we are going to do."

"We're going to have a baby, that's what!" he said excitedly.

"But, that means Katie needs her own room. And what will happen to your office? I'm not ready to be a mother of two. And…"

"Babe, this isn't a fancy restaurant conversation. This is a big brown couch conversation."

"I know. But I wanted us to be alone. I wanted it to be just you and me. And there was only one way to guarantee it was just you and me, and Schroeder asked Nancy to baby sit."

"Schroeder knows?"

"I didn't tell him. All the guys convinced him I was hiding something and he demanded to know what it was and he asked Nancy to baby sit so I could tell you. I haven't told him, but what else could he assume?"

"But you're sure?"

"Yeah, they ran a test right there at the hospital. Doctor Ron did a thorough exam and said everything is fine."

"So…"

"Don't say it! I know what you were going to say."

"What was I going to say?"

"You were going to say, 'How do you feel?' I feel fine. I don't feel any different, except panic stricken. But I feel fine."

The waiter came to our table very French and very apologetic. Rusty asked for our meals to be packaged to go. This made the waiter even more apologetic.

"It's okay, we just have to go home. It has nothing to do with the restaurant or the service. Just package our meals to go."

Lots of French went by at ninety miles an hour.

When our meals appeared they were packaged to go but there looked like there were too many boxes. Rusty took our bags and his bedraggled wife to the front of the restaurant, asked for our car, tipped everybody really well, and drove us home.

First we hit the big brown couch.

"What are we going to do about bedrooms?" I asked.

"We'll figure it out. Katie will probably take my office and the guest room will be a nursery."

"But what will happen to your office? You need a place to work."

"Babe, you worry too much. It will all work out. It doesn't have to work out tonight. We've got nine months."

"Eight."

"Eight?"

"Rusty, I can't keep track of two kids."

"You'll do fine. Just wait and see."

"Are you sure?"

"I've never been surer."

"How can you say that? Everything feels like a jumbled, confused mess to me."

"You've been a jumbled, confused mess for a week, haven't you?"

"Yes."

"If you'd told me a week ago maybe you wouldn't have felt so bad."

"I know, but I was busy being a jumbled, confused mess."

"Do you think you can eat yet?"

"No, I'm still a jumbled, confused mess."

"Okay."

"Plus, it's hard to get enthusiastic about a dish if I don't know what it is."

"Why did you choose François?"

"Because I knew Zeb couldn't get in. I figured he didn't own a tie."

"Babe… here, just be with me."

So we sat there, in each other's arms, me a jumbled, confused mess, him basking in the idea of being a father again. A father of two. And… it was okay. It was right. Rusty made it right. I held on tighter.

French food was not created with microwaves in mind. We were probably committing some French sin taking gourmet food home in Styrofoam boxes and nuking them. Then after the first Styrofoam box started melting we switched to plates. The extra boxes turned out to be pastries. Rusty laughed when he opened the box.

"What's so funny?" I asked.

"Do you know what this is?" he asked.

"Dessert? They must have done it to make up for the commotion."

"This particular dessert is called a divorce."

I found out I liked French sauce, although it kind of covered up the type of meat I was eating. I never did figure out what that was. Lamb maybe?

"So, what do you think?" Rusty asked.

"I think next time I want to go out somewhere, just you and I, I'll let you choose the place."

"Are you doing better now?"

"Yeah, I think I am. I can deal with the present. I have to tell myself that. Right now is no problem, no matter what is happening. Shooting? Tracking? People needing to be found? Screaming kid? I can deal with it. Thinking about the future? About change coming up? I don't know why it always throws me for a loop."

"It's because you try to make it all make sense at once. But it doesn't have to. Not now. Let it make sense a little at a time. If you do that you'll always be in the present, and you'll handle it. You'll see. You'll do a great job."

"We better go get Katie."

"Does she know?"

"No, how could she understand? She'll figure it out as things happen. She likes babies."

"Five more minutes," he said. "Give me five more minutes of couch time. Then I'll be ready. You're sure Katie can't just sleep over?"

"I already feel like I'm imposing on them."

"Okay. We'll go get her. It's just nice to have it quiet."

"It's not going to be quiet in November."

"Hush, it'll be great. Just wait. Everything's fine? You're sure?"

"I'm sure."

Five minutes stretched as we sat in our spot. Neither of us wanted to move but as the hour grew later we knew we had to save Nancy from Katie. I knew Nancy was used to kids. She had grandkids, but none of them were like Katie.

We stood on the Schroeder's porch waiting for an answer within. It took a while. When Nancy made her way to the door she was holding a beaming Katie. Nancy didn't look quite so happy.

"Daddy! Up!" said Katie. Even though Nancy was holding her it was still up higher when Rusty had her.

"You weren't kidding about her wanting to climb," Nancy said.

"At our house her favorite thing to climb is the couch. She likes to jump off the arm of it."

"Here it was the stairs. It took her a good half hour to get up, but then she wanted to jump down! She is so funny. Katie, what does Schroeder say? What does Mister Schroeder say?"

"Kaykins!" said Katie. And she was right, many of the officers called her Katiekins.

"What does Grandma say?" Nancy asked her.

"Go chopping!"

Rusty busted out laughing.

"What does the other Grandma say?"

"Are you hungry?" Katie said seriously.

"That sounds like my mom," said Rusty. "Or Martha. She might identify that with Martha, too."

"I don't know if she still does it," I said. "Katie, what does Big John say? What does *Big* John say?"

"Nodoido," Katie said.

"What did she say?" Nancy asked.

"No radio," I translated.

"She ate a good dinner. I now know what meat looks like. And carrots, and cake, and potatoes. She is so cute."

"Can I pay you for your work?" I asked.

"Pay me? No! And it wasn't work. We enjoyed every minute. All I want is to know what he said."

"That's kind of hard to say. Not that he didn't say anything. He did. It's just that things didn't quite go smoothly in the telling of it. And so the reaction was mixed with the reaction to the commotion at the other table. I guess you could say trouble lived up to its name again. But I'm not having kids until I get it right! With my luck I'd end up with ten kids and still trying to figure out a good way to break the news to Rusty."

"After about three I think I'd be down to, oh no, not again!" Nancy confessed. "What about you Katie? Are you ready to be a sister?"

"Tister! Ready, set, go!" Katie said.

That about summed it up.

"Thank you for watching her for me," I told Nancy. "I don't know when I would have told Rusty if left to my own devices."

"Well, I'm glad you finally did. Now the whole station can know."

Oh man, here we go again.

"I think I get it now," Rusty said. "That whole thing about you wanting me to get a new car was because you were pregnant. Do you really want my old Explorer?"

"It would make a good mom mobile. We've outgrown the Jeep."

"Why don't you get a four wheel drive SUV?"

"Why don't you get a new car?"

"The Explorer is nine years old. I don't want you to take my old car when you could have a new car."

"I like your old car."

"So do I."

"I tell you what, go walk around a car lot with Kelly. I bet there is a car out there just begging you to buy it but you can't hear it because you're too far away."

"No, if I went with Kelly he'd talk me into some Mustang convertible or a Corvette. He doesn't think practically. I need to haul gear around. What about my box?"

He was referring to his toolbox of detective stuff. He also had body armor that took up space in a trunk. He had a lot of job related things he had to have handy for investigations.

"Well, we need to do something soon. I'm going to have doctor's appointments and I need a car for calls. One of us needs to get a car. You're in town every day. Drive by a dealership now and then and take a look."

Chapter 20

It didn't take long for Strict to call with my first real search of the year. It was early. Tourist season was just barely started. But, I learned, this was no lost tourist. A small plane had gone down and the pilot was missing.

"Did you call Schroeder?" I asked Strict.

"Thez is on his way."

"Okay, thanks."

With Zeb in the picture I thought I better look official. I put on my uniform down to the last detail, my hair up in a ponytail, my 9mm in plain sight.

Landon pulled up to the house in his white Mustang. He popped the trunk and I tossed in my pack. Zeb came jogging out of the hills.

"Where are you going?" he asked.

"I got a call."

"Where?"

"Small plane went down. Should be easy."

He opened the back door and hopped in.

"No way," I said. "You are not going along."

"How are you going to stop me?"

I got out and jerked open his door.

"Get out. There is no way Lou Strickland is going to let you go, so you might as well get out now."

"Who is this guy?" Landon asked.

"We don't have time for introductions. Zeb. Out."

"Well, look at you," he said. "The uniform doesn't work somehow. You'd do better to go back to the old look."

"I don't care. Get out."

"You're stuck with me babycakes."

"Oh yeah?" I said and stomped back into the house where Rusty was getting ready to start the day.

"I thought Landon was here. Did you forget something?" Rusty asked.

"I need a little persuasion. Zeb is demanding to go, too. Can you help us out a little?"

When we got outside Zeb was sitting smugly in the back seat, arms crossed, ready to go. Rusty reached in and hauled him out bodily.

"Hey, man! Ease up already!" Zeb said.

"I'll ease up when you leave my wife alone," Rusty said. He leaned down and said through the window. "Lock your door."

Landon hit the power locks and all the doors clicked.

"Take away his gun," I called out as Landon backed out of the driveway.

"Who was that?" Landon asked.

"Tracker, from Wyoming. Thinks he can come down here and do whatever he wants. Only trouble is he has a rather sketchy past and doesn't want to have anything to do with the police. Thinks he can make a living finding people and collecting rewards."

"Is he giving you trouble?"

"No, he's just a pest."

"Why the uniform? You hate tracking in uniform."

"I told Zeb he'd have to become a reserve deputy. I figure I can't make the point stick without living it out, so I wore the uniform."

"Are the rumors true?"

"Rumors?"

"Okay, are you really pregnant?"

"Yes, though it hasn't slowed me down."

"Nothing slows you down. But I needed to know, you know…"

Because he was the EMT. And I was the trouble magnet. He'd had to patch me up before. He'd even saved my life a time or two. He did need to know.

"I know. This should be an easy search. But we need to step on it. You might have your work cut out for you this time."

"I hope not."

We pulled into the compound to pick up a search and rescue vehicle and Thez was waiting for us. We all loaded up into a car together and headed out. We were ready. It was a bit tense. We all felt the time slipping by for this pilot. When we got to base camp I groaned. There it was, the hacked up primer gray truck.

I got out of the car and stalked up to Zeb.

"You are not going along," I said flatly.

"Try and stop me," he answered.

"How did you get here before us?"

"Police scanner. And I didn't stop along the way."

"Oh great."

Strict addressed the group giving Zeb an odd look.

"See that hill?" Strict asked pointing, "You're heading for the other side of it. You'll find officers on site. Your job is to find the pilot."

"That's it? That's all the instruction we get?" Zeb asked and again Strict wondered who this guy was.

To me Strict said, “You’ll find the tracks taped off.”

“Okay.”

Landon opened the trunk and we all strapped ourselves into our packs. I doubted I needed my big pack, but better safe than sorry. Landon always carried a big pack because he also had first aid supplies. The guys looked to me.

“Oh, come on. We’re not tracking yet. Do I have to go first?” I asked.

Old habits die hard. I sighed and set off for the hill. Landon took his place behind me and Thez fell in behind him. Why couldn’t we just walk together? I felt like migrating geese flying in formation.

It only took us about half an hour to get to the other side of the hill. I looked down on the wreckage of the plane and was hopeful. Most of the plane was still intact. I saw no landing gear but the wings were still in place. The cockpit still looked habitable. Men were walking around making notes, talking in quiet tones. I wondered what was going on that they needed to keep quiet. I found a taped off section of ground and walked over to it. It was a much bigger section of ground than I usually got to start out with, perhaps ten feet square, but those ten feet held a lot of information.

“Thez, study this from the other side. Don’t step in. We only have a minute here so take in what you can.” I pointed. “His leg would not support him when he exited the plane. Here’s where his ankle gave way. You can tell it’s his ankle by the twist and the skid right here. He went down to one knee. Here’s his handprint in the dust. Even when he thought he could manage, he couldn’t walk. Here’s blood stains. Here. Here. We need to keep an ambulance on standby. This is going to be a rough one.”

He nodded.

The pilot headed in the direction he expected a road to be. Apparently he didn’t expect to be found in the wreckage or he would have waited for help to arrive. He was in a hurry, as injured as he was. Besides the scrapes and drags his injured body left behind there was an urgency and midway down the hill the flow of blood increased dramatically. I tried to point things out to Thez as we went but I was feeling time slipping away. I totally forgot about Zeb. I became immersed in the trail, pulling everything I could out of it. I knew doing that would rebound on me later but I needed to know what this guy was going through. I had been through a similar accident and I knew the thoughts, knew what it felt like to be banged up, cut up and needing to get away, not knowing how things would turn out. Knowing I just had to do what I could for the moment.

“Landon, call in the ambulance. This is going to be a short trail. It’ll take them an hour to get here. Get them started now.”

“Cassidy, you don’t know.”

"Get them started now. We're looking at broken bones here. His weight is bent over. I'm guessing internal injuries, broken ribs. If he's got broken ribs we could be looking at a punctured lung. This is a lot of blood."

Thez was studying the ground. This was his first real tracking call and he could see it from an EMTs point of view. He didn't feel the urgency I did, but he couldn't read it in the tracks like I could. Sand was scattered in the pilot's haste to make it to the road but he was weakening. He needed help. He was scrambling, now, using his hands to help support himself. In a spot where he rested, briefly on hands and knees blood dripped freely. I pictured him kneeling there, counting the drops, counting his breaths until they calmed enough to continue on.

When we found him he was laying on his back gasping for breath. Landon and Thez rushed in, as did Zeb. At first I backed off. I couldn't take the tension of the moment. But I saw that the guys needed Zeb out of the way. He was interfering.

"Come on man. Don't die on us now. Give me a number!" Zeb said urgently.

I took off my pack and walked over. I tapped Zeb on the shoulder. He looked behind him and went back to his job, to get any information he could out of the guy.

"Zeb. Back off. Let these guys work."

Zeb stood, furious. He got in my face.

The pilot didn't know who was who.

Landon was talking to him like a patient. What's your name? Lloyd. Okay Lloyd what do you do for a living? Farmer. What happened to the plane? Don't know. Engine blew. Something… Where does it hurt?

Then Zeb asking for a phone number.

"Call my wife. Number…" Lloyd didn't know what he was doing.

With Zeb standing before me I warned him, "You get in the way and you'll be arrested. Now let these guys work!"

"I'll take my chances," he said.

Things were getting tense, for me, for the guys, for Lloyd. Zeb pushed me aside and closed in again. When Landon was pushing Zeb out of the way to work I knew I had to do something. I wasn't willing to draw a gun on the group so I walked up to Zeb, grabbed him by the back of his shirt and hauled like hell. My object was to get him away from the group, so I could draw my weapon in a safer place. Zeb tipped over backwards, caught himself with his hands and rushed me, but I was faster than him.

"You better watch yourself, little girl," he spat at me.

I drew my weapon. I wasn't taking any chances. I couldn't take this guy on physically. Maybe, if I could find that cop mode I learned how to fake so long ago, I could accomplish something.

"Zeb, put your hands over your head."

He gave me an *oh come on* look and took a step toward me.

"Put your hands over your head!" I said louder. He did it, but he was smiling. This was not a good sign. "Now, lay down, face first, with your hands over your head."

Thez stood up.

"Frisk him first," he said. "As he's going down is the perfect time to draw on you." Thez frisked Zeb, pulled his pistol out of his pocket, then he took away a hunting knife he had strapped to his leg. "Okay, now… listen to the lady," he told Zeb.

He laid down face first and I cuffed him.

"You can sit up now, but don't move from that spot," I said.

He glared at me and I held him at gunpoint trying not to hear the sounds behind me. Lloyd's breathing was coming in raged gasps now. When he tried to talk he gurgled. Landon was working like crazy, trying to stabilize Lloyd. Lloyd was conscious, but scared. I had to look away from the panic in his eyes. The radio transmissions were a staccato drumming in the background. Codes flew by and I stood, gun pointing at Zeb.

The ambulance closed in and the radio transmissions intensified. The helicopter landed a short distance away and two men jumped out. A quick assessment of Lloyd's condition and he was whisked away to the open doors of the helicopter. I didn't know what I was supposed to do. I could let Zeb go and join Landon. I could haul Zeb in and let Strict deal with him. When I looked to the helicopter awaiting orders I could see the EMTs using the paddles on Lloyd and my morale sunk lower. They looked at the readings. A guy performed CPR. I couldn't hear anything over the clatter of the helicopter. I didn't hear the code for ten forty-five D go by. But I knew. If I'd been alone I would have sat on the ground and wept, but I was not alone. I was still holding Zeb at gunpoint. I still had a job to do.

It felt like I stood there for eons but finally Thez jogged over. Technically he was the senior officer, even if I was the instructor.

"I'll turn his weapons in at the station. If he owns them legally he can claim them. If he doesn't, well, that's his tough luck, he probably won't claim them."

"What do I do with him?"

"Jayce Thompson is on his way. He'll haul him in for you."

"I don't need Jayce to bring him back."

"I don't want you alone with this guy. He's trouble. Wait for Thompson."

Everything went smoothly, with Thompson there. He signaled the helicopter that they could leave as he jogged up, then he hauled Zeb to his feet and pointed him back the way he had come.

"You're going to be sorry!" Zeb yelled. "That could have kept me going for a month. That guy was loaded!"

"What's he yelling about?" Jayce asked.

"He thinks people will reward him for finding them. He was hoping to get there first so he could collect a reward."

"Did you read him his rights?"

"He isn't under arrest."

"He should still know what he says could incriminate him."

"He knows now, if he's smart. Zeb, what brought you to southern California, of all places? I would think the tracking would be better in Wyoming."

"Money. People in small town Wyoming don't have much of it. Just looking at the houses here. You can tell there's money to be had."

"So far it hasn't worked for me."

"That's because you're too nice. People don't want a nice, cute, little tracker. They want someone who can get the job done. Has anybody called you to find somebody, besides your commander?"

"Yes, they have. I found a little dog and a truckload of trouble once. The lady paid me two hundred bucks. I gave it to the search and rescue organization."

"There, you see? You're too nice. Bet she didn't believe you were a tracker when you showed up."

"Results speak louder than words. If Sherry Champlain ever wants a bodyguard you're welcome to take that job. Other than that I've seen very little profit from my tracking except the reward I get knowing somebody's life is back on track."

He stopped and turned around.

"Sissy stuff. You're just following tracks, finding lost people. Sissy stuff. You've never…"

"You have no idea what you are talking about," I told him. "What have I never?"

Jayce steered him toward base camp. Zeb turned back.

"This guy," Zeb said, indicating Jayce, "is here because *you won't shoot*. They know, when it comes right down to it, you're chicken."

I couldn't admit he was right. I didn't want him to know how right he was.

"It's not chicken to hate death. If you ever force me to shoot, you'll be dead as dead can be, just like the rattlesnake. It just might be Thompson came up here to protect you from me."

"Ha! That's a good one. We'll see about that. We're going to be butting heads for a while. We'll see who comes out on top."

"Especially if you keep interfering in police business."

Jayce packed Zeb up into a squad car and we drove off. He dropped me off at base camp. Guess I couldn't complain. Zeb was out of my hair. But I knew Zeb was not going to appreciate being alienated. To him the police were getting in his way, not the other way around.

Strict walked up and put his hands on my shoulders. He knew how hard that D hit me. Ten forty-five D. Patient deceased. Dead. One life, one light, went out in the world. Some farmer named Lloyd. But a new one was growing.

"You okay?" Strict asked.

"Yeah, I'll be fine." It would take a while, but I'd be fine.

I jumped awake and Rusty bolted upright beside me.

"What's wrong?" he asked.

I was still figuring that out. It was a split second dream.

"Nothing. It was nothing. Just a defibrillator."

"Just a defibrillator. Babe, you still haven't told me what happened."

"That's because I'd rather not talk about it. The tracking was… easy, sort of. The tracks were easy to follow. Tough to read. The finding was worse. The finding was horrible. The defibrillator didn't work. Just let me forget it. I don't want to remember that. Hold me. It'll go away if you just hold me."

"If I could, I'd just reach in there and take away all the bad memories."

"It's okay. It'll fade."

In the morning Rusty dropped a key into my hand.

"What's this?"

"You needed a mom mobile. You like my old Explorer. You need wheels that will take you anywhere. Go look."

In the garage was a new Explorer. Four wheel drive.

"Rusty! I wanted *you* to get you a new car."

"I've got the car I want."

"But the insurance money won't cover this."

"It covers enough. Now you have wheels again."

Later in the morning I got a call from Schroeder. He wanted to talk to Thez and I. I was a little nervous about taking the new Explorer. They needed to make prestained mom mobiles. I just knew Katie was going to dump out a bottle on it.

Schroeder didn't beat around the bush, he jumped right into the task at hand.

"You couldn't mistake the trail," Thez told him. "There was more secondary sign than there were tracks. Sometimes I couldn't see the tracks for the blood."

"We didn't take a lot of time for instruction. It was a race. We just got there as soon as we could," I said.

Thez nodded, "It was grim work. The guy didn't have a chance."

"And this guy, Zeb, turned up again," Schroeder pointed out.

"What are we going to do about him?" I asked.

"Well, for now we're going to let him stew."

"You can't keep him if he's not charged with anything," I pointed out needlessly.

"We can always come up with something. Obstruction of justice? Carrying concealed."

"It'll only make him madder and he isn't going to get mad at you. He's going to get mad at me. I was the one who decided he needed to be taken out of the picture."

"No you weren't," Thez told me. "You were the only one capable of it. It had to be done."

"He's got to be sent packing," Schroeder said.

"Dropping him off on the edge of town and telling him to get lost is not going to work. He'll be back. Keeping him in jail is just letting him build up more animosity."

"Then, what do you suggest?"

"You couldn't possibly lose the key?"

"Not possible."

"Have the judge sentence him to six months of police academy?"

"Still not possible."

"I know. I assume, since you've got him in custody, you know who he is now."

"We do. His name is Zebediah Thatcher."

"Is he really from Wyoming?"

"Sometimes."

"Does he have a record?"

"Same record any bar hopping, gun toting, red necked, troublemaker would have, which is to say frequent and minor."

"Well, that's good news in my book," I said and both men looked at me like I was crazy. But it *was* good news. I was used to psychotic murderers. Some bar hoping, good old boy was nothing compared to what I'd seen in the past.

"Thez, you can go now," Schroeder said.

When Thez was gone Schroeder looked to me.

"Do not make light of this," he told me. "Tell me how serious this is."

"So far the guy is just trying to set up shop. He wants to be a private eye, tracker for hire. I have no problem with that except that he can't afford to set up an office and hang out a sign, so he's finding business the same way an ambulance chasing attorney does. We can't have that."

"What do you want to do about it?"

"I need a level one officer. That should be no problem. Jacobsen, Reilly and Thez are all level ones. They all need tracking practice. So, send one of them, just like we planned."

"What about off the trail?"

"Off trail he just seems to be watching for a job."

"Does Rusty know about this?"

"He knows Zeb is around more often than we'd like. He doesn't know he follows me around. He doesn't know he showed up on the search."

"Rusty's going to be more cautious than ever, you know that, don't you?"

"He's always more cautious than ever. I think Zeb will get bored and move on. He just needs to see this isn't a tracker's gold mine. I think he has enough back country boy in him to make him uncomfortable in southern California."

Schroeder wasn't convinced but he agreed to stick with the plan and he was glad to have an excuse to send a level one officer along with me. So… things were back on track.

Chapter 21

I didn't hear from Zeb for a few weeks and then I didn't exactly hear from him. I could just tell he was around in the form of tracks in my backyard. I'd see the cut up pickup truck around.

Katie turned two. She got a backyard playground and a big girl's bed for her birthday. Since she climbed out of the crib there was no use keeping her in it. It was time to make the nursery ready for the new baby. Sometimes Katie climbed into her old crib. I don't think she was quite ready to be a big girl and I was kind of glad. I just had to make sure she didn't climb into it when it was occupied.

She loved the playground, especially the monkey bars. The bars were spaced a little too far apart for her but she still swung on them like a little monkey. I had to watch her on the slide. She was just as likely to try jumping off the top of it as she was to sit down and slide.

Morning sickness came right on schedule but this time I wasn't on a search when it happened. Katie thought it was fun to eat potato chips for breakfast. She didn't seem to know she was eating a real breakfast if she dipped the potato chips into something healthy. She liked to dip them in yogurt. I thought it looked awful. Potato chips and yogurt? She also liked me to make banana boats. The banana slice was the hull and chips were the sails.

Rusty shifted his schedule an hour. That way the worst of the morning sickness was over and Katie was fed before he left for the rest of the day. He had promised me that parenthood and cophood could really work together. He kept his word and I loved him all the more for it.

Early one morning Strict called.

"Cassidy? How are you feeling?"

"Right at the moment? Or in general?"

"Both."

"I feel lousy, but I'll be fine by noon. Why?"

"Morning sickness?"

"Yeah. I can't even sit up in bed for an hour or so."

"I've got a search for you. It's important to get right on it."

"Lou, I can't do anything until this clears. I can't make it go away."

"I know. Who do you want Schroeder to send?"

"Can Jacobsen hit the trail? I can catch up as soon as this clears."

"Right."

"It'll be good for him to go it alone at first. He may not get far but he'll get farther than I will waiting for this to pass. Get him started and I'll be there as soon as I possibly can. Where's base camp?"

"Diamond Springs."

"That's the wrong side of the mountain."

The Joshua Hills team covered the east side of the mountain range and the Glendale/Pasadena team covered the west side. We called them the Glendale/Pasadena team but really it was volunteers from all over the LA area.

"You may run into some of Merrill's men."

"What's the hurry?"

"High profile case."

"Oh no."

"I know you hate the press, but we can't avoid it."

"Don't let this hit the radios!"

"What? Why?"

"It's just the case Zeb has been waiting for. Oh hell. Why didn't I hogtie him and leave him in the desert while I had the chance? He can track, but he's a pest! Arg!" I sat up in my frustration and that sent me over the edge. "Oh shit, hang on!" I said as I rushed off to the bathroom. Rusty picked up the phone and started talking to Strict. Morning sickness was getting to be old hat for both of us.

When I came back to the bedroom, looking a little whiter than I had before, Rusty handed me the phone.

"Keep as much information as you can off the radio," I told Strict. "Make sure all the men are armed and have handcuffs."

"Cassidy, you act like I've never had people intrude on a search before."

"Sorry, I guess it's just new to me."

"Just catch up as soon as you can. I've got to go. After I get ahold of the others I'll call back with details."

"Okay."

Damn. What a time! I was going to be the same tomorrow morning on the trail. And the next day, and the next. As long as the guys knew what to expect and what they were supposed to do I didn't mind being a typical pregnant woman in front of them. But this sure was inconvenient. High profile case. Zeb racing for the recognition at the end of the trail. Me laid up most of the morning. I didn't care about the recognition. Zeb could have that. But what if he got to the end of the trail and his missing person was… like Lloyd? What would he do? I didn't want to think about how this could turn out if Zeb got there first.

"I'll go to town and pick up Bertie," Rusty offered.

"Thanks, she sure likes getting picked up by you. She says she feels like a real classy lady when you pick her up."

"Where is she this early in the morning?"

"The newspaper corner of the library," I answered and then had to rush to the bathroom again. Getting keyed up about things didn't help, either.

"I'm taking Katie," Rusty said, knowing I'd end up on my feet if he left her.

Every time my stomach settled down I'd try to get up and then have to make a run for the bathroom. I felt antsy. I didn't have time to lie around and be sick. I had work to do. I had people counting on me. I wondered if I should call Chase. No, that wouldn't work. We had to get this going as soon as possible. Even sending Jacobsen out was better than calling Chase in and waiting most of a day for him to arrive. I didn't even know if he'd come. It took a special case to get him up to the high desert. Besides, if Strict thought this was a case for Chase he would have called him.

I went to the garage and brought in my backpack. I ran to the bathroom. I did a quick check of my gear. I ran to the bathroom. Arg, this was awful. There wasn't even anything to come up. My stomach was roiling and ugh, it was just awful. I should have just lain back down and waited but I felt the tug of the trail. I added water to the pack. I ran to the bathroom. I put on my uniform. I ran to the bathroom. If this was a high profile search I might need the uniform. I needed to wear it just to make a point to Zeb. I added a can of Pringles to my pack hoping I'd be able to eat them in the morning. Hmm, I took out the oatmeal and hot chocolate. No point in packing that. I ran to the bathroom. This sure was getting old. I halfway made the bed and lay down to wait out the morning sickness.

Strict called back.

"Who are we looking for?" I asked.

"Arthur Chadwick."

"Ummm, high profile case?"

"Yeah."

"Who is Arthur Chadwick?"

"Senator Chadwick."

"Oh. What happened?"

"Same old story, went out hiking, separated from the group and didn't show back at camp."

"Experienced outdoors?"

"He was back in his service years."

"How old is he?"

"Sixty-four."

"He should have known better. And he should know the area well enough to not get lost. He knows LA is west and Joshua Hills is east. How can you get lost with that little bit of information?"

"You know it isn't too tough, or you wouldn't have a job."

"Jacobsen knows he's on his own for a little while?"

"It took him an hour to get on the trail. He couldn't separate out the Senator's tracks from all the others."

"Does he know he's on the right trail?"

"Yeah."

"How does a senator go missing anyway? Don't they have people around watching out for them all the time?"

"That varies widely. Senator Chadwick likes to appear self-sufficient."

"So he goes on a hike and goes missing."

"When you catch up to him try to preserve his dignity."

"Okay."

"Keep your cell phone handy. If Jacobsen gets stuck we might be calling. I'll have to patch you through but we'll figure it out."

"I'll be there as soon as I can. Once I can move about without getting sick I feel fine. I have lots of energy. I can eat anything that doesn't smell weird. It's just the first three or four hours of the day. Maybe if I get up at three AM it'll settle down by seven."

"Don't push it. I'll see you soon."

"Okay. Diamond Springs."

"Right."

I wasn't too happy with the choice of Diamond Springs, either. It would take me forty-five minutes just to drive there. It was a rough, rugged and rock prone part of the mountains. I'd never tracked there before. I was looking forward to it, thinking I should have hiked the area earlier, gotten to know the land and the conditions, but it was Merrill's territory. I never expected to get a call there.

Merrill had a good team. The LA area had more volunteers than the Joshua Hills district. We were kind of the country cousins to the LA rescue teams. While we struggled to get updated equipment they rode around in Hummers that looked like small army tanks.

When Rusty and Bertie arrived I was almost ready to go. It was hard to tell sometimes when the morning sickness had passed. It was kind of like having a temporary flu. First I had to stay flat to prevent the nausea from taking over. Then I could stir around a little. Eventually I could walk around but overdoing it would send me running. I thought maybe driving was safe and once I got to Diamond Springs the morning sickness should be over for the day.

Katie led Bertie into the kitchen and pulled out the drawer where I kept the cookie sheets. That reminded me to take along cookies for the guys. The last search we didn't have much time for cookies but this one might be more than one day and they would have time in the morning to remind me about things like cookies, so I better have some. They'd be welcome to them at that point.

Katie and Bertie loved to make cookies. Bertie liked them warm out of the oven. I don't know how she kept Katie from making a mess of things in the kitchen. I figured that was her problem. She was the one who chose to make cookies with a two year old. I was in favor of Bertie doing anything that would improve her life on the streets. If she craved cookies it was worth all the cookie ingredients in the house to have a ready babysitter.

"This one could be quick but I expect it to take a couple of days," I told Bertie. "This guy has experience outdoors so he might have hiked quite a ways off the known trail."

"How are you going to track in your condition?" Bertie asked.

"Being pregnant doesn't slow me down. It's the morning sickness that does. I'll just send half the guys ahead with my tracker in training and catch up when I can. That's what we're doing right now. I've been on the trail with morning sickness before. I'm just glad my uniform still fits."

Before he left for work Rusty gave me the usual take-care-of-my-girl-out-there lecture and I assured him I'd find my man and be back as soon as I could.

"Katie, be good for Bertie. Mommy will be back soon."

"Bertie make cooky!" she said.

"What kind of cookies should we make?" Bertie asked.

"Chocachip!" Katie said.

"It's always chocolate chip," Bertie said. "But she doesn't seem to notice if I make whatever I want."

"Then make what you want," I told her.

"I need to do laundry, too. I got some new clothes. Winter was hard on these duds. Every Tuesday afternoon they have fifty percent off at the thrift store. I can get twice as much bang for my buck."

"I think I'm ready to go give it a try. I'll see you in a day or two. Or three. I hope not three. Katie, give Mommy a hug!"

I was supposed to go get a search and rescue vehicle from the compound but that would require a trip into town and then back out again. I decided to just park my new Explorer at base camp. All the guys knew me. They would let me in without an official car. I hoped.

The guys stared at the SUV trying to decide who was driving into their base camp. When I hopped out they gathered around.

"Hey Cassidy, what happened to your Jeep?" one asked.

"It burned up in the Elk Meadows fire."

"What happened, though? We could have sworn you'd die a Jeep girl."

"It was time for a change. Two adults and two kids in a rag top Jeep…it was just time for a change and, since I liked Rusty's Explorer and he wasn't ready to give it up, he came home with this."

"Cool!"

I followed the commotion to the main part of base camp. They were making a big deal out of this search. I was wondering how they managed to pull this off without the press breathing down their necks. The map spread out made it look like an army invasion was going on. It looked like they had men out beating the bushes as well as Jacobsen out tracking.

"There's my little tracker," Strict said as he gave me a quick shoulder hug.

"Show me what I'm up against," I asked him.

He pointed to a spot on the map. "This point is that butte over there. Two miles south of that is a small valley. That's the place Arthur Chadwick was last seen. I've got you a lift."

"Nope. The helicopter will wipe out sign."

"It'll save you a lot of time."

"I need that sign. You better have a very long cable if you're going to drop me off up there without messing up the tracks."

"How long will it take you to hike it?"

Sigh, "an hour, maybe two."

"Let them drop you off up there."

It told me a little about the urgency of the search that they would call out a helicopter just to take me to the trail. I felt a little bit like a special delivery package as they whisked me up the mountain. We located Kent Jacobsen and Landon Wilson making their way slowly over the Senator's trail.

"Drop me off down trail, not up trail from them!" I called over the noise of the blades. If we wiped out part of the trail I wanted it to be trail they already covered. "Thanks for the ride!" I told the guys as I clipped onto the cable that would lower me to the ground below. As I dangled there a hundred feet over the forest I felt a little fragile, not really for me. I loved riding the cable. I liked the tension of the mission at hand. I liked the sweeping view and the slight risk. I felt a little spark of fragility inside me. This tiny life I was in charge of. I might enjoy a little risk but I didn't like the thought of any risk coming to my baby. It was times like this that I could understand Rusty's protective nature.

"Boy are you a sight for sore eyes," said Jacobsen. "I sure hope you're ready to take over. In class I could see things easier. Come to find out it was because you were pointing things out to me. Without you here it's all invisible again."

"It's not all invisible or you wouldn't be this far."

"Your friend is back," Jacobsen said.

"Aw shit. Where?"

"I don't know," answered Landon. "I think he's ahead of us. I think he's letting us do the tracking. He's keeping an eye on us but he's ahead of us hoping to find the guy before we get there."

"Great. Just what we need. Zeb is only after the money. I don't know what he hopes to accomplish on his own," I said.

"What money. There is no money," said Jacobsen.

"Tell him that. He won't believe me. Fill me in on the trail. What's it been like?"

"Besides impossible?"

"Tell me what you learned."

"I've learned more from the newspapers and TV than I have from the trail. Chadwick is tall, imposing. He likes to put forth a professional image. On TV he's always in suit and tie. Even if he's touring a disaster area, he's wearing a suit and tie. I hope he isn't wearing one camping. That would be a bit much. I think that would be the point where he'd lose my vote. I think he's dressed a little more practically than that. At least his tracks don't look like dress shoes. They are hiking boots."

"Okay, now we're getting somewhere. What frame of mind is he in?"

"I don't think he knows he's lost yet. He seems pretty calm. Course he might when he knows he's lost, too. He's been in fixes before. He's pretty level headed. He doesn't seem to be doing anything to orient himself."

"Good. I mean it's good for you to think to note that. What was the group like that he started out with? Men? Women? Kids? How many of them were there?"

"It was a large group. That's one thing that gave me so much trouble. There were probably three men about the same size as him. There were a couple of women and a couple of older kids."

"And you're sure you're on Chadwick's trail."

"Yeah."

"Good. Let's go. Track behind me. If you have questions stop me," I told Jacobsen.

The ever watchful Landon asked, "Are you sure you're up to this?"

"We need to take advantage of what time we have. Come morning I'm going to be useless. Right now I'm fine. I could track until dark. Are you prepared to eat lunch on the trail? I'd like to keep going if we can."

"Sounds like we are back on a typical Cassidy search. Did you bring cookies? I might be persuaded to eat those on the trail."

"Cookies are in the pocket on the back. Help yourself."

I turned around so Landon could get the cookies but as soon as he had them I picked up Chadwick's tracks and headed out.

At first, I think Jacobsen rested his eyes. I had noticed in class the constant concentration to detail bothered the guys. It was like looking at an optical illusion for hours on end. After a while I noticed he was trying to read the ground as he walked slowly behind me. When I came to something Jacobsen should be able to read and gain information from I stopped him.

"Take a few minutes to get all the information you can from this spot. Then tell me what you think," I said pointing out a six foot square area where Chadwick had stopped and looked around behind him.

I went ahead knowing I'd be easy to catch up with. Landon and Jacobsen put their heads together over the trail. They talked and pointed and I turned my attention to the tracks before me.

When they caught up again I got a report, or rather, I got their opinion, which turned out to be questions. At least the questions told me they were on the right track.

"You think he was questioning his route?" Jacobsen asked.

"Could be," I answered.

"He sure spent enough time doing it. Why'd he keep going if he was wondering?"

"Apparently he liked this direction better."

"Why'd you have me stop there?"

"The stops can tell you just as much as the walking tracks. The walking tracks show you what condition they are in. The stops tell you what's on their mind. Sometimes the trail does both but you need to really read the places people stop. It could be they just need to rest. It always reflects a decision of some kind, so it's important even if it doesn't appear that way at first."

Another time I stopped Jacobsen, "Tell me what's different about this track."

He studied the track for a long time before catching up.

"Well?" I asked.

"He stopped there again," he said.

"And? What did he do there?"

"Pressure was on the outside of his right foot. I didn't see a left track there. Why?"

"That track verified he was wearing hiking boots. And it told something of how he was feeling. He's not as fresh as when this search started."

"What makes you say that?"

"Took him a long time to decide to tie his shoe. The reason you didn't see the left track was because his knee was down. His right foot pushed outward because he was tying his shoe."

The trail was like this all afternoon; me tracking, Jacobsen piecing together little puzzles that I assigned to him, him reporting back to me as I tracked. We made pretty good progress and he learned as he went. At this point I was more concerned with tracking the Senator than I was with Zeb. It seemed to be an unspoken rule that we not use the senator's title. Perhaps Strict had told the guys to keep quiet. I just didn't want Zeb to overhear anything he might put to good use. I hadn't caught the radio broadcasts so I didn't know what Zeb might have picked up from the police scanner. It wasn't too bad a plan that he had, though, shake the bushes ahead of the people who knew they were on the right track. He just might find the senator before us. But then what would he do?

"If Zeb is a tracker and he's ahead of us, why isn't he tracking?" I asked.

"He's lazy," Landon said. "Or maybe he started out tracking and he didn't want us catching up to him."

"Would you have caught up to him?" I asked.

"We wouldn't have caught up to a snail," Jacobsen said.

"That's not true," Landon said. "We did see a snail."

"That's because it was crossing our path. We didn't catch up to it."

"At least you were studying the ground hard enough to spot him," I observed.

"Well, I'm glad you're on board. I didn't have much hope of catching up to him on my own."

"Practice," I told him as I kept tracking.

Chadwick was definitely tiring. I found a spot where he had stopped to rest. I made Jacobsen read the spot because it held a host of information. He did recognize it as a resting spot but he missed the fact that Chadwick had a bottle of water and that it was still very full.

"How in the world can you know how full the water bottle was?" he asked.

"I don't know for sure. But I can take a guess. Look at the setting. If the bottle was nearly empty and it was knocked over it would tumble down the hill. As it was he knocked it over and it just fell over and stopped. The water sloshed around and slowed its forward motion. So there must have been enough water in the bottle to make it somewhat stable. We can also tell that he has a jacket on. That's good news, too. Let's hope he hangs onto it. It's going to get cold tonight."

"How do you see all these things in one sitting spot?"

"I wonder how people miss it."

Even though the pace picked up we didn't track Chadwick's first day. We just couldn't track as fast as a man can hike. We called a halt at dusk and set up camp slightly discouraged.

"In the morning I'm going to be useless for several hours," I warned the guys. "Landon, remember the first time I had morning sickness? It's basically been like that every morning for the past two weeks. If you guys want to get up and track while it's light, I can catch up to you as soon as I can travel. There's no use trying to track when I have to run to the bushes. I can't even get up for the first hour or two. Doing anything in an upright position brings it on."

The guys nodded grimly. It wasn't the best conditions for tracking but there wasn't much we could do about it.

The next morning went just as expected. Landon unzipped my tent flap so I could get out easily if I needed to. Landon and Jacobsen were slow getting going, reluctant to leave me and reluctant to take on the tracking.

"Go!" I said. "There's nothing wrong with me. I'll catch up. If it would do any good to track like this I'd do it but I'd get nowhere."

It was particularly hard on Landon. Landon had been on a search with me when I had a miscarriage. He'd watched helplessly as I nearly bled to death. A part of him didn't trust trouble to stay away if he left.

"Keep a radio," he said. "It'll help you find us quicker. I know you can track us but it'll be faster if you can just hike there."

He didn't want me to keep the radio so I could use it. He wanted to be able to check on me. In the couple of hours it took for the morning sickness to pass, he checked in twice.

When I caught up with the guys there was a noticeable relaxing on Landon's part. Jacobsen was relieved that he could back off and be the student again.

Midmorning we found the place Chadwick had spent the first night. The trail leading up to it led us to believe he was growing concerned about his situation. He began looking for ways to find his camp. He spent long moments looking at the lay of the land and his back trail. When he spent the night out in the open I thought he would decide to stay put and wait for help, but the next morning he set off again. The tracking was a mixture of the good, the bad, and the ugly. At one point Chadwick climbed a rocky ledge to try and get a better view of his surroundings. It took us hours to find the way he'd gone up, or rather his tracks up top. The guys insisted on using ropes and so Jacobsen climbed up first and set up a belay. They weren't taking any chances. When we reached the top all we saw was more mountains, no hint of a campground, not even a hazy smudge of campfire smoke lying in a valley. Nothing, just like Chadwick had seen.

He had found an open area and spelled SOS with rocks and sat there for a long time. It took me a while to find where he left the area because he had to walk all over the area to find enough rocks to spell SOS big enough to be visible from the air. I was glad to see him stay in one spot for a while. It gave us more time to catch up. When I found his trail leaving the area I was confused. Why go to all that bother and then just ditch it? Something happened that caused him to move on. What was it?

"Hold it guys. We need to do some investigating. Take off your packs and relax a bit. I'll be back."

I left my pack to mark the last known track and I circled the area. I began seeing tracks, or not so much tracks as sign. Sign of another person's passing and when I did follow the sign to a track it spoke volumes. Zeb. Zeb was looking for the senator and Chadwick…Chadwick was trying to get away. Chadwick did not trust Zeb. I followed an odd dance through the woods where Zeb would follow and the senator would back off. It was odd. Very odd. I thought the senator would be glad to be found. I decided I needed Jacobsen's cop sense so I called the guys together. We sat in a circle. The guys munched on trail mix, jerky and chocolate chip cookies. I nibbled potato chips, carefully.

"This is weird," I said. "What it looks like to me is that Zeb found Senator Chadwick, but the senator is evading Zeb like crazy. I'm convinced, by his trail, that if Zeb confronts Chadwick, he'll have a fight on his hands. Chadwick doesn't trust Zeb at all. Why would the senator refuse Zeb's help?"

Jacobsen scratched his head. It didn't make sense to him either.

"Maybe he trusts Zeb about as much as you do," Landon said.

"When you've seen Chadwick on TV is he fit?" I asked. "Could he take on Zeb if he felt the need to?"

"Tough to say. He is able bodied. He's very fit for his age. Whether or not he'd take on Zeb would depend on how threatened he felt. How old is Zeb?"

"He hasn't said," I told them. "I think of him like Chase's little rebellious brother, which I guess would put him in his late fifties. His hair is gray."

"Doesn't mean a thing. I've met thirty year old guys who were gray," Jacobsen said.

"Well, I guess we have no choice but to stay on Chadwick's trail and keep the situation in mind," I said.

"What measures will Zeb resort to, to bring Chadwick in?" Landon asked.

"If he wants any sort of reward he'd have to bring him in peacefully," I pointed out.

"What if that wasn't possible?" said Landon.

"I don't know. I assume Zeb would try and reason with him."

"Well, this is getting us nowhere fast," Jacobsen said. "I say we stay on

Chadwick's trail."

"I don't trust Zeb," I said.

"Good, maybe you'll stay away from him then," Jacobsen said.

We hit the trail but my trouble radar kept giving me false signals. I tried to ignore it, telling myself that Zeb might be a pest but he wasn't dangerous. Jacobsen tracked behind me, and Landon was behind him. As long as the tracking was slow Landon did his best to read sign, too. He never knew when it might come in handy.

When it became obvious we were tracking the same basic area the guys branched out to beat the bushes, while I kept to the tracks.

I thought about the man I was tracking, tall, powerful, on top of his situation. In the service, smart enough to make it up the ranks and afterwards to work the laws and the people of this land until he ran a section of the country.

Suddenly something slammed into me from the side. I'd been focused on the ground, and let my peripheral vision become narrowed. It took me a moment to realize it was a man. We were a tangle of pack and arms and limbs. I reached for my pistol and when he straddled me, pinning me to the ground, he found a gun barrel pointed at his face. It wasn't Zeb. First he saw the gun barrel, then he looked beyond it to the little blond woman he had tackled.

"Senator Chadwick?" I asked.

He scrambled to his feet.

"I…I'm sorry. I thought you were someone else," he said. He offered me a hand up. I got up, thankful I didn't look as pregnant as I felt.

"Cassidy Michaels, Reserve Deputy, Joshua Hills District Search and Rescue," I said extending my hand for a handshake. "Jacobsen! Landon! Ten sixty-five found," I called out to the guys.

They appeared from the trees and the senator pulled back again. He relaxed when he saw the uniforms and I was glad I had chosen to wear mine.

"If you don't mind, sir, we'd like to check you out. Then we'd prefer to take the easy way out. If you'll have a seat, sir," said Landon.

While Landon examined the senator to determine his physical condition I took off my pack and walked around. I had never been on this side of the mountains and I was surprised to find it much drier. From Joshua Hills we often saw billowing clouds, stopped by the mountains, so I expected it to be greener. I watched for deer tracks but didn't find any. When I heard the radio chatter mention a helicopter I began looking around for likely landing spots. My search led me to more open ground. Suddenly there was the sound of a shot and a bullet whisked by my head. I hit the ground.Zeb ran out of the trees. As he drew close he realized there was a gun on him, too.

"If I were you," I said. "I'd freeze and drop the gun. There's two armed officers out there who think you've shot me. You're taking an awful chance."

His eyes narrowed.

"If they think you're a danger to me," I added, "they will shoot first and ask questions later. Standing there, gun in hand over me like that, it would be an easy assumption for them to make."

"You're all just against me. You're just trying to put me away, aren't you?"

"If I was doing that I wouldn't be talking to you. You'd be shot, or at least cuffed and on the ground. No, I keep hoping you'll decide to work with us through the proper channels. Usually I hope longer than I should. Now," I said as I got up, "It's your turn. Hand over your weapon. How many of these have you got? Did you get the knife back, too?"

I wondered if it was a tracker thing to always have a sharp hunting knife on your person. I wondered if his was like mine, if it had been carried since he was twelve years old, if it had saved his life a time or two, if he'd had to scrub the blood stains off and never really could. I wondered if he was linked to it in some way, the way I felt linked to mine. They could take away my gun. I had a harder time giving up the knife. The police took it away a couple of times but I'd gotten it back. Other people had tried to take it away and failed. I wore it under my pants leg next to my calf and it got overlooked a lot. I frisked him and took the knife away feeling a little guilty about it.

"Do I really have to make you lie down to cuff you? Just put your hands behind your back."

"You can't prove anything," he said. "I'll be back. And you should be more careful. This was my big chance. I could have made a name for myself with this case."

"You almost did. You almost made a name for yourself as a murderer who guns down women. I don't think they treat guys like that kindly in prison."

"This was a big case. If you'd just back off and let the reward increase."

"I'm not going to back off. People tend to die when they are lost in the mountains here. Just in case you didn't notice, there's no water and no rain. If people get lost here, you don't just sit around waiting for somebody to get scared and offer a reward. You go. You look. You try to find them before they roast or freeze or dehydrate. When the weather is wacky they can do all three in one day. It's just the way the desert is. Now walk."

"Which way?"

"West."

"Which way is west?"

"That way," I said pointing. "Another thing you need to learn out here is your directions. LA is south, Joshua Hills is north. They are on opposite sides of the mountain. That should give you enough to go on."

Jacobsen wasn't with Landon and the senator when we arrived. I radioed him and let him know he could come back.

"Be nice to these guys." I told Zeb. "Jacobsen? Do you have an evidence bag? I've got another pistol for you."

He produced a plastic bag and I dropped the gun and the knife into it.

"What do mean, another one?"

"Every time this guy messes with one of our searches we take another gun away. I don't know if it's the same one or if he has a stockpile in his truck."

When the helicopter flew over I waved to let them know where I was and I pointed in the direction the guys were. There was radio talk that said they understood. Then they found a landing spot.

After a while two men jogged over. They addressed the senator first.

"Where are we going?" the senator asked.

"That's your call, sir," the one named Mike said.

"Then take me to base camp. I want to meet the men behind this operation."

"Yes, sir."

They conferred with Landon who assured them the senator was physically fit. I noticed he carried a bottle of water and a couple of cookies.

I was glad we were going back to base camp. I expected to end up at the search and rescue compound, a fire station, or in LA somewhere. This was good news.

In the helicopter the senator carried on an animated conversation with Landon and Jacobsen about our search and rescue operations. Zeb was cuffed to a pole and sulked all the way.

At base camp the senator made his rounds of the camp, shaking hands, greeting and thanking each officer. I wondered if he was up for reelection or something.

Zeb was put into a squad car for transport back to the station. I wondered how many trips to the station it would take before they just kept him.

I got into the Explorer and started up the engine. Senator Chadwick jogged over. He signaled me to turn off the truck, so I did.

"Can I have a moment?" he asked.

I got out and nodded for him to proceed.

"I… I'd like to apologize again," he started out.

"There's no need. If you want to make it up to me you can tell me why you were willing to take on an armed man who was trying to help you."

"I didn't know he was armed. And he wasn't trying to help me. He was stalking me. I've had my share of threatening letters. If somebody doesn't like the way I do things, they think they can do better, they fire off a letter. After a while I started ignoring them. I pass them off to my aides and they file them away in some dark file somewhere. I knew people would be out looking for me. But I knew they wouldn't act like this guy did."

"Why, how did he act?"

"It reminded me of being hunted, except he didn't shoot. He didn't speak to me, like a rescue worker would and he kept out of sight. Shortly before you appeared I told myself I was going to get a good look at this guy. I was walking around trying to catch a glimpse of him and then suddenly you were there, and I just did the first thing that came to mind. I hope I didn't hurt you."

"You didn't."

"Your search commander told me it was you who found me."

"Yeah, with some help from Kent Jacobsen."

"You make a good team. I'm proud to have people like you working for the good of the people down here. Not every place is lucky enough to have on call trackers."

"Thanks."

"Well, I'll let you go. I'm sure you have more important things to do than stand around and talk to an old man."

"I've got a two year old and a husband waiting for me."

"And one on the way."

"Yeah."

"You didn't tell me about that."

"It wasn't something you needed to know. I'm fine. Don't worry about it."

"Amazing. If my wife tried to go out on some search and rescue mission while she was pregnant, I'd have locked her in the house."

"Yeah, well, my husband knows I can pick locks. And he knows I'll go. If someone needs me, I can't stay away. I go. But I always come back."

Well, most of the time. I guess I'd always come back from a search. I had gone missing a few times when trouble was being particularly tough on me. But that was trouble. Searches had mostly proven to be safer than everyday life.

I came home to a house in chaos. Well, sort of. My dad would have had a fit if my mom ever let the house get like this. My sister and I had to keep our toys confined to one room, our bedrooms. We were allowed to play in other parts of the house but when we were through everything was picked up and put in our rooms. That was no problem for me. To me play time meant time outdoors. My playtime was tracking, and riding horses.

Katie's playtime seemed to have taken over the house. She scooted around the living room couch on a little, plastic, wheeled horse plowing everything that stood in her way to the side. She plowed toys away in my direction and came to a screeching halt in front of me. She jumped off and ran down the hall.

"Daddy! Daddy, Mommy home!"

Rusty came out of his office.

"Cass, I'm sorry. We were going to straighten things up soon."

"It's okay."

"It is?"

"You think it doesn't get a little crazy around here while you're at work?"

He looked relieved.

"I like it like this," he said. "It tells me there's kids just being kids."

I'd have to keep that in mind. To me there was a balance. We were not adults living in a kid's world. Katie was a kid living in a world of adults. I did think she needed to play but I didn't think we should have to wade through the toys to get from room to room. Next time things were crazy and Rusty was due home, maybe I could relax my rules a little bit.

"Did you find your man?" he asked.

"Yup. He's safe and sound, probably back in his office again."

"Good job. Anything I should know about it before I get to work tomorrow?"

"If you hear there were shots fired, don't worry. Nobody was hit. Zeb's been hauled in again. I wonder how many times it will take to get him to move on. Of course, it's not common knowledge, and it should be kept quiet unless it hits the news, but the guy I tracked down this time was Senator Arthur Chadwick."

"Did Zeb take a shot at you?"

"It's hard to tell with Zeb. I think if he was trying to hit me he could have done it."

"I'm going to talk to him tomorrow. And I'm going to see that he stays put for a while."

Zeb did stay put for a while. I had two peaceful searches, quick one day affairs finding kids who got turned around on family outings. These were months apart one in late spring and one in the heat of summer.

Katie began noticing my big belly and so we started telling her that her baby was in there. She was really curious. She would pat my belly and put her ear up to it.

Once again Rusty wanted to feel every move the baby made. He was there for the ultrasound.

"This baby is going to be bigger than Katie was," Doctor Ron told me.

Maybe it would be a boy. I hoped so. I really wanted to give Rusty a son.

He needed a boy. But we never had enough trouble to merit further testing. Rusty and I wanted it to be a surprise.

One night on the big brown couch Rusty seemed particularly peaceful.

“Things must be going well at work. You seem calm,” I said.

“Things are never calm at work. Do you realize you’ve gone six months without a bout of trouble? I knew you could do it if you set your mind to it.”

“Maybe trouble got tired of chasing after a mom. Maybe he’s gone after some other poor, adventurous girl out there.”

“Just don’t get any ideas. I keep telling you, you’ll get into less trouble if you quit watching for it.”

“I know, keeping track of Katie kind of makes it harder to spot trouble.”

“Kid size trouble. Maybe we can keep it down to kid size trouble,” Rusty said. “Isn’t this about the time the Ben and Jerry’s binges started?”

“It was the whole last month,” I said.

“Month and a half, because it was a month and then Katie came early. So if she’d been full term it would have been a month and a half,” Rusty said.

“Then it’s getting close to time.”

“Why? Don’t tell me you want Ben and Jerry’s.”

“I always like it. But, no, we don’t need to make any midnight runs to town for ice cream. Have you been thinking of names?”

“Of course, but you said, when we were expecting Katie that you wanted to save Kit Carson for a boy. Are you still set on Carson for a boy’s name?”

“That would work. What about a girl’s name?”

“What about Danielle? If she wanted to be a tomboy she could shorten it to Dani.”

“I don’t know. I’ll think about it and see if it grows on me.” We had talked about naming a baby Daniel or Danielle after Daniel Boone. I wondered why we took my dad’s tradition seriously. He always used western names. So far Katie was the first kid to not have an old west name, but the idea was still out there.

As before, my mother called with updates to her shopping.

“I don’t care what you say. I’m hoping for another girl,” Mom said. “Katie can’t grow up with all these boys around her. If she does she’ll turn into a tomboy.”

“What’s wrong with that?” I asked.

“Nothing, dear.”

“She can be a girl and learn to do boy things, too. As many lost people as I’ve found, I’m going to teach her everything I know to prevent getting lost. And I’m going to teach her to stalk deer and be quiet and observant in the woods. No matter what she chooses I want her to be competent."

"That's nice dear. I'm still hoping for another girl."

"Well, I'm hoping for a boy. Rusty needs a boy."

"That's true."

At least she kept her spending in check because we already had most of the baby things we needed.

Wyatt was determined we were going to have a boy this time. He wanted a boy cousin to play trucks and cars with. I wondered about that because, by the time the baby was old enough to play trucks and cars, Wyatt would be beyond that stage.

"You will call me, when it's time," Mom asked.

"The first week in November," I assured her.

Chapter 22

In August academy started. I had to figure out how to teach tracking in a large group. Holding the tracking classes in October was calling it pretty close.

I drove to LA to look over the cadets. Chase met me there.

"You're not laying fifty trails like that," he told me. "You need help."

"I was wondering how I was going to do that. I don't mind the walking. It's laying a trail with the right variety for each person that takes time."

"I'll bring some guys with me. Do you have a set pattern you want them to do?"

"Yeah, I'll do it with them."

"Are you sure you're going to make it through these classes?"

"I'm not due until the first week in November."

"Tell the kid that. You didn't tell Katie. How early was she?"

"Three weeks."

"See?"

"Katie takes after me. I'm always anxious to be somewhere. I always get everywhere early. Maybe this kid will take after Rusty."

"Maybe. I'm not counting on it."

"So, are you prepared to take over if things go awry?"

"I am. But you better be here. I don't trust you. You look different somehow. Something has changed."

"I'll be here. Everything is going to go fine this time. You wait and see."

The cadets all looked so young, although I knew a few of them were older than I was. Many were in their twenties and I had a hard time believing they were ready for the job ahead of them. How could any twenty-five year old kid be ready to take on the job of a cop? And then I remembered that by the time I was twenty-five I had been through the Marines, been married, and widowed. Okay, if I could do that, then maybe they could do this.

I couldn't pick out any one of them that looked like they might be born tracker material. And, really, that's what I was looking for, someone who had to track because it was what they did. Maybe they didn't know it. Maybe they had grown up in the city and never seen a track. But I would know a born tracker if I saw one and, if I saw one; I knew they would take to it. I had very little hope of finding the person Chase wanted me to find. First of all they had to be willing to work in Joshua Hills District. I asked those willing to work in the high desert to step forward I only had fourteen cadets standing before me.

All the action was in LA. The prestigious positions were to be found in the big city. When I asked those fourteen to step forward if they had a particular interest in tracking four of the fourteen stepped forward. Four, who were interested. Not necessarily gifted in it, just interested.

I looked at the four men before me. No women had stepped forward.

"Have any of you had experience tracking?" I asked.

One raised a pinky finger.

"And what was that?" I asked.

"Me and my brothers used to track each other on camping trips," he said.

I glanced to Chase and he shrugged at me. It was better than nothing.

"How many of you are here for a level one?" I asked.

All four were. Okay, I had the information I needed. We were in business.

I learned that my four cadets were Joe Darby, Owen Osborne, Michael Colton and Tex Ward. Michael (Mick) Colton was the camper. I kept them in a separate group, and divided the class into groups of five. They all had to take the basic tracking class, but I wanted the trackers to feed off each other. Those uninterested would pull enough out of it to get through academy. They would learn the value of it, hoped they never needed it, and find they could have used it after they got on the job. It was the ones who wanted to learn that I was interested in.

We met in the classroom where I drew diagrams on the whiteboard. They were very simple drawings of a footprint and lines to indicate where they could expect sign for different movements. A turn to the left showed sign to the right. Each movement had a corresponding diagram. I knew it would still all be invisible once they got out to the vacant lot but at least they had a cheat sheet and they could refer to it. Then I gave them demonstrations on different ways to look at the ground and explained the benefits to each one. I told them to try different viewpoints, different techniques. I had to give them some tools while I had them all together because I didn't know how I'd get that across to them in the field. There were just too many of them. Chase thought it was all very odd. I don't think he had thought about the way he looked at tracks. I described the wide view that most of them had and explained that it needed to be narrowed to suit the occasion. They might have to scan a four foot square and they might need to be four inches away from the track, looking for a centimeter long scratch mark in the rock. They needed to be able to adjust their view for the tracks before them. They needed to see the track, and interpret the sign, which would point them to the next track. There was no point in getting into the reading and profiling of tracks. They would be out there for three hours tops. Reading could not be accomplished in three hours. If Mick, the camper dude, Colton showed any signs of reading I'd nab him for further training.

Chase, five officers and I had crossed and re-crossed a vacant lot following a pattern. I called out commands, “Run! Walk! Turn, turn, pause…” I wanted the tracks to match the cheat sheets so things would be recognizable in the field. I turned the class loose telling them to wave me down if they got stuck. There was a lot of hand waving at first. I moved from group to group. I felt like I wasn’t accomplishing much. How much could they learn from one vacant lot and twenty minutes of instruction?

It was odd how every group had a self-appointed leader. It was never decided that it should be that way, but one man always assumed the role with quiet grace. I took note of these men. These were the guys who would take on the job and become it. They’d wear their job like a comfortable pair of jeans. They’d be the Kent Jacobsen’s.

As I made my way from group to group helping them through the rough spots the other groups listened to my tips and tricks and used them, too. As they put these tools to work the hand waving grew less and I was able to relax a bit.

Mick and Tex seemed to both take to tracking. Mick was a kid again and Tex was his brother and they bent over the tracks talking about the sign. Joe and Owen, took it in but rarely added to the discussion.

“How’s it going?” Chase asked me as I was observing the class.

“Have Michael Ward and Tex Colton go talk to Schroeder after they graduate.”

“What if they don’t?”

“Then…don’t.”

“At least this is better than we hoped.”

“Yeah. I didn’t expect to find anybody.”

“But then you have a better eye for people than I do. That’s one reason I wanted you to teach the class. You see things I don’t.”

After class Chase drove me down to the place where we laid out the second trail. This trail led perhaps a half mile. The terrain was a little more varied than a vacant lot. Here we laid the trail of a fleeing suspect. It went across an expanse, through some brush and down to a creek. It followed the creek and came out the other side and continued on.

When my class had tracked this trail it was a group effort. I’d let the others read the trail and when they got stuck I had stepped in and read it for them. It was this class that Chase knew he had a tracker on his hands. So when I laid this trail I did it with Tex and Mick in mind. I wanted to see what they would catch and what they would miss. I must have been a sight dashing off across the lot, big belly bouncing. The bouncing started up the Braxton-

Hicks contractions that plague every woman in the last trimester, but I continued on. Chase laughed at me but when I was through he nodded his approval.

"I want to do another one," I told him.

"Why?"

"If Tex and Mick bail out the class I want them to try a challenging trail. Not a long one, but one that takes some skill to get through."

Then I laid a trail in another direction being careful to only leave partial tracks. I used objects in my path to hide my tracks. I took my time to create a trail that would really tell me something.

Chapter 23

The class had to be finished during daylight hours and academy didn't start until evening, so we had to get out to the tracking site as soon as possible.

As the class gathered around the start of the trail I could already tell who was interested and who was not. Many hung back. I didn't care. They were probably level twos who would direct traffic when the city held festivals or big concerts. They didn't need to know tracking. It was the ones at the front who concerned me. Tex, Mick, Owen and Joe. I really hoped the level ones would try this trail.

"Consider this trail an apprehension. This is the trail of a fleeing suspect. You should be able to read a bit of the haste put into these tracks. Most people just run, but you will find a few suspects who have time on their hands and they may take the time to try and hide their tracks. You will find a little of both in this trail. We're going to track it as a group until we get to the end. Can I get a volunteer to start us off?"

A cadet stepped forward, a woman. This surprised me.

"What's your name?" I asked.

"Joanna Pierce, sir," she answered.

I had to laugh a bit at being called sir. I was about as un-sir-like as I could get.

"Okay Joanna, let's see how far you can get on this."

She actually did very well on the easy steps. I asked her to describe the trail briefly and I stopped her when the class should notice something. Then I asked for another volunteer. Owen took a turn and then Joe. Mick was waiting for his chance to shine. He was a bit of a show off, enjoying one-upping Tex, so he waited until the trail got tougher before he stepped in.

Mick took his place beside the tracks. He had the first track covered or he wouldn't have volunteered, then he looked puzzled, cleared his throat, and examined the ground. I sensed his unease so I told him, "Don't focus too much on just tracks. Broaden your thinking. When something catches your eye, go with that, see if it leads you somewhere."

When he broadened his view the board laying on the ground caught his eye and he followed it to the next track. He should have caught that, though. Anybody who was used to his kid brothers pulling tracking tricks on him should have seen that board. He fell into a kind of detective mode where he searched the ground for clues. He began poking around under plants looking like a hound dog on the hunt.

When Mick got stuck Tex stepped in. They seemed to have a challenge going between them. It kind of amused me, but it brought out their talents for me to see, too.

Tex tracked more like Jacobsen. He would have to learn how to see again but once he trained himself in the ways to look at the minute differences involved in tracking I thought he would take off with it. If I could keep these two competing against each other. They would make a good team.

As Tex tracked many of the cadets couldn't follow what he was seeing and they asked him to explain it to them. He pointed out things that surprised me. Mick stood back, arms folded, amused at the "beginners." I wondered what working with these two would be like. They were both young. I was glad at least Mick had experience camping as well as simple tracking.

Graduation was in January so I had a wait ahead of me. Then it would be winter and we'd be unlikely to have many tracking calls when the mountains were still cold. And in January I'd have a two month old baby. Gosh, that was still hard to believe, even though time was getting close. Only three weeks to go!

We continued down the trail and I called on other cadets, working my way through as many of them as I could. I started out with the more eager ones thinking if they wanted to try it they should get practice at it. As the cadets were loading up into the big Sheriff's bus I called Mick and Tex over.

"Take a few minutes to try this trail," I told them.

I led them to the starting spot and they looked at the trail knowing right away it was a challenge. Mick looked at me, wondering how much was expected of them. Not much. I didn't expect them to be able to track that trail.

I watched them point and talk quietly between themselves and move to the next track. When all the other cadets were loaded up, I went back and checked on them.

"How is it going?" I asked.

"You're sure this is a trail?" Mick joked.

"Yes, it's my normal mode of walking in the woods."

"Then I suggest you not go missing," Mick said.

"I don't plan to."

"How long is this trail?"

"Not long."

"I hate to keep people waiting" Mick said.

"They're glad to wait. If they are waiting they aren't running."

"Hey, and we aren't, too," said Tex, "track slower, man."

"You're supposed to be doing this, too," I reminded him.

"So, what do you think?" Chase asked me.

"Send Michael Colton and Tex Ward to see Schroeder in January."

"That's it? That's all you're going to tell me?"

"I do want to work with them. For one thing, if they are on the trail Jacobsen can be on the streets. The force needs Jacobsen on the street. I think Michael will take to it easier than the officers in Joshua Hills. If I can get them both to track together they will teach each other a lot. Maybe more than I could teach them. They just have a natural competitiveness that works right. I'm sure they don't know it's there, but it works. I remember when Strict was thinking about whether to add me to the team or not. He knew I could track but he said there were demographics involved. These two are just demographically right. Too bad one of them's not an EMT. They'd make the perfect tracking team with some experience. I think Schroeder would be wise to keep those two together."

"Cops don't work with partners these days."

"That varies. I've seen Jacobsen and Thompson working in the same car."

"Most of the cops with a partner are working with a level two due to budget cuts. I'll see that Schroeder knows about those two."

Chapter 24

A restlessness settled into me when the tracking classes were over. Despite my aversion to LA traffic, I had enjoyed getting out and working with the cadets. Katie and I stayed home, but I could feel the pull of the trail. It was dumb because Rusty would never let me go. Not in my last trimester. I made sure the nursery was ready. I cleaned. I stocked up the freezer so Rusty and Katie would have meals while I was in the hospital and so meals would be easy after I got home. Then, I got a shock. Strict did call. It was unusual for him to call this late in the fall. Tourist season was slacking off. He knew it was iffy calling me at all. But, this girl needed finding. Nights were cold. Time was important. Jacobsen wasn't ready to go it alone. The trail was too old, put down by a light person. The heavier the person the more clues they left behind. He needed a tracker, a real tracker, and he needed it soon. He knew not to call Rusty. He knew he'd get an emphatic *no*. I got the facts. A young girl, fed up at home, ran away into the mountains. The police searched the local streets. She was the adventurous type, maybe she was camped out in the mountains. Strict gave me an address. The house was located in a little bedroom community of small mansions. A few of the homeowners were doctors and lawyers in Joshua Hills. Many of them were based in the LA area. Rich kid tired of being told what to do. She thought she could make her own way. Would I just make sure she really was in the mountains? If she headed for a road the cops would take over again. I thought, sure, why not? Landon will be there if anything comes up. He'll call a lift if I need one. So I made a quick trip into town to pick up Bertie and talk to Rusty.

"Cassidy, why now?" he said after I explained the situation.

"Because kids don't check out the condition of the local search and rescue people before they take off," I told him. "I won't be going far. I'll probably be home tonight. Strict just wants me to verify that the search really is up in the mountains. They say walking is good for you in the last trimester. I'll be back tonight."

"Let me go with you," he asked.

"There's no need. You have work to do. Landon will be there."

"Why do you need an EMT if you're just checking things out?"

"Rusty, it just makes sense. You know Strict sends Landon whenever the victim might need medical assistance. I could do this alone, but he's playing it safe. Bertie is waiting with Katie in the car. The sooner I get up there the sooner I can get back. I need all the daylight hours I can get."

Why did I always leave with a guilty conscious? Because the lives of other people were more important than my feelings, more important than Rusty's needless worry. I felt guilty making Rusty worry, but that didn't change the need to go, so I went.

I dropped off Katie and Bertie at my house on my way up into the mountains.

"I'll probably be back tonight," I assured her. "It sounded like a quick one. This kid couldn't have gone far."

"You go find her. I know you can do it."

I climbed into the Explorer and headed up the mountain. It was a chilly fall day. I was glad I'd brought a jacket and I thought about a kid out in those mountains. Did she have a jacket? Did she bring water? I'd have to find out when I got to the house. The neighborhood I was heading for was up in the pines. I'd driven past it many times. Many kids lived up there. They drove expensive cars to parties in town. The kid I was looking for was too young for that. But she wasn't too young to wish she could take off like the big kids did. I was making my way quickly through the mountains when Zeb's big, gray truck zoomed past. Aw hell, not again. How long had it been since I'd seen him? Months! It had been months. I thought he'd moved on, but here he was. He must have heard about the search on the police scanner. A little way up the road he had pulled off and when he saw me coming he pulled in front of me blocking me from going further. He got out of his truck and walked over.

"Go home," he said.

"I've got a call," I answered.

"Stay out of this. If you go home, let the parents stew, I'll give you a cut."

"No! I am *not* going to let a little kid freeze out there just for a chunk of a reward. If I don't go Strickland will just send out somebody else."

"There ain't nobody else. Those cops are a joke."

"They are not a joke. I know. I'm still alive. I wouldn't be here if they were a joke. They found people before I came on board. They'll find this kid, with or without me. It'll just go quicker if I do the tracking."

"These folks are scared and rich. Give them a day."

"Get out of my way."

"You're not going up there. Every time I turn around you're fouling things up. I want you to see what happens when you just give it some time."

"I've seen what happens when you give it some time. People die. Now move!"

"Okay, I want you to see what happens when you mess with *me*. You go up there and you'll have me to mess with."

"And you will have ten armed officers after your sorry hide. Now move it."

I didn't actually know how many guys Strict had up there. Seemed like there was always more guys up there than actually went out on a search, but they also needed guys on call for things like transport, helicopter drops and pickups.

"You're not going up there," he stated.

Cars were behind him honking their horns.

"You're blocking this way? Okay, I'll find a different way," I said maneuvering so I could turn around. A car heading up the mountain from my direction had to hit his brakes. He honked at me as I sped off back down the mountain. Damn. Was there another way up the mountain? The only one I could think of was half an hour south and then a wide circle back to the west and back north again. I sure didn't want to take that much time. But I didn't want a confrontation with Zeb when I was alone either. I was mad. Mad at this money-grabbing, boor. What kind of a guy would let a kid sit up in the mountains just for a couple hundred dollars? I didn't care what kind of reward the parents came up with. It wasn't the money. It was the kid.

I was driving a little fast, trying to improvise another route, cussing out Zeb, and thinking about all the things that could happen to a kid in these rugged mountains. I'd been attacked by dogs and run up a tree by a bear. I'd been cold and hungry in these hills. I knew what she was going through. It wasn't something a city kid should take on.

I looked behind me and the gray truck was on my tail. When Zeb saw that he'd been discovered he hit the gas pulling up directly behind me. I didn't like the idea of a car chase through the mountains. I got out my cell phone. Strict had an army of help.

"Hey kid," he said. "How's it going?"

"Lou, I've got trouble. Zeb's got it into his head that I am not going on this search. He's trying to stop me. He blocked me from driving directly to base camp. I'm looking for an alternate route."

"Just find the nearest town and…"

Damn cell phones! I knew what he wanted me to do, though. He wanted me to find the nearest public place and wait for an escort. But the nearest public place was not close. It was miles of forest roads away. He'd probably send out a car or two to find me. All these thoughts were jumping around while I was trying to keep an eye behind me. Suddenly the turnoff for a campground came up and I whipped into it bouncing down the rugged dirt road. There were no campers this late in the season. I drove as fast as I could in and out of the little winding dirt roads and then I realized… Zeb had me trapped. I was trapped and he was going to do anything he had to to stop me from getting up that mountain.

I reached the end of the campground and I didn't see the gray truck behind me. Zeb was probably waiting for me at the entrance. I didn't like the position I had put myself in but I wasn't worried yet. I'd just lose him in the woods. If I just had a minute or two he'd never find me.

I took a quick look at my situation and decided to take the time to grab my pack and coat. I slipped on the coat and shrugged into the pack. I didn't bother with the frame pack. I didn't want the weight of three days of gear. I grabbed the daypack containing water and food for a long day on the trail. If I was careful I could make the food last two days, but I didn't want it to come to that. I needed to find a way to the road where an officer could pick me up.

I slipped into the trees, keeping an eye in the direction Zeb might come from. Silently I stalked from tree to tree. I froze whenever I sensed a movement or heard a sound. I hid my tracks, very conscious of the fact that I had a tracker after me. I made my way back up to his truck but I didn't spot him.

My heart was pounding and I didn't know why. I wasn't winded or tired. I was tense, but I wasn't scared, even when I spotted Zeb walking through the campground toting a rifle. He looked comfortable like that. He wasn't tracking. He was hunting. I froze behind the brush that separated us, brush that would never stop a bullet. I turned off my cell phone. If there was one thing I didn't need it was an identifying noise. Rusty and Strict would know, if my phone was turned off, that I needed stealth.

"Cassidy!" Zeb called into the woods, "You can't get away. I'm tired of this. If you won't quit, I'll *make you* quit. I'll track you down. You'll see. You can't run from me! Not on foot. You know I will find you!"

Zeb turned toward me. I silently cursed and made myself small, which was quite a task under the circumstances. I waited until he continued his search, then I found a more solid object to hide behind. If I couldn't avoid Zeb and work my way around him to the road, that meant, to be truly safe, I had to go deeper into the woods. I had no qualms about that, except that it meant giving up on the search. I hoped Strict would call one of the officers I had been training, but he might have to call them in from town. I suspected if he had called one of them to go tracking with me it had been Reilly. We had specifically appointed Reilly if the search was supposed to be short and Reilly hadn't gotten a call since class ended. I hoped he could handle it. I knew he could buckle down and do his best, especially backed by a good reason, but I wasn't sure he could follow a kid's trail. I wished Mick was available. He and Reilly would be a good team, but I had more pressing matters to deal with. I wasn't going to be a help to anybody until I could get out of this fix.

Every time Zeb turned in my direction I froze. I felt frightened, but not for myself. I felt… for the baby. And every time I felt a rush of adrenaline I felt a tightening. It was the false labor, the Braxton-Hicks contractions again.

They happened several times a day and I was used to them. They could get quite strong but they could also be inconvenient. It wasn't something I welcomed when I was trying to concentrate on stealth. If I felt a strong one sometimes I had to stop and wait it out.

Zeb whipped around looking at my hiding spot, not seeing me, but wondering if he had seen something. He lowered his rifle, took aim and fired. Bark jumped off the tree next to me. I had to fight to stay calm. He doesn't see you, I told myself, stay hidden. I had to fight to control my breathing. The shot proved to me, he was trying to stop me permanently. He wanted his chance to be tracker in this area and this was a fight for dominance. If I thought he would work with the authorities, I would back off, but he was a money-grabbing, selfish jerk. He didn't have a heart. This was not a job for a heartless individual. If money drove him, then people would suffer for it.

I decided this Zebediah Thatcher was not going to stop me from tracking. I wouldn't let him. I *couldn't* let him stop me. I had to protect myself and I had to protect my baby. I had to get away and I had to do something to stop Zeb. But what?

Priorities first. I had to stay alive and the best way I knew of to do that was to disappear. I picked my way through the forest, putting space between me and the campground. I kept to cover. I hid my tracks as best I could at a run… and the contractions grew stronger with the bumping and bouncing… and still I ran. When I couldn't run any more I looked behind me. I couldn't see Zeb so I hid in the brush and rested.

Cass, Rusty's never going to let you out of his sight again, I thought, you've really done it this time. Your due date is three weeks away and you're running through the woods, trying to stay away from a gun toting tracker. What do you think you are doing?

Staying alive, I answered myself, just staying alive.

I never did get a chance to evaluate Zeb's tracking skills. He had only claimed to be a tracker. No, he claimed to be a people hunter. If he was a poor tracker I had nothing to worry about. I could find my way to a trail and follow it from there to another campground. I was guessing I was a mile from a road now. I thought about the placement of the campgrounds, roads and trails in this part of the mountains. There was a mountain pass to the north. If I went over that I should be close to the deer clearings that were a mile from my hideout. If I could make it to the hideout, I'd be safe. Rusty would think to look there for me. The mountain pass was a long hike, though, and doing it cross country would take time. I didn't want to be out overnight. Strict would call Rusty, tell him what little he knew. Rusty would know I was on the run. There would be an all-out search for my truck and it was deep within an empty campground. The guys would recognize Zeb's truck first. Then they would discover mine deeper within the campground. They'd put two and two together. They would know where I started out. But how would they find me? Even Chase would have a hard time with the tracks I had hidden. I decided right then and there that I would make it. I'd out-smart Zeb and I'd find a way to survive yet another bout of trouble.

The contractions were not easing up, but I knew the tension of the situation was not helping them go away. Resting helped a little bit but I couldn't rest for long. I needed to get to the top of the pass. If I could find that I'd know the rest of the route easily. I crept out of hiding, watching for any signs of my pursuer. I turned up hill and started walking, careful of my foot placement, treading lightly, using everything I could to hide my faint tracks. I didn't hike straight uphill because it was too hard to hide tracks that way and I became winded too quickly. I walked gradually up the hill at an angle and when I got too far off track I switched directions, making my own switchbacks through the wilderness. I tired quickly. Back and forth, back and forth, I walked ever upward, always cautious, hiding every track as I walked.

When I reached the top I realized I was too far south. I needed to follow the ridge to get to the deer clearings. But I had to stop. I was tired and winded and hungry. I examined my back trail and figured I had time to find more strength. I sat and dug a couple of energy bars from my pack. I didn't use the day pack much. The food in there could have been a few months old. Ick. I ate them anyway. I still had a long way to go.

I tried my cell phone again but there was no signal.

"Oh, come on!" I told it, "I'm on top of a mountain! You should be able to pick up a signal somewhere!"

I sensed a movement. There was no way it could be Zeb. He couldn't possibly track me as fast as I could run. Could it be a ranger? What would a ranger be doing out in the middle of nowhere?

I doubled back looking for a person or a track. I almost melted with relief when I came to the tracks of two men. I followed the tracks along the ridge but the movement must have been a fluke. I tracked the men for ten minutes and never caught a glimpse of them. Based on their trail, I was guessing they were land surveyors. Every once in a while they stopped and popped out the legs on a tripod and their footprints led me to believe they were taking a reading of some kind. It looked like they had been out most of the day. But why way up here? And where did they come from? I wasn't going to second guess the workings of a surveying company's mind. I was glad to have this link to possible help, but then I became nervous when their tracks led back the way I expected Zeb to come from. I decided to backtrack them instead. If I was just tracking to find an object I could do it quickly. I didn't need to profile or put much effort into it. There were two of them, leaving plenty of sign. I walked their back trail until it led to a mineshaft. I circled the mine looking for a road of some kind but the mine was old. If there had been a road the forest had reclaimed it years ago. I looked down into the blackness of the shaft. I dropped a rock down it and heard a faint tap when it hit the bottom.

I found the men's tracks again but darkness came and I was still on their trail. I had to stop and I no longer knew exactly where I was and I was going to have to spend an October night on the mountain with only a light jacket for insulation. Still, I was glad to have that. But I thought about Rusty and Strict and I was cold, lonely, tired and tense and the contractions were still not easing up. They had been going on most of the day. I tried paying closer attention to the contractions, wondering if they were getting closer together or stronger but they didn't seem to be getting more intense. I remembered when Katie was born the contractions got more intense very quickly. It had been a relatively quick labor. Four hours. Four hours was quick for a first time.

As darkness settled into the mountains I felt safer. Zeb would have to stop too. I located a place to bed down. I had to cross rock to reach it so my tracks would not show up. It was deep in the shadows, behind some holly. The holly was scratchy but it also would deter anybody looking for me. I stuffed my pack inside my jacket to create an airgap. I covered myself with leaves for insulation.

As I shivered in the night I thought, if this is warmer I don't want to know colder. It was even colder than the survival trip I took in the snow. When I'd done that I was prepared to be cold. I had mentally prepared myself and the cold wasn't surprising to me. I was by myself, in survival mode, ready to take on the mountains. This was different. I was worried about the baby and about Zeb catching up with me. I thought about what Rusty was thinking. I wanted to curl up on the big brown couch with a roaring fire in the fireplace, but here I was, sad, alone, and tired of trouble.

The baby provided a little company. He moved and poked and kept me awake. His kicks didn't hurt my ribs like they had a few weeks ago. I wondered if he had turned. Or dropped. Hadn't Chase said I looked different? But he hadn't seen me before so how would he notice something like that?

It felt like I was awake all night, contractions preventing any rest, listening, shivering. The contractions were a constant worry.

I started for the hideout as soon as I could see enough to walk. When I grew hungry I found trail mix in the pack. I smelled it. It smelled okay. I snacked as I walked. I was a little nervous because I had to go back the way I came, but I found where I'd changed my plans and got back on track again. When I spotted the rock pillar in the distance I wanted to kiss it. It was a sign of hope. Safety was just down that canyon. Just down that rock strewn, creek tumbling canyon.

The canyon that day looked rougher and rockier than I had ever seen it. Instead of friendly and welcoming it looked foreboding and hostile. I picked my way down and kept to the rocks. Zeb would have a harder time with the rocks, too. Rushing here was not a good idea, so I slowed my pace. At one point I lost a handhold and tumbled down an incline, landing on my backside and hitting my pack. It gave me a jarring I wasn't prepared for. My abdomen tightened with the impact and led to a very long contraction. I folded my arms around by belly and almost cried, not so much with pain, but with tension, frustration, and desolation. I felt so alone. I yearned for Rusty. I needed someone to tell me this was going to turn out okay. Instead, I heard the sound of a rifle shot.

It can't be! I thought. He couldn't follow that trail that easily. Then I remembered the time I spent following the men surveying the land up top. I'd wasted several hours tracking them and giving up on their help. Could Zeb have caught up with me in that time? Oh hell. I pushed myself to my feet and hid in the shelter of the rock. Then I made my way down canyon and when I got to my camp I realized I couldn't use the hideout! The area around it was cleared and sandy. My footprints would show up easily and even if Zeb couldn't figure out how to get into it, a bullet would penetrate the walls easily. It was a death trap, if anybody knew I was in there. It could be shot through, burned… I shouldn't go near it. But what now? This was my one goal. Rusty would know to look for me here.

I fumbled with my predicament. Where could I go? I could continue down canyon to the trail and make my way out to Creekside Campground. That was four miles. I needed a rest before I could tackle that. The contractions were worse. After my tumble, they had gotten much stronger. I hoped it didn't signal a problem. Another one hit and I braced myself for it. If I was bracing myself for the contractions that wasn't a good sign.

I saw a movement up canyon. Oh man, I had to get out of there. I needed a safe hiding place. Not the hideout, not the woods. A place that was defendable. I headed for the side of the canyon. The canyon walls offered hiding places. Defensible little nooks and crannies. As I was making my way down canyon another contraction brought me to my knees. Instead of worrying about the pain, I worried about the knee prints in the dirt. I really needed to stop. I needed rest. When the contraction passed I made my way further down the canyon wall. Then I came to a familiar rock and I looked out over the expanse of the place I called The Boulder Field.

It was not a good place for me to go. If I stuck to the rocks I risked a fall and if I walked below the rocks it was sandy and every track would show. Zeb had proven to me that he was a tracker. Leaving a trail in the sand was a bad move. But the rocks… the rocks were a risk I was unwilling to take. One fall was enough.

There was a cave under the rocks, though. I knew how to get to it. I just needed to figure out how to get to it without leaving tracks. Trent's Cave. The entrance to it was a small crawl space. There was only one way in, so it was very defendable. If worse came to worse I would live. And Zeb would die. But it was my only chance to recuperate. I didn't think I could make it to Creekside Campground before Zeb caught up to me, so Trent's Cave seemed to be my next logical choice. I decided a little time on the rocks would put me in the middle of the boulder field. There would be no tracks going in. The rocks would be impossible for Zeb to track me on, so my tracks would just suddenly appear inside the boulder field. Maybe if I tackled the problem that way Zeb wouldn't venture in there.

I crept over a boulder and felt my way to the next one, making my way closer to the cave entrance. I hoped I could fit through the crawl space. It was tight when I was thin, but then Landon had followed me in and Bradley Sparks was even bigger than Landon. If Bradley could fit through, I thought I could, too.

I didn't like the feel of the contractions. I used the clock on my cell phone to time them but it was rough climbing, getting out the cell phone, noting the time, and keeping track of my back trail. After about a half hour I was guessing they were about twelve minutes apart. But I couldn't remember how frequently the Braxton-Hicks contractions usually were, so I pressed on.

I watched for a rock that would take me under the boulders. The whole area was a jumble of rocks. Huge rocks. And just because I could climb down the one I was on didn't mean I could climb down the one beneath it. It was a rock climber's dream and nightmare rolled into one. It was like a 3D rock maze. Some of the dead ends were not easy to back out of.

I made my way to a tall rock with a big V in it. I knew I could chimney climb up that rock, because I had done it before. If I could climb up it, I thought, I could climb down the V just as easily. I slipped into the crack and lowered myself down chimney-style. A contraction hit and I wedged myself into the crack, the tension of the sharp pain made me push against the rock that much harder. I was jammed in there so tight I couldn't have fallen if I wanted to. When it passed I was able to make my way to the floor of the boulder field.

The next contraction was very bad news. My water broke and the intensity of the contractions took on a whole new life. No! I thought, baby, not here, not now!

Chapter 25

Rusty! He would want to be with me when the baby was born. But more importantly he would want me to be safe. He'd fight through anything to protect us. I calmed my breathing and waited out the next contraction. I needed to stay levelheaded. I had a gunman after me and I was going to be useless. What was I going to do with a crying infant? I couldn't hide with a baby. I didn't have… I didn't have anything. No hot water. No towels. Everything was dirt, rock. I had to rein in my thoughts. I got out my cell phone, knowing it was useless. All this rock. The mountains. There was no way. I started my way down the list. Rusty first. I needed to hear his voice even if I couldn't get anything across, if all I could do was just hear a *hello?* and a *Cassidy where are you?* it would be enough. But I couldn't get through to Rusty. I started on the other numbers Strict. Nothing. Schroeder. Nothing. 911. Nothing. Kelly.

"Hello?" he said.

It was a miracle.

"Kelly! Call Rusty!"

"Cassidy? Where are you?"

"Trent's Cave. Tell Rusty to go to Trent's Cave and bring backup."

"Are you okay?"

"No! Yes! Kel…just send him. I'm scared. The baby's coming. But I'll be safe in Trent's Cave. I have to go. I have to find cover. I need to get in there where I can defend myself."

"Cass…"

"I've got to go, before another one hits. Just call him."

I hung up and ran for the cave entrance. At this point I didn't care about tracks. If Zeb followed me into the cave he was taking his life into his own hands. The next contraction brought me down again. I knelt in the sand and waited for it to pass.

"Cassidy! You still can't get away!" I heard Zeb from far away. His voice echoed off the rocks.

I got up and ran again. It wasn't far. When I found the little tunnel I groaned. Wind had brought in more sand and it blocked the entrance to the cave. I got down on my hands and knees and scraped away the sand. It stuck to my damp pants. I had to get into that cave before the next contraction came.

When I had cleared away the little drift that blocked the crawl space I army crawled through the opening. Army crawling was a lot easier when I had less belly. I couldn't afford to get stuck. I rethought my position and decided to go head first, back down. That way, if I did get caught on the way in I had a gun pointed down tunnel. I lay down and wriggled my way into the tunnel. It was a tight fit. At one point I thought I was stuck but I sucked in my stomach as much as I could and scraped by. Before I could stand up in the cave another contraction hit. I rolled onto my side riding it out, trying to remember to breathe. Breathe, Cass, breathe.

There was no sense timing contractions now. I knew the baby was on his way. All I could do was hang on for dear life and hope it all turned out all right. If it didn't… I didn't know what I'd do. When the contraction passed I took stock of the cave. It was dark, and I didn't have a light. I walked around feeling the earth with my feet. I had to be careful because there was a lot of loose, sharp rock left from the explosion that closed the entrance. I found a spot toward the back that was firm and sandy. I knelt down and brushed away any loose rock that would scrape me. Some delivery room. Didn't there used to be a sleeping bag in here? I couldn't find it in the dark. The only protection I had from the rocks and dirt was my clothes and I was going to need those later. I took off my pants and panties, then my jacket. I was chilly but I wanted to keep it dry. I'd need to wrap the baby in something.

Oh Rusty, where are you? Another contraction. There was nothing to grab. No big strong hands. No reassuring voice. My fingers gripped… nothing, the dirt floor of the cave. The contraction ended and I lay back gasping. I needed to remember to breathe. When the pain hit I forgot all about breathing.

After a while the pain just lodged in my brain. It never seemed to go away. I couldn't think, couldn't remind myself to breathe. I tried to remember what the end of the pain felt like. I knew it was there at the end of it all but that felt too far away.

How many contractions did it take for a baby to be born? Was I in labor all day yesterday? I hoped so. It let me think I'd gotten through part of it the easy way. I hoped I was well into labor when my water broke. I tried to only listen to thoughts that were encouraging. I didn't have an EMT there like I did with Katie. Nobody calling out, "five centimeters, six… nine." Nobody to tell me when to start pushing. I remembered I felt like pushing before I was supposed to. How was I to know when I was supposed to push? It all seemed too big, too hard for one person to do alone. Another wave of pain, tightness. I wanted to cry out but I didn't. I didn't want to do anything that would attract Zeb's attention. My 9mm lay on the ground next to me, though if I had to use it I'd have to time my shot very carefully between contractions. It would take most of a contraction for Zeb to wriggle through the end of the tunnel. I thought if I had to shoot that it could be done. If I had to pull that trigger, though, I had to kill him. If I didn't I'd just make things worse.

After a while I was too exhausted to keep track of the time. All I could do was lay back, and silently cry, and briefly drift off to sleep, and as soon as I found peace another contraction hit and I'd tense up, grip, grip the bare dirt floor, wait, call out silently to Rusty. Wave after wave of oblivious tightening, pain, easing, tightening. They were all running together. All of them were one, all of… oh, oh man, no! Not yet! I felt an irresistible urge to push. But I knew it might not be time. What was that breathing I was supposed to do, to make it so I wouldn't… wouldn't… ARG! I had to! I tried breathing shallowly, like I was told a lifetime ago. It worked for a moment. Oh, but I had to push! Breathe, Cass, breathe. I had to push… it was no use this baby was coming and I couldn't stop him.

I heard a gunshot. It sounded far away but I knew I was hearing it through rock. I couldn't do anything about it except keep my own gun handy, and push like mad. That too, came in waves. Despite the cold, my forehead was damp with perspiration. Oh! Another one! Push! Cassidy, push, the harder you push the sooner it'll be over. I hated that feeling. It overtook all thinking. It felt weird, totally foreign to any other feeling in the world. That urge to push could not be ignored. My fingers were bleeding, my nails all broken from grasping at nothing. I pushed and pushed. Harder. Harder. Harder. Until the moment eased.

There was another shot, a lot of yelling. I was too spent to move. Eventually, just like the contractions I lost track of what was happening. I was trapped in a haze of uncontrollable pushing and dozing and then one of the times I was pushing I felt something give. Oh god, it was the baby's head! There was nobody here to catch him and he was coming. Oh baby, I don't know what to do! Born on rocks and dirt. I pushed and pushed and felt his slippery little body slip gently to the earth. I sat up a little and reached down. I didn't know what to do. What did the EMTs do? What do the doctors do in a delivery room? I wasn't sure. I'd never even seen the inside of a delivery room. Hold them upside down and spank them? I didn't want to do that. Clear the airways, Cass. Do something to clear his airways. I looked at his little pinched face barely visible in the dark. My baby. Less than a minute old still connected to the umbilical cord. I didn't have anything to cut the cord with. I wasn't going to use my hunting knife. It seemed cruel. I stuck my fingers in his mouth, wondering how to start him breathing. I turned him over and massaged his bare back. Come on baby. Breathe for mommy. Please, please breathe for mommy. I became frantic. Rusty! I don't know what to do! Your son is here and I don't know what to do!

"Carson, please… Mommy's here." I reverted to academy training. CPR. I didn't know if it was the right thing to do but somewhere in all that he gave a jerk and cried out. His cry filled the cave and my heart and I wanted to hug him. But I thought the more he cried the more his lungs would clear. I laid back and Carson lay on my chest. I let him cry for a minute then I had to figure out what to do. I still had the placenta to deal with. I remembered that it wasn't an emergency if you can't cut the umbilical cord so I wrapped him up, placenta and all in my jacket. I had no way to bathe him. No way to feed him. I put him to my breast, but he didn't know what to do with it at first. I brushed his cheek and he rooted around instinctively so I tried the breast again. There was no milk yet but soon there would be. He hadn't opened his eyes yet. He was still upset about being born, but it wore off as he warmed up in my jacket. I didn't want to unwrap him and let him get cold again but I felt his little fingers. There were five of them. I bet there were five on the other hand, too.

I heard more shots. I recognized the fact that there were two distinctive sounds to the shots. I worried about the guys out there. Then I heard a helicopter. It was flying in circles. I imagined what was going on in the outside world but I knew the guys would want me to stay put. Going out there would just complicate things. I knew I might have a hike ahead of me so I spent the time regrouping. I dozed, snuggled up tightly with my baby, trying to keep him warm. My legs were cold and wet, but my pants were cold and wet, too. When I heard scraping noises in the little tunnel I hastily pulled on the wet pants and picked up Carson. I held him to me tight and aimed my 9mm at the little tunnel.

"Identify yourself!" I called out, the fear plain in my voice, "Identify yourself or you'll never stand up again!"

Please don't be Zeb, I thought, I don't want to have to shoot. Please don't be Zeb!

"Cassidy?" It was Victor Gomez, my sometimes search partner.

Light bounced around on the rock walls and a head poked through into the cave.

"Victor… where's Rusty? Is he okay?"

"He's right behind me."

"Tell him… he has a son. Rusty! We have a son. He's beautiful." I don't know why I said that. I hadn't been able to see Carson yet. But I knew he was. He was Rusty's boy.

I staggered to my feet in the middle of the cave shivering, holding my baby and Victor stood up, shined the flashlight on me. He shined the light around on the floor of the cave. Rusty struggled through the small opening. I was surprised he could fit, but he was determined. When he pulled himself into the cave and caught sight of me all wet and disheveled, holding our baby, he almost lost it.

"I heard the shots," I said. "Is everybody okay?"

"He will be," Rusty answered, voice reined in tight.

"Who?"

"Ben Tomlin. He'll be okay. As long as he knows you're okay, he'll be okay. Babe… how did you do it? When I saw you go through labor with Katie, I felt guilty for putting you through that and now… by yourself… in this place."

"I didn't have a choice. It was here or the hideout. I didn't think the hideout would be safe. Bullets would go right through it. This was the only safe place I knew. I was on the run…"

"Shh, hush, it's okay. I wish I could see him. Let's get you out of here. Can you walk?"

"I think so. It should be easier than the first time. No stitches."

"Let me see him," Victor said.

I handed Victor the little jacket-wrapped bundle and he unwrapped the folds. Rusty looked over Victor's shoulder as he examined his son in the flashlight beam. Victor suctioned out Carson's airways.

"You did a good job," Victor said.

"I didn't know what I was doing. I was so scared."

"He's fine. A big strong boy. When was he due?"

"Not for another couple of weeks, just like Katie."

"They're going to want to keep him overnight. You, too. Are you sure you're doing okay?"

"I just want to go home."

He took my pulse and blood pressure.

"It's low," he said. "I'm calling the lift back. You're not hiking out like this."

"What happened to Zeb?" I asked Rusty.

"He's going to be gone for a long, long time," he answered.

"So the guys hauled him in again?"

"Yeah, but shooting an officer will put him away for a while."

I was glad they didn't have to shoot Zeb. I'd have to check on Ben when I got out of the hospital. We crawled out of the cave and it was night. Victor signaled the helicopter with the flashlight and they plucked us out of the boulders with a basket. I rode the basket first with Carson in my arms. He was calm again. He didn't appreciate Victor's examination much. I didn't blame him. It was cold in the cave. It was cold in the helicopter, too. The guys rode up and we headed for Joshua Hills. I shivered until Victor handed me a survival blanket.

I had a son. Carson Tomlin Michaels. Victor helped Rusty cut his umbilical cord, with the proper tools. Rusty held the little bundle pulling the jacket back every once in a while to look at him. I had thought all newborns looked alike but Carson definitely looked different from Katie. He was sturdier from the start.

Chapter 26

At the hospital Carson was weighed and bathed and several hours later we got him back wrapped in a little blue blanket and wearing a white stocking cap. Even being early, he weighed nearly eight pounds. Rusty was fascinated.

"I wish I could have been there," Rusty said.

"I called as soon as I could. Kelly was the first person I could reach. I tried everybody."

"He had a hard time reaching me, too. I was out at base camp grilling Strict. He had to drive out there to tell me you'd called. Then I didn't know the way in to the cave. Only Landon Wilson and Bradley Sparks knew the way in. Landon was on the search with Reilly for the little girl. I called the station where Sparks works and they patched me through. He could only give me a general description of where it was. He was willing to come show us but it would take him a couple of hours to get here and then a couple more get to the entrance. I went to the boulder field and followed his directions. About that time Zeb saw officers closing in on the area. He was mad. He started yelling about everybody being against him and how he'd kill us all. So we called in the troops. Every moment we wasted on Zeb all I heard was Kelly's words, 'the baby is coming.' I had to get there and all this commotion was stopping me." He paused. "I've got my girl back. I've got a daughter… and a son. I wonder what Katie's going to say."

"I wonder what my mom is going to say," I said.

While I was alone in the hospital room I worked at making my fingers look as normal as possible. No matter what I did to make them better I had to hide my hands from Rusty. They seemed like a symbol to me of what I had been through and I didn't want him to know that. I should have known better, though. I couldn't hide anything from Rusty for long. When he saw them he grew very still. He took my hand and turned it over. He kissed my fingertips and it took him a long time to find something to say.

"Never again. You'll never have to do that again."

"Don't say that. I would do it again."

"No."

"Rusty you can't say never, especially when it comes to me."

"We've got it all, babe, all we need now is peace. Do you think we could manage that? Can't we just be a family?"

The fingers still bothered him. The nails were rough and the tips were full of scratches and trying to heal. I wasn't going to type for a while. But one thing they could touch was Rusty's heart.

"We can try," I told him. "I've got some trackers to teach. Maybe, over time, we can just be a family."

Katie claimed Carson as her own.

"My baby," she'd say and pat Carson on the head. When Carson cried she ran to me. "My baby hungry," she'd tell me. No matter what was really wrong with him, in Katie's eyes he was hungry.

"Gordon's Quarter Horses," said Martha when she picked up the phone the next morning.

"Good morning Martha, can I talk to mom or dad?"

"It's time, isn't it? Oh, I am so excited! How long do we have?"

"I think I better tell Mom first," I said.

"Just think, this time everything is going to work out perfect. You're there in town. All you have to do is drive to the hospital. This time it's going to work out perfectly! Here she is."

She handed the phone over to my mom.

"Cassidy? You're two weeks early again," Mom said.

"I know, I guess my kids are just in a hurry. Actually Carson was in a little more of a hurry than Katie was. He decided to be born on a mountain. Actually, he was born in a cave."

"You said I could be there!" she said, disappointed.

"Tell Carson that. I had a bit of trouble. But we're both fine. Katie thinks getting a baby was all her idea and she thinks whenever he cries he is hungry. I'm going to have to be careful she doesn't try to feed him."

"When… when was he born?"

"I don't know. Golly, I really don't know. I was in a cave because this guy was after me. And I couldn't tell if it was night or day. I'll have to check his birth certificate!" I fumbled with the papers I brought home from the hospital. "October twentieth. And I don't know how much he weighed either but he was seven pounds fourteen ounces by the time we got to the hospital. He's going to be tall, like Rusty. He's adorable, Mom, you've got to come see him. I'm doing great considering what could have happened. I can sit. Since I didn't have a doctor handy, they didn't cut me. That's a relief…."

Rusty was listening, waiting for his turn to call his mom, too. He could have just called on his cell phone but he wanted to listen in.

"Wayne, we have another grandson!" I heard my mom say, then, "What's his name?"

"Carson Tomlin Michaels."

"Where'd you get Tomlin from?"

"It's a long story. Benjamin Tomlin helped Rusty find me when I was in the cave and he took a bullet in the confrontation. It went okay with the other names…"

"It takes a real wild west baby to be born in a cave with a gun fight going on outside! Wait until your father hears about this! The boys are going to love this story!"

"I hope he's not living up to his namesake," I said.

"And who is that?"

"Kit Carson."

"Oh dear. Maybe you should have gone with Fred."

"Fred?"

"Yeah, someone mild mannered. Like Fred Rogers."

"It's official. His given name is Carson Tomlin Michaels."

"I can't wait to meet him."

"You'll love him. He's got lots of dark hair and he likes to wink."

"Dark hair? Where'd he get dark hair from?"

"Katie had dark hair, too, remember? Then it all fell out and she got blonde hair. There's no telling what color it will be in a few months."

And so it went. She talked for over an hour. Then she packed her bags and came to my house.

Ben Tomlin got out of the hospital before I did. I went to the station and found him working with Tom, his left arm in a sling. He'd taken the bullet in his shoulder. He grinned when he saw us at the door.

"Hey, you made it," he said. "Hey Katiekins! How's the big sister?"

"Fi-fives!" said Katie and Ben held out his hand for her to slap.

"And who have we here?" Ben asked.

"My baby!" Katie said proudly.

"We gave him your name for his middle name. I hope that was okay."

"My name? Why?"

"Because we wanted him to remember where he came from and why he's here. Because he has dedicated friends who are willing to give their all. And when he's old enough to understand what it means, we want him to jump into life and give it his all, too."

After we visited Ben we searched out Reilly.

"I was lucky," he reported. He had been on patrol but stopped by the station to update us. "Wilson and I thought we'd never find the kid. We was tracking as best we could but it was rough. We got about a half mile and then the trail turned back. About that time we got a radio call that the kid had been located at a friend's house. Her friend had let her hide in her bedroom."

"That's good. So everybody was fine. It's kind of ironic that Zeb was after a reward and one never would have materialized."

"The friend's parents called the girl's parents and so we got called off the trail. At least it was good practice."

"Good, keep at it."

"I dunno. I don't think I'm cut out to be a tracker. I mean, if Schroeder says I got to track, I got to track. He's the boss. But there's others out there that'll take to it better'n me."

"Well, keep practicing. You never know when I'm going to be stuck in a cave with a gunman after me."

Rusty's parents were delighted. A grandson. One of each! They made us promise to come to their house for Christmas. It was beginning to sound like we were becoming a normal American family. But I doubted it. How could our family be normal?

We went to the ranch for Thanksgiving. My mom went crazy with the camera. Patrick took Katie out stalking rabbits every day.

"Walk and sneak at the same time," he said.

"Sneak, sneak," said Katie as she squatted down and tried to walk at the same time.

"No, shhh, you have to be quiet or the bunnies will hear you. Walk and sneak quietly," Pat said.

Up on the porch Wyatt was asking me, "How long until Carson can play trucks and cars?"

"Next Thanksgiving," I told him. "Maybe earlier, but for sure by next Thanksgiving."

"How long until he can color?"

"He can try next Thanksgiving. That takes a little longer."

"Does Carson believe in Santa Claus?"

"I don't think he's old enough to know who Santa Claus is. Next Christmas he will."

Katie was more interested in the big horses than the little rabbits. The horses didn't run away when she got close. Patrick had his work cut out for him.

Sleepless nights and draggy days. Walking a fussy baby. Feedings. Diaperings. Potty training a toddler. Family things. Family times.

Christmas with Rusty's family was a blast. With Rusty's mom there to remind her of what Grandmas say, Katie would stand over Carson with a kindly, patient look and ask him, "Are you hungry?"

Rusty's brother, Cody, laughed, "Mom she sounds just like you!"

"That's because she got the phrase from Bev," I explained.

The attic room was snug with four bedded down in it. Katie woke me up bright and early Christmas morning with an excited tug, "Look! Mommy! Come look! Sandy Claus come! Look!"

"Go tell Grandma," I said wearily. "Grandma wants you to wake her up."

I had been up half the night with Carson. I tried to be excited about Sandy Claus but I had to wake up first.

I could hear her scooting down the stairs and wondered if I should have carried her down the stairs. It was too late. Katie had already been downstairs and back up already. I could tell later by the raided candy dish.

"Gam-mama!" she called out at the bedroom door, "Gam-mama! Come! Look!" She rattled the doorknob.

It didn't take long to have the living room full of people. That was because it didn't take many people to fill the room, especially with a ten foot tree taking half the space. It was a paper-tearing, happy bunch of people.

When Chase showed up for lunch he had a hard time wading through the paper.

He sat down beside me at table with a, "That was a mean trail you left for me."

"What do you mean?" I asked.

"I was lucky you got through to Kelly Green. I never would have gotten there in time."

"Chase, you lost me somewhere."

"Strict called me, when the guys located your truck. They looked over the campground and radioed Strict. Strict called me. It didn't take much explaining to know you had trouble on your tail again. So I took out after you. But that trail was impossible."

"It wasn't too impossible, Zeb followed it."

"Then I hope he's out of the picture. He must be half bloodhound."

"So, do you have something cheerful to talk about?" I asked.

"You should have seen the guys," Chase continued. "When Victor made it into the cave somehow his radio was transmitting and all the guys could hear the baby crying. They all stopped. The dads got all choked up. I couldn't see Rusty."

"He was in the cave, too."

"Well!" said Bev cheerfully, "It sounds like you have a story to tell!"

Chapter 27

Graduation ceremonies were held in mid-January. I couldn't be there. Carson was miserable from vaccinations and Katie was determined that she knew just what he needed. A week later I was called in to Schroeder's office. Inside stood Michael Colton and Tex Ward, sharp in their new uniforms. Kent Jacobsen walked in a short time later.

"So, you still want to track for this department?" I asked.

"Yes Ma'am," they said.

"Don't call me Ma'am. Just call me Cassidy."

"Yes Ma'am."

I glared at them.

"Skip the formalities. I'm not the formal type. Once you've been out on a trail with a person a few times formalities get blown by the wayside. Has Sergeant Schroeder told you what tracking with me might entail?"

The two men looked at each other like they thought they might be missing a critical piece of information.

"You have to be ready for anything working with Cassidy," Jacobsen said.

"Anything?"

"Bears, rattlesnakes, forest fires, man hunts through the mountains… anything."

Mick grinned. He looked to Tex. Tex gave an affirmative shrug.

"Yeah," he said confidently. "We're ready… for *anything*."

Chapter 28

Michael and Tex proved to be good choices. I learned very quickly that Michael Colton preferred to be called Mick. Apparently his dad was the Michael of the family and his name had evolved from Mikey to Mick in school. Mick was a talker. It only took one practice trail to get his life story. Still, he was a likeable guy and eager to learn. He tended to show up unexpectedly and he was single so his time was flexible. I just wished I could take off and go tracking as easily as he could.

One morning I was in my side yard stalking the deer, like I did most mornings. The deer all suddenly startled and trotted away. I turned to the house and saw a silhouette in the den window. It was a man and it wasn't Rusty.

"You need to go tracking," Mick announced as he slid open the back door.

"Easier said than done," I said.

He looked around. Katie was stuffing scrambled eggs into her mouth and Rusty had placed Carson's car seat all the way across the table from Katie so she couldn't share without climbing down the highchair and walking around the table. In the time it took her to do that one of us would stop her. Carson was waiting for a bottle impatiently.

"My baby hungry," Katie announced.

"I know, he'll get a bottle soon," I assured her.

"My baby wants eggs."

"He's too little for eggs. Only big girls get to eat eggs."

"We go track?" Katie asked.

"See? The kid wants to go," Mick said.

"They both have to want to," I informed him.

"I thought she liked that backpack contraption," he said.

"She does, but I can only carry so many backpacks."

"So? I'll carry her," Mick volunteered.

"You know, most husbands would worry about their wife taking off into the woods with other men on a regular basis."

"Rusty?" Mick said. "He doesn't care. He wants me to practice. The more I practice the faster I can get called out by Strict."

He was right, still, Mick was getting to be a bit of a pest.

On the other hand he was kind of like the brother that I never had. He stood tall for his five foot eight inches. Part of that was attitude. His dark brown hair was usually combed down neatly for the job but, as soon as he was on the trail and the breeze hit it, it stuck every which way. When he grinned he cocked his head. The habit both appealed to me and irritated me because it could be interpreted in so many different ways. He had a quick grin, a quick brain and a quick trigger finger. Sometimes we went out into the hills and played tracking tricks on each other. I still had to be careful not to truly hide my tracks from him but as long as I walked like a typical hiker he worked through my puzzles. I threw everything at him and I didn't bail him out quickly.

Mick's best friend on the force was a fellow graduate from academy, Tex Ward. And his biggest rival, unsurprisingly, was Landon Wilson. Landon would rather Mick do anything on the force besides track. I thought it was funny that Landon was jealous, but Rusty showed no signs of it. Rusty saw a process going on in the force and somehow it revolved around me.

Police officers are an odd lot. They are family guys, but they have a hard job and sometimes they need to become hard men. With me they find themselves on both ends of the spectrum. I'm their little tracker and my tendency to get into trouble hits them hard. When I am threatened they are up in arms. I've seen them tough as nails and as kind and gentle as a minister. Sometimes they do both jobs at one time. Most people see the tough exterior and react instinctively to the barked orders, the urgency of the situation. But I knew these men. I'd learned that the cop face hid a hope that their barked orders, and raised weapons would be heeded and the weapon would go unused. I saw uniformed officers, family guys, tough, hard, holding onto the hope that society wouldn't force them to be what they were trained for.

Rusty knows if he can spread out the tracking he can spread out the trouble and if he can spread out the trouble I might just live to be forty. I made it to thirty. Some people had doubted I'd live to be thirty. Some people had done their best to make sure I didn't. This crazy trouble gene I was born with never let up. If there was a way for trouble to happen, it happened to me. So Rusty was trying to create a very fine balance where I could have my tracking and safety, too. Mick fit into that plan. So Rusty wasn't jealous. And Landon was.

Mick wasn't in uniform that day, so I assumed he was just bored. After Rusty took off for work I did my best to get Katie and Carson ready for a hike. I put Katie in warm clothes, made her take a potty stop, found her jacket. Then I changed Carson, filled up a baby bottle, found water bottles, changed Carson, packed a few diaper bag necessities in a day pack, grabbed a Ziploc bag of cookies and loaded everybody up into my tan Explorer

"Are you sure we're ready?" Mick asked.

"No, but let's go anyway. We may never leave if we make sure we have everything. Desert or woods?" I asked.

"Woods. Woods have a way of hiding tracks that the desert doesn't."

"Want to make a bet? How much tracking have you done in the desert?"

"Not a lot, but with all that open ground how can it be hard?"

"I feel like tracking the woods, too. How much have you explored these mountains? It's good to know your way around in them if you're supposed to be the tracker."

"I've explored the areas around the popular campgrounds."

"Area? As in miles? Acres? How big an area?"

"I've followed the trails out of them. I've tracked the immediate vicinity."

"You're going to have to get further into them than that. And you need to know your landmarks so you don't get lost off trail, too. Let's go exploring a little by car. You'll see there's more to these mountains than it looks like from a campground."

Chapter 29

To show Mick how extensive and remote the area could be, I took a road that I knew wound deep into the valleys. It began with a little used road that connected to the main highway through the mountains. It branched off and continued on until it ended thirty miles later at an abandoned campground. The last seven miles I had to use four wheel drive and it was even worse than when I had taken the Jeep in there.

"Oh man, how did you discover this place?" Mick asked as I pulled into a weedy, neglected camp spot.

"I just drove until I had to stop. I wish they would maintain this place. It would make a decent campground for remote campers. They'd have to grade the road and bring in new tables. But I kind of like it in here. Deer wander through, and I've even seen a bear in here. Walk around while I get the kids situated."

I let Katie out of her car seat and she ran around the truck while I got Carson out. I put Carson in his backpack and called Mick over.

"Why do I have to carry the squirt?"

"Two reasons. One: the macho guy rule."

"What's the macho guy rule?" he asked.

"Oh, come on… you know the macho guy rule. It says that the *guy* has to carry the pack that makes the *woman's* job easier."

Okay, so that isn't really what it says. It really says the guy has to carry the heavier pack. But I adjusted it a little because Katie was heavier than Carson was.

"Second," I continued. "If Carson needs changing the person in the other pack does it. It's just easier for the person not carrying his pack to get him out and change him. So… you can carry Katie if you want to change diapers."

"Uh, no, that's okay," he said lamely.

I held up the pack and he put his arms into the straps and tightened them down.

"Mommy! Cat!" Katie said.

"Where?" I asked.

She ran off to show me where the cat had gone. She took me to a ground squirrel hole.

"That wasn't a cat," I told her. "It was a squirrel. Can you say squirrel?"

"Quirrl," she said.

"Good girl! Have you ever tracked a squirrel?" I asked Mick.

"A squirrel? They're too small."

"Nothing is too small in the right setting. I've even tracked mice and once I tracked a centipede."

"Maybe the squirrel will come out later."

"We'll check the hole when we get back."

I put on the backpack and knelt down so Mick could lift Katie into it. When she seemed settled I stood up and adjusted the pack to fit me. We set out, me in front, him tracking behind. After a while he said, "Pull on ahead, out of my line of sight, and pull some tricks on me."

"Okay."

I upped my pace and pulled ahead. Katie bounced in the pack glad to be going faster. When I was about fifty feet in front of him I began thinking about what my feet were doing. I found hiding places for my tracks. I didn't trust myself to walk tree trunks with Katie on my back but I managed to give Mick a variety of things to track. I hid my tracks under vegetation. A couple of times I let my tracks appear to go straight while I took a giant step to the side and then kept going. I stepped on rocks. When I figured the kids would be getting hungry soon I made a wide circle and headed back to camp. It took Mick a while to catch up with me. I took off the pack and lifted Katie out. She immediately dashed for the squirrel hole and I ran after her to stop her.

"Don't step on the tracks," I told her. I took her over to the hole and noted that the squirrel had come out while we were gone. I tried luring it out with trail mix but Katie picked up a piece and ate it. I had to hold her and watch the hole from a difference.

"Mommy! Cat!" she said.

"Squirrel," I corrected her quietly. "Don't scare it away."

"Look! Quirrl!"

"Yeah! Shhh, you'll scare him. Just look. Mommy sees him."

The squirrel poked around in the vegetation but it didn't seem very interested in the trail mix.

When Mick walked up the squirrel dashed down his hole.

"There's lots of tracks if you want to try to track him," I said.

"I think this kid needs changing," he said wrinkling up his nose.

"Okay, I'll change him while you check out the squirrel."

I took Carson out of the backpack and Mick set the pack against the truck. He inspected the hole for tracks and poked around in the bushes near the opening.

"Did you see where it went?" he asked.

"Yeah. It didn't go far but it left plenty of tracks for you."

"The only ones I see are right at the entrance."

"I never said they were easy to follow," I told him.

"See. See quirrl?" said Katie. She walked over to the hole and squatted, peering in.

"Well there goes the tracks," I said.

I changed Carson's diaper and then dragged Katie away from the hole.

"I heard they like shiny things," Mick said. "Maybe we can lure it out."

"I think that's just raccoons," I said.

"Nah, lots of animals are curious about foreign objects. Here, let me see your car keys," he said.

I fished them out of my pocket and tossed them to him. He sat next to the hole and wiggled the keys around. At first nothing happened.

"You need to learn some patience. You can't *make* a squirrel be curious. You have to wait for them. It could take hours."

He tried different rhythms. He tried flashing the keys in the sunlight. He tried wiggling them in the sand. Suddenly the squirrel darted out of the hole and pounced on the keys. Mick yelped and dropped the keys and the squirrel grabbed the keys and dove into its hole again.

"Yipe!" cried Mick jumping back. "He took 'em!"

"What do you mean he took them? Squirrels don't steal car keys. I couldn't even get him to take squirrel food!"

"But, he took them! He ran into the hole with them! Now what do we do? I hope you have a spare."

"I do. Rusty's got it."

That was bad news. Rusty was at work in town. It wouldn't help to call him or a locksmith. We were deep in a valley in the mountains. We couldn't even call each other. And even if a locksmith did come out it was one of those fancy computer chip keys that had to be programmed at the dealership. We were stuck. I opened the truck with the combination but we still couldn't leave. I couldn't start the engine. I took the little camp shovel out of the back of the Explorer and handed it to Mick.

"You've got to be kidding," he said.

"Nope, I need that key. We can't call for help. Last time I got stuck back here I was missing for two days."

"How did you get stuck?"

"I couldn't start my Jeep."

"I think I see a pattern here."

"I walked twenty miles up those dirt roads before a ranger found me. Dig fast. I'll take over if you get tired."

He dug… and dug… and dug, but it wasn't going very quickly.

"Watch Katie while I give it a shot," I said.

I'd had more experience with a camp shovel. I had dug out my Jeeps numerous times but I had really built up my digging speed in the Marines. Foxholes were quick business and in Afghanistan the foxholes had come in handy, so much so that I almost preferred my foxhole to my tent. I had dug it to fit me and it fit me well. And so, in the search for my lost keys I dug like it was hard Afghanistan desert dirt and the dirt flew. Mick stood over me, arms folded, head cocked to the side, one eyebrow up.

"Okay, I'm impressed," he said. "I never expected to see that much dirt moved by someone like you."

The burrow was deep. After a while I imagined it filling the whole underside of the mountain and I could just imagine waaaay down deep a little ground squirrel was dragging my keys and saying, "Mommy! Can we keep it?"

And the mommy squirrel saying, "No! You don't know how to take care of it. Take it back up top and let it go." And the poor little squirrel did what I did and hid it in the barn or under his bed.

"You remember Jacobsen telling you you had to be prepared for anything if you went tracking with me?" I asked.

"Yeah."

"Well, this is the easy part."

"Hey, we lured him out with car keys. Maybe we can lure him out with something else," Mick said.

"Not any more we can't, and besides, he's not going to bring the keys with him when he does come out. About all the purpose it would serve is we could shoot him and have some real lunch."

"You wouldn't eat a ground squirrel, would you?"

"Depends on how mad I get at him," I replied.

"I mean, you wouldn't eat ground squirrel *meat*. Would you?"

"Sure, I've done it before. Rabbit, vole and gopher snake, too. Meat is meat."

"You can buy rabbit meat at the grocery store. That seems safe. But out in the wild?"

"Believe me, if you're hungry enough you will eat squirrel."

"How far are you going to dig before you give up?"

Sigh, "I don't think we're going to get the keys back. These little critters know a lot more about digging than we do."

"Mommy look! Ssssssnake!" Katie said pointing.

I grabbed her and leaped out of the hole.

"Holy smokes!" Mick said.

"Snakes like squirrel, too," I said. "Especially baby squirrels down there in their nest."

The snake slithered quickly over the mound of dirt and into the brush. Great, now I couldn't turn Katie loose either.

"You let me dig that hole when there was a rattlesnake down there?"

"I didn't know it was down there and, if you remember, I was the one down in the hole when it came out."

"So now what are we going to do?"

"We can start hiking. Or we can wait here. Or we can split up. There are problems involved with splitting up, though. I've found too many lost people who decided they could do better on their own than they could with the group, then they got turned around. When people are turned around they tend to do stupid things. There are other things to consider. We have limited diaper changing supplies, limited food, limited water. I suggest we sit tight and wait it out."

"But we're twenty miles down a four wheel drive road."

"And I've got friends out there who know all the places I've gotten into trouble. Kelly Green and Rusty both know I've come in here before. They'll check here… eventually."

"How much food do we have?"

"Nothing you would consider a meal, but I doubt we starve. Let's see," I said rummaging through the daypack, "A bag of cookies…"

"Cookie!" said Katie. I gave her one.

"A Ziploc bag of trail mix, four Zwieback cookies for Carson…"

"Cookie!" said Katie.

"These are baby cookies," I told her.

"My baby hungry," she said.

"If he's hungry he'll tell us," I told her.

"Three energy bars, four bottles of water, one bottle of formula."

"How long will that last us?"

"Well, Carson's the one who is going to be in trouble first."

"Don't you umm, like…"

"Maybe."

"What do you mean, maybe? Either you do or you don't."

"Well, it's complicated. First of all he was born in a cave and I didn't know how long we'd be stuck there. I had a gunman after me and no idea when he'd be off my tail. I thought I better start the milk production, just in case. So I let him nurse. But having a job where I have to be gone days at a time doesn't work well for nursing."

"Why?"

"Mick… okay… well… the milk builds up and builds up, you have to have some relief… so you feed the baby. Right?"

"Makes sense."

"If I'm on a search and I can't feed the baby, what am I supposed to do?"

He turned beet red. He had ideas.

"No, I'm not going to do that. Anyway, since nursing a baby and working search and rescue don't really go well together I weaned him as soon as I could. It hasn't been long. I suppose, if I had to, I could nurse him again. And I would before I'd let him go hungry. But I'd rather not. Then I'd have to start all over weaning him again. Another problem we have is… I am only seeing four diapers in here. A baby might go through four diapers in an hour… or a day. There's no telling."

"Hmm, so we need to get out of here in one day, max," he surmised.

"Right, well, diapers are not a life and death matter, but…"

"Umm, yeah, it's the *but* I'm worried about. We could hike for the road."

"It's thirty miles," I reminded him.

"*I* could hike for the road."

"Do you remember the way?"

"What do you mean? We just followed the dirt road."

"There are three intersections."

"Here," he said pulling out my sketchbook from the back of the truck. I kept a sketchbook in case I needed to sketch a track. It helped plant the tread more firmly in my mind. "I'll write a note to alert drivers and then it'll show me the way back, too. I just need to watch for the notes on the trees." He wrote on a page in big block letters "NEED RIDE!" and drew an arrow so the reader would know which direction he went. "That'll work, right?"

"Except that I didn't see any cars on the way in."

"That doesn't mean there aren't any there now."

This kid refused to give up. He just seemed bent on doing something that didn't include changing diapers. It was an odd situation to be in. On the job he outranked me, even though I had five years experience on him and he was a rookie cop. He was a level one and I was a level two, by choice. So if it came to a decision his rank outweighed my seniority, until the kids got involved. If he tried to do something that would endanger the kids he'd have a fight on his hands.

I remembered what it was like hiking out of this place. Two days I hiked. I was down to half an inch of water in a one-liter bottle. I had lived on trail mix for two days. I was tired and hungry and sunburned.

I had faith in Rusty and the rangers finding us but we might get hungry before that happened. My trouble radar was advising me to sit tight. My senior officer wanted to play Dudley Doright and go for help. My experience said don't let him. But, hey, he was young and fit. He just graduated from police academy. He should be able to run five miles, no problem.

So I let him go. I gave him a half bag of trail mix, a handful of cookies, two bottles of water, the sketch pad and charcoal pencil in a daypack and off he went. If all else failed I was still sitting tight. Rusty or the rangers could still find me. If they found me but they didn't find Mick, then I had a tracking job ahead of me. But I could do that, with some supplies.

After Mick set out on foot it was just the kids and I, stuck at the truck, with nothing to do. First Katie got bored, big surprise there.

"Mommy, let's go," she whined.

"We can't we lost the car keys," I explained.

"I find them," she said and started searching the truck. I let her. It was something to do.

Next Carson got hungry. I shook the bottle and prayed he didn't empty it. He nearly did. Then, of course because he had drank a whole bottle he wet his diaper. I felt the fabric and decided this was ration time so I waited. Diaper rash was treatable. He'd probably get diaper rash whether I waited or not. I was thankful Carson did not fight sleep the way Katie had. I didn't have to walk him and rock him and lull him and trick him into falling asleep. About ten minutes of fussiness, a warm snuggle and he was out. Whew!

"Mommy, no keys," Katie reported.

"That's because the squirrel took them," I told her.

"Da quirrel?"

"Yeah, he took them in his house and he won't give them back."

She pouted. Her pout said, "That mean squirrel! What's he doing taking our car keys?" She went over to the, now big, hole and looked inside.

"Keys gone," she said.

"Yup, long gone."

"Where Unca Mick go?"

"He went to find Daddy. Daddy has keys."

Katie lay down in the hole and stuck her arm in.

"No! No, baby, don't do that!" I scolded her. "Mommy squirrels don't like people in their house! She'll bite you!"

She jerked her arm out and stood up. She stomped the ground and said, "Bad quirrel! You come out!"

Oh boy, what a way to spend an afternoon.

"Mommy? Gotta go potty," Katie said.

"Good girl! That's a big girl to tell Mommy when you need to go potty! Good Girl!" I gushed. "When we're in the woods we have to go potty like the animals do."

I grabbed the baby wipes and headed for the bushes with Katie in tow. She looked rather skeptical but she did her thing and I helped her clean up. Then she ran off to explore.

"Nope! We can't run off," I said. "Carson is at the truck. We have to stay near the truck."

"Mommy, go track," she said.

"Maybe when Carson wakes up. He needs his nap, so let him sleep."

About five o'clock I got a surprise. A white van came bumping down the road. Two wheel drive. Plumber's van. It came to a stop on the road behind our parking place and out hopped Mick.

"What did I say?" he beamed. "It worked! Do we still have diapers?"

"Yes. Is there room back there for all of us?" I asked.

"This is better than a ride out!" Mick said, "He says he can get our keys back!"

"A plumber," I said skeptically.

"Yeah, Rupert, this is Cassidy and her two kids, Katie and Carson."

Rupert stepped around the side of the van. He was four hundred pounds of hair confined within a dirty, blue jumpsuit with the name Piper's Plumbing stitched on a pocket. Even the backs of his hands were covered in a light curly fuzz.

"Glad to meet you ma'am," Rupert said. "Where'd the keys go?"

"Right over here," Mick said, very proud of his ability to find help.

Rupert bent over the hole. He scratched at the stubble of a quickly growing five o'clock shadow.

"Hmm, nice piece of diggin' there, Mick."

"Thanks," Mick said, standing taller.

Rupert went to his van and pulled out a long snake. He tied a magnet to the end. He stuck the magnet to the side of the van and yanked it loose.

"Should be strong enough to latch onto a set of keys," he said.

He threaded the plumber's snake down into the ground squirrel's burrow. It took a few tries and some maneuvering but, by golly, it worked! About the fourth time he threaded it down the hole it came back out with my keys stuck onto the end of the snake.

"Yay! Keys!" said Katie.

"Thank you!" I told Rupert. "How much do I owe you?"

"Depends on how much trouble we have getting out of here," he answered. "What were you doing all the way down here, anyway?"

"Hiking," I said. "What were you doing in a plumber's van way down here? I know Mick didn't make it out to the highway."

"I was… You ain't a cop are you?"

"Me? No!" I sort of lied.

He looked at Mick. Hmm. "I was… exploring. Yup. I was exploring. Shoulda been working, but this job is shit. So I was just… driving…"

Mick and I looked at each other. I think we were both willing to let him go. After all, he did help us out of a big bind. But when Rupert went to put away his plumber's snake Mick was right there taking a long look through the back of the van.

"If I get stuck you'll pull me out?" Rupert asked.

"Yup, that was the deal," Mick said. "We'll see that you get back to your road."

"That's a hell of a drive."

"I know, but the van took the washouts real good. How much do I really owe you?" Mick asked.

"Off the books?" Rupert said.

"Yeah, off the books."

"Cause I'm not supposed to be here at all."

"I understand."

"Fifty bucks?"

"That's all? A tow truck would have charged a couple hundred to come back here."

"Yeah, well, I ain't no tow truck. Okay a hundred."

"Umm, can I pay you when we get to that little town up top? I don't have a hundred on me."

"What have you got?" Rupert asked him.

Mick looked in his wallet.

"Umm, twenty eight."

I slapped another forty in his hand.

"Good enough," said Rupert pocketing the cash.

Rupert followed us up the long, washed out, bumpy dirt road. Twice we had to help him over the washouts. When we got past the worst of it he walked up to the window of the Explorer and said, "That oughta do it. I think I can make it from here."

"Okay, thanks again, Rupert," I said. "I didn't think we'd get out of there tonight. Have a good evening."

"'Kay, bye."

"Why didn't I keep my mouth shut when he said fifty?" Mick grumbled as we drove away.

"It's okay. Last time I got stuck in there I couldn't even find a tow truck that would go in and get it. I had to drag out the Jeep with horses. My dad was out two horses and a ranch hand for a weekend. It was a mess. A bear invaded our camp. I think we got out of this pretty easily."

Easily, yes, but not without some repercussions. It took us a good long hour to get back up to the highway and then another hour to get out of the mountains. We were tired and hungry. But mostly I was concerned because Rusty would be home from work. He'd see Mick's car still there, know we were gone all day without supplies for an all day trip. What could have gone wrong? Knowing Cassidy it could mean anything…

When we pulled up Rusty came out the front door. He wasn't worried yet. His hands were not in his pockets nor was he running them through his hair.

His expression was one of patient concern.

"Report in to Schroeder on the double," he said to Mick.

"But," Mick started.

"Your shift is half over. You better salute and call him sir, too."

Mick jumped into his old Toyota Corolla and headed to town, a cloud of doom following him. He always had some fancy sports car in mind that he was saving up for, but so far I only saw him in the old Toyota.

"Will you help bail him out?" I asked. "It wasn't his fault we got stuck. Okay, it was his fault, but he couldn't help it if he was late. We were lucky we got out of there today. I thought you'd call out the troops and we'd be found tomorrow."

"Maybe you should tell me what happened," he said.

"We need to get the kids taken care of first. Katie's only eaten cookies and trail mix and Carson's diaper is full."

"I'm hungry," he said. "I'll call in a to-go order and you take care of the kids."

He called in the order and headed to town. One thing about living in the foothills is that it took almost the same time to cook something as it did to drive there to pick it up. Very handy, no killing time waiting for things to get done.

I gave Katie an apple.

"Don't eat the bones," she reminded herself. She had heard that phrase over and over every time she ate chicken. When she was a baby she did try to eat the bones and the cores of apples and pears, so now she applied the phrase to everything.

I changed Carson and gave him a warm bottle.

Rusty came home to a peaceful house and I thought he had forgotten about the rest of the day, but he hadn't. That night he settled down on the old brown couch and patted the seat beside him.

"Now, tell me what happened."

"We went to that abandoned campground that the Jeep got stuck in. Remember the one we had to take the horses to?"

He nodded.

"Everything went fine. We drove in and hiked and Mick got some tracking practice in and we were going to head back when Mick got this bright idea that we could lure a ground squirrel out of his burrow. Katie wanted to see it and Mick wanted to track it. So Mick dangled my keys in front of the hole and… the squirrel took the bait. Literally. He took my keys to the center of the earth. You had the other one and we couldn't call you. We tried digging. The burrow was too deep."

"I see you got your car keys back," he said.

"Yeah, we lucked out and some plumber who was just driving around in the hills picked up Mick as he was hiking out. The plumber got them out for us. Do we still have that old rod and reel out in the garage? We never use it."

"I think so."

"I'm going to make Mick a special lure for it, and he can go ground squirrel fishing to his heart's content."

Chapter 30

The next day I got out the old fishing rod. I had to replace the old fishing line. It was too brittle to reel in a one pound ground squirrel. I found three old keys, some aluminum foil and some crazy looking yarn that my neighbor, Hazel, had been trying to get rid of. I tied them all together into the most outlandish ground squirrel lure I could think of and saved it for the next time Mick wanted to go tracking.

It took him a while to show up again. Schroeder didn't appreciate his little escapade.

"Cassidy gets into enough trouble without your help!" Schroeder had bellowed.

"Whatever happens," I told Mick later, "just blame it on me."

"I can't do that!"

"I can't lose my job. And Schroeder will believe anything you say. If you tell him I went ground squirrel fishing he'll just hang his head in disbelief. But…he *will* believe you. And the good thing about it is *I don't get in trouble for it.* I don't know why. I guess he just blames the trouble gene but the worst he has done is back off. But then when they need me, they really need me. When you get to tracking good enough to cover their crime scenes they will need you, too."

"Have you ever seen Schroeder, really, really mad?" he asked.

"No, and I doubt you have either," I told him.

"Oh, man! I don't want to see him when he's really, really mad then."

"I doubt being half a day late for work would tick him off that much. When I've seen him mad he's gone all quiet. I bet he was putting up a mad front because you're still new. He knew he could get his point across."

"Damn right, he did. Are we tracking the desert today? You said you'd show me how tough the desert can be."

"Okay, but first I have something for you."

"Oh, no. We are not having ground squirrel for lunch. I won't eat it."

"If I was bringing ground squirrel for lunch I wouldn't tell you what it was until it was too late."

"Oh. Okay. Then what is it?"

I went to the garage and got out the old fishing pole and brought it to Mick.

"Here, fish for ground squirrels all you want," I told him.

He busted out laughing. "Are there ground squirrels in the desert?"

"You're kidding. You really want to try it out?"

"Sure! Why not? This could be entertaining."

"Well, okay… why not?"

Boy, did I make a mistake. I should have taken him to some remote hill in the middle of the desert, but I wanted to go someplace we wouldn't have to hike three days from if we got stuck. I went through all the contortions it took to get both kids ready again and we all got into the Explorer. I figured ground squirrels liked people food and people food could be found at picnic grounds so I drove to Devil's Punchbowl. Surely there were ground squirrels around the picnic grounds.

We hunted around for a little while until we found a squirrel burrow under a bush with a picnic table nearby. Mick settled in, sitting on the picnic table with his "bait" dangling in front of the squirrel's hole. Katie got bored so I put Carson in a backpack and we walked around the picnic grounds.

"Mommy! Quirrel!" she said pointing.

"Yes! Squirrel!" I said. "Too bad it isn't where Mick is."

Five minutes later, "Mommy! Quirrel!"

Everywhere we turned we were seeing ground squirrels. I kept an eye on Mick. A ground squirrel was sniffing for food under the picnic table but Mick couldn't see it because he was sitting *on* the picnic table. He jingled the keys. The ground squirrel cocked its head. This could take all day. I decided to lay a trail for Mick while he was distracted. I took off up the hill and let Katie run just a little ways ahead of me. I kept to the side of her so the tracks wouldn't be confusing to Mick. I led him over hard pack and rocks, sand and gravel. I was careful how I put down my tracks to give him just enough challenge without making my footprints invisible. Then I called Katie and headed back to the picnic ground. About half way back I began hearing voices.

"Yee haw!" said Mick loudly. "I got one! Cassidy! I got one!" There was excited scrambling around and I came on a scene from… okay, from I don't know where. There was Mick, standing on the picnic table, gazing down the ground squirrel burrow. And there was the ranger, standing just behind Mick, arms folded over his chest, looking decidedly unhappy. Mick was oblivious. He let the line play out as far as the ground squirrel would go. The ranger probably thought he had a nut case on his hands. When the line had played out Mick got down off the picnic table reeling in the excess line. He stood directly over the hole and began reeling the lure back in. Slowly, slowly. It looked like the squirrel was fighting him a little but that just made him more enthusiastic about getting the lure back, so he could really see if the squirrel would fight for his treasure.

About this time the ranger roared, "Boy! What in tarnation do you think you're doing?"

Mick nearly jumped out of his skin. I imagined a poor ground squirrel underground getting yanked into the roof of his house.

"Fishing for ground squirrels!" Mick said. Big mistake.

"And do you have a squirrel fishing license?" the ranger asked.

"Um, no sir! You see, I'm not going to keep them. This is more like catch and release fishing!"

The ranger frowned. "Ten pound test line. How big a squirrel were you planning to catch?"

"Hehe, that's a good one, sir."

Warren Randolph did not joke. He glared at Mick and narrowed his eyes.

"Do you have a squirrel hunting license?" Randolph repeated evenly.

"No, I'm not going to hurt the squirrels."

Being in law enforcement, Mick decided about then that he might be in just a little bit of a pickle.

"And how do you know you aren't hurting them? What are you using for bait?"

"Car keys," he blurted out.

While he was talking to the ranger the end of the pole was dipping and moving about.

"Let me see," the ranger said.

Mick buckled down to the task at hand. Feeling the steely glare of the ranger behind him, he reeled in the hapless critter who was fighting the line every bit of the way. When Mick pulled the ground squirrel out of its burrow it was hopping mad. It was chittering and chattering and its tooth was caught in a strand of yarn. Now what was he going to do?

"So, this is a catch and release program, is it?"

"Yes, sir."

"Then I suggest you do just that."

Mick stood over the angry squirrel. He needed thick leather gloves for what he was about to do, but he didn't have any. He grasped the squirrel gently but firmly over its shoulders. The squirrel darted out of his grasp. He reeled it in tighter and tried again. This time when he tried to grab hold of the squirrel it jumped backwards making Mick jump, too, but it was just the motion needed to free the squirrel. It dashed away still chattering like mad. Mick sat back with a huff.

"I think I'll give up ground squirrel fishing," he said.

"Good idea," said the ranger as he got out his citation book. Mick recognized that motion and his heart sunk.

"You can't write me up," Mick said.

"Who says I can't?"

"What are you going to cite me for?"

"Well, now, I don't know. Fishing without a license?" Warren said,

"Poaching?"

"But I didn't actually catch anything!"

"You don't have to catch something to be fishing."

I was a little worried about bailing him out, but at least I knew the ranger and he knew odd things were going to happen with me around.

"Warren? I gave him the fishing pole as a joke," I said walking up.

Warren Randolph rolled his eyes.

I had him.

"Trouble, what are you doing here?"

"We came up here for a tracking lesson, but our last tracking lesson went awry when a ground squirrel stole my car keys. I gave Mick the fake squirrel lure as a joke and he wanted to try it out, as a joke. He's not taking up poaching or squirrel fishing. He was just seeing if it would actually work again, just this once."

Randolph grunted in frustration. Of all the rangers he was the most regimented. Most of them were easygoing guys with a job to do. Warren Randolph was almost like a game warden, ready to jump on any misdeed with his famous citation book. Ninety percent of the citations issued came from Warren's book and he was proud of it.

"Look," I said, "confiscate his weapon, take it back to headquarters and give all the guys a good laugh. But don't write him up for a joke."

"Look Mommy! Quirrel!" said Katie.

"Yes! Nice squirrel, isn't he cute?"

"Quirrel's house?" she said toddling over to the ground squirrel's hole.

"Yup that's where he lives," I said.

Katie managed to smooth out the confrontation without even trying. Warren watched this little kid enjoying the great outdoors and he softened considerably. Katie batted her big blue eyes at him, grabbed his finger and pulled him toward the hole.

"Look! Quirrel!" she said pointing.

Carson helped by taking two big chunks of hair and pulling with all his might.

"Well, well, sport, that doesn't look very comfortable for your mom. Here, let go."

I was used to the pulling but I'd let Warren disentangle me if he'd forget about the squirrel fishing.

"Unca Mick, come on!" Katie said toddling off towards the tracks.

I was still tangled up with Carson and Randolph so Mick set down the fishing pole and ran after Katie.

"Uncle Mick?" Randolph asked.

"Katie thinks everybody is her uncle," I explained.

"Then who is this character?"

"He's a rookie cop. He showed some promise for tracking at academy so I have been teaching him to track."

"He's a cop, but he fishes for squirrels illegally on park property?"

"I told you, it was just a joke. There are no tourists around. Nobody's going to suddenly think squirrel fishing is a great sport. This was a one-time thing. Take away his fishing pole but don't write him up. It'll be a black mark on his record."

"How much of a rookie is he?"

"He graduated in January."

"*Humph*, when *I* graduated I had the code memorized. You wouldn't have caught me…"

"Yeah, I know and you can only eat one potato chip, too."

He snatched up the fishing pole, turned on his heel and marched off to his truck.

"Squirrel fishing…" he muttered as he got in. He drove away without stirring up dust.

Whew! That was close.

Chapter 31

"You let him take the pole?" Mick asked, incredulous.

"It was just an old fishing pole with some keys, foil and yarn tied to the line. I'm sure we can make another one, if it's that important to you. It was better than having you written up. Imagine standing before a judge and trying to explain why you were ground squirrel fishing! You'd get fined and laughed at and then it would hit the station. I think giving Warren the pole was the easiest way out of this."

"He's a jerk," Mick said.

"That's what every person says when you give them a ticket."

"Yeah, I still remember that first ticket like it was yesterday. In fact, it *was* yesterday. Thompson pulls the car over and he says, 'this one's all yours'. I think he must have known that gal. Usually he likes to talk to the girls. So I get out of the car and saunter up to the driver's window and I ask the woman for her license and registration. She was cute! Drove a cute car, too! And she stares at me and she says, '&%#$@!' and I repeated the request, patiently, like Thompson said I had to. I don't think she said much of anything I could understand. I figured I was never going to get a date, so I wrote her up."

"You mean if you thought she'd go out with you you'd have gone easy on her?"

"Well... I had to give her a ticket for something. Thompson pulled her over. So I was kind of stuck giving her the ticket."

"You gave out your first ticket yesterday?"

"Yeah, I hope they aren't all like that."

"No, you get all kinds. There are the scared ones who call you sir and apologize all over the place. There are the guys who just say, 'oh damn, not again.' Then there are the little old ladies who are glad to get pulled over so they can talk to a man in uniform. Here. Track. We want to get back by lunch time."

By then Carson was back in the backpack and pulling on my hair again and Katie was running circles around us. Maybe Katie would wear herself out. She approached a cactus slowly and carefully.

"Mommy! Ouch!" she announced.

"That's right! Don't touch. That's a cactus. It's sharp! Ouch!"

She reached out with one finger and touched it gently, then jerked her hand back.

"Ooo, ouch," she whispered. The cactus had earned her respect.

Mick was glued to the trail and I was glued to Katie. The tracking progressed very slowly.

"So what do you think of all this wide open dirt?" I asked Mick.

"It doesn't give," he said.

"Sometimes. Sometimes it can be so sandy you can't read tread. The wind erases tracks real fast in the desert."

"How much tracking have you done in the desert?" Mick asked.

"A lot. I've tracked more coyotes than people. People aren't attracted to the desert for some reason."

"I wonder why?" he said sarcastically.

"I've had a few, though, one kid went out dirt biking and crashed. Another kid took off trying to let the desert kill him. We talked him out of it. It's not a nice way to die. Antonio's wife went missing. I tracked down Eva and their baby. You have to be prepared to track in any setting."

"You ever get called *here*?"

"To Devil's Punchbowl? I've hiked here from the back way on a search, but most of the calls here don't require tracking. The calls here are to help tourists who fall off the rocks and hurt themselves. There's people around to call a ranger, so there's no tracking involved."

"What did you do *here*?" he asked about the tracks he was studying.

"You give up too easily. If you were on a search and I wasn't there, what would you do?"

He didn't mind having to figure things out for himself, another thing that made him good for this job. When you're the tracker you're all there is. No EMT is going to bail you out. It's read the tracks or beat the bushes. So far reading the tracks had paid off no matter how stumped we got.

"We haven't had a call yet," Mick said.

"Tourist season will start when the weather warms up. We'll get plenty of calls then."

As time wore on I began helping him more. I was going to have two hungry kids, soon.

When we got home he didn't want to stay for lunch.

"I better get going. Don't want to be late this time."

Katie and I ate leftover spaghetti for lunch and Carson fell asleep with his bottle. Katie fell asleep two minutes before Carson woke up, so it was a long day.

That evening I had two kids raring to go and I was ready for my nap. I cooked dinner. I always cooked extra so there would be something in the refrigerator for lunches.

This day my leftovers all disappeared. We were just sitting down to dinner when the doorbell rang. Rusty got up to answer it. When Rusty came back he was followed by Kelly Green grinning ear to ear.

"Are you missing this?" he said holding up the rod and reel.

"I'm not. But Mick Colton is," I said, setting out another place setting.

Kelly joined us at the table. "I never saw Warren Randolph laugh so hard," he said.

"Warren Randolph laughs?" Rusty asked.

"He walks into the station, oh umm, sorry, into *headquarters*, and says, 'Any of you boys ever caught yourself a ground squirrel fisherman before?' and we all agreed that was a new one to us. He shows us this rod and reel and the outlandish lure on the end. 'Believe it or not it worked!' He says, 'this rookie cop out at the punchbowl hooked himself one mean little varmint. He was lucky he didn't get bit.' We asked him if he threw the book at him and he huffs, 'nah, Trouble showed up and bailed the kid out. Her and them kids. First I got me a fishin' without a license charge and next thing I know Trouble's got me hogtied. I just couldn't do it.'"

"So how'd you end up with the fishing pole?" Rusty asked.

"When Warren got his story out I said, 'hey, that's my fishing pole! I lent it to Cassidy last summer!' so he gave it to me."

"Well, take it back. Put it in the Bad Idea Museum. If I take that back Mick will be out trying it again. So far his luck has been pretty good. Once the squirrel took his bait and the next time he actually caught one."

"It was a fluke," said Kelly. "There aren't that many squirrels that will go for a bunch of keys."

"Still, I'd rather not deal with it. I'm trying to teach him to track, not get him in trouble."

"What made you come up with this?" Kelly asked holding up the lure.

"Trouble. And I was trying to make it as a joke. Mick just carries a joke a little too far for Warren Randolph."

"Everybody carries a joke too far for Randolph," Kelly said.

"I saw a quirrel!" said Katie.

"You did?" said Kelly enthusiastically. "Was he a big one?"

"I saw his house!" Katie said.

"Where does a squirrel live? High in a tree? Down on the ground?"

"He lives in a hole," she explained.

"Remember that old campground we had to pull my Jeep out of?" I asked.

"Yeah, how could I forget? You were missing two days. I didn't even know it was down there until you showed it to me. I'm supposed to know those mountains inside out and then you find a whole campground I was never told about."

"Well, if I ever go out tracking and don't show, keep that place in mind. I almost got stuck in there again."

"Seems to me," said Rusty, "you'd best stay out of there."

"But, it's a cool place. The animals know it's safe. Deer visit it. Katie saw a squirrel. It's peaceful…"

"Until trouble shows up," Rusty said.

"Anyway, it's just something to keep in mind."

"Katie, what does a squirrel say?" Kelly asked.

Katie thought about it. It took a while for her to decide. She knew it wasn't moo, or meow, or neigh, but she couldn't remember what they said exactly, so she said, "Yummy! Keys!"

I should have thrown the rod and reel away, or at least hidden it back in the garage. But it sat around and Mick saw it on his next visit.

"Hey! You got it back. All right!"

"I thought you were through ground squirrel fishing," I said.

"I was. But then I got to wondering just how deep those holes go. If I can get another ground squirrel to take the bait I'll let him carry it into his hole and put a mark on the line. Then when I reel him in I can tell exactly how far he went."

Oh no, not again.

"I can only talk Randolph out of writing you up once. If he catches you again it's a repeat offense. He can do whatever he wants."

"Okay! So I won't let him catch me," he said.

"Take the pole home. You're on your own with this one," I said backing out of the whole situation.

"Thanks!" he said and put the pole into the trunk of his car.

Next thing I knew he was coming back with pictures.

"Look," he said excitedly, "my girlfriend took these."

I leafed through the pictures. One showed him holding the pole above his head and a tiny speck of black in the sky.

"What did you do?" I asked.

"I caught a raven! He liked the shiny keys and snatched it off the ground. I was flying him like a kite!"

"Mick, you've got to put an end to this. It was a one-time joke."

"I'm just having a little fun with it. I found out how deep a ground squirrel burrow is. We'd have had to dig for a long time. I'm glad we changed our plan on that one!"

"So, how deep is a ground squirrel burrow?"

"Oh, about twenty feet. Unless you count the last squirrel I caught. He ran into his hole and out his back door. I didn't see him get away and the line is going out and going out and then it stops. Aha! I thinks, this is going to be good! I put a mark on the line, and I start reeling in the lure. There's no squirrel on the end but about ten feet away I see the brush moving. Something's in the brush! Maybe I can track it! So I put the pole down and the critter stops. I didn't want to scare it away so I went back to the pole and when I reel it in the critter starts up again! I inched over that away and I'm reeling the line and the critter moves and I can see it! It's… it's the lure. The durn old squirrel hauled the lure through his house, out the back door and into the woods. He pulled a fast one on me."

I smiled, imagining him trying to track his own lure.

"So, now that you know how deep a ground squirrel burrow is I hope you will drop the whole thing."

"Oh, I did. Only now Tex wants to give it a try."

"And you let him?"

"Yeah."

"Did you warn him that he could get arrested?"

"Umm, no."

"We're not doing any tracking until you call Tex and at least warn him about the consequences of playing with that thing in the wrong place at the wrong time."

He gave me a *spoiled sport* look and went out to his car to get his cell phone.

When he came back in he said, "He's on his way. When he found out we were tracking he wanted to come, too."

"Why don't you two go tracking then?" I said.

"Aw, I promised him cookies."

"You can't promise him cookies. What if I don't have any?"

"Of course you have some. You always have some."

I'd have to remember that.

Chapter 32

Tex and Mick were in about the same boat as far as wheels went, except while Mick drove a beat up old Toyota Corolla, Tex drove a beat up old GMC pickup with a big star of Texas sticker proudly displayed on the back window. I could hear the truck long before I could see it.

When he rang my doorbell he stood back, ready for anything. First was Shadow. For some reason Shadow knew Tex's truck. And I don't think it was the sound of it. I think it had something to do with a food smell associated with it. Shadow looked at Tex expectantly.

"What does he see in you?" Mick asked.

"It's the smoker," Tex said.

Mick looked at him like he was crazy.

"I got a smoker in the bed of my truck. I make jerky in it."

"You make jerky? As in cooking? Aw come on man, you got better things to do than cook tough meat."

"You wouldn't say that if you had some. Hey pooch, you want some jerky?"

Shadow recognized the phrase *you want*. He barked his answer. Tex reached into his pack and tore off a small piece and tossed it to Shadow. Shadow snatched the little bite out of the air.

"So, are we just standing around or are we tracking?" Tex asked.

"We're getting ready to track," I said. "You can't do anything quickly with two kids involved."

"Hey, Tex gets to carry the squirt," Mick said.

"What? Why me?" Tex answered.

"Because you have the shortest hair," Mick informed him.

"What does my hair have to do with it?"

"If Cassidy has to carry that kid very far her hair's going to be shorter than yours. The little guy pulls it out."

"And that's supposed to make me want to carry him?"

"Okay, I'll carry him," Mick said. "If I carry him I don't have to change diapers."

"What kind of a tracking day is this?"

"I'm just going tracking. You two can do what you want," I said pulling Katie's coat onto her.

When I went to get Carson he had fallen asleep on his blanket. I picked him up and put him in his car seat.

"Pray he stays that way," Mick said.

"He'll last about fifty-five minutes," I said.

"Then step on it," Mick said.

I decided he was right so we drove some place close. I drove down Lost Hills Road and turned on a dirt road about two miles down.

"This is where I saw my first mountain lion," I told the guys.

"Cool, what was he doing?" Tex asked.

"Umm, eating," I said vaguely. "I stood and watched him for a while because I was scared he'd see me if I moved."

"You were not." Tex said. "From what I heard you're not scared of anything. The guys kind of wish you were."

"There are some things I am scared of. And some things I used to be afraid of, like dogs. I'd had a pack of fighting dogs turned loose on me, and for a long time after that I was scared of dogs. Not my dog. But any big, powerful dog. German shepherds, Dobermans, pit bulls. I made a point of getting over that. I like dogs, I really do, but for a while I had to force myself not to turn tail and run."

"I think the stories are exaggerated," said Tex. "You couldn't have survived all the things they say you did."

"That's fine with me."

"They couldn't possibly be true," Tex said.

"Okay."

"That's all. Just okay?"

"Yeah, I don't care if you believe them or not."

"You don't?"

"No."

"Hell, I would! I'd want them to believe that I was kidnapped and jumped out of the van and survived by my wits hiking for two days up a river and eating gopher snake to stay alive."

"Why?" I asked.

"Well, because, it's adventure man! You'd be, like, a legend!"

"And?"

"Umm, well, you mean that's all?"

I pulled over and turned around. Katie was disappointed but she didn't speak up. Something was up.

"I'd rather forget it, if it's all the same to you. The hike and the survival tricks are nothing. I can remember that. It's the smell of greasy tires, the feeling of being driven to who knows where, memories of being beaten, gagged and tied up with a pillow case over my head I can do without. I'd like to forget the impact of the road when I jumped out of a van chugging thirty miles an hour up a steep hill and I'd like to forget the instant of decision it takes to jump off a cliff rather than face some guys that were going to haul me away to be beaten some more."

Two sets of eyes stared back at me. Nobody said anything, so I turned around and I was going to start the Explorer up again but I thought better of it. I turned back around and told the guys, "If you hear these stories, and you want to know if they are true, don't ask Rusty. It's harder on him than it is on me. When he remembers one of those times he becomes… protective. I guess that's the kindest way to put it. Let him forget. You have to remember that when I am going through one of these trouble bouts I am busy dealing with it. And he is… he's scared to death it's going to be the end of me. Being a detective, his brain goes into overload. He knows what could happen, what would happen to most people in my situation. You can't blame him for his reaction. He does his best to find me, to stop whatever situation I have fallen into. But there is always that chance that this time he might not make it in time. I might not be able to jump from the van and tumble down a cliff. So… don't ask Rusty. Okay?"

Gulp. "Okay," they answered.

The stories were true, they thought.

Damn. Couldn't even a rookie take me just for who I was? A mom. A stay at home mom who could track.

Tex was on a roll, though.

"You took down a guy who was shooting up a school?"

"I was the only armed person nearby."

"You were that girl trapped in a mine for three days after an earthquake?"

"A very dark camping trip with a kid from north Texas. Trevor."

"Do you know how the whole country hung on that news story?"

"I know how Rusty hung on minute by minute progress. I know I couldn't see a thing when they pulled me out. I know everybody else was a lot more keyed up than I was."

"I saw your wedding on TV!" Tex said, realization dawning. "I was at my mom's house and she just had to watch it."

"And I found the minister on a search. He was one of my ten sixty-fives."

"Hey, I know a celebrity!" Tex said.

"You don't know the half of it," I said.

"What do you mean?"

"All that hoopla over the wedding and they missed the honeymoon. The plane crash, survival in the woods of Minnesota… Let's go tracking. I'll feel better if I can get out and track a little."

I started the truck again and pulled back onto the dirt road. About a quarter mile farther up there was a little clearing.

"Oh man, this is going to be tough tracking. You can't even see the ground," Mick said.

"Another thing you have to deal with on searches," I said. I put the truck in park and pocketed the keys.

"I'll carry Katie so my tracks have more weight to them. That will help a little."

"We don't need help," Tex bragged and Mick gave him a warning look.

"You don't?"

"No."

"Okay, I'll carry Katie because I'm the mom, how about that?"

That sounded reasonable to him. I put the pack on and Mick lifted Katie and set her into it. Everybody knew their job.

"Go Mommy, Go!"

"First we need to put Carson in his pack, too."

Carson was still sleeping deeply. I picked up his limp form and put him in the other backpack, then lifted it so Mick could get his arms through the straps.

"I wish I could sleep like that!" said Mick.

I held up the daypack, "Who wants to be in charge of the c-o-o-k-i-e-s?"

"Cookie!" said Katie. Shoot, I couldn't even spell it any more.

"That sounds like a job for Tex Ward," Tex said. "Okay fearless leader, give us some tracks and don't go easy on us."

"Tex, you don't know what you're asking," Mick said. "If she does that we won't get out of sight of the truck."

"Ha, we'll see about that," Tex boasted.

While Mick tried to talk some sense into Tex I took off into the woods. I walked normally, not the heavy footed walk I usually did for Mick. The two men looked around on the ground.

"You asked for it. *You* track her," said Mick. "You'll have to get down close to the ground to see any sign of a track at all."

I didn't look back to see Tex confidently standing over the tracks, then go *hmm*, then bend over the tracks and finally get down on hands and knees. I did check back after the guys never caught up to my slow walk and I found them twenty feet from the Explorer.

"How far did you go?" Tex asked.

"Not far, maybe a quarter mile. What's wrong? Having trouble?"

"Me? No, not at all," Tex lied.

"Good! Mick, do you want your own trail?"

"No, I'm having fun watching Tex."

I let Katie out of her backpack.

"Don't walk on the tracks," I told her. "Come this way. Let's look for squirrels." Then to the guys, "I'll stay within hearing distance and I'll rescue you when Carson wakes up."

"Quirrels?" said Katie.

"Yeah, find a squirrel house," I told her.

She started poking around the bases of trees. At least she had learned something about squirrels.

Half an hour later the guys had moved on, about five more feet. They were bent over the tracks quietly saying things like, "What do you think? Is that it? It's so hard to tell..."

Mick's up and down movements were jostling Carson around so I took him out of the pack and went to the truck.

I pulled out the diaper bag and opened the back hatch to give me a changing area.

"Hey there! Carson! Peek-a-boo!"

He smiled and winked and kicked his feet.

"Those are Cassidy's tracks, good luck." The voice wasn't Mick's or Tex's. "It's easier to look for non-tracks when you're tracking Cassidy."

"What do you mean non tracks?" Tex asked.

"With Cassidy you look for flat spots. See how the dirt has more texture to it here, but not here? It's been flattened. That's Cassidy's track. She's not going to leave tread or lines unless they are disguised by natural things to distract you from the real track."

"Yes, sir," Mick said.

I looked up and there was Chase Downing talking with Mick and Tex. I finished changing Carson's diaper and bundled him back up again.

"You don't have to call me sir unless we're in uniform. Today I'm just Chase. Got it?"

"Got it."

"Where did *you* come from?" I asked as I walked over.

"Just checking on the progress," Chase said.

"How did you know where we were?"

"I stopped by the house. Nobody was home," he said as if that explained everything.

"Where's the Bug?"

"It's hiding. Just like I taught it to."

"Unca Chase! Do it again!" Katie said.

"Do what?" I asked.

"I swear that kid has the memory of an elephant. Let me see, I have to see if there is one," he said as he fished around in his pocket. He palmed a quarter and then pretended to pull it out of Katie's ear.

Katie looked at the quarter wide eyed and shook her head. She poked her finger in her ear. No quarter.

"I have it?" she asked.

"What are you going to do with it?" Chase asked her.

"I don't know."

"Then let's let Mom keep it for you," he said handing me the quarter.

"Me see!" Katie said so I handed her the quarter. She examined it carefully and then placed it back in my open hand. I stuck it in my pocket.

"I see you've been working with them," Chase said, indicating Mick and Tex.

"Yeah, Mick shows up about once a week and we manage to get a little tracking in. We're kind of limited on time with the kids along."

"Are they able to track that trail?"

"No, but Tex asked for it. I figure if he wants to try a challenge it's good for him. It gets him to think. They'll get more of a variety when tourist season starts. You didn't come all the way up here just to check on a couple of rookies."

"I came up here… because I shouldn't be down there," he said.

"Why? What's going on down there?"

Down there was San Diego and the California/ Mexico border. There could be a dozen reasons why Chase might have to lay low for a while. It didn't surprise me that he had cleared out. It just surprised me to see him down a little dirt road in the Angeles Forest when he had no clue where I was.

"The price has gone up. I rake my yard every night."

"That's a big job."

Chase's yard stretched to the highway one direction and across the desert to a mountain the other direction.

"I don't rake all of it, just enough so I can tell the place has been checked out. And I use the Bug and drag a board over it. I don't take a little garden rake to it. The wrong tracks have been appearing in the wrong places. I'd like to live a while longer, so I cleared out."

"How is Rusty's family?"

"Fine, Cody's been working at the zoo until the kayak place opens up again. He likes the safari uniform. He has his picture taken with girls and a giraffe or elephant in the background."

"Sounds like he's right at home there. How's Greasy Joe?"

"Greasy."

"How's Slick?"

"Slick."

"How's Juan Garcia?"

"Slick."

"The Border Patrol and the BORSTAR guys?"

"Fine, Taz suggested I get lost for a while. I was making things difficult for them. So I gave them a break."

"Hey, you want a break. Why don't you choose a trail and take these guys out on a real tracking lesson. They need to learn these mountains. Take them out of Creekside. Show them the hideout and Trent's Cave."

"Trent's Cave is gone."

"Ha! You just think it's gone. Carson will tell you it is very much there. He was born in it. I've been there twice since the big explosion. In fact, I'll make you a bet you can't find the way in."

"How'd you find it?"

"I tracked a curious little kid. She thought it was a pirate cave."

"She'd be right about that."

"So, what do you say? You want to take a tracking trip up the canyon?"

Chase eyed the two rookies.

"I'll talk to Schroeder," Chase said.

"Stay for dinner tonight."

"It's a deal. Now, let me show you how to track Cassidy. You can't treat her trail like any lost camper. For one thing she always knows exactly what she's doing and you have to put yourself in her moccasins."

Chase helped them track the short loop I laid for them.

"That's it?" he asked when they were back within earshot.

"We're working with the attention span of a three year old," I informed him. "When the kids get hungry we have to clear out."

"Just give her a c-o-o-k-i-e," said Mick.

"Cookie!" said Katie.

"Yeah, cookie!" said Tex.

"Hey, I'll take one, too," said Mick.

"Galleta," said Chase.

"Yeah, I guess that's the next step," I replied.

"A guy ate a what?" Mick asked.

"A cookie," Chase said.

"Cookie!" said Katie.

I gave up and passed the cookies around.

Chapter 33

Rusty enjoyed having Chase stay for dinner. He got to catch up on the family news and hear the latest stories from the police force down in San Diego.

Katie liked having company, too. Things were different when company came. People were more animated. They played with her. When her plate was mostly clean she asked me, "I get down?" and I hesitantly said yes and took her out of her high chair. She ran around the table and stood before Chase.

"Do it again!" she said expectantly.

Chase fished in his pocket again and pretended to pull the quarter from Katie's ear. Her smile was instantaneous and she took the quarter from Chase but when she looked at the quarter her little brow furrowed.

"Not mine," she said. "Mine gots a horsy."

It had been hours since Chase pulled the first quarter out of her ear. How could she possibly remember which quarter was hers? I stuck my hand in my pocket and brought out her quarter. Sure enough, it was the Kentucky state quarter and it had a horse on it. I passed it to Chase and he tried again. This time when he pulled "her" quarter out of her ear she was jubilant. She clapped her hands and held it up for all to see, "Mine horsy!" she announced.

To me this was very odd. I didn't even expect Katie to remember Chase and not only did she remember him and his magic trick, but she remembered what coin he had pulled out of her ear that morning. Why would a three year old care what was on a coin? I mentally filed this little incident away and paid closer attention to the workings of my daughter's mind.

Though it seemed to the other officers that Mick and Tex got to go on a mini vacation, Schroeder approved the tracking trip with Chase and the guys scrambled to find camping gear. I couldn't loan them my search gear. I might need it if I got a call from Strict. But I looked out in the garage for backup gear that I kept. Good useable camping gear was never discarded. Since I'd had such a variety of mishaps in the woods I knew it was possible at any time to need a new stove, tent, or sleeping bag. I kept old gear around as long it might serve a useful purpose. So, I was able to loan Mick Rusty's old sleeping bag and pack. I assume they found the other gear they needed because next thing I knew I had peace and quiet around my house. It was just the kids and I during the day. Wow! How long had it been since I had a day without a call from Mick, either asking a question, or wanting to go out tracking. The first day I kept expecting the phone to ring and I expected to have to pack up the kids and hit the trail. I couldn't believe I was relieved to be able to stay home. Usually I had the opposite problem being cooped up at home with the trail calling. I stuck a load of laundry in the washer, washed up the dirty dishes and… and…

"Jump!" Katie called from the living room. About the only purpose the living room served was it looked nice, and contained a climbable sofa that Katie loved to jump off of. I ran to the living room and got there a half second too late. Off the arm she jumped and landed flatfooted, bursting into tears.

"Waaaahhhh Mommmmmy!"

I sat down on the floor next to her. "It's okay kiddo, it'll go away in a minute. That's why I don't like you to jump. Jumping can hurt."

In a few minutes she was still sniffling but her feet had settled down.

"Jump again?"

"It'll hurt again," I said but watching her jump convinced me maybe she was big enough to learn her lesson the hard way.

About that time there was a cry from a bored Carson who wondered where I went. Even at home I was on call.

"Let's go outside and play," I suggested.

I picked up Carson and Katie ran to the back door. They only got to play outside when I was there to watch them. I thought Katie would stay in the yard but I didn't trust wild animals to stay out. Katie ran to the slide and climbed up lithely.

"Slide down!" I told her as I climbed up with Carson. After she slid down I slid down with Carson on my lap.

"Can I slide with Carson?" Katie asked.

"Climb up," I told her. When she got up top I placed Carson on her lap. "Hang onto him and I'll catch him at the bottom. Wait for me to get to the bottom."

I jogged to the bottom of the slide and stood, arms outstretched.

"Okay!" I called to her. She pushed off and Carson slipped, wide eyed. Katie tried to correct and they both ended up slipping down the long, slick slide sideways. About halfway down Katie had slipped around totally backwards and Carson was flailing around. Uh oh! How was I going to catch two kids at once? I braced myself for a tangle of crying kids. Katie hit first knocking me over backwards and then Carson got launched off the end of the slide and I caught him as he finished pinning me flat to the ground. I went down with an, "*ooof!*"

Katie laughed, "I do it again! Please Mommy!"

"No, not until you can hold onto him. You need to be a little bigger. Eat your vegetables and maybe you'll be bigger soon."

"Can I slide by myself?"

"Of course, as long as you slide and don't jump. You can only jump if Daddy can catch you."

Katie climbed off me and I struggled to my feet holding a squirming Carson. As I stood up an odd track caught my eye. It was a man's footprint. I ruled out Rusty, Chase, Tex and Mick. It was small for a man. I put Carson in the baby swing and gave him a good long push then I took a closer look at the track. I followed to the next track and the next. I had an uneasy feeling. People didn't accidentally stumble across my house. It was by itself on a rural road. My closest neighbor was a quarter mile up the road.

Having two kids complicated these things. If I'd been alone I would have followed the tracks and drawn as much as I could out of them but I didn't want to do that with two kids in tow. I didn't know what I'd find at the end of the trail. I couldn't think of any good reason for a person to be poking around the back of my house. My trouble radar pinged lightly. I went back and pushed Carson again. As long as he was moving he'd be happy. I took note of all the information I could draw from the few tracks visible from the kid's playground. Small man, size six shoe, hundred forty pounds, worn shoes, not tennis shoes, not boots, not dress shoes, something with little tread that was similar to dress shoes, an old work shoe of some kind, wide toed, worn heel, occasional drag to the right foot, not enough to make me think he was injured, more like the tired walk of a man who was used to walking. The stride led me to believe he was little taller than I was. Asian? Hispanic?

"Mommy, what you doing?" Katie asked.

"Just tracking," I answered her absentmindedly.

"Me track, too!"

"We're not going for a hike. We need to stay home."

"Me track, too!"

"Can you see the track?" I asked pointing at the ground. "See the shoe print? It's a track."

She squatted down and looked at the dirt.

"Tha's a track?"

"Yeah! Can you see it? It looks like a shoe."

"I see it!"

"You do?"

"Yes!"

"Can you trace it? Show me what it looks like. Trace the lines."

"Huh?"

I reached down and started the line that made up the side of the shoe.

"See? Trace it. Like Mommy."

She poked her finger into the dirt and tried to follow the line around. She wasn't very successful, but she came close enough to show me that she did indeed see the track.

"When people walk they leave tracks on the ground," I explained. "When Mommy goes tracking I am watching for tracks like this on the ground. This is a man's track. Put your foot in the dirt and push down."

She stuck her foot out and pressed her track into the dirt.

"See? There's Katie's track!"

"Mine? My track?"

"Yeah. You make Katie tracks whenever you walk in the dirt."

This was news to her. She started walking around in the dirt watching behind her to see her tracks forming. She was fascinated by them just as she had been by her shadow when she first noticed there was a mysterious darkness that followed her every move. At first she was worried about her shadow. She tried to pick it up, and trick it by moving when the shadow wasn't looking. Rusty's mom had home movies of Katie trying to catch her shadow. Her discovery of her tracks was similar, though not as alarming to her. She knew she made those tracks herself so they weren't scary.

"Mommy! Can I see Carson's tracks?"

"Sure, after the swing slows down."

She ran over and grabbed the chain on the swing and it came to an abrupt halt yanking her off her feet. She got up and dusted herself off.

"That wasn't nice. Carson likes to swing," I scolded.

"Show me!" she said.

Sigh, I took Carson out of his swing and set him down feet first in the dirt. Katie got down on all fours to examine the little footprints.

"Carson's tracks are feet!"

"That's because he isn't wearing shoes. He'll wear shoes when he starts walking."

This was a new discovery, too. She sat down and yanked off her shoes and ran around making barefooted tracks, giggling to herself.

"Look Mommy! Feet tracks! Show me your feet tracks!"

I sighed and took off my shoes and walked around barefooted, too. She examined my footprints and announced, "Big," then to her footprints, "little" and to Carson's "littler."

"And Daddy's are bigger," I explained.

She laughed, "Big, big daddy feets!"

Rusty was a bit puzzled when he walked in the front door and Katie dragged him to the back door telling him, "Take your shoes off, Daddy!"

He sat down on the old brown couch and took her in his lap. She squirmed out and grabbed at his foot.

"What's going on?" he asked.

"Katie discovered foot prints today. She wants to see your tracks up against mine. She knows mine are big but she wants to see that yours are bigger."

"Oh, okay," he said and took off his shoes. He tended to be a bit tender footed outdoors, but he followed her out the back door anyway.

"Come here, Daddy," she said leading him to my footprints. "See? Mommy's feet! Mine feet! Carson's feet! Daddy feet!"

I wondered how she remembered where the tracks were. Most people would just see a very busy patch of dirt and I bet that's what Rusty thought when he saw it, too.

"Walk, Daddy, walk feet tracks," Rusty walked around tender footedly and let Katie follow them and see what they looked like. She seemed pleased. She squatted down and traced one of the tracks. "Big Daddy feet," she said to herself. I went back to the kitchen.

"Well, that was different," Rusty said as he came back in. "Were you like that when you discovered tracks?"

"No, I was older and I figured them out myself. I got curious about what the marks were on the ground and when I followed them there was frequently a ranch hand on the other end making more of them."

"When is Chase due back?" Rusty asked.

"Probably tomorrow. You know he is never very specific about his plans but I doubt Mick and Tex can be gone more than a few days. The only reason they got the time off at all is because it is more of a training trip than a camping trip."

"I wish he'd get here. He's making me nervous."

"How can he make you nervous by being away? He's away most of the time."

"I think he has a tail," Rusty said.

The odd tracks I'd seen earlier came to mind. I wondered if there was anything left of them after Katie's barefooted exploration of the back yard.

After dinner and cleanup I waited until Rusty was busy playing with the kids and I slipped out the front door. The guys had taken Mick's car on the tracking trip. The Bug was a two seater Baja Bug rebuilt for taking Chase deep into the desert on the California/Mexico border. Tex's old truck had a bench seat, but for some reason guys aren't comfortable being buddy buddy close unless it's buddy buddy close with a cute girl in between. The Bug sat next to my driveway in an area that wasn't sure whether it was part of the lawn or not. There was some grass, but patches of dirt fought for dominance. It was a little hard to read because Chase had arrived a few days ago, but in a way that helped my cause. Chase's tracks were faint but the more recent tracks stood out. Whoever had been in the backyard had been particularly interested in Chase's Bug. I noticed that Chase had worked on it since the last time I rode in it. The windows were gone and there was webbing over the windows like there is on some racecars. I wondered why Chase would do that. It seemed like a bad move. The car would be cold in the winter and terribly windy to drive. Then I saw the ragged edge of glass down in the door panel and understood. He hadn't removed the windows. They had been knocked out. I ran my finger along the bottom of the window opening and a hand reached out and grabbed mine. I jumped back, yanking the man into the door of the car, but he hung on tight.

"Wha' choo know about the man who drive this car?" he asked.

"Nothing," I said nervously.

"I know. You know dis man. Or he no come to your house."

"Let me go," I said.

"I tink not. I tink you tell me."

"I'm not going to tell you anything."

"Look," he said, "I find dis in the de car. Very useful, I tink."

He tried to slap a handcuff onto my wrist but I yanked him into the door again. His head smashed into the webbing. I gave it a kick and yanked my hand free. I ran toward the house. I had a rifle hidden by the front door. He opened the door of the Bug and ran after me tackling me and smashing me into the front door of my house. The noise alerted Rusty and he came to the door to investigate. When he opened the door I fell into the living room and the scruffy Mexican man stood face to face with Rusty. One hit and an old 9mm pistol clattered to the porch, a reach and a pull by Rusty and the guy was face against the wall of the house. Rusty took the handcuffs from him, bent his arms behind him rather painfully and cuffed his hands.

"Thanks for bringing your own cuffs," Rusty said. "I hope you brought the keys, too, or you may be stuck for a while. Now what are you doing here and, more importantly, what have you done to my wife?"

"I do not ting!" he said nervously.

"Cass?" Rusty asked.

I couldn't say anything without giving information to both parties so I only stated things the guy already knew.

"He was hiding in the Bug," I said.

"And what were you doing at the Bug? Ch…"

"Ten twelve!" I said quickly cutting him off. Rusty's eyes narrowed at his captive. Ten twelve was the code for radio transmissions that said to be discreet, that there were other ears. It was the only thing I could think of in an instant to stop Rusty from telling the guy about Chase. In a way, even that gave him more information than I wanted him to have. It said these people know the code, just like Chase Downing.

"Go get me the telephone and then take care of the kids. I'll take care of this," he said.

I went into the house and grabbed the telephone and Rusty's sidearm and took them to the porch. I didn't think a cuffed, unarmed man would try anything with Rusty but I wasn't going to trust him anyway.

"Mommy?" Katie said looking for an adult.

"Be careful," I told Rusty, then to Katie, "I'm right here, baby. Daddy will be right back. Where's Carson?"

"Carson wants a cookie."

"Oh, he does, does he? Are you sure it's not Katie that wants a cookie?"

"Okay!"

"You just had dinner."

She looked disappointed and led me to the den where Carson had tangled himself up in his blanket. I untangled him but my thoughts were outside.

"What was Daddy playing with you when he got up?" I asked.

"Hide and seek," she said.

"Who was hiding?"

"Daddy."

"Do you want to hide?"

"Okay!"

"Just don't go outside."

I hid my eyes, counted to twenty picked up Carson and walked around the house talking to him.

"Carson, where's Katie? Where do you think she hid? Is she under the crib?" Look. "No, she's not there. Is she in the closet?" Open the door. "No! She's not there either."

There was a giggle from my bedroom.

"I think I hear Katie," I said stalking around the house. "Is she in the bathroom? Hmm, no, what do you think Car? Where did she go? Maybe she's in my closet." I hoped not. Katie didn't know about the secret room yet and I'd rather she didn't know.

I took as long as I could to find her. I was surprised at her patience. When I saw flashing lights in the front yard I went and found her in the window seat in my bedroom. The seat was hinged for storage and there was a large kid-sized space in there. It was a favorite hiding spot for Katie.

"You're a good hider!" I praised. "I thought I'd never find you!"

There was a knock on the front door.

"Uh oh! Who could that be?" I said to Katie even though I had a strong suspicion.

Yup, it was Jayce Thompson. Jayce usually patrolled this side of town. I opened the front door and he stepped in.

"Rusty wants me to get your report," he reported.

"Jaycee!" said Katie excitedly.

"Hi Katie! How's the big sister?"

"Sit down. There's not much to tell," I said. "I was playing with the kids outside this afternoon when I spotted strange tracks. So after dinner tonight I went out to look around. I noticed Chase's Bug was different than it used to be so I went over to look at it. Next thing I know there's a guy inside the Bug trying to cuff me and asking me questions, so I yanked him into the doorframe, gave him a kick to the head and took off running. He slammed me into the front door and then Rusty took over."

"Are you sure you didn't give him any information?"

I replayed the conversation for him and he nodded. "Okay, well, we're taking him in. We'll at least find out who he is. Send Chase to the station when he gets back. Put some ice on that lump."

"What lump?" I said feeling my head. "Oh, that lump. I must have hit it on the front door."

Jayce escorted our intruder to town and Rusty came in clearly perturbed with me.

"What were you doing out there at night?" he asked.

"Tracking."

"You can't track at night."

"The motion detector sheds enough light on the driveway area. I couldn't do it before dinner because Katie would follow me."

"What made you think to check the Bug?"

"I was just looking around because I'd seen strange tracks today. I wonder if I ought to take a trip up the canyon to warn Chase."

"Why didn't you just tell me?"

"Because I was reading tracks. I wasn't hunting down trespassers. One just happened to be out there."

"Next time just tell me. I'll check it out."

"I thought there were only tracks to check out. You want me to tell you to check out tracks? I thought tracks were my department."

"Cass, you should know by now, trouble leaves tracks."

"It was just minor trouble. If it saved Chase some major trouble it was worth it."

He ran his hands through his hair and it fell back down over his forehead just like it always did when he was frustrated.

"If the phone rings in the night, let me get it," he said. "I told them I wanted any information they could squeeze out of that guy."

About ten o'clock the phone rang. Rusty picked it up. I tried to stay out of it. But Rusty fell into a trap. A Cassidy trap of his own making.

"Can you outfit me for a trip up the canyon?"

"No. Mick has your camping gear."

"Let me use yours."

"That would work except that you don't have a pack until the guys get back."

"You lent him my pack?"

"You haven't used it in years."

"Can you just pack up a day pack, then?"

"And how are you going to find them? They could be anywhere within a few miles of the hideout."

"If I camp at the hideout they should show up."

"Not if they're through camping. Let me go. If they aren't at the hideout I can find them. What's up?"

"That guy was a bounty hunter."

"But if you've got him locked up he shouldn't be a problem, right?"

"If he's the only one, no, he wouldn't be a problem. We've been in touch with Taz and it's pretty clear there's an all-out race for Chase's head. He can name three people besides the guy we picked up. If they communicate in any way, Chase should not come back here."

"Then where would he go?"

"That's Chase's problem. But he needs a warning. If he comes here he's taking a risk."

"I can hike in at first light, without being seen. I can check out the hideout. If they are gone I can figure out which way they went and find them. Chase may not be very trackable but Mick and Tex are. Tracking Tex is like tracking Thez. He's so cocky even his feet are cocky. Thez walks like a model in a tennis shoe commercial. Tex walks like he's modeling his badge. It's funny when he's in uniform but it's worse when he's out of uniform. When he's in uniform at least people know he's just a rookie who's full of himself. Out of uniform it's kind of puzzling."

"Put him in a tense situation and he won't have time for badge modeling. Give him a couple of those and he'll be grounded. Sooner or later it happens to us all."

"Let me go. I know you can hike in and camp but you'd be shaking the bushes. If I go I'll just locate them and warn Chase. It'll be a lot simpler if I just go in by myself."

"What if you're followed?"

"We can take precautions. If I go to the station, I can catch a ride up there. Nobody is going to tail a police car."

"I can't let you do that."

"You can't just let Chase walk into a trap. If he does it's going to happen in our front yard. That would be worse than being followed into the woods. In the woods I can lose them. You know I can. They aren't going to hurt me if they think I know where Chase is. They'll just follow until I find him. If I am followed I can use the radio if I need help. There are other things we can try. Have the officers create a diversion. While I am making my way to the police station for a lift to the trailhead, have a couple of guys move Chase's car. If they see something happening with the car they will follow that instead."

He hated when I said things that made sense. He knew there had to be trouble in it somewhere and he knew if any trouble hit it would strike me. It always did. But he also knew I could get in and find Chase.

Other than the moccasins, I felt like I was back in the Marines again. Camouflage, bulletproof vest, pack, rifle, pistol. He'd have made me wear a helmet if he thought I'd keep it on. I considered hiking boots. But if I found a need for stealth I could hide my tracks easier in moccasins. Before the sun came up Rusty was seeing me off and I slipped away and headed to Creekside Campground. While I was still in the foothills a black and white pulled in behind me and followed me for a few miles, then pulled me over. I followed his movements in my rear view mirror. Big John Jankowski.

He walked up to the window. He wasn't smiling.

"You're stuck with me," he said.

"What do you mean?"

"You're not going up there alone."

"You're not going with me," I argued. "The whole point of me going is so I can slip in and out without being followed or spotted. If you go I might as well phone ahead and *tell them* I'm looking for Chase."

"What's that supposed to mean?"

"Umm, don't take offense, but, John, you aren't exactly… stealthy. Everybody within a half mile knows you are coming."

"You're still stuck with me."

"I'll lose you within five minutes."

"Wanna bet?"

"Sure, under one condition."

"What's that?"

"If I lose you, you turn back."

"What if I win?"

"Then you can go."

He nodded agreement, but he'd never had to keep me in sight when I wanted to disappear before. Big John followed me up to the campground and parked beside me.

"Did you bring your Adventure Pass?" I joked.

Any car traveling in the National Forest had to have an Adventure Pass if they parked. If you were just passing through you could do just that. But park and you had to have a pass. Restroom stop? Maybe they thought their restrooms were a real adventure. You needed a pass or risk a ticket. I bought a year-long Adventure Pass because I was up in the mountains a lot. I took out my pack, stood it on the tailgate and slipped my arms through the straps. I tightened them down and fastened the hip belt. I belted on the pistol, slung the rifle over my shoulder, closed and locked the Explorer and headed up trail.

"Hey wait!" Big John called after me.

"You want to go with me? Then go. But you'll have to keep up. Good luck."

"Cassidy!"

I smiled and motioned for him to follow then turned and continued on. He scrambled to catch up but John's scrambling was more like a bull in a china shop. I walked quickly, careful to place my tracks so they were nearly invisible, then when the trail turned I went straight into the woods and found a place to hide. When Big John didn't appear I found another tree, keeping an eye down the trail. This was too easy.

"Cassidy!" John called down the trail. I continued on through the trees, keeping plenty of woods between John and me, being careful when I exposed myself to view. He hiked the trail alone. Every now and then he took a look around but the camouflage and busyness of my gear made me blend in with the woods. He looked down at the trail. No tracks. He looked to the woods, no Cassidy. I took off in a fox trot through the forest to put some distance between us.

John stayed on the trail. I could hear his steady footfalls. Thump, thump, scrape, thump.

After a while I began to hear another sound. A human sound. Leaves crunching. Twigs snapping. My trouble radar began pinging and I stopped to assess my situation. I backtracked a bit until I found a place I could observe the bounty hunter from. I found him easily, just by following the sound.

After my trip down into Tecate any number of people might recognize me and connect me to Chase Downing. It didn't bother me, until now.

If this guy was from the part of Mexico I saw, he wasn't used to getting around in the forest. I noticed that he wasn't looking at the ground so he wasn't a tracker. He was a hunter. Armed. But I didn't think he wanted to harm me; he was hunting Chase. As long as he thought I was leading him to Chase I thought I was fairly safe. Only problem was I couldn't let him *find* Chase. I decided I better lose this guy.

Losing him turned out to be easier than I thought. I simply found a hiding place, and let him pass me. He found the trail and pretty soon he was stalking Big John instead. Big John continued down the trail oblivious to the silent interaction around him. He plodded along, hot and thirsty.

When I got to the place where the creek crossed the trail I debated. I could let John lead the bounty hunter on, but it would take me a couple of hours to climb the canyon and find Chase. In that time a lot of bad things could happen to Big John. I decided I owed him a warning.

It took me a half mile to catch up and pass the two men. I found a thick bramble off the side of the trail and settled in. As soon as John got within earshot I said, "Keep walking, you've got a tail. Keep your gun handy. Watch your back, and go back to town."

"Cass…"

"Shh! You don't see me. Now get out of here!" I almost whispered.

I shrunk back into the brush, making myself small. John was almost on top of me and still hadn't spotted me, but I wasn't taking any chances. He looked flustered then decided on a plan and kept going up the trail. After the bounty hunter passed me, I slunk back to the canyon.

I found my pack, and put it on, then found a discreet way up the canyon where rocks and trees would hide me from below. I didn't want to be followed by John *or* the bounty hunter. Either one would complicate things. I hurried to the camp knowing where Chase had planned to stop. It was the only flat spot in the whole canyon, had a creek close by, shade, and it was a short hike from Trent's Cave. It was very possible that Chase took my bet and was looking for the entrance. When I drew close it was obvious that the guys were no longer there. I crawled into the hideout to see if it had been used. Everything was stowed neatly and the shelter smelled of earth and damp vegetation.

I sat in the hideout thinking. Which way did the guys go last? They could have gone up canyon or down, but Trent's Cave was neither. I had to locate the boulder field to check for tracks there. If they had looked for Trent's Cave I was sure I would know it because the ground under the boulders was very soft sand. I climbed down into the sandy bottom and walked to the path that Trent had used to get there. That was the entrance Chase would have looked at first. I found one set of tracks that went directly to the dynamited front entrance and back out again. Chase had satisfied his curiosity there and simply walked out. But Mick and Tex hadn't gone with him.

I backtracked to get the whole story and decided they hadn't been worried about being spotted by someone following them. If Chase did expect a tail his tracks would have been invisible and he would not have led the guys into a canyon that would confine their movements. So, I decided, Chase had felt entirely safe on this trip. That was a good sign. It was puzzling, though, that he hadn't chosen to use the one good camping spot in the canyon. I looked the camp over again and found no flattened areas or tent peg holes where a tent might have been set up. The most activity I could pinpoint was a brief rest and a trip to the creek. Hmm. Why did Chase come to this canyon at all if he wasn't going to take my suggestion or my bet about the cave? The tracks leaving camp were Mick's and Tex's hiking tracks, but they were not tracking anybody. If Chase had been teaching them tracking I would find very slow walking tracks and frequent stops. It was obvious they were just hiking through the canyon on their way somewhere else. I found tracks heading up canyon and followed their trail to the top and then across the ridge. As I walked along, very aware of the openness of the ridge, I thought about the many times a bounty hunter could have taken Chase down from a hiding place below. I hurried, only keeping track of the trail, not bothering to profile.

I was stopped in my tracks by a lone shot that echoed off the mountains. It was high pitched and sharp, not a 45. The sound of the 45s was ingrained in my mind. This was more like my 9mm. So it wasn't Big John's shot. Damn. I dashed down the canyon again. I didn't know whether to worry about Big John or Chase and the rookies.

I wove my way down Shadow's path. My dog wasn't much of a rock climber so I had learned long ago there was a walking route down the canyon. I didn't want to take the time to climb carefully so I ran recklessly. By the time I got to the camp again I had my rifle in hand and I'd reverted to my scouting stance, running crouched over, eyes ahead scanning the brush. The farther I ran the more cautious I became until I was running from tree to rock, stopping and scanning, listening carefully. Finally, I had to turn to the ground for some clues. I found John's tracks at the bottom of the canyon, and followed them hurriedly. They left the trail, and there was a swath through the forest like a rhinoceros had charged through it. This was normal for Big John. Nothing stopped him. He just barreled his way through. I barreled after him in a much more refined fashion. I found him crouched behind a tree that wouldn't even come close to hiding him. He turned suddenly raising his rifle and then abruptly stopped.

"Cassidy! Get out of here," Big John hissed.

"Are you okay?" I asked.

Zing! Thwap! I threw myself at the ground and army crawled to Big John's hiding place.

"Damn it Cassidy. Are you all right?"

My right shoulder stung. I examined it, finding a neat hole in my shirt. I was glad Rusty made me wear my bulletproof vest.

"I'm glad they are firing from a distance," I said. "Why is he shooting at you? Doesn't he know you could lead him to Chase? I thought you could keep him busy while I found Chase but I wasn't planning on you getting shot!"

"Then get out of here," John said.

"Too late. What are you trying to do?"

"Avoid a bullet."

"What are you trying to do in the big picture?" I asked.

"I was told to stick to you until you finished what you came in here to do. But now it appears I'm arresting a man for attempted murder."

"You got backup coming?"

"Yeah, but they'll be a long time coming."

"Nah, they'll come by airmail. Where is he?"

"See those rocks?"

"Damn, I was hoping to get behind him."

"No," John said. "You're not taking any more chances."

"If I could get back there, we'd have him."

"What part of *no* don't you understand?"

"I'm hearing dyslexic. When you say *no* I hear *on*. So, we're *on*, right?"

"No!" he barked.

"All right!"

I slipped out from behind Big John and glided over to the next sheltered spot I could find. I kept my eyes on the rocks.

"Cassidy! Get back here."

I needed more freedom of movement so I stashed my pack in the brush before moving on to my next target. Each move brought me around to the side of the bounty hunter and I began catching glimpses of him watching for Big John's movements. I hoped Big John would stay put. I could count on him staying in one spot about as much as he could count on me. So I expected him to be unpredictable. To surround the guy, though, we needed John in front and me behind. I was sure John could see that. The closer I got the tenser and more careful I became. If I spooked the guy he might shoot first, think later.

I had closed the gap to maybe thirty feet when I noticed movement on the trail. At first I worried unsuspecting hikers were stumbling on a surprise they were not prepared for. Then I realized it was Mick and Tex. They had heard shots and gone into rookie cop mode. And Chase… where was Chase? I didn't want him to be spotted or he would be dead before he knew what happened to him. There was a whistle from the woods and Mick and Tex stopped and looked around. I could hope that Chase was in veteran cop mode. So here we were, five to one. I still had to get around behind the rocks to spring the trap, though. Big John made his way over to the two rookies. This was a good move because now they would know what was going on. They spread out forming a semicircle around the front of the gunman and I continued around back. I had to be silent. I only moved when I knew the man was distracted. But after a while he became so paranoid he was constantly looking around him.

"She needs a distraction," Mick whispered.

I barely heard what Mick said and I hoped the bounty hunter spoke mostly Spanish.

Mick and Tex exchanged glances. I took a look at my goal. There was movement in Tex's vicinity and the next thing I knew I heard a *Zzzzzzzzzzzz, plop, jingle*. What was that?

That's what the bounty hunter thought, too. He looked around. Then he focused about ten feet in front of him. He was instantly alert. There was a rustling in the brush. The bounty hunter eyed the brush warily and I took the opportunity to find the next closer hiding place, silently gliding into place and standing statue still.

More rustling, then a branch began jerking violently and the bounty hunter became concerned. This animal was bigger than he thought. What kind of animals did they have in the mountains of America? As the branch danced around I was able to advance in a low crouch to ten feet beside the man but as I noted the movement of the branch I also recognized the movement for what it was, a lure caught on a branch and being jerked around by a fishing pole! Tex had been ground squirrel fishing! I almost laughed that the confiscated fishing pole might just have saved a life.

The bounty hunter was getting truly worried now. If he had seen an animal right then he would have shot it, but no animal appeared. I slipped in closer, shouldered my rifle and…

The bounty hunter sensed movement, turned and fired catching me square in the chest. Another shot caught me on the way down in the shoulder. I was thrown back, stunned.

I sensed movement and confusion but I couldn't breathe. I knew what had happened. He'd hit me dead on but the vest had stopped the bullet. Stars danced around before me and I struggled with the decision of what to do next. As things became clearer I began hearing voices and they were all very much alarmed but calm enough to follow procedure.

"It's not hopeless yet," John was telling Mick. "She has a vest on."

There was a calming, a reordering of the minds, an okay, so now what do we do attitude.

"I wish Chase was here," Big John said. "He probably speaks Spanish."

In the meantime the bounty hunter bent over me.

"Una chica Americana?"

"Speak English," I gasped.

"Why?" he said. "You die anyway."

"No, I won't. If you knew who I was you'd doubt it, too."

He drew back, amused. This girl thinks she can outsmart me? A bounty hunter. I think he still thought he could bring in the legendary Chase Downing.

"Wy?" he said. "Who *are* you?"

"Have you ever heard of… Señor Grande?"

He laughed, but it was okay because now I was providing the distraction.

"You… Señor Grande? Señor Grande es un big bad man."

"Oh yeah? When Chase Downing escaped who did they say helped him? A big bad man?"

He looked doubtful.

"Un chica Americana?" I asked.

Bingo.

"No." he stated. "I not believe it."

"He was held in a bus. He was chained to a bench, a school bus seat. He was shot. There were explosions in the night. There was an American girl shouting things in the night. The children! Señor Grande has the children! You remember that night?"

He grabbed me by the shirt front and hefted me to my feet. He held me in front of him and put the gun to my head.

"Señor Chase! You want dis girl back? Señor policía, put your weapons down. You want dis girl to live."

"No! Don't!" I yelled.

He grabbed my arm and twisted it behind my back. I got mad and stomped on his foot. He twisted again. I stomped again. He twisted again and I threw my weight into him backwards. It hurt like crazy but his footing was unsure and he stumbled. I heard a bang and a ruckus as I was pulled down on top of the bounty hunter. I rolled off him, gasping for breath, and my brain fuzzed out.

"Never, ever, do that again," Chase said beside me.

I couldn't answer him.

"This is the second time you've put your life on the line for me. I won't have it." He looked at me. "Are you there? Cassidy, you're turning blue."

And stars were dancing around in front of me but I couldn't draw a breath. I was fading. All I could do was wait it out. Fighting it just made it worse.

"Somebody do something!" said Mick.

I wasn't out for long, just long enough for Big John and Tex to pack our prisoner off to jail and scare Mick half to death. Unfortunately, Chase had seen me like this before.

"Take it easy, kid," Chase said. "What do you think you're doing out here?"

"War…" I had to stop, swallow. I tried again, "Warning you. Not to come to the house. This is the second bounty hunter we've hauled in."

"You were a little late."

"At least he didn't find you first."

"Did you hear what I told you earlier?"

"Yeah, next time I scout out a bounty hunter it should be for someone else."

"That's not what I said."

Mick sat down beside me. He had been nervously pacing.

"Okay, I believe the stories now," Mick said. "But I sure hope you're not planning on doing this often. I don't think I could take it. How was I supposed to know you were wearing body armor? I thought he'd killed you. Twice!"

"Twice in one day. Chase, is that a record?" Twice in a week isn't unusual but I didn't know if I've done it twice in a day before.

"You need a new vest," Chase said, then he stood up. "Ready to give it a try? If your ribs hurt don't push it."

"Yes, Daddy," I said, still hoarse.

Oh, man, did my ribs hurt.

"Where's your pack?" Chase asked.

"I'll find it," I told him as I accepted a hand up.

"No," Chase said. "Mick, find Cassidy's pack."

"How am I supposed to know where she left it?"

Chase just looked at him.

"Oh, yeah… right."

Mick set out to find my tracks.

"Now, tell me, what are we looking at here?" Chase asked.

"One guy was staked out in your Bug. You need to get the windows fixed so you can lock it. I found tracks in the yard, checked out the Bug and ended up with a gun in my face. When he was hauled in and the police did some checking around they found out there were three other bounty hunters all in a race for your head. I was coming up here to tell you not to go back to the house, or the station."

"I meant, you. You going to hike out of here?"

"Yeah, no problem. But I need to change clothes first. I'm not going home with three bullet holes in my shirt."

"You think Rusty won't find out?"

"No, I know he will, but I'd rather the bullet holes aren't the first thing he notices."

"Don't hide things from him. He cares."

"He cares, too much."

"Really?"

"He cares, too much for his own good. He blames himself for letting things happen to me. If he sees the bullet holes he'll think he should have stopped me."

"He should have. It wasn't worth the risk you took."

"It was to me. If you'd walked up to your Bug like I did, you'd be dead right now."

"If you hadn't worn that vest you'd be dead right now. Don't do that, not for me."

"I'd do it again," I stated stubbornly.

He tried to think of a response. He ended up staring at the ground, hands in pockets. "We should be getting back. I better go bail out Mick."

Mick had spent the entire conversation looking at the same tracks near the place where I was shot. The tracks leading up to it were placed while I was in stealth mode. It was almost useless trying to track that.

"Soak up whatever you can of tracking Cassidy. If you can track Cass, you can track anybody… and she needs someone around who can find her."

Half an hour later Chase found the pack. I pulled my extra t-shirt out of the bottom pocket of the pack and went to the bushes to change.

"Mick, let her be," Chase said.

He held up my pack so I could slip into it easily. "You sure you want to pack this thing two miles?"

"Hand it over."

"You're just being stubborn."

"It's what I'm good at."

He took the tent off my pack and strapped it to his. It wasn't unusual for Chase to camp without a tent. He hefted the pack again, still didn't like the weight of it but he held it up for me and I slid my arms through the straps. It took some time to get things arranged right. I tightened the hip belt. If I pulled the shoulder straps tight everything ached. If I left them loose the pack pulled backwards on my sore collarbone.

"Let's go. We can make it in an hour or two if we keep at it."

I've found that even with three trackers hiking, the woman goes first. It's one of those rules. The guys think they need to let the woman go first, so she can't be left behind. I think they just like to watch women walk, though I can't imagine there is much to see with a heavy hip belt on and bulky pack blocking most of the view.

I've found miles are not all the same size. Depending on the situation, a mile can be very long, or very short. At the gym I could walk a mile in fifteen minutes. Bruised and battered, sandwiched into a pack, the miles felt endless. I debated stopping and taking the pack off and then chided myself. It's only discomfort, Cass, it's not going to kill you to keep going. Suck it up and keep those feet moving. I made up a little hiking cadence in my head.

"When the trail gets long, keep on moving, don't slow down, if you're sore don't show it, you might get home before the setting sun. Keep those eyes, to the trail, read those tracks before they're stale, follow those prints, until the day is done."

It bugged me that I didn't know where the tune came from. I knew all kinds of songs. It could have been rock, country, a marching cadence I learned in the service, a song Rusty had sung to the kids…I wasn't too picky about the music I listened to except that I'd turn off a song real quick if it triggered flashbacks. I didn't let flashbacks stick around. I gave them the boot as often as I could. And then I thought it was sad. If any person told me that they had to keep a constant rein on their memories I'd think they needed a different life. This line of thought wasn't unusual for me either. But I couldn't find a way out of this life I'd created for myself. Even a minor thing like hiking in to find a friend and give them a message turned into an all day, life threatening situation, a memory to block.

I was glad this little stunt of mine hadn't landed me in the hospital. I was very tired of hospitals. I gave my thoughts the boot and tried to turn to something more positive.

"What are you going to do when we get back?" I asked Chase. "You can't go to the station. You can't go to my house. They could both be watched."

"Drop me off at the Bug."

"I don't know where it is," I said. "Rusty might have moved it. Since we knew it was marked, we thought it might help draw the eyes of the bounty hunters to move it around."

"Then drop me off at Schroeder's. It will be late enough. He'll be home. I can make arrangements from there."

"I'd rather not," Mick said. "Schroeder's already on my case about getting Cassidy stuck in the woods. I don't want to be around when he hears about this."

"I'll give you a ride," I said.

"Are you doing okay?"

"Yeah, I'm always doing okay. If I'm not I just tune it out and keep going."

"Then stop for a bit."

"If it's all the same to you I'd rather keep going."

"Cassidy, stop. You've been through a lot today."

"What? What have I been through?"

"Taking those shots, even in a vest, is a shock to the body. Don't push your luck. I didn't think the vest was going to do the trick that last time."

"I didn't think I'd ever breathe again. Now that I've got it figured out, I think I ought to keep at it."

The Explorer and Mick's old Corolla sat peacefully in the parking lot, oblivious to the drama that unfolded that day. I fumbled for keys. Gave up. I tried the combination and had to punch it in twice. I opened the door and hit the lock to unlock the back hatch. I went to the back crawled in and laid down. The hard floor of the truck made my ribs ache.

"I told you to slow down," Chase reminded me.

"I know, I'm slower now."

"Do you want me to drive?"

"Yeah, if you want."

Guys almost always preferred to drive.

I felt every bump on the way into town and I wasn't looking forward to the drive home from Schroeder's house. Chase pulled up and handed me the keys.

"Thanks for the lift."

"Call Rusty to find out where your Bug is."

"Will do. You going home?"

"Yeah, I think I better."

"Be careful."

"I will."

He pulled his pack out of the back of the Explorer, closed the hatch and walked to the Schroeder's front door. I waited to make sure he was asked in. When Schroeder answered the door I started to put the key into the ignition but Schroeder motioned me in. Shoot. I did not want this. I unbuckled my seatbelt and got out of the Explorer as carefully as possible. I walked slowly, jarring as little as possible. Since I had sat still for a while my bones had settled into a constant ache. I was going to be moving slow for a few days.

"Good evening," Schroeder said.

"I hope so. I could use one," I said.

He held out an arm for a shoulder hug and I knew to refuse or ask him to be gentle would give me away so I leaned over and braced myself. He felt the vest. Looked me up and down. I was glad I changed shirts.

"I want you to leave the vest with me," Chase said.

"Why?"

"We need it as evidence. We can get an attempted murder charge added to the list."

"Cassidy… come in," Schroeder said. "Sit down."

"I'll come in, but I'd rather not sit down."

I went to the little powder room down stairs and took off the t-shirt and vest. Oh damn. I didn't know how bad it would look. And I wasn't even a cop. Schroeder would know exactly what had happened when he saw that. If I thought the vest looked bad, it was nothing compared to me. I couldn't see my back but I knew it was worse than my front. I slipped the t-shirt back on and took the vest to Chase. I handed it over without a word. When Schroeder saw it he frowned and crossed his arms over his chest.

Nancy walked in and gasped, "My word, Cassidy! What have you been doing?"

"Just delivering a message to a friend."

Chase wasn't much of a help. He laid out the vest and proceeded to list the distinguishing marks on it.

"These are from the firing squad in San Diego, right?"

"Yeah, I think I better save up for a new vest. I was lucky the chest shot today was from a distance. I doubt it would have worked point blank again."

"These are from today, right?" he said pointing out the marks at chest, shoulder and back.

"Yeah."

"Did anybody tell you you're supposed to *avoid* being shot?" Schroeder asked.

"I think most people just naturally avoid it when possible," I said.

"I know… you're not most people."

"I do avoid getting shot. Believe me, I don't enjoy it. It hurts, even in the vest."

"Fighting with a guy who has a gun to your head isn't exactly avoiding a bullet," Chase informed me.

Schroeder sat down with a huff. He didn't want to hear this.

"I wasn't going to play the helpless woman hostage. I was afraid you'd give in."

"When we do have a helpless woman hostage we spend the whole time praying they don't do something stupid and get themselves shot."

"Well, it all worked out," I said lamely. "I need to get home. Rusty's probably starting to worry about both of us. After all, if I didn't find you in time, you'd be the one to walk into a trap."

Chapter 34

"Mommy! If you dip Gummi Bears in ketchup they taste yucky," Katie said as I walked in the door.

"Okay, I'll remember that," I said wearily.

"And if you eat them with French fries the fries get stuck in the Gummi Bears and they get gross."

"Ah, I see."

"And jumping off the back of the couch is really high!"

"It's not nice to the couch to climb on it like that."

My favorite voice in all the world rumbled across the room and enveloped me, "Babe, you're home," Rusty said with arms open wide.

"Gentle," I told him as I wearily stepped into his embrace.

"What did you do to my girl this time?" he asked.

"I'm sorry. I'll be okay soon. It was a rough day on the mountain."

"Is everybody okay?"

"Yeah, I think I got the worst of it. Did Chase call about his car?"

"Not yet."

"Mommy, you want my Gummi Bears?"

"What are they mixed with?"

"A samitch."

"You're eating a Gummi Bear sandwich?"

"It's good with peanut butter an' jelly an' Gummi Bears."

"Okay, I'll try it. I'd just about try the Gummi Bears and ketchup right now."

"Okay!"

"No! I'll take a sandwich, no ketchup."

"Babe, you don't have to eat Katie's concoctions for dinner. We can come up with some real food."

The Gummi Bear sandwich wasn't half bad. They kind of blended in with the jelly. It was a bit chewy but I'd had much worse dinners than that before.

"You like it?" Katie asked.

"Yeah, that was good," I told her.

"Want another one?"

"I can make it," I said.

I made a peanut butter and jelly sandwich and only pretended to put Gummi Bears on it. Katie seemed pleased that her culinary talents were appreciated.

"Cassidy, why do you do that? I bet you hardly ate all day."

"It's okay, she's learning. Everybody learns differently. If she wants to learn what not to eat with Gummi Bears it's fine with me. I'm just glad I didn't have to go through the learning process with her this time."

"She wanted to make the sandwich with cookies, peanut butter, jelly and Gummi Bears."

"Sounds good," I said halfheartedly.

"Cassidy, what's wrong?"

"I'm sore and tired and still have a ways to go before bed time."

Just then the phone rang. I hoped it wasn't Chase or, even worse, Schroeder. Rusty got it.

"Hello?… yeah, she's right here…. Everything's fine, why?… no… I'll find out and let you know tomorrow."

Shoot.

He didn't jump on my case. He didn't fret. He stayed close and he wrestled Katie to bed while I gave Carson a bottle and lay down on the couch. When both kids were asleep and the house was peaceful he came to me and offered me a hand up. I shook my head no.

"Fifteen minutes," I said. "I need fifteen minutes of couch time, first."

Even though I was already stretched out on the couch I got up and he sat in his spot. I sat in his lap with my head on his shoulder and he wrapped his arms around me and put a kiss on my head. This was our comfort spot. The place where nothing in the world could go wrong. We might tackle some tough issues and we might hurt a lot, but this was a safe spot. And it was ours. And nobody could take that from us. It was one of the few constants that we could count on. The old brown couch. I swore the old brown couch would always have a place in our home, even if it got relegated to the secret room. I needed this couch, these arms.

After a while Rusty felt some of the tension easing and he broached the subject at hand, like I knew he would.

"What happened today?" he asked.

I took a moment to think. "Thank you for making me wear the vest today."

He took a moment to think, too. He knew if he played his cards right we'd be closer and if he didn't I'd get defensive.

"Thanks for wearing it."

So far so good. We had never actually fought. We'd butted heads. We'd disagreed, but we had never come down to an all out lovers fight before. We were not going to do that now. I think we both respected each other too much to allow that to come between us.

"I need a new one. It was a rough day. Almost a standoff. Almost a hostage situation. Not quite, but I took a hit for it. And I still hurt. I'm still not convinced I didn't crack a rib. The shot was too close."

"Hon, I think you should start at the beginning."

So I did, I explained it all to him so he could see why I did what I did, why it unfolded like it did and when I finished he wrapped me gently in his embrace and he buried his face in my hair and he took a deep breath.

"My girl. My precious girl. I came so close. Again. Stay with me. Stay with me tonight." We sat on the old brown couch for a long time and when I showered before bed he came into the bathroom so he'd still be close. That was okay. We had an unspoken rule; if the bathroom door was open it was an invitation of sorts. For play, for sex. To sit and watch and take comfort in the fact that we were still together. That night Rusty came in and saw me undressing. He saw the bruises, knew what kind of a hit would cause a bruise like that. He undressed, too, then followed me into the shower. He soaped up his hands and gently massaged the aches. He couldn't make them go away but he could help me forget why they were there. Though it hurt, it hurt with the gentlest caring, and I was able to put the cause away and wash the day from my mind and so we emerged from the shower tired but refreshed. We dried off and went to bed certain of one thing; we still had minutes to share.

Chapter 35

It was a somber Tex who showed up at my door the next day. He didn't come in right away when I opened the door wide.

"So," I said. "You were warned. You have to be ready for anything when you track with me. Are you still ready?"

He tossed a tiny piece of jerky to Shadow and walked in. Carson was fussing in the den so I went to pick him up.

"My baby's hungry," said Katie.

"We'll see. If he doesn't settle down maybe he is."

Tex wandered around the living room while I calmed down Carson. He was looking at the photos Mark Mireau took of me on Santa Cruz Island.

"Take it down and read the back," I said.

He read it, hung it back up and went on to the next one, then to the shadow box with my honeymoon souvenirs in it.

"You're an interesting lady," he said.

My honeymoon souvenirs consisted of a parachute, a rabbit skin and a homemade snare we used to catch the rabbit. Framed pictures from our honeymoon hung inside the shadowbox with the parachute as a background. Nobody understood the significance of those objects except Rusty and I. Five days in survival mode, no camping gear and lost in the woods. All we knew was there was a lake north of us and on that lake was a honeymoon cottage with our name on it.

Carson was still fussing so I went to the kitchen to make up a bottle. I lay him on his blanket and he screamed louder. When the bottle was mixed up and in the warmer I picked him up and the volume settled down again.

"Mommy, why do babies cry so much?"

"Because they don't know words yet."

"Carson doesn't know words?"

"He will. We need to teach them to him. You're still learning words. There are lots of words you don't know, but you're talking real good for a little kid."

"I am not little. Carson is little."

"You can help me teach Carson words," I told her.

"How do you do it?" Tex asked. "Yesterday you were stalking a bounty hunter through the woods and getting shot. Today you're walking a baby like nothing happened."

"Yesterday is past. It's today we need to worry about. Today I have a fussy baby and a curious toddler."

"I'll never forget that shot."

"Tex. Not in front of the kids. Okay? I don't want them to grow up thinking that stuff like that is normal. It's only normal for me. I don't want it to rub off on them. Tell me how the tracking went."

"It went… interesting. That guy is about as easy to talk to as a wall."

"Chase talks. And when he does you need to pay attention. You need to listen on multiple levels. Often what you can infer from his words will teach you more than what he says."

"He knows his tracking, though. We tracked hikers. Then we climbed up a canyon. He left me and Mick at that camp while he checked something out. He was gone for maybe half an hour and came back without a word. Then he just keeps on up the canyon, so we took out after him. We tried to track Chase as he hiked but he's about as hard to track as you are and we had to keep up."

"Can you show me, on a topo map, where you went?"

"I can try."

"I can show you where the camp is to start you off."

I jiggled my fussy baby on the way to the bedroom/office and pulled a very worn topo map from the bookcase. I tossed it on the dining room table and went to check the bottle. It was warm enough for me. Hopefully it was warm enough for Carson. Tex spread out the map.

"The campground is just off the edge of this quadrant. Here's the trail out of it," I said pointing. "You followed this trail until you got to this junction. Then you followed the canyon this way. Here's the camp. I know you hiked to the top of the canyon. I tracked you that far. That's where I was when I heard the shot and went back to check on Big John."

"What was Jankowski doing up there?"

"He was going to tag along and keep me out of trouble but I shook him pretty quick."

"So what was that bounty hunter doing up there?"

"He was following me because he thought I would lead him to Chase. Then when I lost Big John I lost the bounty hunter, too. He followed Big John instead."

"And Big John ran into trouble."

"I don't know what triggered the shooting, but I couldn't turn my back on Big John if he needed help."

"Big John needed help as much as he needed a trouble magnet."

"Well, you have to admit we got him."

"Seems to me, he got you."

"Nah, can't get me down that easily. He wouldn't have spotted me at all if you hadn't made him paranoid with that fishing lure. He thought there were animals in the brush and when he caught a movement he just opened fire."

Tex sat down at the table. He wasn't sure how to take that.

"I'm not blaming that shot on you," I told him. "You were trying to distract him so I could close in. You couldn't help it if the guy's first reaction was to shoot."

"Here!" said Katie plopping a sloppy sandwich in front of Tex.

"What's in it?" I asked

"Peanut butter, jelly, and Gummi Bears," she answered.

"Why the sudden fascination with Gummi Bears?" I mumbled to myself. "It's really, not too bad," I told Tex.

"Mommy! Member the nanaboats you used to make?"

"Yeah," I answered warily. When I had morning sickness, and I could only eat potato chips, I made Katie banana boats by cutting a banana in half for a hull and then stabbing potato chips in it for sails.

"Can I make some so the Gummi Bears can have boats?"

"Next time I go grocery shopping," I told her.

"Can I have a fork?" asked Tex, "And maybe some whipped cream."

"I get it!" said Katie cheerfully.

"Now, show me where you went," I said.

"We didn't stop in the canyon because Chase said there was not enough variety there, so we kept going until the canyon topped out and we followed this ridge. Basically we just kept hiking and when we stopped I don't know why we stopped. It was just an open area. We spent Saturday tracking each other. Chase was weird. I could tell he knew what he was doing, but he was very tight lipped about it. He made us think good and hard before he spoke and then, when he did, he didn't actually tell us anything, just tweaked our thinking in a certain direction. Mick and I, we're talkers. We talk about everything on the trail. Chase said we were as bad as a ladies' quilting bee."

There was a crash in the kitchen and a "oops!" from Katie.

I went in to assess the damage.

"How many times have I told you not to climb the refrigerator shelves? They are made to hold up milk. You're much bigger than a gallon of milk."

She looked around on the floor and picked up a can of whipped cream.

"I got it!" she said and ran around to the dining room, whipped cream and fork in hand. I picked up a bottle of apple juice and put it back on the shelf and closed the door. I sat down at the table and burped Carson.

I guess the tracking had turned out about as I expected, but I still had questions.

"How did you happen to show up where Big John and I were?"

"We were tracking our way back to the car when we heard the first shot," Tex said as he sprayed whipped cream all over his sandwich, "We didn't think much of it because we're all used to hearing shots, people out shooting at cans and bottles. So what if they weren't in a place where that was legal. It's so common. We all go out shooting with friends, do target practice in the hills. So we just kept on but after a while Chase starts heading in a different direction. I don't know why. So Mick and I just tracked Chase that direction and then all of a sudden he starts hurrying and then he gets all weird on us and he vanished and we couldn't track him anymore. About then we saw Big John and we were wondering what in the world he was doing out in the forest by himself. So we go check it out and see you there and this Mexican guy and we can see there's something going down. We all kind of went on automatic falling into our ranks like we would at work. I didn't know what Chase was up to. I knew he was around. Don't know *how* I knew. It was just a feeling I had. He was headed that direction and he was worried about the goings on, so I knew he'd be there."

"Chase is like that."

Tex cut off a bite of sandwich with his fork and stuffed a bite into his mouth.

"Jump! Jump!" Katie called from the living room.

Plup, a quick giggle, "I didn't fall! Mommy! I didn't fall!"

"That's good," I said. "Don't climb on the furniture."

"Is she alwugh thi acve? Arr my mouf ig stuck."

"Yeah, she's always one step ahead of everybody. What did Chase do while all the action was going on?"

"I thingk he wars…hode on…"

"Can I get you something to drink?"

"Wha disolgs peanug butter?"

"Coke? A bottle brush?"

"I'll tage da Coke."

By the time I got back with a glass of Coke he'd managed to swallow most of the peanut butter.

"I think Chase was coming up on the scene from behind, like you were trying to do. But I never actually saw him do it. I do know that when we all closed in he was right there. And he was mad. If he could have had steam coming out his ears he would have."

"What was Chase mad at?" I asked.

Tex cut up the sandwich into very small bites.

"It's hard to tell with Chase. At first he was mad at what you had tried to do. Then he was mad at the guy. I think, in the end, he was more mad at himself."

"Why is it guys always blame themselves when I do something stupid?"

"Because it's easier than blaming you."

Hmm.

"I'm going to hit the road for a while," Chase said.

"Wha! Where'd you come from? I didn't hear the door. I didn't hear you come in," Tex said.

"Tex, calm down," I said. "That's normal when Chase shows up."

"Unca Chase! Do it again! Do it again!" Katie said running up to him.

Chase looked worried. He didn't have a horse quarter.

"Let me see," he said peering in her ear. "Uh oh. No horses. Katie, the horse is gone."

"No it's not."

"Yes, it is. I can see it. It's a bird this time."

Katie poked her finger in her ear trying to feel the bird.

"Can I see?"

Chase pretended to pull a quarter out of her ear.

"See? See the bird?" Chase said holding the quarter out to her.

Her eyebrows shot up and she ran over and showed me the quarter. "Look, Mommy! A birdy!"

"So I see!" I said. "Where are you going? It's not like you to run."

"I'm not exactly running. I hate travel. Maybe I'll go check in on Elan and Patrick. I don't want to freak out your dad, though."

"Nonsense, they'd be glad to have you."

At the same time I said it, I thought I better give Dad a little warning.

"Hello, Martha?" I said.

"Cassidy, dear! How are you?" Martha said.

"I'm fine, how are you?"

"Wonderful, dear, like always. As long as the ranch is running smoothly I am doing fine."

"Could I talk to Mom or Dad?"

"Of course. Let me see, who is here? … Mister Gordon? It's Cassidy."

"What happened this time?"

"I don't know, sir. She only asked for you or Betty."

"That's a good sign. Cassidy?"

"Hi Dad! How are you?"

"It depends."

"Everything is fine. I was just calling to warn you, you're going to have company."

"Isn't this Martha's department?"

"Not exactly. Chase is coming. He won't be any bother. He is just checking in on Patrick and Elan. I thought you'd want a heads up."

"Chase. The beach bum?"

"Dad! He's not a beach bum. He's a police officer." Well, a retired police officer.

"Humph."

"He means well, Dad, just be nice to him, okay? And tell Mom he's coming. She always likes company. I doubt he'll stay in the house. When he's at my house he sleeps in a hammock strung up in the gazebo."

"Humph."

"Dad! Just be nice to him. Okay?"

"Okay."

Next thing I knew Mom was on the line.

"Cassidy! What happened this time?"

"Nothing, Mom, I don't have to be calling because of trouble."

"How is Rusty, how are the kids? When can you come for a visit?"

"I'll ask Rusty. He and the kids are fine. Katie has been doing cooking experiments with Gummi Bears. Carson is still wishing pushups caused forward movement."

"Is he still a little snuggle bug?"

"Yeah, I'm so glad he takes after Rusty. He's such a good baby."

"When are you going to get Katie a horse?"

"When she's old enough to take care of it."

On and on she went catching up on news of her grandkids.

"Mommy? Who you talkin' to?"

"Grandma."

"Can I talka Gramma?"

"Oh, yes! Put Katie on. I love talking to little kids on the phone. It makes them feel so grown up."

I handed Katie the phone, "Hewo?" she said. "I'm free," she said holding up three fingers. "I can count. One, two, free, four…" she counted up to twenty-nine and couldn't remember thirty. "He's at work…he catches bad guys." Simple enough. "Mommy went tracking and she got shot." Damn, how'd she know that? There were raised voices on the other end. I'd have to talk to Katie later.

"Tell Grandma I didn't get hurt."

Katie handed the phone back to me with a surprised look.

"I think you're in trouble," she said.

"Hello, Mom? I told you, I'm fine."

"Katie said you got shot!"

"Katie is too observant. One of the officers was talking about a search we went on and Katie overheard a short sentence. I made him stop talking about it because I didn't want Katie to hear but I guess she heard enough."

"But did you get shot?"

"Yes and no. I was wearing my vest. It took the hits and I'm fine."

"Hits? Cassidy, you've got to avoid people with guns. Trouble magnets and guns don't mix."

"I know, Mom. When I went on that search I wasn't planning on getting into trouble. It just happened."

"What kind of trouble do you have going on there that you got shot?"

"It's not my trouble. It's Chase's. And it should be over."

"Katie, we need to talk."

"Am I in trouble?"

"No, of course not. Why, what did you do that you might get in trouble for?"

"I dropped the Gummi Bears and Dadow ate them all."

Oh, yuck. Now I was going to have to make sure I let him out before he pooped rainbow diarrhea all over the house.

"That was an accident," I told Katie. "Next time if you drop something say, 'leave it!' and he might leave it alone long enough for you to pick them up. What we need to talk about is something else."

She looked at me seriously with big blue eyes. Rusty's eyes.

I asked her, "Do you worry when Mommy gets shot at?"

"No," she answered. "Shots hurt, but you don't want to get sick, so you hafta have them."

Huh? She thought I was getting booster shots? Immunizations? Okay, I decided quickly, she could think that. It was better than what I thought she was thinking.

"If your arm hurts from the shots," Katie said. "I'll sit with you. It always helps me to sit on your lap when I get shots. I don't like shots. Does Doctor Ron give you a lollipop?"

It always touched me how Katie took her shots. She knew it was going to hurt but there was no whining, crying or fighting the nurse. She just buckled down and took it and when it was over she kept her misery to herself. She would curl up in a comfortable spot and ache by herself or play quietly instead of exploring like usual. But when I noticed things being unusually quiet and picked her up, she gladly accepted any comfort I might offer.

"No," I told her. "Adults don't get candy for being good."

"Well, they should. Do you feel better now?"

"Yes, I feel much better." My mom might not, but I did.

Chapter 36

"Cassidy, have you started dinner yet?" Rusty asked when I answered the phone.

"No, I was thinking about it. Why?"

"The Schroeders asked us over for dinner. We haven't gone in a long time. We should. Nancy has hardly met Carson."

"Sounds good to me."

"Meet me there?"

"Okay."

"Katie, what do you want to wear to Schroeder's house? Do you want to be a princess or a cowgirl?" Those were Katie's two distinctions in clothes. Play clothes were cowgirl clothes and dresses were princess clothes.

"What's Carson wearing?"

"Play clothes. We don't need to dress up."

I took her into her room and started pulling out outfits. Every time we did this I sorted out a couple of outfits that Katie had outgrown before she even wore them. My mother bought anything Katie looked cute in and she looked cute in almost anything. I held up a dress.

"No, I do it!" Katie said.

"Okay, don't make a mess. We have to leave in half an hour. I'm going to get dressed."

Hmm, I thought looking through my closet, do I want to look like a princess or a cowgirl? I decided I better be prepared for anything. Jeans won out. I'd just pulled them on when I heard Carson fussing in the den. I'd left him on his blanket with several toys to keep him company. I knew he'd miss me soon but this was a different cry. This was an uncomfortable cry. I zipped up and pulled on any old shirt so I could run out there and check on him. When I got to the den Katie was kneeling on the floor stuffing Carson into a white and navy blue western shirt. She had on a cowgirl shirt and denim skirt. The skirt was backwards and unzipped. Carson did not like being dressed by a three year old.

"Katie! What are you doing?" I asked even though it was obvious.

"I want to match!" Katie said.

"You and Carson can match but you need to be gentler. Don't make him cry. Come on. We'll change his clothes gently."

When all was said and done they made a cute pair. Each kid wore a white western shirt with red piping and a navy blue yoke. Katie wore a denim skirt and cowgirl boots. I didn't like her to wear boots. Her feet were still growing. She didn't need to cram her feet into those pointy toed clompers. And Katie did tend to clomp in her boots. I needed to teach that girl how to walk quietly. I refused to put boots on Carson but I let her choose socks for him that matched her boots.

"Will you curl my hair?" she asked.

Arg, I was the world's worst hair stylist. It was cases like this where I wished I could call on my sister. But Jesse lived four hundred miles away.

"Your hair is already curly. It's cute. Let's just brush it and hair spray it and you'll look gorgeous."

"I wanna curl it!"

"You can't. The curling iron gets too hot. You have to be a big girl to use a curling iron."

"How big?"

"Eight," I said picking a number out of the air. I figured an eight year old would learn from their first burn.

"Free, four, five, six, seven, eight," she counted on her fingers. She looked disappointed. I was sure she hadn't done the math even though she was holding up six fingers. I got out the curling iron and curled her hair. It looked almost exactly the same as it had to start, but we'd gone through the motions, and sprayed it, so she felt pretty.

I quickly changed into a blouse and put on a little makeup. I checked the diaper bag.

"Are we ready?" I asked.

"We need cookies," Katie said.

"Why?"

"'Cause Shoder wants cookies," she said matter-of-factly.

"Okay," I said taking a bag of cookies out of the refrigerator, "You give them to him." I handed her the bag and loaded the kids up into the Explorer.

All the way to town she sang, "The wheels on the truck go round and round all the way to town…"

We pulled up in front of the Schroeder's house, but Rusty's Explorer wasn't there yet.

"Now, be nice to Mister and Missus Schroeder. If they tell you to do something you obey them," I reminded Katie. "Don't climb the outside of the stair rail. If you jump down the stairs only jump one step at a time. If you jump far you will scare Missus Schroeder and she'll make you stop. Try to eat a little bit of everything. If you don't like it, you don't have to finish it, but you have to taste it. Tell her what you like best. It's polite to compliment the cook."

"What does Carson have to do?"

"Stay happy and not fill his diaper in the middle of dinner."

"That's easy. How come I have to do the hard stuff?"

"Because you're a big girl. You got to do the easy stuff when you were a baby. There are advantages to being a big girl. You know how to do fun stuff that Carson can't do. Do you want to ring the doorbell?"

"Yeah!"

"See? Carson can't do that."

Katie ran to the front door and rang the bell before I could even get Carson and the diaper bag out of the truck.

"Katie! Thank you for coming to dinner!" Nancy said, "Did you come all by yourself?"

"No. I brought my mommy and my brover."

"Go on in and find Mister Schroeder," she said.

Katie marched into the house carrying her bag of cookies.

"Here, let me help you with all that," Nancy said. "With all the things babies need nowadays it's a wonder anybody could carry it all. I heard this little guy is a lot calmer than Katie is."

"He's more like a baby than Katie ever was. He hasn't picked any pockets or caught a bank robber yet. This guy wants to interact on a more personal level."

"Come here, Carson," said Nancy. "My what a big name for such a little baby."

"Little? He weighs three pounds more than Katie did at his age. He's going to be a big boy."

"Like his daddy," Nancy said. "Let me see you, you big boy you. He… takes after you in some ways and Rusty in others. Katie sure got Rusty's eyes, didn't she!"

"She sure did. I have a feeling Carson will look more like Rusty by the time he's grown."

"I hope so… I didn't say that… you didn't hear me say that, did you?"

"It's okay."

"I mean, if a boy had a choice to look like you or to look like Rusty, I'm sure a boy would… umm."

"It's okay. I sure wouldn't choose to look like me if I was a boy and in a way I was the boy of the family. I did all the horse training, and hunting, and tracking, and my sister did all the sewing, and arts and crafts, and babysitting. At least she grew up into a respectable wife and mother. I grew up into a trouble magnet."

"Oh, Cassidy, you're a wonderful mother. Just look at these two. As different as night and day but wonderful children. You're doing great."

"Katie's a little chatterbox now. She'll talk your ear off if you let her. If you want to put Carson down he'll be fine on a blanket in the living room."

"Put him down? Why would I want to do that? I've got a baby! I love holding babies! Let's go make sure Katie found Schroeder."

Not only had she found Schroeder, she had him over a barrel.

"Shoder? What's that?" she asked.

"It's a piano."

"It's big."

"That's because it has lots of parts. A good sound board is big."

"What's that?"

"A sound board helps the piano make music."

"Can I see?"

"It's not something you see. It's something you listen to."

"Can I listen?"

"You have to make the music yourself."

"Yeah, Schroeder, can we listen?" I asked. He knew I'd been wanting to hear him play the piano. Still, he looked embarrassed. "Show Katie how it works," I suggested.

He opened the cover and sat Katie down on the bench.

"You push these keys and the piano plays notes. See?" He pushed a white key and a note came out. Katie looked at the keys.

"Can I push it?" she asked.

"No pounding, be gentle."

She pushed a key and a note barely sounded.

"Okay, push a little harder," Schroeder said.

Katie pushed a different one a little harder and gazed in wonder that she could make a note.

"You put lots of different notes together and it makes a song," I explained to her. "Mister Schroeder knows how to play songs on it."

"Can you play the ABC song?" Katie asked.

"How about if you play it?" Schroeder asked.

"Uh uh!" she said. "You do it!"

"Push this one," ding, "Again," ding. She'd never hear the tune at this rate.

Schroeder took her hand and helped her plink out the ABC song.

"I did it!" she said clapping her hands.

"Now let Schroeder show us how to do it," I said. He'd gotten himself into this. The only way out was to play the piano.

"Cassidy…" he tried to back out.

I pulled out an old music book from a nearby bookcase and turned to a page with lots of penciled in notes.

"Here, play this," I said, "It looks easy."

"That's because it's my first solo book. I haven't played anything in there for forty years."

Forty years? I quickly took the book back and found a more recent one.

"Here," I said handing him the book, "You choose something."

As he looked through the book, I was leafing through the beginner book. I found a page with notes jotted on it and examined it closely. It wasn't Schroeder's handwriting. It was a woman's hand. Probably a music teacher. There were brackets with notes like "slow down here" and "forte!!!" and "BIG FINISH!"

I turned to another song with notes on it. I found a note that said "Left hand has the melody here," and one that said "Good Job, Lenny!"

Lenny? Was that Schroeder's first name? Lenny? Lenny Schroeder? Leonard Schroeder? I just couldn't picture Schroeder as a Lenny. Or a Leonard. I looked at the cover of the book and then inside the front cover. There, penciled inside the front cover was the name Leonard Harrison. Rats! Well, I was kind of relieved. Schroeder just didn't seem like the Leonard type. However, if there was one note with a name, maybe, just maybe there was another. I didn't hear music so I looked up. Schroeder was watching me amused.

"You won't find it in there. Lenny Harrison was my neighbor growing up. We had the same piano teacher and we traded books back and forth."

"You better play something or Katie's going to use her hound doggy eyes on you."

"That's no fair," he said. "Using your daughter like that."

I put the book back and chose another old piano lesson book. This one had much more complex music in it. I checked the cover. No name. I checked the inside cover. No name. I looked through the book but only two pieces had written notes on them and they consisted mostly of dates at the ends of movements. Looked like it took about two months to work through a whole four page song. Some of the movements were long, some just a line or two. Still, no names in this book.

Schroeder put the music book up on the piano and looked nervous. He put his hands to the keys and tensed up.

"Nancy's the only one who usually hears me play anything," he said.

"I can't play the piano. I wouldn't know a mistake if I heard it," I said.

Just then the doorbell rang.

"Saved by the bell," Schroeder said.

"Nope, you stay there. It's just Rusty. I'll get it. Katie, ask Schroeder very politely if he'll play a song."

I laughed as Katie batted her big blue eyes at Schroeder. As I walked to the front door I could hear Katie saying, "Please, Shoder, show me how you play the piano." If there was one thing Katie was good at it was hound doggy eyes.

"Hey!" Rusty said as I opened the door.

"Shh, Katie's working on Schroeder to play the piano," I said.

He gave me a kiss and then followed me into the den.

"Please, Mister Shoder?" Katie said.

"Oh, man," Rusty said. He knew what Schroeder was dealing with. He cratered to Katie's hound doggy eyes every time. It was his fault. They were his eyes.

I picked up another old music book. I decided the older they were the more likely they would be to have a name written in them. This one had Jaime Schroeder printed neatly on the inside of the cover. Jaime? Somehow I doubted this was Schroeder's first name either. He didn't look like a Jaime. This was probably a sister. It looked like girls' printing.

"Oh, come on Schroeder," Nancy said, "You have entire pieces memorized. You don't need a book to play something for Katie."

"It's not Katie that makes me nervous."

"Play *Pop Goes the Weasel*," Nancy said.

"No don't!" said Rusty. "Katie will be singing it all night."

"And she has to jump whenever she says *pop*!" I added.

"How darling!" Nancy said. "Play it Schroeder! Please?"

Now he had two girls after him, and two parents against him. Rough, gruff Sergeant Schroeder was between a rock and a hard place and the only way out was through Katie. Katie settled it.

"All around the coppinter's bench the monkey chased the weasel! The monkey thought it was all in fun *POP!* goes the weasel! Please?" She looked up at him and he sighed and rolled his eyes. He played *Pop Goes the Weasel*. Then he played it country style, then blues style. Katie danced to the tune, and popped up whenever she heard *pop*. Nancy was thoroughly entertained.

When Schroeder was finished Katie walked over to the piano and poked a key. She squatted down and looked under the keys. She liked to know how things worked but this piano wasn't giving her many clues.

"Do it again!" she said.

"Yeah, play something to make her forget *Pop Goes the Weasel*," Rusty said.

The next song didn't help. Schroeder played *Linus and Lucy* and the fast pace of the song sent Katie running around the couch. She jumped up and down and clapped her hands. When he was finished we all clapped, and Schroeder looked uncomfortable.

"You shouldn't be embarrassed to play," I told him. "You play beautifully."

Katie snatched the bag of cookies off the floor and presented them to Schroeder.

"Katie, what do you say to Mister Schroeder?" I prompted.

She paused a moment and then brightened, "I brought cookies!" she said.

"Thank you for playing the piano for us," I said to Schroeder.

Rusty held out his arms to Carson and Nancy handed him over, then went to check something in the kitchen. Rusty tossed him up in the air and caught him a couple of times. Carson drooled on Rusty's forehead and Rusty wiped it off with is hand and went to the kitchen for a paper towel.

Dinner was Chicken Parmesan. Katie was happy. She got "pasketti." She sampled the salad. She dug into the spaghetti and I added little chicken bites to her plate.

"Dinner is delicious," I told Nancy.

"Save room for dessert," she said.

"Me too?" asked Katie.

"Of course! We wouldn't leave you out," Nancy said.

"Carson, too?"

"He's too little," I said.

"Then I'm glad I'm big."

"We'll have dessert right after dinner to give the sugar time to wear off," Nancy said. "I tried to think of something Katie would like so we're having brownie sundaes. I have a sundae bar all ready to go. All we have to do is scoop out some ice cream."

Katie was in heaven presented with that sundae bar. She started out with a brownie. Schroeder added a scoop of vanilla ice cream. She added chocolate sauce, crushed up Oreo cookies, sprinkles, Gummi Bears, whipped cream and a cherry.

"Gummi Bears!" she exclaimed.

"Where did her sudden fascination with Gummi Bears come from?" I asked Rusty.

"I was wondering that, too. Why did you buy so many packages of them?"

"I didn't. I thought you did. They were in the house when I got back from my trip into the woods."

"They were there before you left."

"No they weren't."

"Katie, where did we get all the Gummi Bears from?"

"The store!" she said.

"What store?" I asked.

"The food store."

"I didn't put Gummi Bears in our cart."

"*I* did!"

"I don't remember putting Gummi Bears on the belt at the store."

"*I* did!"

"I don't remember paying for all those Gummi Bears."

"You *did*."

"I don't remember putting them away when we got home."

"*I* did! I put them in my room. But then I dropped them and Dadow ate them."

"Next time ask me before you add things to the cart."

"But you would say *no*."

"Maybe, maybe not. How many Gummi Bears did we buy?"

"A box."

"Gummi Bears don't usually come in boxes, they come in little plastic pouches."

"A box has lots of them."

"Okay, I'm really slipping. I thought I was overly alert and come to find out my three year old smuggled a case of Gummi Bears behind enemy lines without being caught."

"Am I in trouble?"

"No, you're not in trouble, but next time ask first."

Rusty declined dessert but I didn't think it had anything to do with his diet. It was a common thing, Katie heaped up her plate and Rusty bailed her out when she couldn't finish it all. After a short time Katie began slowing down.

"What's the matter, Princess?" Rusty asked.

"I'm full."

"You need some help with that?"

"Uh huh."

Rusty pulled her into his lap and scooted her bowl over. After a couple more bites she asked if she could get down.

"Let's go wash your hands," I said. "You're probably all sticky."

I led Katie to the powder room but Nancy stopped us, "Use the one upstairs. That one smells like wet paint."

Katie was glad. She dashed up the stairs.

"Where we going?" she asked.

"Just to the bathroom," I said.

We found the bathroom two doors down on the left. Katie went inside and I started the water and found the soap.

"No, I do it," she insisted.

"We need to get all the stickies off."

"I do it!"

"Okay," I told her, "but use soap, rinse off, and dry your hands."

I walked out into the hall and started looking at the family pictures on the wall. Nancy was a very organized person. She had picture frames that hold school photos for every school year, for each of their three kids. She was sentimental, too, saving kindergarten handprints for all five family members; two blue ones for Schroeder and his son and three pink ones for Nancy and the two girls. Nancy's and Schroeder's were obviously older. The frames were mismatched. The kids' handprints were in identical frames. Schroeder had long fingers as a kid, good for playing the piano. Penciled on his handprint was C or was it L? It might even have been an E. Hmm, G? It was a first initial and a last name, Schroeder. It was smudged and yellowed with age. I looked up and down the hall at the pictures to see if there were any other identifying marks, but didn't find any. So many little clues, yet I thought, I'd never learn Schroeder's first name.

"Let me see your hands," I said to Katie when she came out. "Oops, we need to wash your face." I dampened a washcloth and wiped off a squirmy Katie. If there was a kid who liked to have their face washed I hadn't met them yet. "Okay, you're clean again," I said releasing her. We rejoined the group and Katie tried to be patient with the adults, but she finally got bored.

"Can I play the piano?" she asked.

"No pounding," Schroeder said, prepared to be sorry he let her.

Surprisingly, she started trying to pick out the tune for *Pop Goes the Weasel*. She could tell she was starting off on the wrong note. But she knew how to go up and down on the scale. After a while she slipped down and came back to the table.

"I can't do it. Can you show me?" she asked.

"Have you ever thought about piano lessons?" Schroeder asked.

"She's too young. And I don't know how to play anything except a bamboo flute. I can't read music."

Schroeder went into the den, sat Katie on his lap and helped her tap out the tune. Even sitting at the piano she jumped when she got to the *pop*. He did it again adding harmony with his left hand. Katie bounced and clapped her hands, pleased with her efforts.

"Do you want to see the train?" Schroeder asked her.

"Yes!"

He took her into his study and pretty soon we could hear the train clacking over the tracks and Schroeder began a game I'd seen him play with his grandson.

"Katie, see the little people? Here's a lady and here's a man. Can you find a doggy?" He held her over the train board and she looked and looked for a dog. After a short while he gave her hints. "It's by a house and near a tree." When she had found the dog he asked her where the horse was, then the red car.

We sat at the table and visited with Nancy.

"Tourist season is coming up. Does that mean you will be on the trail more?"

"Yeah, but I've got a couple of rookies I'm training. I'll be going out with two guys at a time."

"I should shoot you for giving that crazy fishing pole to Tex," Schroeder called from the other room.

"I didn't. Mick Colton gave it to him. I gave it to Mick as a joke."

"Yeah, well, those two could take a joke on a world tour. I'm tempted to confiscate the thing."

"It's fine with me. When Warren Randolph took it away the first time I was relieved, but then Kelly Green brought it back to me. It's the fishing pole that won't go away. It's a boomerang pole."

When Katie was tired and rubbing her eyes they came out of the study. Schroeder put her down and she ran up the stairs. So much for being tired. She jumped down them one at a time.

"Oh, Cassidy, she's going to fall. I just know it," Nancy said.

"She'll be fine as long as she takes it slow. It's when she tries for two at a time that she falls down. If you try to help her she just insists on doing it by herself."

"Just like someone else I know," said Rusty.

"If she tumbles down those stairs, I'm going to cry, too," Nancy said.

Hop, hop, hop Katie went down the stairs. When she got to the bottom she climbed back up.

"I'm tired just watching her do that," she said.

"She'll fall asleep on the way home," I said.

"And what about you?" Nancy said to Carson. "Will you fall asleep on the way home, too?"

"Hopefully," said Rusty.

"How are you feeling after taking those shots?" Schroeder asked.

"Moving a little slow. But I'm feeling better."

"Mick and Tex almost quit on you."

"Yeah, Tex showed up this morning. He didn't want to go tracking so he must have just been checking up on me."

"That's not a nice thing to do to a rookie cop. Their first couple of weeks and they watch you get gunned down. Reality stinks when that happens."

"Reality stinks sometimes when you're a trouble magnet. You can't get away from it. All you can do is make the best of it."

"Is that what you were trying to do?"

"We were trying to surround the guy. John had him covered from the front. We needed someone to get around behind. I could do that. I almost did. Then Tex and his famous squirrel fishing lure thought I needed a distraction so he cast the lure out there. The bounty hunter was jumpy, so when he saw the movement of the lure through the brush he got worried. When I moved he just fired. He didn't know what he was firing at. All he could see was that the brush moved around a lot. Wham, bang and I was on the ground."

"And you say that guy was a bounty hunter after Chase Downing's head."

"Yeah."

"Where is Chase?"

"He's making himself scarce."

"But where is he?"

"Last I heard he was driving up to check on Patrick and Elan, but he sure didn't like the idea of staying on the road. He's not the tourist type. He'd like to be at home in San Diego, with his ornery old cat and his surfer friends at the beach, prowling around the desert tracking."

"Where does he stay when he visits the ranch?"

"He's welcome to stay in the ranch house. There's plenty of room, but I bet he tosses out his sleeping bag in the tree house."

"And if we need to get hold of him?"

"Call his cell."

"What does he know about these men who are hunting him?"

"He knows they need the money and they don't much care what happens to him as long as they get it."

"And people who get in their way?"

"They don't care what happens to them either."

"And how do these guys link you to Chase?"

"I went down to Mexico to get Chase out of a fix. They didn't like losing him when they had him. I guess they are trying again."

"Why don't you go check on Patrick and Elan, too?" Schroeder suggested.

"Patrick is having a blast with Chase up there. I don't want to throw a monkey wrench in the works. Why?"

"We haven't seen the end of this."

"I can't stay at the ranch until this blows over."

"Why not?"

"Because! Umm… I'll go nuts there. My mom will buy every toddler outfit in town. I'll have to buy a new house for Katie's clothes!"

"Cassidy, you're exaggerating," Schroeder said.

"Only just barely," Rusty said.

I glared at him even though he took my side.

"Cassidy, maybe you can chance running into these guys, but most of the time you've got Katie and Carson with you. What'll you do if you have a run-in with the kids along?"

I didn't have an answer for that. It was one of my big worries, too.

Katie was hopping slower down the stairs.

"We'll talk about it when we get home," I told Schroeder. "I've got two kids who are ready for bed."

Rusty took the cue and said, "Nancy, dinner was delicious as usual. Thanks for inviting us. Katie, can you come tell Mister and Missus Schroeder thank you for dinner?"

Katie hopped down the last two steps and came over to the table.

"Thank you for dinner," she said.

"You're very welcome," Nancy said.

"What did you like at dinner?" I prompted Katie.

"I like the brownies and the piano."

"Yes," I added. "Thanks for playing the piano for us. Will you do it again some time?"

He shrugged. Big tough policemen weren't supposed to play *Pop Goes the Weasel* on the piano.

As we started loading up, Katie asked, "Daddy? Can I ride in your car?"

"We'll have to switch the car seats," Rusty said.

"But I want to ride with you."

"We can just swap keys," I suggested.

After thanking Nancy and Schroeder one more time I climbed into Rusty's Explorer and headed for home. He had a little more buckling in to do, with two kids and a diaper bag. I took the most direct route home.

Chapter 37

When I pulled onto Sunset Road I was wishing I'd held off a little bit. The foothills were dark. And when I pulled onto Lost Hills Road I realized I hadn't left the porch light on. Finding a dark driveway on a dark street on a dark night was nearly impossible. I drove mostly by muscle memory. When I thought I found the driveway I started turning, watching the headlight beams. I was glad we had motion detector lights when they came on, because they startled a man waiting in my driveway. He was leaning against the garage door under the motion sensor so he wouldn't set it off. I threw the Explorer into reverse, backed out of the driveway, and called Rusty.

"Don't take the kids home. There was a man waiting for us, just standing there in the dark."

"Where are you?"

"When I saw him I didn't stop. I just backed out and kept going. I'm circling around to the other end of Sunset Road."

"Okay, I'm hanging up so I can call this in but I'll call right back."

We hung up and I made my way around Lost Hills Road to where it connected with the other end of Sunset Road. I turned left and caught up with Rusty at the other intersection of the two streets. He was pulled off the road waiting for an officer to show up. I could see the relief in his eyes as I pulled up. I got out of the truck and walked over to his window.

"Thanks," he said, "for just backing out."

"I didn't want you to follow me into a situation. You'd have your hands full with the kids."

"Switch cars with me and take the kids to Kelly's house."

"Can't we just…"

"Yeah, we could. Or you could stay out of the way and we cannot worry about you. Or the kids. Take them there and bed them down on the couch. I'll call ahead. Kelly would rather you were there than here in a confrontation."

"I know, but I feel like such a wimp."

"Sometimes it's better to be wise."

He flipped open his phone and there was a quick conversation.

"Kel? I'm sending Cassidy over…She'll have the kids with her…Just a piece of couch…I don't know, could be an hour, could be overnight…She'll come. She'll do it for the kids…I'll see you in a while…bye."

I grumbled all the way over to Kelly's house. The kids slept soundly in the back seat. I wondered how stocked up the diaper bag was after the evening at Schroeder's. Oh well, I could always run down to the little general store in the morning if I needed to.

Kelly's road was dark, too, but it was a different kind of dark. It was a kind of dark I was used to in the woods, where the trees held a tiny bit of moonlight no matter how dark the night. The dirt road was perhaps a quarter mile long and three other houses shared it. His was a small A-frame with a stack of firewood outside the front door. His Kelly green Charger sat in front of the woodpile. I pulled up next to it. There was no real driveway to tell me where to park. He opened the door wide and light spilled out into the night.

"Trouble, you're losing your touch. What happened?"

"It's a long story that started in Mexico. Help me get the kids in. Here, take Carson."

"You go ahead. Katie's heavier."

"No, if you pick up Katie she will wake up right away. I don't know how she knows the difference in her sleep. Rusty and I can carry her around but if anybody else picks her up she wakes up fast."

I set Carson in his arms and then went around the truck for Katie. I draped her over my shoulder and grabbed the diaper bag. She slept soundly.

"Here, put her here," Rhonda said as I came in the house. I laid Katie on one end of the couch where Rhonda had laid out blankets. I settled her in and then made a little bed for Carson on the floor. He was used to a hard bed and he was used to playing on the floor. I plopped into a chair with a frustrated sigh.

Kelly sat on the arm of the chair. "Now tell me what happened."

"Chase Downing got himself in hot water and there's drug dealers in Mexico who have offered a reward for him. They know Chase has connections with me so I've had bounty hunters calling on me, looking for Chase. Border patrol down there advised him to clear out so he came up here. They followed him up here so he took off again. Only problem is the bounty hunters haven't caught on. One of them was waiting for me when I got home."

"Don't they just ask a few questions and go on their way?"

"They are a little more forceful than that. The first guy put a gun to my head. The second guy showed up while Chase was up in the mountains. I hiked in to warn Chase and ended up with a bounty hunter on my tail."

"I'm glad you came here. No sense in tempting trouble. What do you need?"

"I'm fine. I'll wait a while and see what happens. If Katie wakes up in a strange place I need to be here. Rusty will let me know when the coast is clear."

It was frustrating not knowing what was going on at home. I knew Rusty would wait for help to arrive, but I also knew he was used to walking into situations like this. He'd be right up front.

Carson woke up and I changed him and made up a bottle. Rhonda's kitchen adjoined her living room so everything was handy. I curled up with Carson in the chair and he ate and played with my hair. I fell asleep still curled up in the chair with Carson lying in my lap.

I heard the doorknob turn and came awake quickly. Rusty let himself in and walked quietly into the room. He saw Katie sleeping peacefully on the couch and took Carson from me so I could stretch out. He shook the bottle a little to get an idea of how long Carson would stay asleep.

"How did it go?" I asked.

"We didn't find anybody. It was too dark. He must have slipped into the trees."

"I can tell you in the morning, if that's the case."

"No. I don't want you walking into a trap."

"But if I go home they will come knocking on the door again."

"I'll go home with you in the morning. We'll pack up some things."

"No, Rusty, I don't want to leave. They can't drive us out of our home."

He just looked at me. Okay, maybe they could. I was willing to risk it, but I wouldn't risk the kids… so maybe they could. While one part of me rebelled another part of me thought Katie would love going to Grandma and Grandpa's house. She could ride a horse again. She might even be able to ride Patrick and Wyatt's little pinto. I'd ridden when I was her age, but there wasn't much of a way to stop me from doing what I wanted to do. If they hadn't put me up on a gentle horse I'd have climbed the fence and hopped on any one I could.

"Will you? For me?" Rusty asked.

"I don't want to leave you. They'll come looking and find you there. What will they do? I know you can't come, too. You have too much going on at work. Why won't these guys just accept the fact that we don't know where Chase is? You can't get information out of a person if it isn't there."

"No, but they can try. And the fact is, you do know where Chase said he was going."

"I wouldn't send them to the ranch. That would just transfer the problem to innocent people." Then I got to thinking, "This may be a long term problem. If the reward for Chase is worth it to these four guys who is to say more people won't step forward if they fail? I think to stop this we need to stop the guy with the money."

"Cassidy, you're talking about things that are happening in another country. You think the police in both countries are not trying to get the drug problem under control? If the guy behind this could be stopped easily, he wouldn't be out there in the first place."

"I know, but what if this is something we need to find a solution for? What if they won't stop until they get Chase?"

"Let's take care of today first. You look at such a big picture, it gets to be too much for anybody, any agency, any country to take on. Don't worry. Just take care of my girl and my kids."

I had to do it, even though I didn't want to. I had to take the kids out of harm's way. Or be prepared to protect them. I'd rather look like a chicken than have to protect them. So far, by the looks of things, protecting the kids could involve firearms.

Chapter 38

"Gordon's Quarter Horses. This is Martha speaking, how may I help you?"

"Hi Martha."

"Cassidy! Hello dear, how are you?"

"We're all fine. Just thought I'd let you know you might have three more at the ranch for a little while."

"Oh, your mother will be thrilled! I bet the kids are getting big! How long can you stay?"

"It might be a few days. It could be longer."

"What does Katie like to eat these days?"

"Peanut butter, jelly and Gummi Bear sandwiches."

"Oh my. I think I need to make a run to the store."

"No, Martha, don't do that. She'll eat whatever everybody else eats. She's just been experimenting with Gummi Bears ever since she smuggled some home from the grocery store. Don't buy more. Maybe she will forget about them."

"What do *you* like to eat these days?"

"Anything without Gummi Bears in it."

"I think I can manage that."

"Daddy come with us," Katie said.

"I can't, Princess. If I can I'll drive up for a visit."

"Today?"

"No, not today."

"But I will miss you."

"I'll miss you, too, sweetheart. You be good for Mommy. You can play with Patrick and go shopping with Grandma. You can ride the horses." He picked up Carson and held him close. "Okay Sport, you be good for Mommy, too. Cass… take care. Let your mom help with the kids."

"Do I have a choice?"

"Thanks for doing this."

"You'll call?"

"I will. Believe me, this isn't easy for me either."

"How will we know when it's safe for the kids?"

"I wish I had a good answer. If you're still up there when I wrap up this case I'll drive up. Plan something fun."

I couldn't even answer him right then. All I could do was hold onto him and fight back the anger. That bounty hunter was wise to stay away that day. If he'd shown his face he would have had an emotional basket case on him in a second. But no, one of the reasons I was taking the kids away was so they wouldn't see that side of me. I didn't want them to know trouble. I wanted them to grow up thinking the world was a good place. So I'd go show Katie the horseys and the bunnies and the doting grandma, and pretend people who hunt other people don't exist.

Rusty gave Carson a kiss and put him in his car seat. "Be careful," I told Rusty. He gave me a strong hug.

"I'm always careful. You take care of my girl."

"I will."

He gave me a long kiss and then there was a long awkward moment of silence and we both knew it was time for me to go, but I still didn't want to. I climbed into the driver's seat and talked myself into starting the engine. He kissed his finger and put it up to the window. I took the kiss and sent one the other direction. Gosh, I hated doing this. It wasn't that I didn't want to see my family. I did. I just wanted everything to be the same. I wanted us to be a normal family where the kids didn't go to Grandma's house to escape bounty hunters trying to take down a friend. Rusty followed us until we exited onto the freeway and then pointed his Explorer toward work.

"Mommy, don't be sad," Katie said.

"Okay, let's do something happy," I said. "What can we do that is happy?"

"Let's sing the Grandpa song."

"The grandpa song?"

"Yeah! Daddy taught it to me at bedtime. You know… Grandpa Gordon had a ranch EIEIO and on his ranch he had a horse EIEIO with a neigh, neigh here and a neigh, neigh there…"

She went through horses and dogs and bunnies and then couldn't think of any other animals that Grandpa Gordon had.

"Does he have cows?" she asked.

"We had some baby cows when I was a kid. We used to practice calf roping, but when they grew up we sold them to somebody who raised cattle."

Half an hour down the road Carson got bored. Katie tried to play with him but to Carson play meant being held.

"Maybe he's hungry," Katie said.

There was a basket full of toys between the kids. We brought coloring books and storybooks that Katie had memorized. She liked to "read" them to Carson. She never turned the pages at the right spots but he didn't know that.

I pulled off at the next exit and went through the baby routine of changing, feeding, burping. I put him in his car seat and started up a CD of kids tunes. Katie sang along and Carson was content for another half hour.

"I wish he'd learn words so he wouldn't cry!" Katie said plugging her ears.

"Teach him some words," I suggested.

She tried but Carson just wasn't interested in vocabulary building. He just wanted to be held but there wasn't anything I could do for him without stopping and then I couldn't hold him for long. It was a long, weary drive. Four hours to the ranch. Katie and I were both glad when we finally pulled up the lane and followed the white fence to the big ranch house. Patrick was at the barn doing chores and he ran up to the house to greet his favorite cousin.

"Hey Katie! High five!" he said. "Aunt Cassidy! Guess what!"

"Chase is here," I said.

"How did you know?"

"He was at my house before he came here."

"I've had so much school and chores I haven't had much time for tracking. Chase has been working, too. Martha finally convinced him to sleep in the house."

"How did she do that?"

"After working with the horses he needed a shower and the way to get a shower was to take a room."

"Has Grandpa been nice to him?"

"They don't see much of each other. Chase knows more about horses than I ever thought."

"He grew up in Arizona. There were horses around. Elan's family had horses. I bet they rode every once in a while. Do you think Katie could ride Snoopy?"

Snoopy was Patrick and Wyatt's little white and black pinto horse.

"You don't have to know how to ride a horse to ride Snoopy," Pat said. "All you have to do is sit on him. You don't have to rope him because he follows you. Once you get him going he seems to know what to do. I don't ride him anymore. I ride Buck. Since Dad has me doing more work around here I had to have a taller horse. Steve and Randy have switched to Apache. I still miss Mack and Chet. They were good horses."

"They still are. They're doing well at the riding school. Does Apache still startle when he hears loud noises?"

"He's getting better. Steve and Randy know his quirks."

My mom bounded down the steps and nearly tore off the door of the truck.

"There's my Katie!"

Katie was working on her car seat buckle so Mom unlatched it.

I took Carson out of his seat. He was still fussing. He needed a change, a bottle, and a snuggle on the couch. I had a feeling I'd get to do the changing and the feeding but my sister would show up in time to do the snuggling.

"Welcome home, Cassidy," said Martha. "Can I get you some dinner?"

"Just a little. Katie, too. We'd have been here sooner but we had to make frequent baby stops. Let me take care of Carson first, though."

"Katie," said Patrick. "You want to help me feed the horses?"

"What do horses eat?" she asked.

"They eat hay and oats. Aunt Cassidy, can Katie come with me?" Patrick asked.

"Don't let her go in the stalls or eat the hay."

"She wouldn't eat hay, would she?" Mom asked.

"If it's good enough for the horses…"

Patrick and Katie took off for the barn.

"Okay, baby, you're next," I told Carson.

My mom had taken one of the bedrooms in the ranch house and turned it into a nursery/playroom. There was a crib, a twin bed, a bookcase full of books in a variety of age levels, and two big shelving units full of toys. The grandkids were ten, eight, three and four months. Patrick didn't have much to do with the room until Katie showed up. He was too grown up to play with toys. Carson wasn't. Carson was going to have a ball in there. When he was changed I put him on the floor with a toy car. A new toy! Oh boy! I left him in the playroom and went downstairs to prepare a bottle. His curiosity about the toy would last just about long enough.

Martha was in the kitchen when I went looking for a pan to put hot water in.

"Can I do it?" she asked. "I haven't held a baby in so long!"

Sigh, it starts. Carson was all taken care of. Katie was busy with Patrick. I walked the house. Nothing had changed except the playroom. The house was full of guest bedrooms. It was like a bed and breakfast inn. When it was built customers came from all over the country and the nearest hotel was thirty miles away. Rich people stayed with us frequently when I was growing up. I wouldn't say things had calmed down over the years, but perhaps Dad had. He was more settled, less set on making his first million. I guess by most people's standards he was rich. He'd offered me money to go to college. He'd offer to pay for Katie and Carson's college when the time came. But I'd made my own money off his horses. Maybe I wouldn't need his money to put the kids through school. Even though I'd grown up a rich kid, I didn't think like a rich kid. I'd groomed horses. I'd fed them and watered them and mucked out their stalls. I'd helped train racers and workhorses and helped with foaling. I'd exercised so many horses in so many different stages of training I thought I could stay on any horse. Of course I'd taken my share of tumbles, too. With chores and tracking and hunting and training I didn't have much time to think about money. When I thought about the cost of my own three bedroom house and thought about what it must have cost to build this house… how many bedrooms did it have, anyway? Six upstairs. Four downstairs. Just the house was worth a couple million. Yeesh, Dad…

I walked out onto the big wrap around porch. I saw the barn down the road. Beside it was the bunkhouse. It seemed odd in these modern times to have a bunkhouse but Dad had wanted some of the hands to be available twenty-four seven. And the single guys really didn't mind. It was free room and board. They had a bed, a bathroom and a room they could do what they pleased with. It contained a pool table, a card table and a punching bag. The hands rarely had use for the punching bag. They didn't use it like I did. When I got frustrated I tended to take things out on it. But, if the hands used it at all I suspect it was to keep their reflexes quick. One had to be quick some times in dealing with horses. I'd lost a lot of pocket change at the card table and I could play a decent game of pool at one time.

I walked the fence line that bordered the road. The road came in from the "big road", the highway, and curved around leading to the house and then continuing the arc to the barn. It was a very short walk. There was room to park tractors and trucks between the house and the bunkhouse and then the barn was beyond that. Six horses grazed in the paddocks between the driveway and the big road. I didn't recognize any of them except Snoopy. Snoopy was bought for Patrick and Wyatt to ride. He was more like a dog than a horse and he had markings like Charlie Brown's famous dog, so his name became Snoopy. I ducked under the top rail of the fence and stepped through. I crossed the first paddock and ducked into Snoopy's paddock. I wanted to check out this little horse. Did I trust him with a three year old on his back?

Snoopy trotted up and nuzzled my pocket. Oh, rats. I bet Patrick always had a carrot for him. I raised his head and looked at him eye to eye. His long forelock blew into his eyes and he tossed his head. He nuzzled my pocket again.

"Okay, boy, I can take a hint."

I walked to the barn and Snoopy tagged along. It was hard not to like this friendly, little horse. When I got to the gate he started to follow me through it and then I realized there was a worn lead rope draped next to the gate because Snoopy insisted on going anywhere he was allowed. I clipped the rope onto his halter and let him follow me to the barn. Satan charged his stall door as I came in but it didn't faze Snoopy. That was a good sign.

"Aunt Cassidy, what are you doing with Snoopy?" Patrick asked.

"I just visited him but he thinks I have a carrot so I'm getting him one."

I looped the rope over a stall door and went to the little refrigerator in the office and got out a carrot. I broke it in three pieces so he'd be getting three treats. I gave him one piece on the flat of my hand and he munched happily. Since I was at the barn, I decided why not just saddle him up and see what he will do? So I found a saddle and a bridle and had him ready for a ride in the corral in just a few minutes. He stood patiently and when I got into the saddle he turned and looked at me, surprised. I knew he wasn't used to adults riding him, but I didn't think I was too heavy for a quick ride around the corral. A kick and he started forward at a sprightly walk. He turned sideways so I could unlatch the gate without dismounting, then he moved forward so the gate could swing. This little horse was a mind reader. I rode through the open gate, not bothering to close it. He started around the outside of the corral so I decided to not follow his routine. I turned him and he shook his head and then obeyed. Patrick put Katie on the gate and told her to hold on then swung the gate back and forth.

"Look! Look Pat! Mommy ride a horse!" Katie said.

"You want to ride the horsey?" Patrick asked her.

"I ride! I ride, too!"

"Okay, wait for your turn."

Snoopy was attentive and responsive but jerky, like many small breeds. I stopped by the gate and held my hands out for Katie.

"I do it myself," she said.

"First you ride with Mommy. If you do good, you can ride by yourself."

She held out her arms and I hauled her into the saddle in front of me.

"These are the reins. You use them to steer the horse. Hold them like this," I said positioning the reins in Katie's hands. I held her wrists and gave Snoopy a little kick. He walked forward slowly. "Okay, turn," I said moving her hands to the right. Snoopy walked to the right. "Okay, other way," I said moving her hands to the left.

"Go! Go fast!" she said.

"Nope, first we learn slow. To go fast I have to steer. Okay turn right." With each turn I had to move her hands for her but she was getting the hang of it. How old did a kid have to be to learn their left from their right? I'd taught many a child how to turn a horse. I knew Katie would catch on much quicker. Most of the kids I had worked with previously had learning disabilities of some kind. We walked around and around the corral, we did a couple of figure eights to get more steering in, but Katie got bored at a walk.

"Okay, let Mommy steer and we can go fast."

I took the reins in one hand, put a steadying hand on Katie with the other, and kicked Snoopy into a trot and then a lope. Katie hung onto the horn.

"Nope, let go and balance. If you feel unsteady, hold on with your feet.

You'll get used to it."

"I do it myself," she said.

"Okay, but you'll have to do it slow."

I stopped Snoopy and got off. I placed Katie squarely in the saddle. Her little legs stuck straight out. There was no way she could hang on with her feet but the advice was still solid. All her riding days she needed to know to grip the horse with her legs.

"Are you ready?"

"Go!"

"Kick with your feet," I told her.

When I saw her feet move I pulled gently on the bridle and led Snoopy forward at a walk.

"Okay, turn."

I watched the direction she jerked the reins and pushed Snoopy that way. After a while Katie wanted to go fast so I had her kick Snoopy again and I broke into a jog. Snoopy picked up his pace and I watched carefully as Katie bounced in the saddle. When she started slipping I quickly let go and grabbed her before she could fall. Snoopy slowed to a walk again. Katie laughed and laughed.

"That was bumpy!" she laughed.

"Let's let Snoopy rest and go find some dinner."

When I turned to lead Snoopy back to the barn I saw the fence was lined with ranch hands.

"Hey Trouble!" Randy called out.

"Hi!"

I looked down the row. Patrick, Randy, Steve, Chase, Elan, James, Zack. Patrick looked older than his ten years when he stood tall with the men. He might have little boy features but he had a discerning eye, a quick hand and sharp mind. He'd be as good a hand as any of them. They stood there in Levi's and Wranglers, boots and western shirts. Well, all except Chase. I doubted he owned a western shirt. Chase wore khaki cargo pants, moccasins, and a worn t-shirt that advertised a gun company. He'd been working. He had a bandana tied around his head. He looked mean. He looked sunburned. I wouldn't want to tick him off in a bar. But he smiled when he saw me, a mixture of amusement and concern. He knew I wasn't here for a visit. Something had prompted this turn of events. He also knew to save that conversation for later. There was a calm patience hiding in that man.

"Welcome home," Steve said as he came up beside me and put an arm around my shoulders.

Randy plucked Katie from the saddle and asked her, "Are you a cowgirl like your momma?"

"Not yet," Katie said. "I'll be a cowgirl when I grow up."

"Your momma was a cowgirl before she grew up."

"How old do you hafta be?" Katie asked.

The guys all looked at each other.

Patrick answered the question, "You can learn to be a cowgirl when your feet reach the stirrups."

"Katie, do you remember everybody's name?" I asked.

She pointed, "Unca Chase, Teve, Ranny, Pat, umm… Unca James…"

"And Zack," I filled in.

"Why is Chase an unca and I'm not?" Randy asked.

"All the officers are uncles," I said. "She sees Chase more often than she sees you."

"Unca Chase, do it again!"

Chase felt his pockets, "Shoot, anybody have a quarter on you?" he mumbled. Everybody stuck their hands in their pockets. A quarter got passed discreetly and Chase stole a glance at it. He looked in Katie's ear."

"Is it a horsey?" Katie asked.

"Nope."

"Is it a birdie?"

"Nope."

"What is it?"

"It's… a buffalo."

"What's that?"

"It looks like a big fat cow."

"Can I see?"

Chase pulled the quarter from Katie's ear and handed it to her.

"A buflolo! I show Gramma!"

Randy set her down and she ran toward the house.

"Do you think she needs help?" Steve asked.

"I don't know, but I have a horse to turn loose," I said. Patrick ran after Katie to make sure she got into the house.

I led Snoopy to the barn and took off the saddle and bridle. He didn't do much work so he only needed a light brushing to put him right. He followed me back to his paddock and I gave him the other two pieces of carrot before closing and latching the gate and draping the rope over the fence again.

"What's going on in Joshua Hills?" Chase asked after I turned Snoopy loose.

"We've had some unwelcome visitors. Rusty worried about me. I worried about what I might have to do with the kids present. So I came up here. Where kids don't have to worry about their mom gunning down a bounty hunter."

"Cassidy… I'm sorry."

"It's not your fault. I just wish…" I wished a lot of things. "I wish the world was a peaceful place. At least for people who can live that way. The kids still think it's peaceful. When Katie heard I got shot, she thought I had to have booster shots at the doctor's office. It didn't even enter her mind that I had been shot with a gun. I'd like her to stay that way."

"How long are you here for?"

"I don't know. I can't think of anything that can be done to stop the problem back home. Rusty can't really assign guys to watch the house and pick up bounty hunters. They can't haul in everybody who comes calling." I walked to the bunkhouse. "Steve, do you guys mind?"

"What do you want, Cassidy?"

"I just want a few minutes with the punching bag."

"Go ahead."

I hadn't been in the bunkhouse for years. I tried to ignore the guy's stuff lying around. I stood at the bag for a moment but it really wasn't in me. I sighed and turned around.

"What's wrong, Cass."

"I'm not mad enough yet. I guess that's not the solution."

My cell phone rang about the time Rusty would be getting home from work.

"Hi," I said when I answered the phone.

"Hi. You doing okay?"

"It was a lousy drive. Carson cried half the way here. I had to stop in every town. Katie's having a good time, though. She got to ride Snoopy. I rode with her and then I walked beside her while she rode him by herself."

"Do you think that's wise?"

"I was right there. We were just walking around the corral, little more than a pony ride at the fair. She needs to learn how to balance. I haven't seen much of Carson. Mom, Martha, and Jesse keep passing him around."

"It sounds like everything is going great."

"Yeah… great."

"Babe, it hasn't even been a day."

"It's been the longest day."

"Just hang in there. You'll be fine."

"You won't run up here real quick-like and spend the night with me?"

"Would you like that?"

"More than anything."

"I wish I could."

"I'd make it worth your time."

"Cassidy!" Jesse said behind me. I didn't know anybody else was around.

"Me talk too!" said Katie.

"Go ahead and put her on."

"Hewo? Daddy! When will you come here? It's fun. I got to ride a horse. I got to feed them hay. Hay tastes yucky. Why do horses eat hay?... If I get a horsey tongue will I like hay?... I can't like ice cream and hay both?" She laughed, "A horsey has a big tongue! I couldn't talk!... I okay, I'll stay a little girl... I love you, too. Bye bye." She handed the phone back to me.

"In case it comes up again horses like hay because they have different tongues than we do," he said.

"Okay, I'm glad she decided to stay a little girl."

It was a rather melancholy conversation. I tried to be upbeat but I was so lonely. I just wanted to pack up and go home. He'd had a meeting with Mick and Tex and they said they would practice without me while I was gone. I knew their police duties would override their tracking practice. It only made sense. If duty calls you don't go following a bunch of tracks on the ground. They were supposed to do a patrol of my house each day and report any odd tracks. That might provide a smidgen of practice.

Mom took Katie shopping. I let them go so they could try on outfits to their hearts content. I finally got to visit Carson because Jesse is a natural born shopper, too. Wyatt came along and wanted to play cars with Carson.

"Carson can't crawl yet."

"It's okay, he still likes to see the cars zoom around."

"Okay, run upstairs and get some cars and I'll put him on a blanket."

I spent an hour watching Wyatt crawl around Carson on the floor. Trucks dumped loads of building blocks and buildings appeared on the floor. Race cars drove too fast and wiped out block buildings. Carson thought it was great, personal boy-type entertainment.

When Jesse came back and Mom and Katie were "doing hair" I got Shasta out and headed for the hills. In a few minutes Chase caught up with me. He was riding Apache.

"You know the history on that horse?" I asked.

"He's just like me. We're both a might jumpy."

"Let's go hunting," I suggested.

"It's not hunting season."

"Let's go hunting this guy who backs the bounty hunters."

"Easier said than done and illegal as hell to boot."

"Why can they hunt us, but we can't?"

"Cassidy, you know the answers. You just don't like them any more than I do. I've been dealing with this shit for forty years."

"I don't have forty years to put into it. I have two kids and I don't want them to know this happens. How long can I keep them from it? Do I have to run to do it? Which is better, running or getting a dose of reality? I want to give the kids a reality they can deal with. They shouldn't have to deal with this."

"That's why *I* deal with it. I didn't mean for it to rub off on you. Over the border issues are always touchy. It's not something any one person can do alone. You can't wipe out the drug trade by taking out one hot shot with a load of dough. You take him out and that just makes you marked by the ten who are waiting in line to be the hot shot when he's out of the picture."

"Who is this guy? Does he have a name?"

"He does."

"What is it?"

"I'm not telling you."

"Why?"

"Because, this is eating at you. I don't want you to focus on a man. It's too easy to hate a man and it does no good. It hurts you worse than it does him. Make the best of what you've got here."

I jabbed Shasta in the sides and he leapt to a lope. I urged him faster. Chase had no trouble catching up. I knew Apache was a much faster horse than Shasta had ever been. Shasta enjoyed stretching his legs for a change. I worried he'd step into a gopher hole so I pointed him toward the deer flats and I pulled him up when we got close. When I could see deer off in the distance I got off Shasta and told him to stay.

"Cassidy…"

"Shh, no talking here."

"Cass…" I glared at him. I nodded toward the deer and walked away. I doubted I would get very far the way I was feeling. To stalk deer I had to focus on the deer, which was one reason I decided I should do this. I couldn't be mad at drug dealers and be peaceful with the deer at the same time. One or the other would win. I hoped it was the deer. I didn't worry about the deer seeing me. It was scaring them that I needed to avoid. I walked until all heads came up, ears pricked forward. Okay, here we go. I froze. Freezing was always the beginning of going forward with deer. It was a long, quiet, peaceful game of Mother May I. It was give and take with nothing changing hands. Freeze. Freeze. Wait. It was much like surfing. You had to catch a fleeting moment. The deer decided I was no threat and bent to graze. When their eyes followed their noses I stepped forward, one, two crouched steps. Start and stop. No blinking, barely breathing, waiting, two more steps, okay, one more. Good. Three was good. Freeze again. The closer I got the lower I crouched. I chose a doe and made my way her direction. It's okay, I silently told the deer, I'm not here to hurt you. I just want to be near you. Don't run away. Then I had to settle my mind because she seemed to know when I was thinking and when I was stalking. For some reason, they tended to prefer stalking to thinking. The doe looked up and stared me in the eye. I froze. Her gaze was peaceful, but alert. She seemed to know she could easily outrun me. It took her a long time to look down again. She seemed to be studying me. This was an odd situation. I decided to give her some time. Next time she looked down I smoothly lowered myself to the ground. I lay on the ground, eyes peeking over the grass. She could still see me but when I was smaller I was less threatening. I lay there watching her and after a while Mexico was miles away, not a threatening hunter who could be just around the corner. I crawled a few steps closer. She startled a little so I lay back down. If I dashed forward I could touch her. But I didn't want to do that. I wanted the touch to come with respect, not a threat. So I waited and waited and inched forward, still flat on my belly in the dirt.

"Cassidy…" I heard off in the distance.

It had a warning tone to it. The deer's heads all pointed toward Chase. What was he warning me about? I waited. No sense in panicking. It was just deer. If anything they would just run away. The doe startled and I shrunk lower.

"Cassidy," Chase repeated. It still had a warning tone but he seemed to respect my wishes and stayed out of the picture. I peeked over the grass again and I saw… the buck. He pawed the ground as he glared me into the ground. His glare said, "What do you think you're doing with my does?"

I thought about my options. I could quietly back out, or I could jump up big and threatening and scare him off.

I rose to a squat, ready to bolt if I needed to. I held out my hand like I would to a dog. I'd never come nose to nose with a protective buck before. His glare intensified. He meant business. I looked away from him. I wanted to let him know he was the boss here so I gave way and let him dominate. Then I stood. I knew Chase was ready in case I ran into trouble but I didn't want him to shoot. Even if the buck charged me I didn't want him to shoot. I decided to trust the buck, so I turned my back to him and walked away. He could have run me down easily but I left him to his does and I hoped he would let me go. Ten steps and I glanced over my shoulder. He was still glaring so I kept walking. It reminded me of walking out of the ring when I'd tried to leg my first calf over and it butted me in the stomach. All those people watching. Me clutching my stomach, kicking at the dirt, knowing Steve would throw an arm over my shoulder and encourage me to try it again. He threw an arm over my shoulder, not around, because I was eleven years old. The calf probably weighed more than I did. It was a losing battle. I didn't feel that bad this time but I could feel the eyes boring into my back. When I was a safe distance away I turned again and waved to the buck. He tossed his head at me.

Chase holstered his pistol.

"It wouldn't have worked from this far away," I said. "If you had shot him you'd have a different kind of problem on your hands." I looked him in the eye, the kind of look I knew not to give the buck. "In that situation… don't shoot. I don't care what he's doing to me. Don't shoot. I was on his turf. He has the right to protect his does."

He didn't argue with me. And I knew he'd shoot if he had to. I wondered at what point he would have to. We climbed into the saddle and headed back to the ranch at a walk. I was calmer now. He knew it. He wasn't going to stir up the ashes to see if the fire was out.

"Thanks," he said.

"You could have come with me."

"No, it was much better that I didn't."

"I think I've taken advantage of the free babysitting long enough."

I rode slowly into the barn and dismounted. I took care of Shasta carefully going over him, checking for rocks in his hooves, brushing him down. I remembered doing this so many times. At one time he was my best friend. Brushing him, getting ready for a ride and coming home from a ride was our hellos and see ya laters. And one day it was good bye, I'll be gone for a while. And now I was this woman who showed up and he didn't remember the attachment, but I did. Oh man, but I remembered it like it was yesterday. Knowing I was getting on a plane, walking away from the only life I knew, walking away from my horse, my family, my room, my hills just because I was… stubborn. That was it. I threw myself to the mercy of the Marines out of stubbornness.

I walked to the racetrack and then started walking around it. I opened my cell phone and called Rusty.

"Hey babe, is everything okay?"

"Yeah… are you busy?"

There was a long pause and I think he decided he better not be busy.

"No."

"I just wanted to hear your voice."

"Okay."

"I should be in the house. I just got back from the deer flats. I should go see how the kids are doing. But I'm not ready."

"Were the deer there?"

"Yeah, I had a good stalk. The buck drove me away, but it was still a good stalk. I'll email you some pictures of Katie. She went shopping with Mom and they were styling her hair when I left."

"I'll be checking my email. Cassidy, you're just sinking deeper."

"I can't help it. My past, present and future are all fighting it out here. And you know what? I don't like it. I'm the same stubborn kid who ran off to the Marines."

"No you're not. You're my girl."

"You're girl is all screwed up."

"Stop it."

"What?"

"You're making my arms ache."

"You max out the machines at the gym but I'm making your arms ache from four hundred miles away."

"Different kind of ache. Think of a happy time and tell me about it. It's been three years. Remember when you were coming home from the ranch and you were in labor with Katie? It was a race to see if I'd be there when she was born, and then it was a race to see if she'd be born in the ambulance or at the hospital."

"We didn't make it to the hospital."

"No, but it's okay. I was there. I got to see her take her first breath. Do you remember how we felt that day?"

"It's kind of different for a woman. I was just glad labor was over. I was relieved. And I was scared to death. I didn't know how I'd learn to be a mom and I knew I had to learn fast."

"And you did. You've been a wonderful mom. I knew you would be."

"I wish you could have been there when Carson was born."

"I know. That was under less than favorable conditions. Do you remember trying to get his birth certificate? There was no doctor, no EMT to verify his place or time of birth. There was no witness that could state that, yes; this baby belongs to this mom. We're lucky we have connections."

"Once we got up here Carson has been fine. Jesse likes to spend time with him. Seems like Patrick adopted Katie and Wyatt adopted Carson. Wyatt's determined Carson is going to play cars with him. Are you sure you're not busy."

"Don't worry about it. You're sounding better."

"I told you I just needed to hear your voice."

"This summer we need to take a surfing trip. I think you've got the hang of it if you can just get to the ocean every once in a while. You always seem to feel better at the beach."

"We can go to the beach any day you can get away."

"We'll go as soon as the weather warms up enough. While you're at the ranch get out and do things. Even if it means watching Katie try on a hundred outfits at the mall. At least you won't be dwelling on things. Scrapbook with Jesse. Take on some ranch chores. You've had too much time to think."

"I know. But I only have patience for so much shopping."

"Shop for you. Find something to surprise me with."

"I'll try."

I had to laugh when we hung up because, surprisingly Rusty wasn't alone when he had that conversation. He must have been at work, but whoever he was with understood our situation. It was Tom. Before he pushed the *off* button I heard Tom say, "You're a brave man, telling your wife to go shopping."

And Rusty saying, "In this case, it's pretty safe."

Pretty safe because he knew I didn't like shopping and because my mom would pay for everything.

When we hung up I felt like a whole new person. Well, not quite but, I was sane enough to approach the kids and not scare them.

"Mommy! Where did you do go?"

"I went for a ride. I visited the deer."

"Aw, that's no fair!" said Patrick.

"Pat, have you ever stalked deer and had that buck challenge you?"

He laughed, which meant he had. "Kind of a wimpy buck, isn't he?"

"Have you seen him with antlers?"

"Yeah."

"How old is he?"

"I don't know how to tell his age. He isn't a youngster, though. I keep telling Steve he can't shoot him. Isn't he cool!"

"Yeah, he's cool. And he has a respect for people who respect him."

"That's another reason I won't let Steve shoot him."

"Patrick won't let us hunt the deer flats." Steve said. "If a deer comes from the deer flats he won't eat it. So we had to find another herd."

Wow, the power of a kid. But I could understand. He wouldn't eat a friend. Made sense to me.

"I was a little worried that Chase would shoot him today," I told him. "I was stalking a doe and the buck came up and stood over me. He didn't like me messing with his does. But he backed off when I did."

Shopping. I worried about shopping. Every time I went to the mall something bad happened. If there was a crime planned for the mall they looked at my schedule and planned on doing it while I was there. I'd brought down a bank robber, a purse snatcher, I spotted a man who was trying to kidnap his son from his ex. Maybe, if I just hung out in the women's clothes section, and only looked for something to surprise Rusty with, I'd be safe. Or they would be. I guess they usually got the worst of these shopping trips.

I knew finding something to surprise Rusty with was not a practical thing to do. He wanted me to buy a dress and then the only time I would wear it again was if we made a point of going out on a date where we both got dressed up. Even when we did go out on a date I preferred casual places. Still, I didn't mind picking out a dress to surprise him. It usually had the desired effect.

"What are we looking for?" Jesse asked.

"Something that will surprise Rusty."

"He's a detective. He's probably seen it all by now."

"He doesn't want that kind of surprise."

"Victoria's Secret? Fredrick's?"

"We can look. Are you sure you want to walk down the mall with me, though. Remember what happened last time."

"You stopped that guy from stealing that woman's bank deposit. At least you accomplished something that day."

"I don't like surprises at the mall."

"Cassidy, you're getting superstitious," my mom said.

"Okay, if nothing at all happens while we are here I'll admit I am just superstitious. But if something does happen then you have to admit that I am a major trouble magnet. You go to this mall all the time and nothing happens. The only time anything out of the ordinary happens is when you come here with me."

Jesse said, "Mom, you have to admit…"

"Don't even say it! We'll see. You *can* go to the mall without disaster striking."

I looked through Victoria's Secret. I tried on a few things. Katie held up a teddy and said, "Mommy, look, pretty!"

"It won't fit you. This is a store for grown-ups."

Katie looked around as if she was thinking, well, why shop here then, if there's nothing for me?

"The only thing in here that would surprise Rusty would be this black gothic looking thing and I think you're supposed to have black fuzzy handcuffs to go with it."

"Oh! I know where to get those," Jesse said.

"No," I replied. I'd had enough of being tied up and cuffed.

"You mean you've surprised him with all these other things already?"

"No, but it's hard to use fancy lingerie when you have kids in the house."

"Tell me about it," Jesse said.

"I'm not going to go into the bedroom and put something like that on.

Even if I managed to get it all the way on it would just come right back off. Might as well skip that middle step."

"You're too practical for your own good. You know that, don't you?" Jesse said as Mom paid for her purchases.

When we got out of Victoria's Secret Katie dashed across the mall.

"Hey, Kate! Wait!" I said dashing after her. She stopped midway at a grand piano. On weekends it had a piano player at it entertaining shoppers and pointing them to a music store further down the mall.

"Look Mommy! Can I play it?"

"No, it's just here for display. It's not for kids to play."

"But I won't pound. I'll be nice to it."

"Sorry, you still can't play it. It's against the mall rules."

"Unca Shoder lets me play his piano."

"Then you'll have to wait until we go to Uncle Schroeder's house again."

"Does Katie want to play the piano?" my mom asked excitedly.

"Yes!" and "No!" Katie and I said in unison, so I added, "Give her three years. If she's still interested we'll think about it."

Mom got excited.

"Just think! We could have a *musician* in the family. That would be wonderful! We could put a piano in the living room. I can just picture everybody in the living room around a crackling fire and piano music filling the house."

"Mom, before a person can be a musician, they have to be a beginning musician. Are you sure you want to listen to all the bad notes and mistakes leading up to that?"

"If I can keep up with a steady flow of icepacks from your dealing with wily horses all these years you'd think I could deal with a few sour notes. At least she doesn't want to play the trombone."

"What's a trombone?" Katie asked.

Oh no.

I looked at lingerie, dresses, and tops. I was getting shopped out and finding nothing.

"Cassidy, you're just being too picky," Jesse said, "There's been three or four outfits that would be perfect, but you just don't see it."

"Outfits tend to pick me. I don't pick them. I'll know the right one when I see it."

"For someone who doesn't like shopping, you sure are taking your time."

"We can go home any time you want," I said.

"I haven't given up yet," she said. "As long as you're looking for something for you, I can look for something for me. At least I am having better luck than you."

"Look Gramma! Teddy bears!" Katie said. I was trying to hang onto a wiggly Carson so I was glad when my mom followed her into a store where customers make their own teddy bears. When I caught up, Katie was looking at little, limp teddy bear bodies.

"What's wrong with them?" she asked.

"Nothing, sweetheart, they just don't have their stuffing in them yet. When you buy one they put the stuffing in them. See? That man is buying a teddy bear. Do you want to make a teddy bear for you and one for Carson?"

The man took his foot off the pedal, felt the teddy bear, he stuck his hand into his pocket and then felt inside the bear. I thought it was odd for a man to care how the stuffing in a teddy bear felt. Katie watched him.

"If I get a teddy bear they won't be sick anymore?"

"Katie they aren't sick, they just aren't stuffed," I said.

She watched the man as he continued to fill the teddy bear then reach into his pocket. Katie walked up to him.

"What'cha doing?" she asked the man.

"I'm buying a bear for my brother's kid," he said rather gruffly.

"Why do teddy bears need shiny rocks?" Katie asked innocently. She held up one of the shiny rocks. My mom took it from her.

"Oh, my word! It's a diamond!"

"What's a dimon?" Katie asked as the man began glancing around with a desperate look on his face.

"Gimme that!" he snapped. He snatched the diamond out of Mom's hand. He reached into his pocket stuffed something into the bear. "Okay, just sew it and let me out of here."

"But sir! Don't you want to name it? Little Jennifer would be pleased to know her bear had a name."

"I just want to buy the damned thing!" he snapped.

Mom covered Katie's ears.

A teddy bear full of diamonds? This didn't smell right.

"Mom, watch the kids. I'll be right back."

"Where are you going? You're *not* going to get in trouble are you?"

"Not if I can help it. Here." I handed Carson over and sprinted down the mall looking for a uniform. Security… security where are you when we need you? Just then the man passed me, teddy bear flopping around limply under his arm. Oh shit. I took off after him hoping a security guard would pull me over for speeding in the mall.

"Hey! Watch it!" an angry woman snapped as I ran past.

"Stop that teddy bear!" I yelled.

Everybody stopped and stared. At least when everybody stopped it slowed the guy down. He had to weave around people instead of passing them. I put on a burst of speed saw a couch in the middle of the mall, jumped onto it and launched myself at him. Oh shit! I fell short, scrambled to my feet and kept after him. As I fell face first to the marble floor one man said, "Ooo, that's gotta hurt." Darned right it did.

"Stop! Damn it! You're not getting away. Somebody call Security! Stop that man!" I yelled.

He ducked down the hallway that led to the bathrooms. I worried that there might be an exit at the end of the hall. He burst through a door and I burst through right behind him. I thought I'd have a race through the parking lot but I bounced off a very surprised man walking toward the door zipping his fly. I must have been running pretty fast because we both went down.

"Ma'am, do know where you are?" he asked.

I looked around and I didn't see cars lined up in a parking lot. I saw things lined up all right. Urinals. The reactions were mixed. Some of the men turned scarlet. There were a few smirks. I was still in pursuit mode.

"The man with the teddy bear! Stop him!" I said.

"*Cassidy*?" I could hear Jesse looking for me in the hallway outside.

"Jesse! Go get a security guard!" I called back to her.

"Cassidy! Are you in the *Men's Room*?"

"I thought it was an emergency exit! Go find a guard!"

I looked from man to man. Teddy bear man must be in a stall.

"Ma'am, if you'll just wait outside, I'm sure he'll be out momentarily," the man said.

I backed out. There was no way he could get out without me seeing him. Now I had him. He was trapped.

The man zipped his fly and followed me out.

"Are you all right?" he asked.

"Yeah. I'm getting used to chasing men through the mall. This is only a slight variation. Never caught a diamond thief before, though."

"I thought you said he had a teddy bear."

"A teddy bear full of diamonds."

"Umm, are you sure you're all right?"

Just then Jesse rounded the corner and pointed to me.

"You called for Security?" the officer asked.

"There's a man in there. He's carrying a teddy bear and inside the bear is a handful of diamonds."

Zipper dude shrugged.

"Is this him?" the guard asked.

"No, he was just my latest victim. Sorry."

"It's okay, I'm just curious how this is all going to turn out."

A man came out of the restroom, glanced around at the crowd, shouldered his way through and went off to join his wife again.

Another man came out, looked around at the crowd, took in the uniforms, glanced back in and walked off down the hall.

"You'll tell me when he comes out?" the officer asked.

"I probably won't have to tell you," I said.

A boy came out. His eyes got big.

"Is that a real gun?" he asked.

"Run along son," the officer said.

One after another men came out of the restroom. Men were not anxious to go in when they saw the uniforms standing guard over the door.

How many men fit in one restroom? I knew the women's restroom could fit fifty on a holiday weekend. But I thought the guys had a drive through in there. Finally I figured the room must be empty. I looked to the guard and he looked to me.

"Look, if I was armed I'd do it, but I'm just shopping."

"A man with a teddy bear?"

"Yeah."

The guard looked to Jesse. "Did you see a man with a teddy bear full of diamonds?"

"Well, not full of, but… yeah. Enough to be suspicious," she said.

The guard took out his sidearm and pushed his way into the restroom. It appeared to be empty. The guard went from stall to stall doing the TV cop thing, pushing in the door and standing there gun poised. Nothing. Damn.

"There's nobody in there," he reported.

"Are you sure?" I asked.

"Yeah."

"Mind if I take a look?"

The two guards exchanged glances, looked down the hall. There was a crowd of men standing at the end of the hall waiting.

"You have thirty seconds," the guard said.

As I walked into the men's room again Jesse said behind me, "Cassidy, this is so embarrassing."

I looked over the long line of urinals, walked from stall to stall, and glanced up. The vent was loose. There was a movement above. I walked out of the men's room.

"Okay! You're right, he's gotten away," I said loudly.

"All right everybody clear out, the actions over," the guard said.

"Nope, wait. Get the customers out of here. Station yourselves at the exit and the end of the hall. He'll be out as soon as he thinks we've gone." I said quietly.

The guard gave me an "oh come on look" but he said, "Excuse me, ladies, gentlemen, if you'll just step out to the end of the hall, there's another restroom in JC Penney and Dillard's. I'm sorry for the inconvenience."

The hallway went still. I heard the sound of shoes hitting tile floor. The guard shoved me behind him and out strolled a lone man. He walked down the hall and met a gun, turned around and met another. Bingo!

"Put your hands over your head and hand over the teddy bear!" the guard barked out.

"What teddy bear?" the man said with his hands over his head.

The guard frisked him and he came out clean.

"Check his right coat pocket," I said.

Still clean.

"All right, hold him here. I'll be right back."

I went back into the men's restroom, climbed from the toilet to the toilet paper dispenser to the top of the stall wall. I pushed the vent cover out of the way and poked my head up inside. There was the floppy tan teddy bear leaning against the side of the duct with a small manila envelope next to him.

"Anybody have rubber gloves?" I called down. A security guard produced a pair. They had to carry them in case they had to collect evidence or deal with a bleeding suspect or victim. I put them on and pulled out the bear and the envelope, handed them down to the waiting guard and climbed back down. Teddy bear man struggled when he saw the bear but he was caught. Finally.

"If you'll just follow us, ma'am," the guard said.

Oh great. The endless questions and paperwork. I had to reiterate the whole story and they thought I was nuts until they felt the teddy bear and found out there really were a couple hundred diamonds inside.

"And you say your three-year-old pointed out the diamonds to you?"

"Yes, she even picked one up and showed it to us."

"Mommy look, I got a teddy bear just like the man's and he has a heart inside him and his name is Dimon. And Carson got a doggy like Shadow. And his name is Too."

"Too?"

"Yeah, like, he is Shadow, too. And Too has a heart, too. They have more love in them when they have a heart. And mine got a dress to wear but dogs don't wear dresses. So Too, just got a collar."

"Okay," my mom admitted. "You really are a trouble magnet."

Filling out the paperwork took over an hour and both kids were tired and hungry. I was shopped out. Except for not finding a surprise for Rusty it was a typical shopping day for me. Diamond and Too came in bulky house-shaped boxes so we clumped along down the mall until we found our exit and we piled into the Explorer and went back to the ranch.

"Hey babe," Rusty said when he called that night. "Did you get to go shopping?"

"Yeah, we went to the mall."

"Any surprises?"

"No, not at all. Not the kind you're thinking of either."

"There are two kinds?"

"Well, if I told you I took down a teddy bear toting jewel thief you wouldn't be surprised, would you?"

After a moment of thought he said, "No."

"I didn't think so. So, no, I didn't find any surprises for you. Maybe next time."

"Don't try *too* hard. I'd rather have you back in one piece than have that surprise."

"Okay."

Chapter 39

"I liked that little gauzy number Katie showed you," Chase said as I was walking through the barn.

"You *followed* me? On a shopping trip to the mall? And you didn't die of boredom?"

"It got real entertaining right there at the end."

"And you didn't help bring that jewel thief in?"

"It looked like you had things under control."

"Under control! You… you let me run right into the *men's* room!"

"You were a little hard to stop at that point. I bet the guys in there rather enjoyed it."

"Enjoyed it? You think they enjoyed it!"

"I bet they talk about that over the water cooler at work for days. And I did help you. I pointed security down that hallway before Jesse found them."

"Well, I'm glad you thought I had things under control. If Rusty asks you about it I trust you'll keep the story straight."

"I see Katie got a teddy bear."

"Katie can get anything she wants. Why would you follow me to the mall?"

"Checking your trail."

"So did I have one?"

"Only me."

"That's good."

"If you had a tail we'd both be in trouble. Has there been news back home?"

"No, Rusty calls every night, but he hasn't reported any progress. I haven't exactly pressed him for news. We mostly just talk. About the kids, about what happened that day. Little stuff."

"Little stuff is what makes the world go around. The big stuff just tries to mess up the little stuff."

That got me to thinking, though. How would I know when it was safe to go home if I didn't ask?

The next day was pleasant. Katie and I rode Shasta around the corral.

"When can Carson ride a horse?" Katie asked.

"He could ride today, but he would do the same thing you did when you were his age."

"What did I do?"

"You just chewed on the saddle."

She laughed at that. How silly she'd been when she was a baby. It would be years before she realized she was perfectly normal.

"Katie, when you saw that man at the teddy bear store yesterday, where did you find that shiny rock?"

She grew very quiet. It didn't take a rocket scientist to figure out what that meant.

"Tell me," I said. "You won't be in trouble, if you tell me the truth. You might get a talking to, but you won't be punished. I've got the talking to all planned out and I think it won't be too bad."

She got quieter.

"Kaitlyn Elizabeth," I stopped Shasta and got off.

"Why are we stopping?" she asked.

"Because you obviously can't talk to me while we ride. So hop down and talk to me. I want to know where you found that shiny rock."

It was a long way down. She held out her arms and I lifted her down and carried her to the fence. I sat her on the top rail where we would be eye to eye.

"This isn't a scary thing. This is just Katie and Mommy having a talk."

"I found it…" she debated. There was an easy out. Would she take it? Or would she fess up? "I found it… in his pocket."

I wanted to give her a high five and say, "Yes!" but I didn't. She'd broken a rule.

"You know it is wrong to take things from people's pockets."

"But he didn't even know…"

"That's worse. Just because you are able to get things from people's pockets without them knowing doesn't mean it is right to do it." I wasn't raising my voice. I was determined this was just a mommy/daughter talk.

"Why was it bad?"

"Because a man's pockets are a part of his personal space, and the things in his pockets are his possessions. If you take something from his pocket you are stealing that thing from him and the thing you took might have looked pretty and tiny, but it was worth a lot of money."

"Why did he put the shiny rocks in the bear?"

"He was trying to disguise the diamonds. It is very suspicious for a person to have a lot of diamonds, so he probably stole them. He knew he'd get in trouble for stealing them so he was trying to hide them in the bear. He could carry a bear around and give it to someone without getting in trouble. No one would know the diamonds were in there unless he told them. So he was hiding something he stole. After he sold the diamonds they would take the diamonds out of the bear."

She gasped. Get the diamonds out of the bear! Why… they would have to take him apart!

"I just want you to see that it isn't the smart thing to take things from people's pockets. This time it was a diamond. What if the man thought you were *stealing* his diamonds? He could call the police and then you'd really be in big trouble. I don't want you to get in big trouble. I want you to…" ignore reality and save sickly under-stuffed teddy bears. "I want you to leave people's pockets alone so you will be safe. And not get in trouble."

"Did I do a bad thing?"

"You broke a rule. Mommy and Daddy don't have rules except to keep you safe. You have to remember: no pockets."

"Did I do a bad thing to name my bear Dimon?"

"No, why?"

"I don't want my bear to be in trouble."

"Your bear is fine. He's a loveable bear. And you were nice to give him a good home. You take good care of him. Okay?"

"Okay."

"And Katie?" She looked at me expectantly. "Thank you for telling me the truth when I asked for it. I'm proud of you for telling me the truth even though you might have gotten in trouble."

She looked thoughtful a moment, then she said, "Can we ride some more?"

"Yeah, we can ride some more."

After a couple more laps around the corral I put Katie up on the fence with Steve and let Shasta run. Katie bounced and clapped her hands. I set up a low jump and took Shasta over that a few times.

"Can I do it too?" she asked.

"When you get bigger. You have to know how to hold on with your feet."

After school Patrick took Katie out stalking rabbits.

"Okay, are you ready? Can you sneak and walk at the same time?" Patrick asked.

Carson and I watched as Patrick led Katie into the paddock and they found a little cottontail nosing around in the grass.

"Katie, sneak up on the rabbit," Patrick whispered. "See the bunny? Go sneak up on it."

Katie put on her Dangerous Tracker Baby look and started sneaking. Katie didn't know there was a reason to sneak. She didn't know she was trying to get as close as she could without being spotted. The hope was when she figured that out she'd have the posture and the movement down so everything would click into place. Katie wasn't going to tag a rabbit that day, but she had fun following it around the grassy paddock. When her attention turned to the horse grazing in the distance Patrick picked her up and they went over to pet it. It was so peaceful. It was hard to picture bounty hunters staking out my house. I decided I'd ask Rusty what Mick and Tex had been finding. Maybe they hadn't found anything. Maybe I could be home.

"Starting early, isn't she?" Chase said.

"Ask Steve that. He was here when I was her age. It doesn't look too early to me. Oh sure, she doesn't know what she's doing out there…"

"My worry is that she does."

"It's just a game to her."

"And what is it to you?"

"Okay, it's a game to me, too. Unless I've been without food for a couple of days. Then it's skill, or a meal. Even if it's only a game to her it might come in handy later."

"So you're teaching Katie to stalk."

"I'll teach her anything I think she might use. I've used stalking in many different ways."

"What are you going to do when she can stand right in front of you without being seen?"

"Been there done that. My mom learned I'd show up when I was good and ready, so she just waited. I always got whatever she had in mind for me. I just got it when I was ready to receive it."

"Interesting. Have you gone tracking with Patrick?"

"He's been too busy."

"You should. You'll be surprised."

"Have you talked to the officials up here? Do they know they have a tracker they can call on?"

"You don't want Patrick to get involved in that."

"He'd love it. I assume they wouldn't send a kid on a dangerous call, but if it was a matter of finding someone and an adult went with him, it would do him good to put his tracking to use."

"They wouldn't take him seriously."

"Until he proved himself. So they have some guys beating the bushes and they have this kid with a partner out 'tracking'. Who is going to find the ten sixty-five first?"

Rusty didn't call that night. I worried a little. I missed him a lot. But I knew his job frequently called for long hours and when it got too late he would figure I was asleep and not want to wake me up. He'd pace the house wondering if he should anyway. He'd wonder if I was waiting for his call. Sometimes he called when that happened and sometimes he let me rest. But I wasn't resting. So I worried and paced and finally went to bed lonely.

Chapter 40

"Do I hafta eat eggs and meat and pancakes?" Katie asked Martha.

"No, dear, you just have to eat healthy."

"When we visit, my mommy says I have to taste a tiny bit of everything."

"You're not visiting. You're family. If you ate everything on the table here you'd burst. I make eggs for the guys who like eggs and I make a stack of pancakes because some of them like something sweet. They work all day. They can stand to eat a couple of pancakes with syrup and jelly. But you don't have to eat anything you don't want to."

"Then can I just have the syrup and jelly?"

"That wouldn't fill you up. You can put it on a pancake."

"Can I have coffee?" Katie asked.

It was right about then that I walked into the kitchen.

"I'll make it," I told Martha and Katie looked disappointed. "You know you can't have straight coffee. I'll make you a Katie coffee."

I got a cup and quickly filled it halfway with milk, then I slowly poured in a couple tablespoons of coffee so it looked like more coffee than it was. I added a little sugar, stirred it up and gave it to her. She sipped it just like she saw Daddy do over his breakfast. With coffee, sugar and syrup in her she was quickly ready to start the day. And I figured as soon as the sugar rush wore off she'd be ready for a nap, too.

"Let's get you dressed for the day," I told Katie.

"I do it!" she said.

"Cowgirl clothes. You need play clothes today, not dresses."

"New clothes?"

"If you wear new clothes bring them to me so I can take the tags off."

I heard Carson wake up, so I followed Katie upstairs. I heard the front door bang open and Patrick saying, "I have to catch the bus!"

He dashed to the dining room loaded up on scrambled eggs and shoveled them in.

"You better hurry young man," Martha said.

"Patrick! I go too!" said Katie running out the playroom and standing at the top of the stairs.

"You can't go to school. You're not old enough." Patrick said as he dashed out the door.

Katie rushed after him, "Pat! Pease! I go too!"

"You can go to school when you're a big girl," I said. "You'll start school when you're five. Right now you're only three."

"I want to see what they do there."

"They read and write and do math."

"I can do those."

"You think you are doing those, but you're doing little girl versions of the things the big kids do in school."

"I *can* do those!" she said adamantly.

"After I feed Carson I'll show you what reading is."

I changed Carson and took him downstairs. I started a bottle warming, then figured bottle time was as good a time as any to read a book. So I told Katie to go upstairs and find a book that she liked to hear. She brought one back downstairs and as I gave Carson his bottle I told her to open the book.

"You know this story. One fine day in the summer sun, Billy Bunny went for a run. How do you think Mommy knows that the bunny's name is Billy? And how do I know what kind of a day it was?"

"The pictures."

"The pictures show a fine summer day but how do I know the bunny's name is Billy?"

"Cause you made it up!"

"No I didn't. I know the bunny's name is Billy because these words at the bottom of the page tell me. See? This word says *one*, this one says *fine*," I kept pointing and saying the individual words. She seemed puzzled.

"This part of the story is words?"

"Yes."

"Like words we talk?"

"Yes."

"I can read words we talk?"

"If I wrote them down. That is what writing is, it's putting words on paper."

"Somebody talked these words and wrote them in the book?"

"Sort of. Somebody thought these words and they thought a kid would like to hear them, too, so they wrote them down for kids to listen to and read when they get bigger."

"Patrick can read?"

"Yes, Patrick is a good reader."

"Can Wyatt read, too?"

"Yeah, he learned to read in school."

"I want to go to school!"

"I told you, you can go to school when you are five."

"I want to go to school now!"

"You can't, they only let you in when you're five." Then you're stuck there for thirteen years, I thought.

"But I want to read stories, too!"

"You do?"

"Yes!"

"It takes a long time to learn how to read. First you have to learn your letters and the sounds they make. Then when you see the letters lined up you can figure out the words."

"Okay!" Just as simple as that. Is that all there is to it? Okay! Right then she didn't even have the ABC Song right. She sang *emelenopee*. Rusty, help! I've got a three year old who wants to jump into kindergarten! At the same time I knew that as long as a kid wanted to learn they would *try* to learn. So what was the harm in teaching her? It would give us both something to do. So as I fed Carson I taught Katie the ABC song being very careful to get the L-M-N-O-P part just right. Then after breakfast I wrote all the letters out, big and small in the order of the song.

"In the ABC Song it is not exactly words. It is the letters that make up words. See this? This is a big *A* and this is a little *a*. What's the first word in the ABC Song?"

"A."

"Right! And the next one is a B so here we have a *B* and a *b*, so as we sing the song, look at the letters."

We sang the song very slowly as I pointed out each set of letters. Golly, I had a new respect for kindergarten teachers already.

"When you know what each letter looks like then we can learn what each letter sounds like. And when you know what the letters sound like you can start to read."

"Okay!"

I folded the paper in half and asked her to find each letter as I said them. Find an A. Find a C. Find an F…We did this for a little while and some of the letters took a lot of thinking. I wasn't in any hurry. She didn't last as long on the other half of the paper. She started getting bug-eyed. So I made her take a break. But every once in a while she would see a label or a sign and she'd say, "Mommy! I see an A!" She remembered A, that's for sure.

"When you want to learn some more and we're both not busy, bring me the paper and we'll do some more."

By mid-morning Rusty still hadn't called. I thought if he had a late night at work he would sleep in a little and then call but I didn't hear anything. I tried calling his work cell. It went straight to the message service. That wasn't unusual if he was working. If he couldn't be interrupted or a ringing phone would cause a distraction he turned his cell phone off. I tried his office and got the answering machine there, too. I tried calling home and a woman answered.

"Michaels' residence."

"I'd like to speak to Rusty Michaels," I said.

There was a pause, no, "Rusty, it's for you."

"I'm sorry, he can't come to the phone right now," she said.

"Tell him it's his wife."

There that ought to do it.

"I'll give him the message and he'll call you back as soon as he can."

Okay, Cass, no need to freak out. Just because there's a woman at your house and she won't let you talk to Rusty. No cause for concern. Just because he sent you away for three days and now you can't get hold of him and there's a woman at the house is no reason to jump to conclusions. So just be nice and give him two minutes.

"Okay, thanks," I said and hung up.

Two minutes passed. Two hours passed. I wasn't the jealous type. I knew women were after Rusty all the time. He was just a chick magnet. Maybe that's what I got for marrying a chick magnet. But he'd always been so loyal before. He was worse than loyal. He was loyal, protective, devoted and, so far, totally trustworthy. It was too much to expect, I thought. On the other hand I was far too observant to not notice anything fishy before I left for the ranch. If anything was going on with Rusty I was sure I'd catch it. Nothing seemed odd except for the behavior of these bounty hunters and even that was not odd. Except they didn't seem to use bounty hunter logic. They seemed to be after me personally. I was thinking myself in circles so I decided to find something better to do. I walked down to the barn and looked over the horses. Katie tagged along.

"Look, Mommy! Satan's name has a's in it!"

"Yup," I said, "S-a-t-a-n. Now you know how to spell his name and when you learn the sounds you will know an *s* sounds like *ssss* and the first *a* sounds like *ay*. *T* sounds like *t…*"

My whole day was spent in conversation like this as Katie noticed words everywhere. She didn't need to know that Satan got his name because he was a devil horse. She knew that horse was *mean* with a capital M.

After lunch there was still no answer at Rusty's work and no answer at the house either. What was going on? I went to my dad's office and he was busy doing paperwork. I knocked softly. He looked up, surprised it was me.

"Yes, Cassidy?"

"I was wondering if I could send an e-mail. It will only take a minute."

"Sure, come on in." He pulled out a writing surface and turned the keyboard so it fit on top. "Drag that chair over."

I lugged over an easy chair and sunk into it too low to make typing easy so I knelt on it instead. Then I was too high.

I logged in and clicked the box to start a new message. Then I remembered I was supposed to send Rusty pictures of Katie with her hair all done up. I typed in the message I intended to:

"Hey there! Is everything okay? I haven't gotten through anywhere. Give me a call."

Then to lighten it up a little I wrote:

"Expect your conversations with Katie to get a bit weird. She is bugging me to teach her to read so she is learning the sounds of the letters. Pictures to follow. Love, Cass"

"Is everything okay?" my dad asked.

"I hope so. That's why I e-mailed. I told him I'd send him some pictures of Katie, too. Do you mind if I do that?"

"No, as long as you do it soon. I'll need my computer in an hour or so."

I ran off and found Mom's camera, took out the memory card, and stuck the card into Dad's CPU tower. I followed the prompts and opened the folder. I looked through the pictures, all four hundred and eighty two of them, and found three of Katie to send. Mom had done Katie's hair in little ringlets. I found a few pictures of Carson dressed up like a cowboy. He'd only worn the outfit for an hour, and then I decided he looked too uncomfortable, so I changed him into play clothes. The pictures were cute, though. Then, just in case he needed a reminder, I added one Mom took of Katie and me riding Shasta. It took a minute for the pictures to go across the net, and I wondered how long it would take him to download them. Maybe I should have made them smaller. He would probably receive them as he was heating up dinner anyway. When I was away he frequently picked up dinner from town and ate it at home, if the kids were there, or at Kelly's house if they were not. Hmm, Kelly's house. I wondered if Rusty had been there in the past few days. I didn't want to call there, though. I didn't want to be checking up on him. I was supposed to trust my husband, right?

I did. I really did. But what woman wouldn't question what was going on at home after calling home to find another woman there. Any woman would at least be curious, many irate. I was taking this well, wasn't I? Many women would run off to their sister's house and eat Ben and Jerry's and rant about their no good two timing… okay, so maybe I wasn't taking this very well. I actually had considered the Ben and Jerry's route minus the ranting.

"Cassidy? What are you doing?" my dad asked.

"Huh? Oh, stewing, but I guess I ought to go check on the kids."

"If Jesse spends much more time with that baby she's going to decide to have another one."

"She needs a little girl."

"Oh, no she don't."

"I'll go take him off her hands."

I looked around the house and Katie was being fitted for a dress. Carson was nowhere to be seen so I walked down to Jesse's house. She was mopping her kitchen floor and Carson was asleep on the couch. I stood there watching her for a bit. It wasn't a big kitchen. It wouldn't take her long. When she had wrung out the mop and put it away I asked her, "What else do you need to do?"

"Need? I don't *need* to do anything. Why? What do you want to do?"

"I need a distraction."

"Okay. Sit down and tell me about it."

"No, I just need to be doing something. Shopping, riding, scrap booking, mucking out stables, exercising horses. It doesn't matter."

"Yes it does. Tell me about it."

"I called home and a woman answered the phone. Now find something for me to do."

"A *woman*? Why that…"

"Jesse, that's why I didn't want to tell you. Because you'd jump to conclusions. *I'm* not jumping to conclusions. I'm just finding a distraction until I can get a reasonable explanation."

"A reasonable… a reasonable… how could there be a reasonable explanation for a woman to be at your house while you're away?"

"You're not helping and you will *not* say *anything* to *anybody*. Even if he is up to no good I don't want Katie to hear about it."

"You have to admit, any girl in the world would go after him."

"I think I'll go riding. At least then I only have one person telling me all these things. I don't need two," I said as I walked out of the house.

"Oh come on, Cassidy. There's bound to be a reasonable explanation. Though I don't know what that would be."

As she said that a blue and white patrol car rolled past Jesse's house to the big house. I looked at Jesse and Jesse looked at me. This was not good.

"Call Mom and tell her to keep Katie upstairs," I said as I walked down the lane to the house.

Chapter 41

The driveway to the ranch was not long, perhaps an eighth of a mile, so it didn't take me long to catch up with the patrol car even on foot. The officer was exiting his vehicle as I approached.

"Can I help you?" I called out before he could get to the front door.

"I'm looking for Mister Gordon or Steve," he said. He must have been around for quite some time to know the people at the ranch on a first name basis. To the people in town Dad's first name really was Mister Gordon.

"Can I ask what this is about?" I asked. "It'll help me decide who you should really be talking to."

"This is concerning Mister Gordon's daughter."

"Then you're looking for me."

"I don't think so Miss."

"I am Mister Gordon's daughter and I want to know what happened."

"Miss, could you just direct me to the man I am trying to find?"

Sigh. This was aggravating. Cops tend to get goal oriented. Target fixation. And they are a stubborn lot. Once they are given orders it's impossible to make them believe their orders might not change a little depending on the circumstances. So I took him to Steve. Better Steve than my dad. I found Steve's most recent set of tracks and I followed them out to a paddock and then I followed him and the horse to the corral behind the barn. The officer followed me wondering why I didn't just check all the outbuildings, but I fell into tracking mode and forgot. In a way it was a relief that that had happened. I was beginning to wonder if I was losing my tracking ability, if maybe motherhood somehow overrode stuff like that.

"Steve," I called out over the corral fence, "There's a man here to see you."

Steve looked up and saw the officer standing there.

"Orrel? What has Trouble been up to now?" Steve asked, walking over to the fence.

"Trouble?"

"Cassidy here. Usually if the cops show up she's involved somehow."

"Cap'n Howard asked me to come by and check on things."

"Oh yeah? Why?"

"We've been asked to put the ranch on patrol."

"Why? What are you watching for?" I asked.

Orrel ignored me and kept his eyes on Steve. Steve was irritated.

"Why? What are you watching for?" Steve asked on my behalf.

"Suspicious activity."

"Cars bearing Mexican license plates?" I asked.

That got Orrel's attention. He turned to me.

"Now how would *you* know about something like that?" he asked.

Damn, how did they find out?

"You got your orders from Captain Howard? Who received word from Joshua Hills? And who called from the Joshua Hills station?"

"Answer the lady," said Steve.

"You'd have to ask Captain Howard that."

"Okay, I will. Is the station where it's always been?"

Steve grinned. "Yeah, it's where this one has always been."

"Okay," I said exasperated. "Then where is it?"

"It's not where you think it is. It's across from the bank."

"Can I take Chase along?"

"He's in the barn."

I jogged to the barn. I stuck my head in and called out, "Chase, follow me. We're in for it."

He put down the hoof pick and exchanged glances with Elan. Elan gave him a nod and Chase fell in behind me.

"What's up?" he asked.

"That's what we've got to find out." I said.

"What car?"

"The Explorer."

He punched in the combination and hopped in the passenger's seat. It didn't surprise me at all that he knew the combination to my new truck. I ran inside for the keys. I grabbed them off the dresser in the bedroom and then stuck my head into my mom's sewing room.

"When the patrol car leaves the coast is clear," I said. "I'll be right back."

I took off before she could ask any questions.

"What's with the cop?" Chase asked when I got back to the truck.

"They've decided to put the ranch on their regular patrols."

"Why?"

"They wouldn't say."

"But…"

"But it involves watching for cars with Mexican license plates. I want to talk to the guy who talked to Joshua Hills."

"You can't just bust into the police station and demand to talk to some unnamed individual."

"We'll start with Captain Howard."

Chase and I fell into silence, each speculating about what this turn of events might mean. When we got to the compact brick structure across the street from the bank we saw quickly that this call had been the big news of the day. A case! Something to do! Something besides sipping coffee at the corner café or talking to the men outside the barber shop.

The whole building consisted of a room with two wooden desks, and a hallway that appeared to contain four offices. One of the rooms must have contained a cell or two.

"They *upgraded*, to this?" I wondered aloud.

I think I came in the front door a little more forcefully than most people did. Two uniformed men jumped to their feet.

"I'm looking for Captain Howard," I said.

"That would be me," one of the men said. He had a calmness to him that only came from experience, or small town life.

"I have some questions. And I have a very good reason for asking them so I'd appreciate straightforward answers. When did you get a call from the police station in Joshua Hills?"

He scratched his head and took a moment to figure out how he wanted to proceed. He was neat, every piece of his uniform pressed just so, tails tucked in, every button buttoned, shoes shined, belt full of all the gear he needed for a siege. He had maybe three deputies under him, maybe a detective. He probably had one guy in charge of forensics.

I was wondering what kind of a picture we made standing there. I was glad Chase wasn't in his usual cargo shorts and ratty t-shirt. He was in ratty jeans, boots, and Henley shirt with a denim shirt over it. I was in not quite as ratty jeans, a knit top and boots. At least we looked like we just rushed away from Gordon's Ranch.

"Ma'am, I don't believe we've met," Captain Howard said.

"I'm Cassidy Michaels, Wayne Gordon's daughter. And we have met, though it's been a while. This is Chase Downing, this concerns him, too."

"Captain Howard," Chase said. "Cassidy and I are involved in law enforcement. When your officer appeared at the ranch, we knew something had to be behind it. He wasn't giving out any information."

"Sit down," Howard said, "no use in getting all up in arms over this. You're both in law enforcement?"

"I'm retired but I volunteer my services in San Diego. Cassidy is a reserve deputy based in Joshua Hills. Her husband is a detective, also based in Joshua Hills. Cassidy and I are the trackers for our respective stations."

"Why are you armed?" Howard asked Chase.

"I've reason to be."

"Cassidy Michaels. So it was your husband I spoke to?"

"Yes! What did he say?"

"He said he didn't want to worry you, asked that I step up security around the ranch, said he'd call Mister Gordon about hiring a security guard."

"Why?"

"Now, that I'm not sure I should tell you."

"Captain, if we are in danger, we want to know what to watch for," I said. "Something happened back home to trigger a decision like this. I want to know what happened. If you won't tell me what it is, I'll hop in my truck and go find out for myself."

"I wish you wouldn't do that," Captain Howard said. "The danger would only be worse there."

"Then tell me. I'm not afraid of the danger to me."

"I'd tell her if I were you. She's not kidding," Chase said.

Captain Howard stared at his shoes.

"Ma'am…"

"Don't you ma'am me like I'm some little housewife who should be home baking brownies for the kiddies in the neighborhood. I know what I'm up against here. I tracked Chase into Mexico and distracted a bunch of drug dealers so we could escape. Remember the Peccati case? A little blond woman holding a man at gun point. Then, all hell breaking loose. Your men might have been the ones to take him down. That little blond woman was me. I have two kids to protect now. I have a right to know what their dad is dealing with. It only makes sense to know what I am supposed to be watching for."

"I think it'll help more if you tell me. What am *I* watching for?" Howard asked. "What happened back home that brought you up here?"

"Bounty hunters are looking for Chase. They know they can find him through me so they targeted me, too. I faced two of them before taking my kids up here."

"Well, apparently they haven't given up on finding Chase through you," Howard said. "Your husband came home to a ransacked house. So far all he can tell is that two pages were ripped out of your address book: the pages with your family's and your search partner's information. Landon Wilson has been informed. Orrel went to warn your father. Your husband has been busy dealing with the investigation…"

"Thank goodness!" I said.

"What do you mean, thank goodness? This is about the worst news we could get," Chase said.

"Not the worst, just bad."

"Then what would the worst be?"

It was my turn to look at my shoes.

"I tried calling home, when a woman answered the phone I didn't know what to think. But I thought something anyway… I'm glad she was just investigating a crime."

"You mean you thought Rusty…"

"What was I supposed to think? She just said Rusty couldn't come to the phone."

Chase was enjoying the situation. I was not. Chase stuffed his amusement into his pocket and got down to business.

"Adding the ranch to your patrols is a start. Any vehicle from south of the border is worth checking out. Suspicious activity of any sort, especially by Hispanic males, should be noticed and investigated at the very least. They will be well armed and you should consider them dangerous."

"How are we supposed to catch these men before they catch you?" the Captain asked.

"Foot patrols. I know your men have neither the time nor the inclination to hike around the ranch. I think Cassidy and I, being trackers, have a better chance of knowing when we are targeted."

"You want us to do nothing?" Howard asked, surprised.

"No, do as Detective Michaels asked and if you do happen to spot any cars from outside the US I'd appreciate a call. If you happen to get a call from us be prepared for quick action. Have roadblocks planned out ahead of time. If they take Cassidy they'll pump her for information and they won't be nice about it. If she won't give them the information they want, she may be tortured or taken to Mexico to be used as bait. If they take me, they'll head for Mexico any way they can get there." It was unusual for Chase to talk this much. He was really concerned. He looked me straight in the eye. "If they try to take you I want you to give them any information they want."

"No."

"Cassidy, it's not worth what they will put you through. If you disappear I'll be heading for the police, helping them do what we can. You won't have to worry about me."

"I can't send them to the ranch."

"Do you want me to clear out?"

"Not if you don't want to. Now that they have the address… I'm more worried about the kids."

"I don't think they would target the kids. Make sure they are always with an adult that isn't you. Don't leave the ranch alone."

"Shit."

"Did you bring your 9mm?"

"I don't want to carry it. Katie will ask questions."

"Where is it?"

"Locked in a box in the Explorer."

"A lot of good it will do there."

"It won't do any good at all. The only way I'd use it would be a life and death fight."

"They lay one hand on you and it's a life and death fight. You got that?"

I couldn't say yes. I knew to say no was a big mistake. I would not open fire at the ranch. I would let them take me first.

"Cassidy, if you get taken, and they use you for bait, it's going to work. If I have any assurance that they will really let you go I'll turn myself in."

"No!"

"*Don't* let them take you. You're a Marine. You're an officer. You can do it."

"I could. If it weren't for Katie."

"You'd rather her mom be taken away than explain to her how sometimes you have to do bad things to accomplish some good? I'd hit the road again but it wouldn't serve a purpose. It would just make it so you really don't know where I am and they wouldn't believe you. If they do show, I want to be where I can do some good."

"They could be here already. If they took the page yesterday. They could be here."

"Are you scared?"

"No. I'm just mad."

"Do me a favor and get scared."

Captain Howard learned more from listening to Chase and I than he did from asking his own questions. He had work to do, at last, but he didn't seem pleased with the prospects. He handed Chase and I each a business card.

"If you need help quick don't call 911. They take five minutes to figure out which town is closer and who they should call, which departments they should send. You want a car and you want it now you call that number. I'll call the guys in and report what's going on. We'll formulate a plan."

That didn't give me a whole lot of assurance, but I didn't let on.

"Thanks, we can use all the help we can get," I told him.

Chapter 42

When we left the station I didn't head straight for the ranch. I was bummed out. And I wanted some insurance.

"Where are you going?" Chase asked.

"We're going to visit an old friend."

"You want to drop me off at the ranch first."

"I thought you didn't want me going anywhere alone. You might want to visit this friend. It could save your life."

I pulled up outside an office building. The outside held no clues as to the type of business it was until we walked up to a brass plate that said Carr's Private Investigation and Personal Security Specialists.

"No quips," I warned as I reached for the door.

"Me? Quip?"

"One of the guy's names is Rashawn. Rashawn Carr, get it?"

"Now who's quipping?"

"Other guy's name is Desmond."

I pulled the door open and walked into the same cherry wood reception area I had been in five years ago. There was a different receptionist, in a neutral colored business suit, just like before. She glanced up as if she expected me to have an appointment.

"May I help you?" she asked.

"Yes, I'm interested in some personal security."

"Could you be more specific?"

"At one time I rented a personal tracking system from you. I'd be interested in that again. I was also hoping you had access to some body armor."

"Very well," she said. "If you'll have a seat I'll call Mister Carr and I'm sure we can arrange something to suit your needs. Sir? May I help you?"

"I'm with her," Chase said. "Where do you come up with these places?" he muttered to me.

"I had a drug lord after me. I needed to be findable."

"Do you make a habit of this?"

"No, do you?"

"I try not to. I'm beginning to wonder."

I found a seat and Chase sat down two seats from me. I picked up a travel magazine. I opened it to a picture of a couple on the deck of a huge log cabin styled house overlooking a lake. They held wine glasses. They were smiling. I showed it to Chase.

"This is some other world," I said.

"Not mine," Chase answered.

"The ranch is almost like that at times."

"Not this time."

Sigh.

"Katie wants me to teach her how to read."

"Oh no."

"Why?"

"Just what we need a toddler who can read."

"It'll take a while, she's just now learning her alphabet. She's been finding A's all over the place."

"You know she's as smart as you are?"

"I'm not sure I'd call myself smart. A smart person wouldn't do the things I do."

"Okay, intelligent. She's as intelligent as you. She's going to be reading before you know it."

"I can't really stop her now. Patrick can read so she thinks she needs to read, too. She sees things, she asks questions. I can't refuse to answer good questions."

"Cassidy Michaels," the receptionist said. "Right this way."

She led Chase and me down a hallway to Desmond Carr's office. Desmond was a large black man. His brother, Rashawn was more slender. Both men, when in the office, were impeccably dressed in suit and tie with a matching handkerchief in the pocket. This was not a rent a cop office. This was personalized personal security. When last I saw Desmond he was patrolling my father's ranch as a nighttime security guard, not in suit and tie. He had proven a very practical and capable man. He performed his duties flawlessly. It had been I who fouled things up.

"Mister Carr, it's good to see you again. I wish it could be under better circumstances," I said.

"Missus Michaels," he said as we shook hands.

"This is my… coworker. Chase Downing, Desmond Carr. Chase and I find ourselves in similar circumstances."

"I hope this proves to be less dangerous than the last time you employed our services."

"I'm afraid not. In fact the circumstances are very similar. I was hoping to buy a similar tracking device to the one I used last time. And I was hoping you could provide us with some protection from firearms."

"A body guard?"

"No. Do you stock body armor? Bulletproof vests? I'm afraid a bodyguard wouldn't do much good in our case. We expect either a bullet from a distance or abduction. Body armor would up our odds a bit."

"You seem very calm about all this. Perhaps a little history might help."

"Chase, you'll have to start this. I don't know how it started."

"I track down illegal aliens and drug runners. They decided to turn the tables on me. There, does that cover it?"

"Tell them about last year."

"That's your story."

"Last year Chase went missing. I tracked him down to an old school bus in a little village in Mexico. With a little gunpowder and a faulty camp stove I managed to create enough of a distraction to sneak in and free him. We crossed the border with a posse of angry Mexicans after us. Now the people who abducted Chase the first time have upped the ante. And they know I have information about his whereabouts. We've had two bounty hunters fail but the officials down south can name a couple more we need to be wary of. Recently a bounty hunter broke into my house and managed to find the address of my family up here."

"And that's where we stand?"

"That's where we stand. Except this time my children are involved."

"And your children are how old?" Carr asked.

"My daughter is three and my son is four months."

"And your husband?"

"He's at home trying to sort this all out from his end while the kids and I are supposedly out of harm's way visiting the grandparents."

"And you wish to *buy* the tracking system, this time?"

"It saved my life once. I'm willing to invest in it if it will do what we need."

"Are you aware of the price of the items you are inquiring about?"

"I know they don't come cheap and I know if you have a cheap one I don't want it. I want one that will work. Over distances. If these bounty hunters get their way we could have a state-wide search on our hands."

"Then you are talking about a GPS. A tracking system doesn't even come close to the range you need."

The talk went round and round. We never did find exactly what we needed but we did come up with a system that would help, with two transmitters and two bulletproof vests. I paid them half my life savings, hoped Dad's horses continued to win and vowed to go back to the races. The only reason I had enough disposable money to buy a system like it was because I'd won a trifecta. I can't really claim any luck or skill in betting because I let Steve do my betting for me. He just had my money to play with.

"Cassidy, this is probably as much as the reward those bounty hunters would get for bringing me in."

"So you think I should take you on a little trip to Mexico and recoup my investment?" I asked.

"No, I'd appreciate if you didn't. I'd have a hard time fighting you."

"Wear your vest. I'll wear mine. Carry a transmitter. I'll carry mine. If one of us goes missing the other takes the receiver to the proper authorities and we go from there. Right?"

"You need some instruction on who the proper authorities are. I know you don't like working with Slick but he's probably your best bet if the action's moving south. If things move really fast you'll have to go straight to Monty. He may be BORSTAR but he's got connections north and south of the border with Border Patrol and the police. He's got experience as a Navy Seal. You can't go wrong with Monty."

"And what is Monty's real name again?"

"Alfredo Montez."

"Okay, got it."

"One more thing. After you hand off the receiver, go home. I don't want you involved in this any more than you are right now."

We stood there glaring at each other, a battle of wills, and I backed off, but it didn't mean anything and he knew it. I would turn it over to the authorities. And I might stay out of it. And then again I might not. It all depended on circumstances.

Chase and I doubled up on caution and kept a sharp eye on the tracks around the ranch. An odd track didn't have a chance with both of us watching. Chase was armed twenty-four seven. He slept in the bunkhouse instead of the big house. I tried to get him to change his mind but he wouldn't listen. He refused to draw the eye of potential bounty hunters to the house. The guys kept firearms in the bunkhouse as well, though they didn't wear them doing their chores.

An officer checked in twice a day. Everybody was on edge. When I went outside I made sure each kid was assigned to a responsible adult. It felt like the changing of the guard.

I was relieved to finally get a call from Rusty.

"Hey, it's good to hear your voice again," I said.

"Sorry I didn't get to call yesterday. Things were a mess here." No mention of the break in, just things were a mess.

"It's okay." No mention of spending a day ranting silently about another woman at the house. "I missed you. Guess it's going to be a while before you can break away for a visit."

"No, actually I was thinking it sped things up."

He's worried, I thought.

"What do you need to get done before you come?"

"Cassidy, I don't mean to put you off, but could I talk to Chase first?"

"I'm in the big house. I'll have to track him down." As I was walking through the living room Katie spotted me.

"You talking to Daddy?"

"You'll have a turn. Stay with Grandma." Then after I got out the front door, "When you talk to Katie she's going to go on and on about letters. She likes A's. She sees the letter A on every sign she spots. She thinks that because Patrick can read she needs to be able to read, too. I taught her to sing the ABC song right and we are matching the letters in the song to written letters. Then I'll teach her the sounds that go with the letters so she can sound out words. Chase thinks I'm nuts to teach her to read."

"How is she doing? Isn't she a little young?"

"If she was too young she wouldn't be asking the right questions. We've only been doing this for a day. On paper she recognizes several letters but when she's out and about she notices the A's. I'm not pushing her. It's all very easy, natural learning for her. I'm not teaching her to write them, just recognize them. It's not so different from recognizing different kinds of animals. She knows a horse goes neigh so why not teach her that letters say things, too?"

"Cassidy? What are you doing out by yourself?" Randy said jogging up.

"Rusty wants to talk to Chase."

"Check the back gate."

"Thanks."

"Why did Randy want to know why you were by yourself?" Rusty asked.

"Because your call to Captain Howard has the whole ranch on edge. I can't even turn around without bumping into somebody."

Relief flowed through the line. I still say there are all kinds of silences. This was a relieved silence.

"I only asked them to keep an eye out, to add the ranch to their patrols."

"Well they did that. Two times a day an officer comes and knocks on the door and asks if everything is all right."

"I didn't ask them to do that, but it's good that they do."

"When I went down to talk to Captain Howard it looked like they welcomed some work to do. I think they fight over who gets to come over because once Martha had leftover cherry pie. I told her it's easy to spoil cops and she better quit or keep baking, one or the other."

"If a patrol car shows up twice a day that's a good visual deterrent. Do they always come at the same time?"

"It's only been a day. They haven't had time to establish a routine."

"Let's hope they don't. They should try to be unpredictable."

"I've got Chase's tracks. He's doing a patrol around the backside of the ranch. He sure is easier to track in boots. He's been helping the guys around the ranch. He seems to know as much about horses as he needs to fit in. He rides well."

"Thanks," said Chase beside me. "What's up?"

"Nothing. Rusty wants to talk to you."

"Go back to the house."

"I'll be in the barn."

"Go back to the house."

"Chase, I'm a big girl…"

"Hold on," he told Rusty. He took me by the arm led me a short way ahead and pointed to the ground. He stood over me, watching the hills as I read the ground at our feet.

Chapter 43

The tracks didn't belong to any of the ranch hands, that's for sure. I'd have to follow them for a bit before I'd get paranoid about them. I started down the trail and Chase let me track it a bit before turning me toward the house again.

"Is it them?" I asked.

He jerked his head toward the house.

"If it is, I'm not leaving you out here in the open," I said.

"Get in there. If it is them and they see us together, they'll think they hit the jackpot. I'll track it later. Go home."

Chase headed back to the ranch so I'd go back, too. He went into the bunkhouse to talk, so I went to the Explorer and got my 9mm out of the lockbox and ducked through the back fence behind the house. I looked around for a trail knowing the person who left it had not been thinking about their tracks. I didn't want to be out there long. I knew it would take Chase and Rusty two minutes to have a half hour conversation. And when I got the phone back Rusty would know I knew everything. I was probably saving a lot of time and explanation by letting Chase talk first. I found footprints and followed them in stealth mode, making myself small, keeping to cover as much as I could. I backtracked the person so I would be less likely to be caught and I could find out where they had come from. When the tracks stopped I looked to the ranch to see what the person had seen. Damn, they had a pretty good view of the property. They could see the road coming in, the back of the house, the area between the house and the bunkhouse and a small area near the barn. I figured I better get back before I was missed.

I slipped back through the fence and stalked my way around the side of the house. At the corner of the house I scanned the driveway and paddocks for strangers before stepping onto the porch and going in the front door.

"Mommy! You said I could talk to Daddy," Katie said.

"You will, Uncle Chase is talking to him now. You'll still get a turn."

It felt odd changing from tracker to Mommy with the closing of a door. I climbed the stairs two at a time and hid my pistol on the top shelf of my closet and went downstairs to be a mommy again.

The scene in the living room looked so peaceful compared to the goings on outside. Carson played on a blanket. Wyatt had once again set up an elaborate system of roads and block buildings and Carson was watching him push cars around making *vroom, vroom* noises. Katie had her own car and it had somehow jumped from the floor to the coffee table and couch. Soon I realized there were imaginary bridges.

"Look Mommy, the car has an *A* on it," she said. She held up the car and sure enough, there it was at the end of Tonka.

"That word says Tonka. Can you hear the *a*? In this word it sounds like uh."

"What does this letter say?" she asked pointing to the *T*. She made me sound out the whole word. I never realized how many words there were around us until Katie started finding them. I was relieved when Chase briefly entered through the front door, handed off the phone and slipped back outside. I was glad I'd gotten back to the house before he brought the phone to me.

"Hi," I said to Rusty.

He wasn't sure where to start.

"I'm glad you're taking precautions."

"Do you think it's an overkill?"

"I wish you wouldn't put it like that. How much, no, I'm not going to worry about that."

"I took it out of the winnings."

"How much did you win?"

"Enough. Frank's Choice bought it all."

Frank's Choice was one of Dad's racehorses. He had some pretty long odds at first because he had hokey looking knees. Nobody would believe he could win with knees like that, so he was a long shot. I had bet on him, and he didn't let me down.

"We went with a different system this time, one that has a broader range. Chase and I both wear transmitters."

"Let's just talk. I'm glad you're thinking. You're giving us tools. I just want to hear how you're doing. I'd like to hear things are normal."

"Even the normal things aren't going to sound very normal to you. The kids are fine. Carson is playing cars and trucks with Katie and Wyatt. Katie wants to talk to you. Katie makes me sound out every word she runs across. She doesn't seem to know that some of those words can be ignored. She doesn't need to know what the care label on her clothes says, or what the fiber content of her pillow is. When I read them to her she says, 'what's polyester?' or 'what does *like colors* mean?' I end up explaining all these tedious things that don't mean a thing to her."

"It must not be too tedious to her or she wouldn't keep asking."

"Just wait until you talk to her."

"Me talk!" Katie said.

"Are you ready?" I asked Rusty.

"Sure, put her on," he said.

Katie took the phone and looked at it a moment.

"Daddy! What does m-e-n-u say? … You mean like at a restwant? … Why does a phone have a menu?"

I couldn't help it, I laughed. Rusty was getting a good dose of what I'd been going through. She looked at the phone again.

"What does o-f-f say? … So if I push it, it goes off?" Oops, too late. She'd hung up. "Daddy?"

"Here, give me the phone. You turned Daddy off." I hit the speed dial for Rusty.

"Hello?" he said.

"See what I'm dealing with? Here she is again."

I went to the kitchen. I heard enough of Katie's questions just talking to her. I didn't need to hear her questions to other people, too.

"You should have seen her when she discovered everything in the pantry was labeled," Martha said. "I had to read all the cans and boxes to her. She took each can from me and shook it and tried to feel if it really was peas or carrots."

"I've created a monster," I said.

"I think it's cute. Only your father is bothered by it."

"Why? What did she do to Dad?"

"She tried to get him to read the titles of all the books in his office library to her."

"Oh no, maybe he should close the door for a few days until she gets tired of it."

"You think she'll get tired of it? I think she's going to ask until she knows everything. You think you weren't as bad as she is? At least most of her questions are easily answered. You wanted to know *why* things were the way they were. Instead of reading a label and saying there are peas in the can I had to explain why people put peas in cans."

"Mommy? Mommmmmy," said Katie.

I went into the living room and took the phone from her.

"I see what you mean," said Rusty.

"Don't let her sit up front in the car or you will have to sound out every word on the dashboard."

"Is Carson sleeping through the night?"

"Sometimes. He settles down quick when he does wake up, as long as I go through his routine."

"Tell you what. I'll try and tie up loose ends. Maybe I can be there tomorrow night."

"Really?"

"Yeah. Thanks for the pictures you sent. They made me homesick. I want my girl back. I want my kids."

After all the worry I'd been through it took me a moment for it to register. He wanted me. He really wanted *me*!

"I haven't found a surprise for you yet."

"That's okay, if it's risky going out don't do it."

"What did Chase think about the tracks he found?"

"He hadn't followed them far when you found him."

"I'll ask him later. He probably went back after he talked to you. I wish he wouldn't go by himself."

"It's what he does."

"I know and it's what got him in trouble in the first place."

"Now you know how I feel when you do things like that."

"Do we know what kind of a reward this is for Chase? Do they want him dead or alive?" I asked.

"I think this Morales character would like to execute Chase himself. But I'm sure if the only way they can bring Chase in is dead that could be arranged, too. Tell you what, you let me finish up here and I'll do my best to be there tomorrow."

"Okay, I'll be counting on it."

"I love you."

"I love you, too."

"Bye."

Sigh.

Chapter 44

When I turned around Chase was standing at the doorway watching me. I'd never seen a look of affection from him before, but I came close that time, though I don't think it was meant for me. He'd been a Michaels family friend for many years. I think he just liked observing a life he never had, but would have enjoyed had the opportunity presented itself. Then it clicked off and he nodded toward the yard. He'd found something.

It seemed dumb to be sneaking around my parent's house although I had spent most of my childhood doing exactly that. He led me into the oak woods behind the ranch. The farther we went the stealthier we became until I crouched over a hiding spot. Someone else's hiding spot.

"What do you make of this?" Chase asked.

A person had lain there, for some time. They had brought a pack, not a full backpack but a daypack or a rucksack. They had a canteen. The indentations were plain in the scrubby grass and sand. And they had binoculars. I was guessing at that because there were elbow prints the right width apart to have held binoculars up at eye level. I followed the line of sight and it included the driveway and porch of the house. They could see our comings and goings. Hopefully they had seen Orell checking in on us that morning. Hopefully they were not on their way to take up their post again soon.

"Did you finish this?" I asked.

"It ends at the highway. Looks like someone dropped them off and picked them up. I'm going to stake out the highway, get a car description and a plate number. Are you thinking what I am thinking?"

"I don't know, what are you thinking?"

"They're watching the patterns of the house. They're taking notes so they will know our habits. They're trying to form a plan they can spring when the fewest conflicts might arise. Is that what you were thinking?"

"No, but I agree with yours."

"What were you thinking?"

"I was hoping you were doing the thinking."

"Go to the house. I'm going to follow the trail to the highway and find a place to watch from."

"Be careful. Don't try anything."

"Don't try anything you wouldn't try?"

"Don't try anything. Period. All it would do is draw attention and they would know they've been found out."

"You don't think they should?"

"If they don't know they've been discovered they will stick to their old pattern. Then we can set up to catch them. We can bring Howard and his men to stake them out and maybe they will haul them in and leave us bounty hunter free."

"Sounds too easy."

"First get the information on the car. That will allow us to learn more about the owner."

"Go home. I just wanted you to see what we're dealing with here."

"Okay, now I know. I'm tempted to plant more trees in this part of the wood. I sure would like more cover."

"It would just give them more cover, too."

I went home, stealthily moving from hiding place to hiding place and when Chase was convinced I was home again he moved off toward the highway. I spent the rest of the afternoon listening for gunfire. I didn't expect it, but I dreaded it nonetheless.

Dinnertime came and Chase wasn't there.

"Aunt Cassidy, are your adventures always this boring?" Wyatt asked.

"Unfortunately, no, Wyatt. I wish sometimes they were. You weren't out tracking with me and Chase this afternoon. It might have been a little more interesting then."

"No fair!" Patrick said. "I wanted to go, too!"

"Not this time. The woods behind the ranch are strictly off limits. I don't care what your reason is to need to go back there, you will not do it."

"Aw, why not?"

"We'll know more when Chase gets back."

There was a knock on the door and Martha got up to answer it.

"Don't just answer it," I told her. "Look out the peep hole first."

"Cassidy, you're being silly. Most people just walk into the house during daylight hours. They know they can make themselves at home in the sitting area. Even town folk know that. The only reason they even knock is because it is past five."

She opened the door and there stood Ashton Sheffield. He was two years ahead of me in school. Not many of the kids from school stayed in the area, because there were no jobs. In fact, after further thought he had to have moved away and come back because there wasn't a police academy around for a couple hundred miles.

"I see I still have perfect timing," he said. "Is everything all right?"

"Not quite," I said. "I'll fill you in after we fill you up."

"It's a deal."

Sheffield was a big, broad man with gold rimmed glasses and a car salesman's grin. Straight brown hair was just a little longer than regulation but he looked sharp and this was a small town so nobody complained. He sure didn't need a ranch dinner. I was wondering how I was going to dodge the officer's questions and Katie's questions, feed Carson and still eat.

"Are you a police?" Katie asked Sheffield.

He bent over Katie's high chair. She didn't really like to be in a high chair but it was easier to keep her near me and it made more room at the table.

"Why yes I am," he said, "and who are you?"

"I'm Katie. My name has a *A* in it. See, Kayayaytie."

"You're right. How old are you?"

"I'm free," she said holding up three fingers.

"Katie," my mother said. "Be a good girl and eat your vegetables."

"I don't have any," Katie said.

"Yes you do," I told her. "These are your vegetables."

"Those are chicken," she said.

"Eat one, I bet they are vegetables," I told her.

Sheffield smiled and found a seat next to Zack. Katie popped a chicken nugget in her mouth and chomped down.

"Ewe, it is," she said wrinkling up her nose.

"What? You don't like it?"

"What is it?" Katie asked.

"It's squash," Martha said.

"Why did you squash it?" Katie asked.

"Katie, you're monopolizing the conversation," my mom said.

"I am not. I don't even know how to moloplizize anything."

Randy laughed, "She got that right!"

"What Grandma said is it's time to give the adults a turn to talk."

"Oh," she said and then perked up, "Did I eat my vegetables?"

"Two more, now hush for a bit. Quick, somebody over twenty think of something to say."

"Ashton, here's a plate," Martha said.

"Ash, ash, hey! Your name has a A in it, too!" Katie said.

"Where's the duct tape," I asked.

"Cassidy, if there's something not right around this ranch I think we all should know about it," Dad said.

"Chase is checking on that right now."

Dad looked around the table.

"Where is Chase?" he asked.

"He'll be in as soon as he finds out what we need to know."

"And what is he hoping to find out?"

"The make, model and plate number of a car that dropped off a scout."

"You mean a boy scout?" asked Wyatt. "I want to be in boy scouts."

"An admirable goal," said Sheffield.

"No, not a boy scout. A grown up bounty hunter type scout."

"Oh boy!" said Wyatt.

"That's why it's dangerous to go into the woods behind the ranch."

"Cassidy, you don't mean… that they found you?" Mom said.

"I don't know. That's why we are waiting to find out what Chase learned." I really needed a change in topic so I said, "If all goes well, Rusty will be here tomorrow night!"

"Daddy!" said Katie. "My Daddy is a police, too."

"Uh oh," said Patrick warily. "That means he's worried."

"Patrick," my mother said, always the optimistic one, "Maybe he just wants to see his family!"

"Would somebody like to take a plate out to Chase?" Martha asked.

"No!" I said quickly. "Nobody should go out there, especially, not Chase."

"Then why does he get to go?" asked Wyatt.

"Nobody tells Chase what he can and can't do," I said.

"What if something happens to him?" Mom asked.

"Do you want me to check on him?" I asked.

"No!" my mom said as quickly as I had.

"I can check on him without leaving the house."

I went upstairs and got out the GPS receiver. I set it to pick up Chase's transmitter. It showed him somewhere in the middle of the state. I narrowed the view until it showed him as a dot beside a road.

"He's okay," I said. "He's within a mile of here. If they had him he'd be half way to Mexico by now."

"Good!" said Martha. "Now, let's eat."

After dinner I was playing with Katie and Carson on the floor in the playroom. Katie pointed to a toy and said, "Look Mommy, another A!"

"Yup! That one is in the word Playschool."

Sheffield and Dad came to the door.

"Cassidy, can we talk to you?" Dad said.

"Yeah, sure, I'll be downstairs in a minute."

I picked up Carson and followed them out. Dad led us to his office but he didn't sit behind his desk. That was a good sign.

"I want to know why you bought that GPS," Dad said without preamble.

"We had good luck with a similar system when I was having trouble with Pecatti," I said.

"You're worried," he stated.

"I'm a trouble magnet. When you're a trouble magnet sometimes it pays to be worried. Chase would prefer I be scared."

"Chase knows what he may be facing?" Dad asked.

"He does."

"What? What is Chase facing?"

"Torture and execution."

"And you? What is it that has you worried?"

"They know I have information about Chase. They would try and get that out of me. Then they would use me for bait. But that isn't really what has me worried. It's Katie. If something happens to me, don't tell Katie. I might be a trouble magnet but I'm doing my best to give Katie a trouble free childhood. I do worry about Chase. If they use me for bait he's already said he would turn himself over to them, that if there was any hope for my release, he would take my place. But I don't want him to do that. So… Dad, I do worry."

"I'm with Chase. I'd prefer you to be scared."

"I've found fear blocks logical thinking," I said.

"Been scared a time or two have you?" Sheffield asked.

"You might say that. Did Captain Howard come up with a plan to set up some speedy roadblocks?"

"He did, but there are only four of us. We'll have to hope that if anything goes awry they choose a main thoroughfare to get away."

"I think they will. They aren't familiar with the roads and some of these streets can wind for miles and seemingly go nowhere. If they have seen one of those roads they will not chance getting on one. They will head south and they will do it quickly. Dad, do you still have a good map of the area?"

He went over to his bookcase and pulled out a road map. He spread it out on his desk and the three of us bent over it.

"Do they make one of just our area?"

"Only a little tourist one that they use at the motel to show tourists where they are in relation to the rest of the area. Even that shows mostly outlying areas because people mostly come up here to visit the vineyards."

"Do you have one? After all, we are in the outlying areas near vineyards."

"I think I picked up one. I keep it for out of towners who come to look for a horse. Often they want to know where to go for lunch or dinner afterwards." He went to his desk, opened a drawer, and leafed through a stack of papers. "Here we go."

"Hey," I said. "Tony Macaluso got his vineyard on the map. I thought it took longer than that to develop a decent crop."

"He's done well for himself."

"Okay so if Tony Mac is there we're about here," I said pointing. "So, show me what the plan is."

"Is this your only copy?" Sheffield asked.

"It doesn't have to be." Dad went over to his printer and made a copy of the map side of the paper.

Sheffield took a pen from his pocket and found the spot on the map where the ranch was. He put a dot there. Two major roads went south, one went north, one west. It took a jog north or south to get a major road east.

"These two roads are obvious choices for road blocks. Then the west branch we figure we have to block because it gives access to the 101. We aren't too worried about the northerly route. Orrel will be stationed here, I'm taking this one, Cap will hit the western route. Junior is so damned hot to trot he wants to patrol."

"Junior?" I asked.

"He's just the youngest one of us. He got the nickname when he was a rookie. It just stuck. He hates it."

"How old is he?"

"Twenty six but if you want a good car chase he's the best of us. It makes sense to have him patrol. He was a race car driver in another life."

Sounded like Tex. I wouldn't mind having Tex up here on my side so I nodded my approval.

"Why hasn't Chase turned up yet? Doesn't that guy ever eat?" Dad asked.

"You wouldn't know it if he'd come back. Do you want me to find out?" I asked.

"What, with that fancy GPS gadget?"

"Or I could walk down to the bunkhouse and ask."

"Never mind." He picked up the phone on his desk and hit a single button.

"Yes sir?" Steve asked.

"If Chase is there send him up here," Dad said.

"Yes sir."

"You have a line to the bunkhouse now?" I asked.

"And barn," Dad said. "You moved out." In a way it felt like a compliment. When I was a kid I'd been Dad's messenger boy. I was sent to bring back any hand Dad wished to speak to. Most times the hands looked at me like the bringer of doom, though my dad was seldom unfair or unreasonable. Everyone dreaded a call from The Boss.

We never heard the front door open or close but Chase appeared at the door to Dad's office.

"You hungry boy? Go grab some grub and come back."

"Don't call me boy." Chase said and turned around.

When Chase came back with a plate full of leftovers Dad asked him,

"Why shouldn't I?"

"You call me boy? When my hair is grayer than yours?"

Dad looked at Chase, perhaps for the first time. I knew Dad had looked at Chase before, because he commented on how Chase looked like a beach bum. This time Dad looked again.

"Mister Gordon, I joined the force when I was twenty two. I put in thirty-five years. That's many more than I needed to retire. It was in my blood. I didn't know what else to do. So when I retired I volunteered. And I'm still at it. I figure it'll be the death of me. But it's what I committed my life to. I've seen the best of it and I've seen the worst of it. And Cassidy's been both. She's sealed that for me. Now I figure I've seen everything. If these hunters deliver my one-way ticket to Mexico. Then I'll add one last item to the list and be done with it."

I'd never seen Dad quite like I did that day. I think his respect for both me and Chase was upped a notch. This man, this beach bum, saw something in his daughter. Yes, daughter. He'd always thought of me as a son, but no, I was a daughter. He had two daughters. He had to focus.

"What did you find by the highway?" I asked.

Chase looked for a place to set down his plate to eat. He walked around Dad's desk, set down his plate on Dad's leather desk pad, plopped himself in Dad's thick, leather chair, and stuck a biscuit in his mouth. It was the first time I'd ever seen anybody in Dad's chair except Dad. I thought he would hit the roof. I thought he'd give Chase the boot. The audacity! But he didn't.

Chase chewed and swallowed. "Nothing," he said. "I found where the car pulled up and I saw where someone had gotten out and gone to the stake out spot. But nothing happened while I was there. I'll check the area for other places like that as soon as it gets light."

"So what do you think about that stake out spot?" I asked.

"I think it bears staking out."

I guess it's what I expected.

"We may have another set of eyes up here tomorrow night. Rusty's coming," I told him.

"He's worried," Chase said.

Chapter 45

I was upstairs in the kids' bathroom giving Carson a bath, when I heard Martha walking down the hallway looking for me.

"I'm in here!" I called out.

"Oh! There you are. Would you talk to Jesse? She's worried about Pat."

"Pat? What's going on with Pat?"

I pulled Carson out of the water and wrapped him in a towel. Martha took him from me and handed me the phone.

"Hey Jess, what's up?"

"It's Patrick! His teacher called to see if he was sick! He isn't sick. I sent him out to do chores and I thought he got breakfast at the big house. It never occurred to me that he would skip school! When I get my hands on him… but I can't find him. I thought maybe you could take a look around."

"Okay, let me get Carson dressed and I'll go look. Where have you already looked?"

"I walked the grounds. I poked my head in the barn. If he is really skipping school I can't imagine where he would go. He can't hide anywhere on the ranch. He'd have to go out to the hills or to town. He wouldn't go to town. It's too far and he'd get picked up."

"Okay, I'll see what I can do."

I diapered Carson and pulled a play outfit onto him. I put a jacket on him and went downstairs. When I got to the front door Katie ran up.

"Me too!" she said.

"Katie dear, would you help me in the kitchen?" Martha asked.

"Go see Martha!" I told her. "Thanks!" I called as I hurried out the front door.

Now where would that boy be? I knew he had fed the horses in the paddocks. There were little straggling pieces of hay where once there had been a flake. I picked up his trail at the last paddock and followed his tracks to the barn. I searched the barn and stuck my head into the tack room and office. I glanced up into the rafters knowing I had frequently hid up there to watch the goings on below. I circled the barn catching Patrick's tracks going out the backdoor. My alarm grew when his tracks went to the back gate and into the land beyond. I had no more taken two steps from the gate when Chase said, "Oh, no you don't!"

"I'm looking for Patrick. He didn't show at school today."

"Check the bunkhouse," he said.

"You let him skip school?" I asked.

"I had a better lesson for him," he said.

"And what was that?" I asked.

"To not stick his nose where it didn't belong."

I walked to the bunkhouse. It was locked but it was possible to unlock it from the inside. I knocked.

"Patrick?" there was no answer. Chase grinned.

"Chase, unlock the door," I said.

"I don't have the key. You'll have to get it from James or Steve."

"Why would James have a key? He doesn't use the bunkhouse."

"No, but he might wonder why he has it when he has to go looking for his son. I just told him to hold onto it for a while. That he might need it."

I turned and stalked off to the office in the barn. I went to a wall of keys and looked for one that might fit the bunkhouse lock. I pulled down four different keys and went back to the bunkhouse. I tried two of them before the third one fit. James might have had one but I preferred not to involve him in a Patrick/Chase confrontation. I expected to open the door and find a hopping mad kid, maybe scrubbing the floor with a toothbrush or something of the sort. What I saw both amused and irritated me. Patrick was neither mad nor scrubbing the floor. He couldn't, because he was handcuffed to the bedstead. A sheepish grin appeared when he saw it was me. He knew he was still in trouble but at least I could understand the situation he was in. I looked around for Chase but he'd disappeared. That figures, I thought.

"I should have known I'd get caught," Patrick said when I sat down next to him.

"Why did you go into the woods behind the barn? You were told in no uncertain terms that it was dangerous to go back there. We're not talking about danger like maybe seeing a rattlesnake. We're talking about danger like men back there who might just decide they can use you for their own purposes. If they did that then you would be in real danger. We'd have to call in the police, all of them. It would mean hostage negotiations and closing off the roads, locking down the ranch, calling in backup from neighboring towns, containing the area. But even more important than that, Chase wouldn't let them have you. They are ultimately after him."

Gulp. He knew what that meant.

"When you go back there, thinking you can hide so good they won't see you, you're putting Chase's life on the line. I don't go back there because I don't want to endanger Chase. Chase goes back there because he takes his life in his own hands. It's a risk he's willing to take to protect *us*. He's found evidence of people being back there. That should be enough warning to keep you on this side of the fence."

"What will they do to Chase if they get him?" he asked.

"They will pack him off to Mexico, and turn him over to a drug dealer down there. That man is looking forward to making Chase as miserable as possible before he kills him. I know they are very capable of making a man miserable. The conditions I found Chase in last time they had him were appalling. No man should be kept like that. I think one reason Chase decided to leave you here is because it would remind me of that day. He was chained to a school bus seat bolted to the floor, much like you are cuffed to this bed. The area was about as big as a closet. There was a blanket on the floor but it had been there for months. It was filthy. He didn't have a restroom. He had to go there in that little room. He was shot. He hadn't had a bath in a week. He'd been beaten. He had nothing to eat but beans and tortillas. He was supposed to be taken further into the country to be killed. I managed to find him the day before they were going to move him. If I had waited one more day before going down there, if I couldn't find a flight, if I'd taken a day to get properly outfitted, Chase would have disappeared into Mexico never to be seen again. Do you see what we're up against with these bounty hunters?"

"Why don't the police just catch them?" Pat asked.

"Because they haven't done anything wrong until they try to hurt one of us and when that happens it will be too late. They are going to wait for the ideal chance and when they spring the trap it won't be until they have their plan perfected. Our best chance at getting through this is to be as boring and unpredictable as possible. If they can't decide on a plan they will resort to something less than perfect and maybe we can stop them. But your job is just to lay low. Don't be a target. When you went behind the ranch you made yourself into the perfect target. Now, what's the procedure for getting you to school with the least amount of trouble?"

"I have to sign in at the office. I need a letter from my mom or dad saying why I was late."

"Okay, so help me here. Why were you late?"

"I was tied up?"

"They would want to know what was more important to you or your parents than attending school."

"Dear Missus Falway, Patrick could not be at school on time because he got distracted by some tracks behind the ranch and spent the morning being punished for his carelessness. Please make sure he comes home with makeup work, enough to keep him busy through dinner time."

"You really want me to say that?"

"It wouldn't be too far from the truth and it wouldn't be the first time I got distracted by tracks and ended up late for school."

"Why do you want all that makeup work?"

"It won't be that hard and I can do it with Katie."

"You can't do anything that involves words without Katie looking for all the A's in a paper."

"Why does she do that?"

"Because she knows you're a big kid and you can read. She wants me to teach her to read. She can identify lots of letters but she's stuck on A's for some reason. She makes people sound out words for her. She's getting to be a pest."

Patrick was excited. "Can I teach her to read?"

"First let's get you uncuffed, then let's get you to school. You can think about how to teach Katie to read after you finish all that make up work."

I got the cuff key from Chase, wrote out an excuse letter and forged Jesse's name on it. I asked Zack to go with me to take Patrick to school and then I went in to the office with him and pretended to be mad and told him his mom was going to give him what for as soon as he stepped off the bus. He tried to look contrite, but a grin slipped through, then off he went.

When I got back to the Explorer Zack asked, "Why did you let him off the hook? He could have got himself killed."

"And he knows it now. He's a good kid. He won't do it again. It wasn't his fault he was late for school."

I stopped the Explorer at Jesse's house and told Zack to leave it at the big house. I took Carson with me as a peace offering. He was getting tired and a little fussy so he'd provide a good distraction.

"Pat's fine. I took him to school. He'll probably have lots of homework this afternoon."

"Where was he?" she asked as she took Carson from me. She set him on her lap and started playing baby games with him. He settled down at first but he was probably due for a bottle and a nap.

"He'd gotten distracted by some tracks and then he got tied up when Chase caught up with him. Chase wasn't too happy. He gave him a lecture and then he got one from me too. I think he's had enough lecturing for one day."

"That boy. What am I going to do with him?"

"Nothing. He knows what he did was wrong and he won't do it again."

"This isn't the first time he got distracted by tracks and been late for school."

"I think if that's all you have to worry about you should count yourself lucky. He's on the right track. Don't worry so much."

"Just wait until he gets home."

"Jesse, don't be too hard on him. He's already heard it three times. You know what it is like. When you did something wrong, you'd hear about it from Mom, then Martha, then Old Frank. When I did something wrong I'd hear about it from Steve, then Old Frank, then Dad, then sometimes Mom, too. I need to take this kid to the house and make him a bottle. I bet he's ready to settle down to serious baby work, like eating and sleeping. When he's down for this nap I need to send Katie through the bath. I want them to be semi clean when Rusty gets here."

"Wait a minute! Patrick needed a note from me to get back in school," Jesse said.

"He had one," I said.

"You forged a note from me?"

"Yeah."

"Why… you're worse than he is! You're a bad influence!"

"Thanks. I'll see you later."

She stood there in the doorway hands on hips as I walked up the road to the big house.

"Mommy, you took a long time!" said Katie.

"Sorry, sometimes auntly duties go beyond the norm."

"Everything you get involved in goes beyond the norm," Martha said.

Chapter 46

"When is Daddy going to be here?" Katie asked as she splashed in the big bathtub. The beach towel on the floor was bordering on sopping wet. I wondered if there was more water inside or outside of the tub.

"Tonight."

"I want him to come now!"

"Me too. He'll come as soon as he can. Are you going to be a cowgirl or a princess today?"

"Can I be a cowgirl and then a princess?"

"Sure, but don't expect a lot of time with Patrick today. He has a lot of work to do today."

"Boys always hafta work."

"Girls get their share, too."

"Girls have work?"

"Of course, everybody needs work to do."

"Then I want to work, too."

"Your work is keeping your toys picked up and learning how to read."

"Teach me more letters."

"You're taking a bath."

"So? Look! Letters!" she said handing me the shampoo bottle.

I sighed and started quizzing her on the letters that were on the bottle.

"What's this one?"

"J!"

"What's that one?"

My mom came to the door.

"Cassidy, ease up already! She's only three!"

"It wasn't my idea. She asked for it."

"Oh. Is Rusty supposed to be coming tonight?"

"Yeah."

"And you haven't found a surprise for him yet."

"No, but I don't think now is a good time to go looking."

"Why not?"

"Because that would be tempting two kinds of trouble at one time. I have bad enough luck with just normal trouble."

"What if we just went to a tiny shop downtown? I know a shop that might have just the thing."

"We're not supposed to go out by ourselves."

"We'll take one of the men with us."

"You can find a ranch hand that is willing to go downtown to a ladies clothing boutique?"

"They will if I ask. They can go to the feed store. It's just a few doors down."

"Oh goodie, a feed store."

"Oh don't give me that. Who was it that used to drag me in there and drool over saddles?"

Okay, that would be me, but I doubted the guys were in the market for a new saddle.

"They would rather go to town with us than do chores," she added.

"Okie dokie, Katie!" Randy said as he unbuckled Katie's car seat buckle. She pulled her hands loose from the straps and climbed out of her car seat.

Randy went around to the back of the truck to find the bridles he'd brought along for mending. Mom and I climbed down from the old ranch truck and Katie climbed around inside the cab of the truck. I reached into the rear passenger side to unbuckle Carson when I noticed the truck rolling. Katie was standing on the driver's seat. Her foot slipped off the seat and she grabbed hold of the steering wheel. The wheel turned and she slipped under the seat. The truck was rolling! I tried to run around to the driver's seat, but the door slammed me to the ground and the truck continued backwards into the street. Katie grabbed the steering wheel to climb back up to the window and the truck turned again. Cars honked and passersby waved a warning at motorists who were unaware of the drama unfolding. I got up and ran after the truck. Drivers that had stopped for the truck started up again when they saw it pass them. I wasn't too worried about Carson. He was snugly strapped into his car seat and the speeds were slow, but Katie was standing on the front seat. Why did we have to live in such a hilly place? I grabbed hold of the truck door and it dragged me off my feet. I pulled myself back up and launched myself into the truck. I pulled Katie down onto the seat and lay in front of her just in time to come to a loud crash into another car. I was thrown against the dash and Katie was thrown into me. She started to cry but she wasn't sure if she was hurt or just startled. She sat up and then climbed to the seat.

"Look! Mommy! A A!"

I groaned and pulled myself out of the floorboards. I took Katie in my arms and hugged her close then looked out the windshield. Sure enough, there was an A on a white, very foreign license plate. A Mexican license plate. The car was empty.

"Hey come back here!" yelled a witness as the driver fled on foot. The man walked up to the open door of the truck. "Are you okay?" he asked.

"I think so. What about you, Katie, are you okay? Did you get hurt?"

"I drove the truck!" she said.

Red and blue flashing lights closed in on the site and pretty soon Ashton Sheffield stood at the door. A rescue squad pulled up. Wow, this was quick. Was every department in town as bored as the police station had appeared?

Mom ran up. "Katie! Are you all right?"

"Gramma! Let's go shopping!"

"Not yet sweetheart. Come here, let the rescue guys do their job."

I took Carson out of his car seat. He liked seeing all the different faces in the crowd that was gathering.

"Are you a policeman?" Katie asked the paramedic.

"No, I'm a fireman," he said. He felt Katie's arm for broken bones. She watched him. He shined a light in her eyes.

"Mommy? What are they doing?" she asked.

"It's okay. You have to do this whenever you crash a truck."

"I didn't do it! It did itself!" she said.

"They're just making sure you didn't hurt yourself. They're going to do the same thing to me." Because I am going to be a good girl and serve as a good example to my daughter instead of insisting on signing their little waiver form.

When they put the blood pressure cuff on her and started pumping it up she asked, "Can I squish it, too?" She tried to give it a couple of squishes but didn't accomplish much so they released the pressure and started again.

"Who was driving the truck?" asked Sheffield.

"Nobody. We were getting out of it and Katie knocked it into gear."

"And who was driving the car?"

"They took off before we got ourselves sorted out, but if I were you I would find out. The car has Mexican plates. The information might do us some good."

"If we do find these guys we can pick them up for leaving the scene of an accident."

"Search the car, too. You're likely to find weapons in there."

"What will we find if we search the truck?"

I looked in the back of the truck.

"A shovel, a bunch of dirt, a lead rope…"

"Ma'am, if you'll sit down," the paramedic said. "Does it hurt anywhere in particular?"

"Yeah, but I think the vest protected me from most of it."

"The vest?"

"Yeah." When I sat down the stiff vest rode up.

"What are you doing wearing a bullet proof vest? Our *cops* wish they could have one."

"Hopefully not getting shot."

My mom stepped forward. "You have to understand, Conner, my daughter is a bit of a trouble magnet. She's been shot at several times. Right now we are watching for bounty hunters."

"Missuss Gordon, are you okay?" Conner asked. "Were you in the truck when it crashed? Did you hit your head? Folks around here don't even know what bounty hunters are, much less dress in case they are shot by one."

"Humph, no I wasn't," Mom said. "And I'm not the nut case you make me sound like."

About then I heard the click, click of a camera. I looked around and there stood the reporter for the little local newspaper. Oh boy, we were going to be the talk of the town.

The old ranch truck was undamaged but nobody was really sure what was going to happen to the other car. When they opened the trunk they found two high-powered rifles and a baggie full of marijuana. I was relieved it was just the two rifles, although it was possible they had firearms on them when they left the scene, too. I had pictured an arsenal. However, the officers said the car would be taken to an impound yard where it would go unclaimed. In the meantime the police were finally doing something. It was suggested that, if the men driving the Tsuru were without wheels, perhaps they would try to rent some. So the attention was shifted to any car rental office within twenty miles.

Dad looked puzzled when I told him about the incident. "A Tsuru? I never heard of a car called a Tsuru."

"They're sold in Mexico but not up here. That's one more thing that proves it could be linked to the people who are out to get Chase."

"How much damage was there?"

"If you look at the ranch truck you can't tell there's any more dings than there were before. But the other car was all caved in."

"Any injuries?"

"The police are checking the local medical clinics and car rental offices. So far we haven't heard of any injuries."

"You know, this could have been very serious for Katie. If she had been standing up when the truck hit she could have been grievously injured."

"I know, Dad. That's why I chased down the truck. I think I got the worst of it, and we're all okay. I kind of consider the crash a lucky break. It revealed a few things to us that we wouldn't have otherwise known."

I walked out to the paddocks and waited for Chase. I knew his trouble radar would sense news.

"Read the newspaper in the morning and then hide it from Rusty," I said.

"Is that all you're going to tell me?"

"They won't be driving a Mexican car for a while and they are minus two rifles."

"Great. Now they are going to look like every other illegal alien in the state."

"Sorry."

The trip wasn't a total loss. After the accident was cleared up Mom, Katie and I did go to that boutique and the woman working there had an eye for what looked good on a person. She was excited to have a new victim and plied me with every outfit she thought went with my eyes, or would look perfect with my figure or would bring out my sparkly personality. I was trying to lay low and be as unsparkly as possible. However, I did find an outfit that would surprise Rusty, and my mom said it was just darling, but we'd have to do my hair. That meant I could spend a few hours laying just about as low as a person can get, but I'd still be ready for Rusty when he arrived. I could kill two birds with one stone and keep Mom happy and busy, too.

At dinner Chase was still looking for more news but he was his usual quiet self so he was glad when Steve said evenly, "Heard you ran into trouble in town."

"Katie did," I said. "Why don't you tell Steve what you did in town today, Katie?"

Katie perked up, "I drove the truck! I drove it down a hill and I crashed it!"

"You drove the truck?" Patrick asked.

"She accidentally knocked it into gear and it rolled down a hill," I said.

"That's not driving," Patrick informed her.

"Is too!"

"Is not. To drive the truck you have to have control of it."

"Mommy?"

"He's right, kiddo. You have to have the key in and start the engine and control the truck at all times."

Then Randy added, "Of course, if I remember right, Patrick didn't control the truck very well on his first try either. Took out a section of fence."

"I tooked out a car," Katie said proudly.

The doorbell rang right on cue and Martha got up saying, "I should just plan on another place at the table for breakfast and dinner."

"No, don't." Chase said. "I'll talk to them. They need to break up their visits more. If they fall into a pattern we become too predictable."

Martha answered the door and in walked Junior. He walked into the house and leaned against the wall to the dining room with his thumbs hooked through his belt loops. That in itself was quite a feat because police belts were wide and thick and held a plethora of gadgets, weapons, cuffs, baton, pepper spray, extra ammunition, and sidearm. Maybe a cop's belt expanded as they aged because they were allowed to use more gadgets and their ability to use them depended on their girth. Nah, that wasn't it. But I still thought it was odd that Junior had no trouble doing the belt loop thing. It looked like he did it a lot. Maybe his belt loops were stretched.

"Got a name on that car," Junior said.

Chase sat up straighter, paused over his dinner.

Junior waited, enjoying the expectation.

"And it is…"

"Not something I should talk about in public. It's proprietary information."

"Guess I need to prove I'm the master of propriety, but this isn't my table. Shall we step out back?"

"That isn't necessary," Martha said. "Sit down Roger."

"This will only take a minute," Chase said as the two men stepped out of the room. I was tempted to go, too, but I knew Chase would cryptically pass along any information I needed to know.

When they came back Chase seemed no different. The information, or lack thereof didn't seem to affect him in any way. Roger sat down and added a few things to his plate but he ate sparingly. Unlike the older men, Roger seemed to have a little restraint when it came to his diet. I thought he could probably run farther, too.

The doorbell rang again. Mom and Martha traded questioning glances and Martha went to the door again.

"Check the peephole first!" I called.

"They aren't going to come up and knock on the door with a patrol car out front," Randy said.

Then the most wonderful voice said, with its familiar deep rumble, "Am I interrupting something?"

I was out of my chair in an instant and across the living room. Katie was trying to climb out of her highchair calling out, "Daddy! Daddy!"

Mom pulled her out and brushed her off and set her down. She jumped up and down beside us as Rusty crushed me in the best hug ever, then he picked up Katie.

"Princess, you're getting so big. How's my baby girl?"

"I'm a big girl. I can read."

"You can?"

"I can read A's."

"You need to eat a good dinner so you grow up big and strong like your mommy."

He put her in her seat again and looked around for Carson. He was sitting on James's lap. James stood and passed Carson across the table.

"Sit down, Rusty, golly, our little group is growing by the minute."

"You weren't expecting me," Rusty said.

"Nonsense, sit down. You're always welcome."

"I'll just step upstairs and get rid of this coat and wash up."

When Rusty headed for the stairs Chase slipped away from the table and followed him.

"Hey sport…" Rusty said to Carson as he took the stairs two at a time.

They were gone longer than the time it took to wash up and take off a jacket. I suspected Rusty was getting an official update. Something seemed to be going on behind the cheerful family smiles and animated dinner conversations. An undercurrent. Maybe it was just Chase. Chase seemed to create an air of tension about him without realizing he was doing it. I think that's what made him get along in the cop world and be out of place with most of the rest of society. When Rusty came back to the table a little more somber, I was irritated. Just let him enjoy a cheerful homecoming! This was celebration time. He shook hands all around the table. Junior didn't need an introduction. He knew Rusty was involved in law enforcement just by the handshake. Or maybe he was cuing off Chase. When Rusty sat down Katie started climbing out of the highchair again.

"Katie. Honey you need to eat," Mom said.

"I eat wif Daddy!" she said.

"Let her loose," Rusty said. "It's okay."

He loaded his plate as much as he could before Katie stood next to his chair expectantly. He repositioned Carson on one leg and Katie climbed onto the other one. He had to eat carefully but he didn't mind. He had his kids. Every once in a while Katie would lean forward and take something from his plate and he didn't mind that either. He could always get more. If he could move. When my plate was clean I got up and took Carson from him and then Katie switched to his left leg.

Conversation flowed but it was just the normal questions. How was the drive? Was the weather good? He complimented Martha on the dinner. I let it flow counting down the minutes until we could go upstairs and close the door. No bounty hunter was going overshadow my joy.

One by one the ranch hands departed to tend their last chores, and make the rounds. Patrick ran home and came back with an armful of books, still working on make-up work. Katie handed Rusty the, now ragged, paper with the alphabet written on it. She climbed up into Rusty's lap and said, "Ask me a letter."

"Okay, which one is H?"

"Huh, huh, H. That one! That's a big H and that's a little h."

"Good job! Can you find the D?"

Some of the letters she had sounds for and some of them she could only identify, but they ran through several letters before she hit a glitch.

"You're doing so good, sweetheart. You're so smart, why do you want to read?"

"Patrick can read."

"He couldn't when he was three."

"I like to read."

"Okay, as long as you like it, I'm glad you are learning it."

But that night he had a different story.

"Cass, isn't Katie going to be bored stiff in school if she goes in already reading?"

"Try holding her back."

"Can you imagine what the teachers are going to go through with a bored Katie in class? She'll drive the whole class to distraction."

"I can't stop her from reading. Spend an hour with her and you'll end up sounding out a dozen words. Everywhere she goes she spots letters she recognizes. You'll see. You can't stop her from learning. She's got a sharp eye and a sharp mind and she uses both."

"I knew *that* from the time she was two months old."

"Just have patience with her and go with the flow. She'll learn at her own pace. Now, set that aside. I haven't gotten all my welcome hugs in. I missed you every minute."

All I could do was luxuriate in the fact that I had him here and I was whole again. At first it was quiet and tense. Neither one of us had left pleasant circumstances to be where we were that moment. He'd just finished a tough case, put back together a thrashed house. He knew, despite my overwhelming joy that things were tense at the ranch. So it was touch and go at first, dodging the uncomfortable subjects we'd have to deal with later, trying to focus on right now and tomorrow.

"What do you want to do while you're here?" I asked.

"I want to see you be happy. I want to play with the kids. I want to hug you without the vest on."

"That's all?"

"I want you. I just want you, anyway I can get you."

He had me. From the second I knew he was there, this moment had been pulling at me. I wanted to lose myself in him.

The Velcro had such an impersonal sound ripping loose. It was a police sound. A utilitarian sound. It wasn't the sound of a woman undressing for her man. And the unyielding vest coming off felt clunky, but as I set it aside I felt free. I was me again. I was soft and ready and he wrapped his arms around me again and even that sent an electric charge through me. He ran his hands through my hair and brought my face up for a kiss. He smiled.

"Slow down," he said.

"I haven't done anything."

"Oh yes you have. You're a coiled spring."

"I know, I'm sorry."

"Nope, no sorries, take it slow. It'll be so much better if you take it slow."

Carson woke up in the night and Rusty rolled out of bed and pulled on some pants and a t-shirt. The cries escalated.

"Hey buddy, have patience. Mommy and Daddy are here. We just got distracted. Come on, settle, settle."

Carson would settle down as soon as he fell into his routine. I pulled on a robe and went downstairs to start a bottle. Rusty brought the baby back to the bedroom and I brought the bottle upstairs. Katie wandered into the room rubbing her eyes.

"Carson woke me up," she said sleepily.

"Okay, come lay down. Carson will be asleep soon."

Rusty walked the room holding the bottle for Carson. I lay down and Katie curled up with me, still rubbing her eyes. She watched Rusty pace and jiggle Carson. She reached up to play with my hair and let it fall sleepily to her side. Rusty lifted her arm and put it in a more comfortable spot. We were a family again. Even though it was the middle of the night and we all wished we were asleep, we were together. We were content.

Chapter 47

In the morning I saddled up Snoopy and Shasta. We were going to show Daddy what a big girl his princess was. Katie sat tall and proud in the saddle as I walked Snoopy around the ring. Mom stood at the fence snapping pictures. When Katie demanded to go faster I climbed into the saddle and held onto her as Snoopy did his choppy little canter around the corral. Katie clapped and laughed and Rusty grinned ear to ear.

"Can I ride Shasta, too?" she asked.

"Not by yourself," I answered.

I climbed into the saddle and Rusty handed Katie up to me.

"There's no horn so you have to balance," I told her.

"Where is it?"

"This is a different kind of saddle. It doesn't have one. It's a big girl saddle. Put your hands on your legs and balance. Follow the movements of the horse."

When Katie had enough of riding I turned her over the Rusty and put Shasta through his paces. I wasn't sure being up in the saddle was a good idea considering Chase's discoveries, but I wanted Rusty to see things be as normal as possible.

Chase and Randy joined Rusty at the fence. I wondered how the two men could work together. They were about as opposite as guys came. I thought Randy's constant banter would drive Chase crazy.

"Unca Chase, do it again," I heard. How many quarters did one man have?

"Trouble, I got a new horse for you to try," Steve said as he led a new horse to the gate.

"How old is she?"

"Three."

"Trained?"

"Semi."

"She racing or working?"

"A teenage girl has her eye on her."

"Pleasure riding?"

"She's never been in competition before but she likes the idea of trying."

"Okay, roll out the barrels."

He opened the gate and I rode Shasta out. I dismounted and walked over to introduce myself to the newcomer. She was pure red from head to toe. Even her mane was the same red color. Usually a horse will have a white blaze or white socks or dark streaks in the mane. The horse looked like it was professionally dyed. I knew she wasn't but I couldn't help but run my hands over her looking for impurities. I didn't find one. She was gorgeous.

She stood still while I put my foot in the stirrup and pulled myself up. When I was seated she came alive. She felt like she was spring loaded. I wasn't even convinced she was one hundred percent quarter horse. It felt more like she had some of the Arabian spunk to her. I pointed her through the gate and touched her sides and she lunged into an easy canter. She should have waited for further orders before taking off but the bunching of her muscles and the easy way she went into the gait felt wonderful. This horse was a joy to ride. Randy and Steve rolled barrels out into a cloverleaf, and I brought the filly back to the start.

"Okay girl, come on, let me see what you can do," I told her. "Ready? Set? Go!" I came down with my heels and she leaped forward. She took the first barrel flawlessly. I aimed her at the second barrel and it went a bit rough. She swung wide. The third barrel was a little better. With practice and a steady hand she would shape up well. I wasn't sure a teenage girl had the focus to keep training to a steady, firm pace. I was curious if the horse was stuck in a barrel racing mindset so I began at the start again, took her around the first barrel, aimed for the second one then didn't turn her when the barrel came up. She continued on straight.

"Good girl!" I praised. She *had* been listening to commands. She liked speed so I let her gallop around the ring once before pulling her up.

"She's a dream to ride, but she's not from our ranch, is she?"

"How did you know?" Steve asked evenly.

"She's got a different bearing to her. She's lighter on her feet."

Steve wasn't too sure he liked that comment. It meant that I could feel a difference, that our stock needed refining. And maybe it did. We had good solid horses with good solid training but he didn't want solid to mean rigid.

Steve and Randy had a silent conversation. I'd thrown a monkey wrench into the works.

"We can't buy her out from under Michelle," Steve finally said.

"Why not. If we offer more," Randy said.

"She'll throw a fit and her sister will never go out with you again."

"A horse is a horse."

"And a woman is a woman. They stand together. If you buy this horse you can kiss Victoria goodbye."

"Wait a minute. This debate is a girl problem?"

"Depends on which way you look at it," Steve said. "Randy doesn't seem to think so. Michelle had her eye on this filly and so her big sister, Victoria, had Randy work with her and decide if she'd be a good match for Michelle.

We'd been debating and leaning towards recommending Michelle buy Sky, but then we liked the looks of her."

"And Randy likes the looks of Victoria," I said.

"If Tori is going to let this get between us then maybe I *should* kiss her goodbye."

"Ah, but can you? I think that's what this boils down to. You have to decide if the relationship is worth the price of a horse. If you buy Sky she won't even be your horse. But Tori could be your girl."

Now this was interesting. I thought Randy would never find a girl. He'd been so stuck on me while we were growing up and then when I left for the Marines he'd taken it personally. The fact was I never planned on getting serious with Randy. I was glad to hear he was seeing someone.

"I say Michelle buys Sky and we make an offer on Sky's sister," Steve said.

"Sky doesn't have a sister."

"But she could."

"Now you're talking three years before we have a working horse and there's no guarantee her sister would be the horse Sky is," Randy argued.

"And what will you be doing three years from now?"

"Depends on if we buy Sky or not."

"This is your decision," said Steve.

"Crap," said Randy.

"Mommy, can I ride the princess horse?" Katie asked.

"Double cr** even Katie can see the difference," Randy grumbled.

I pulled Katie into the saddle and we rode once around the corral and then I turned Sky over to Steve again. As he led her away I was sorry Dad wouldn't be able to keep her. She was a fine horse.

Rusty was determined that his family was going to be a real family for just a few days. In the afternoon he drove us to one of the neighboring towns that was big enough to have a park. We picked up some burgers and had a picnic and played on the playground.

"I like my slide better," said Katie. "When are we going home?"

"I don't know sweetheart. Grandma and Grandpa sure like it when you visit. We don't get to see them very often. Don't you like it at Grandma and Grandpa's house?"

"I like it. I like Patrick. I just miss…"

Home. Rusty knew, too. We were just homesick. We hadn't managed to lose the bounty hunters. We'd complicated things further. We had gotten the family involved. But we couldn't run forever. Chase could hit the road. We could go home, but the problem would follow us.

We tried to have a fun day. Katie chased Rusty around the playground and swung on the swings, which went higher than her ones at home. I pushed Carson on the baby swing. We walked the quaint little downtown area and ate dinner overlooking the coast. I loved eating at seafood places in interesting places like wharves where I could watch the comings and goings of old salty fishing boats and sleek yachts, chunky tourist boats and little motorboats taking men on harbor errands. It was a whole different world on the water. I liked getting snapshots of other worlds. I had done that in Mexico, taken little mental snapshots of village life that I would cherish always. Even though I now had bounty hunters breathing down my neck I was grateful for the things I did take from that trip. I found out tortillas don't really grow in little plastic packages on the grocery store shelves, and some kids would do anything for a chocolate bar. I found out there were kind people in places you never expected to see them and they came in all ages.

That night we had a meeting in Dad's study. It was different from Dad's office. We called it a study, but really, it was a room upstairs with a big TV and plenty of couches, a few bookcases. It was all dark woods and leather furniture so it felt like a study. It was one of those public access rooms of the house. The ranch hands were allowed in there, just like family. It was more comfortable and informal than meeting in the office. Captain Howard, Dad, Chase, Steve, Rusty and I were bouncing ideas off each other, trying to decide what to do.

"I say there's safety in numbers," Dad said.

"To who?" Chase asked. "I don't want to involve folks who have no business worrying about my problems."

"Too late," Dad said.

"Dad, it wasn't Chase's fault they found us here. They got the information from my house. And the information they did find didn't lead them to Chase. It led them to me. Chase was just a bonus."

"What have you found in your scouting forays behind the ranch?" Howard asked.

"We've been watched. There are three vantage points they like. I could confront them but nothing says they shouldn't be back there. It's public land. All confronting them would do is make myself vulnerable and let them know they were in the right place at the right time."

"We can't just sit here waiting for them to make a move. When they do make it, what's going to happen?" Dad asked.

"What they would prefer is to take us alive to their head honcho down in Mexico," Chase said.

"So you're talking about abduction. That isn't an easy thing to do with as many people as we have around here," Howard observed.

"Unless they get tired of waiting for an opportunity. If they wanted to they could knock down the door and storm the place."

"How many people are we talking about here?"

"Not enough to storm the place. These guys like to work alone. It's the money. They don't like to share. I thought it was unusual, witnesses said two men ran from the car Katie hit."

"That was a lucky break, to find that car and get those statements from the witnesses. I'd thank Katie but I don't think she should be encouraged," Chase said.

"Encouraged to what?" Rusty asked.

Rats, he didn't know about that.

"Katie knocked the truck into gear and it rolled down a hill. I managed to catch the truck and pull her down but it was a mess getting the accident all straightened out."

"It didn't help that the folks in the other car hightailed it," Howard said. "Things have been mighty peaceful around here considering the threat. Are you sure they are out there? And if they are, why have they never been out there when you scout back there? Seems like that would be the ideal time to take you down. Alone, in the woods."

"I have seen them. It's tempting to take them on but all you could do is take them in for questioning and deport them if they are illegals."

"What about the driver of the car?"

"The name we got when we checked the plates was for a US citizen."

"But the car was registered in Mexico," I said.

"A US citizen can register a car in Mexico. Many people have dual residency. It's not unusual," Chase explained.

"Did the name mean anything to you?" I asked.

"The owner of the car and the driver of the car were not the same person. The owner is Anglo. The driver is Hispanic."

"So… stolen car?" I asked feeling my way through the police logic.

"If it was, it wasn't reported," Chase said.

"Borrowed?"

"Likely."

"Who would lend their car to someone who was going out of the country? That sounds a bit suspicious."

"Not to someone involved in the deal, or afraid of the person doing the borrowing."

"We are just speculating. What are the facts?"

"We're pigeonholed."

"No we're not. Let's just wave good-bye, let them know we are clearing out and disappear again. At least the ranch will be done with them," I said.

Rusty and Dad jumped on that one.

Rusty said, "And where would you go?"

And Dad said, "I still say there's safety in numbers."

"We're getting nowhere. We need to come up with a plan."

"Their plan is to take one of us alive. So let's bait them," I said. "As soon as they make a move we can nab them."

"No," said Rusty. "It's too easy for something to go wrong and, if it did, it would go wrong for *you*."

"I'm getting to the point where it's worth a little risk to put an end to this."

"That's just where they want you. The only place you are moving to from here is a safe house."

"No, it would be like jail."

"That can be arranged, too," the Captain said.

"One thing you can do, Captain, is tell your men that arriving at the ranch at precisely breakfast and dinner time does nothing to discourage bounty hunters," Chase said. "Break it up some. Sometimes come back in an hour or two. Don't let your men become predictable."

"They aren't going to want to hear that. They rave about Martha's cooking," Howard said.

"I'm sure they can see the reasons behind it," Chase said.

"Well, at least there is one thing we can do for a few days. We can move around and keep them guessing," Rusty said.

Oh, yay! I thought, that means he is going to be here a few days!

We never did come to a consensus that night. We just beat the subject to death until we didn't even want to think about it anymore. All I knew was something had to change.

Chapter 48

Rusty and I had a wonderful time going out on little day trips. As we drove around I thought Rusty paid more attention to the road behind us than he did in front. If we ever had a tail he didn't let on.

Things at the ranch settled down to a different kind of melancholy feeling. It was Randy. He'd take Sky out and work with her and each time he did he got more frustrated, not with the horse, but with the circumstances. He was loath to give up Sky and he was obviously very attached to Victoria as well. I thought he was working with Sky, looking to find some reason the horse would be a bad choice for Michelle. The problem was he couldn't find anything. Sky was the ideal horse. She had been expertly bred, raised and trained and Randy couldn't find fault in her no matter how hard he tried. He battled what to do if he decided to keep her as well. She wasn't like many mares. He couldn't see breeding her. She was too good for just a brood mare. She was too good for a workhorse. She wasn't a racehorse. For the next few years her best bet was pleasure riding and competition, maybe dressage. She would be a stunning dressage horse, but then again, all those were things Michelle would do, but not Gordon's Quarter Horses. It seemed Sky was destined to be Michelle's horse.

Randy counted down to dooms day. Michelle was going to come to the ranch, fall in love with Sky all over again, ask Randy's opinion, and he'd choke on the words, but he'd get through it. Then Michelle would buy Sky and that would be it. Randy would spend years trying to find a horse like her.

Chase fell into a different kind of mood. I can't really call it depression because it wasn't exactly an emotion. He was in hyper stealth mode, like everywhere he went he couldn't be seen. It wasn't that he was afraid of the hunters. It was more like watching a man handling a ticking time bomb. He wanted his hands on it as little as possible. Walking from the barn to the house he watched the gap between the buildings, made sure the coast was clear, appeared at the door of the bunkhouse and slipped inside, checked the window out the back of the room without stepping in front of it, leaving no profile, no shadow on the window. When his inspection of the area behind the ranch was as complete as possible he appeared soundlessly at the front door. Once inside he avoided all windows. I knew if I tracked the area behind the ranch I would find no sign of Chase's passing. I was tempted to go back there but I didn't tempt trouble. If Chase said the bounty hunters had stake out spots back there I believed him. I didn't share his caution, though I had a caution of my own. On the ranch I felt comfortable walking around. I searched my surroundings for things that seemed off or odd. Movements caught my eye until I identified them. Once identified, I relaxed.

Katie asked to go riding every day. I would take her riding around the corral but I made sure we were never alone. I wore the vest even though it was uncomfortable. Katie was used to feeling its bulkiness under my loose clothes.

The officers broke up their visiting times though they were beginning to wonder if we were pulling their legs. When they arrived everybody greeted them and chatted with them and updated them that everything was going well. I bet if Martha didn't keep a steady supply of desserts on hand they would have found more important things to do.

"Oh, do sit down and at least have a slice of pie," she'd say.

Then she would get any news from in town and stall so the patrol car was outside long enough to get noticed. I don't know if that was her plan but I was glad to have the car out front.

The day finally arrived and the whole ranch was abuzz, which I thought was odd because I thought this was mostly between Randy and Victoria. I thought the only reason Steve was in on this was because Randy needed fatherly advice.

Mid-afternoon everybody gathered at the corral, even Mom and Martha.

"Isn't she the prettiest thing?" Mom asked.

"Yes, she is," I agreed.

Randy had gone to extra trouble to groom Sky until she shown. There wasn't a fleck of dirt on her and her hoofs were polished, her mane and tail combed. She was full of herself prancing around like a beauty queen in a fashion show.

Victoria drove up first in a black Ford 250. She pulled up between the house and the bunkhouse like it wasn't the first time and she stepped out, a long legged denim-clad woman. I was guessing she was a little younger than Randy but not by much. She was fashionable and sharp looking. Her brown hair was curled and bounced as she walked.

A silver Toyota Camry drove up the road and parked beside Victoria's truck. Out bounded a blonde teenager of about eighteen. She was much like Victoria except she obviously shopped in the Junior's section. She wore low-rise jeans, bleached and distressed in interesting places. There was a flower and curlicues tattooed just above her pants line. Michelle's father came forward and shook hands with Randy first and then with those within reach. He wore navy twill slacks and a green polo shirt.

Michelle went straight to Sky and petted her, looking into her eyes.

"There's my beautiful Sky," she said.

Randy was trying to be cheerful and friendly but it wasn't coming across to those who really knew him.

"How did she do?" Victoria asked Randy. "Did you try her out? Tell me how she reacted."

Randy took a moment before starting. "She handles well. She, um… Tori, I couldn't find a thing wrong with her. I tried her on the barrels. I ran her on the track. I rode her most every day and she responds well. Steve rode her. Cassidy rode her. Cassidy even tried to trick Sky but she wouldn't be tricked."

"Cassidy. Who is Cassidy?" Victoria asked.

"Mister Gordon's older daughter," Randy answered.

Victoria examined the crowd. Her gaze settled on me and she sized me up.

"What do you think, Cassidy? How well do you know horses? Is Sky the horse we're looking for?"

"I grew up on Dad's horses," I answered. "I've trained, broke, competed, won a bit, tested racers, mucked out stables, you name it; I've done it. And I think Sky would be perfect as long as she is worked, ridden, talked to, groomed and trained every day."

"You think she needs training? I thought you rode her."

"I did. She's a dream horse. But she'll only stay that way with a dedicated owner who will give her time and keep her mind and her body busy. That takes daily work. You can't just throw hay at a horse and ride it if you feel like it and expect it to stay fit. Sky is the way she is because a talented trainer has worked with her every day for over a year. If you can't keep that up you'll find yourself with a backyard horse that's nice to look at and hard to ride."

Horses were not for everybody. It took a dedicated person to keep horses. Any starry eyed girl would do precisely what Michelle did when her father asked her squarely, "Do you think you can do all that?"

She gave her daddy the most pitiful look and said in her best not-quite pleading voice, "I'll do anything Daddy. I'll feed her and groom her and train her myself."

The dad saw the look, but he wasn't quite convinced, and neither was I.

"Lead her around a bit," the dad said.

Randy bowed his head and Dad boomed, "Cassidy, would you hop up there on Buck and lead Sky around a bit."

I got on Buck and took Sky's lead rope. I held her head high so she'd present a good profile. I felt guilty doing it, but Dad had asked me knowing I'd do Sky justice. I was curious how this would play out. What was Dad's interest in it? Did Dad have his eye on Sky, too? I think Mom and Martha were just caught up in the horse versus girl drama. I watched Sky as I led her around. The sun glinted off her shiny coat. Her mane and tail flowed gracefully behind her. I walked her back and forth in front of them and then led her away from them so that, if they knew a thing or two about a horse's legs, they could examine her for movement problems or weaknesses. Then I trotted her around so they could see her muscles work.

"Michelle, try riding her," her father said.

Steve walked off to the tack room to get a saddle and bridle. He was careful of his selection. The saddle was broken in, but the leather had been polished up. In a few minutes Sky was ready to go.

Michelle hadn't ridden much. I could tell just by the way she took a few tries to pull herself up. She took a minute to get comfortable in the saddle. She held the reins with one hand the saddle with the other. Lightning wasn't going to strike if you used the saddle to help balance, but it was telling, if you used it automatically. Dad could see her inexperience.

"Cassidy, show her a thing or two," Dad said.

I rode Buck around the corral moving from a walk to a trot to a canter. Before I went further I checked to see how Michelle was handling the canter. She was managing. I didn't think it was wise to make her gallop, though. Then I corrected my thinking. If Sky was too much horse for Michelle maybe the dad would see it. So I had Buck break into a gallop and Sky followed. Michelle shrieked. I slowed down. Slowed to a trot, then to a walk.

"If you're wanting to compete you're going to have to train at a gallop. Sky handles the barrels well, but it takes communication from you. You're the boss. If you can't be the boss then you won't make it at barrels. If you want to try her at jumping it's all teamwork. You have to judge your horse and her abilities at each speed, so you know how to take the jumps. If you want to work in dressage that takes even more fine-tuning. You have to know each other and you have to cue off each other constantly."

"Can I just ride her around a little and get used to it?" Michelle asked.

"Sure," said Randy forlornly. "Go for it."

Michelle walked Sky around in the corral for a bit and then wandered out the gate, her blonde hair bouncing with every breeze and every movement. As I watched I thought Michelle was not ready for a horse like Sky. She walked and trotted her up and down the area between the barn and the house. She worked up to a canter again. I was beginning to change my mind about her when there was a sharp crack and Sky stumbled and Michelle fell in the dust of the farmyard. Sky bolted and took off running, afraid of something, she wasn't sure what. Since I was sitting on Buck I put my heels to his sides and he lunged toward the gate.

Rusty and Chase were better at handling medical emergencies so I took out after Sky. She ran until she got to the back fence then turned around. I got a rope loose and I was getting ready to lasso her when she turned and ran at the back fence again.

I cussed out the young horse as I frantically got the rope ready. Sky ran until the fence came in view and handily sailed right over it. Could Buck do that? I didn't know and I didn't want to chance it in a clunky Western saddle. I unlatched the gate and jumped into the saddle again. In no time I was galloping through the open gate after the wayward filly. Only problem was Sky was much younger and much more fleet of foot than Buck ever was. I wound up the rope and hung it on the saddle as I followed Sky into the oaks behind the ranch.

Chapter 49

Riding full tilt through the oaks, I caught a movement to my right. A man stumbled out of the brush and watched me ride away. Then he looked behind him and found cover again.

Sky was enjoying the chase. She hadn't been truly free for a long time. She was ready to stretch her legs, see the countryside and she wasn't eager to be caught. She seemed to know how long a rope was, or how far it could be thrown. Whenever I got close enough to give it a try she would toss her head and smirk at me and run off again out of reach. I couldn't get up much speed in the trees. If I could push her out into the open I could get up some speed but Sky was much faster than Buck was. I had to outsmart her somehow.

When we came to Tony Macaluso's vineyard Sky was still going strong. I was glad she chose to go around the vineyard because it was easy to get hung up on vines, supports, and wires. It was not a good place for a horse to go.

I tried to figure out what might be going on at the ranch. Dad would assure everybody that I was capable of catching Sky. Rusty would step in and organize the group, and call for any medical attention Michelle might need. Chase would head for the back of the ranch. His instincts would tell him something had happened back there, and he would worry that this was meant to target me. That started a whole chain of thought that I didn't like the looks of. What if they *had* targeted me? Perhaps the ensuing chaos allowed them to learn something or create a diversion. Shoot, I should be watching my tail.

Off in the distance I could see a rider making his way toward me. I took comfort in the fact that we could team up and it would be easier to catch Sky so I set my mind to finding a way to box her in.

It was when the rider was about a quarter mile away that I realized this wasn't a ranch hand. They were riding Apache. Without a saddle. Of all the horses on the ranch, Apache was a good choice. He could probably catch Sky but any ranch hand would take the time to put a saddle on him and come properly outfitted. How had somebody else managed to get into the barn and take a horse? And why would they? If it was the bounty hunter trying to catch me, what could he do? We were miles from the ranch and the nearest road was a couple of miles away. Oh… I thought… no, the road past the Macaluso place was only a half-mile west. I tried to pinpoint my location and that reminded me about the tracking device. Chase, Dad and Rusty wouldn't see a need to check the GPS yet. They wouldn't get concerned until they decided to send a hand out and they discovered Apache missing. I ran my hand over my pocket and felt the little lump of a transmitter that I now carried everywhere I went. Before they could get closer and recognize what I was doing, I took the transmitter out of my pocket and placed it under my left breast, inside my bra. If they frisked me they would be less likely to find it there. If they tried to touch me there I had good reason to protest.

I took stock of my situation. What did I have to work with and what were the goals? I had the transmitter. That was just insurance. I had two horses, well potentially. I had a rope. I had my wits about me. I counted Sky amongst my assets because she was faster; it was possible that she was even faster than Apache. I decided I had a better chance with Sky than I did with Buck. I looked behind me and the rider was making steady progress. I gave Buck a solid kick and he surged forward. Sky lithely leaped to a run to stay out of range. The problem was I didn't have time to play Sky's games. I needed that horse if I was going to get away. Catching Sky was a chore to begin with, but it was time I put my determination into overdrive, and if you ask the guys at the station in Joshua Hills about what happens when I do that, they would say, "Oh no."

I took out after Sky like a tornado was on my heels. Now the thing to do if a tornado is on your heels is to find cover and make that cover as strong as possible. Then there's those fools among us who think they can outrun a tornado. Buck was running just as fast as he could in the cramped quarters of the woods and Sky felt equally hemmed in so she headed for more open ground. I goaded Buck.

"Come on, boy, you can catch her. Isn't she the cutest little filly you ever saw, you rickety old grandpa of a horse you? Go get her! Yeah!" Slap, kick, "You can do it…" I leaned over the saddle making myself a smaller target.

Sky took time to see how far behind we were and Buck closed the gap a bit. I could hear hoof beats behind us. I knew how skittish Apache could be. Any surprise could startle him. When I saw the gun come out I knew I had to do something. I pulled hard to the right and Buck swerved in front of Apache. Apache lunged to the right to avoid a collision. I knew I was dealing with a horse person when the man gripped with his legs and followed Apache's movements expertly. I aimed for Sky again and urged Buck on. She had slowed, thinking we had given up the chase so when Buck came barreling out of the trees towards her she shied away but we were able to catch up. I got a loop ready and brought Buck up alongside. I threw the loop over Sky's head and pulled it tight. I continued pulling until the two running horses were side by side and very uncomfortable about the situation. If I had time I would have stopped, switched horses and turned toward home but I had an armed man hot on my heels and Buck was slowing us down. There was nothing for it but to pull Sky in as close as possible and switch horses on the run. It was dangerous as hell, and I was glad Rusty couldn't watch. I slid my leg over the saddle, riding sidesaddle, one foot in a stirrup I leaned over and grabbed the horn on Sky's saddle. I switched the foot that was in the stirrup, made sure I had the rope, pushed off from Buck with all my might and hauled on Sky's saddle for all I was worth. When I was standing in the stirrup on Sky's side I yelled, "Good boy! Go home Buck! Go on home!" It was a magic phrase that every horse seems to know that meant, we're through, time to go back to the nice comfortable barn. If we were in the saddle and said it the horses automatically turned around and headed for the barn. I was counting on Buck showing up and drawing enough attention to get the guys going.

"Good girl!" I told Sky, "Now take off. Let's go! You can shake this guy. I know you can. Come on girl!"

I didn't bother looking back. I was hightailing it as fast as Sky would go. I was lucky the first part of this little adventure had been more of a game to her but she took my commands seriously and lit out at a good, fast pace.

Apache was a fast horse. I'd had experience trying to catch Apache before and in the end I had to trick him. I never would have caught him by chasing him. I decided, now that I had Sky's help, I should be findable so I started a wide U-turn and headed back to the ranch. Bad move, the bounty hunter was taking no chances. He began pushing Sky closer and closer to the road and when Tony Macaluso's vineyard came into view he tried to force Sky into the rows of grape vines. Tony's land was deep and, though I could see the house, I doubted anybody at the estate would see what was happening beyond the fields. More and more we were wedged in until Sky had had enough. She reared and lashed out at Apache. She became tangled in a vine and down she went. She was all flailing legs and all I could do was roll under the grapes until she found her footing. Off she went leaving me in a tangle of grape vines, rope and wire. I crouched under the grape vines and tried to make my way farther into the vineyard. The vines were thick and it didn't take the bounty hunter long to walk down a row and find me. I heard the gun and looked up. He spoke to me in Spanish, but I only caught one word, which I thought meant *go*.

"No," I said, "I'm not going with you."

"You go. Or you die," he said.

"We'll see about that," I told him.

I thought if I had a few seconds of inattention I could run, but he walked up to me, stuck the gun to my side and noted the stiff vest under my shirt. He waved the gun at me.

"Take eet off," he demanded.

"No."

He aimed the gun at my head.

"Take eet off."

"If you want me alive you won't shoot me."

He growled at me reached out and grabbed me by the shirt and physically dragged me to the end of the row. I slipped out of the shirt and scrambled to my feet, but he dashed after me and grabbed me by the arm.

Apache had been a good horse, unfortunately. He had stood patiently and waited for his rider. The man grabbed the rope up, forced me to the ground and tied my ankles. I kicked him and punched at him and he ignored it all. When he had my ankles securely bound, he made a loop on the other end, put it over Apache's head, ran the rope down Apache's back and hoisted himself up. He sat on the rope trying to keep it positioned so Apache wouldn't get his legs tangled in it. Then he rode toward the road, dragging me along behind him. I counted my lucky stars he hadn't demanded my vest. It took many of the bumps and protected me from the sand and rocks. I had to be careful to keep my arms and head up. At a walk it wasn't too tough but when the pace picked up I couldn't help but roll around. Damn but I was in trouble now, and worse, Chase was in a fix, too. I prayed he wouldn't turn himself in for me. I'd figure something out. I'd get away, and when I did, I wanted to go to San Diego, or Joshua Hills, or come back to the ranch and find Chase as he'd always been. I tried pulling myself up to work at the ropes but, when I did, I was dragged on my side or my rear which was much harder. Rocks tore at my shoulder when I was on my side and on my rear when I managed to stay upright. It didn't take long to reach our destination but it took hundreds of rocks, scrapes and bumps. I was bruised and scraped by the time he stopped Apache at a white Impala parked just off the dirt road.

I repeated the license plate number over and over as I was bound and gagged and stuffed into the trunk. I heard him slap Apache on the rear, sending him home, then he walked to the driver's seat, opened the door and got in. I heard the engine start and knew I was in for a long, rough road. For the first half hour I repeated the license plate number over and over as I took stock of my situation. I looked for a trunk release cable. It had been cut. No surprise there. Bad news, too. It meant they had thought ahead a little. I looked for a lever that would fold down the back seat. There wasn't one. I pushed on the back seat and it gave a little. Maybe both sides were not latched properly. I didn't want to use that escape route unless the car was empty. If I appeared in the back seat while the driver was there I'd be discovered and he'd fix the seat.

It was cramped and hot in the trunk. I knew to keep calm. It was the number one rule when dealing with trouble. In fact that rule, reworded a bit, was my acronym to remember the license plate letters. PNP, Panic Never Pays.

I was lying on a loose piece of car carpeting so I scooted as far against the seat as I could and pulled the carpeting toward me, then I stuffed it in a corner out of the way. Underneath was a pressboard panel that covered the spare tire. There could be tools in there. A crowbar or lug wrench or jack and jack handle. Any of those things might come in handy. If I was extremely lucky, there would be a screwdriver. It wasn't easy in those cramped quarters to move, especially with my hands and feet tied. There was barely room to move the panel. All I could do was lift it and feel around underneath. I decided I needed my hands and feet. As we bumped and jostled along I worked the rope that bound my feet, because it was easy to reach, and the way I was tied I pulled the ropes on my hands tighter whenever I moved my feet away from my hands.

The rope was a tough one to loosen. It was a well-worn ranch rope and it was made to hold horses, to stay tied even with a horse lunging against it, so pulling and tugging did nothing. I had to patiently work the knots. By the time I got my feet free I knew we were a long way from home. I hoped we were not going to Mexico. But… maybe I should. Maybe the border crossing was my chance to attract attention. They would have to inspect a car that had something thumping and banging in the trunk.

I knew it would be several hours before we could reach the border. I vowed to keep my ears peeled for chances to attract attention, then that reminded me that I better keep going at getting untied, because part of my plan involved knocking out the tail lights of the car. To prioritize I developed a to-do list. I found it helped to do that in these situations. If I had things to do I wouldn't have time to worry about things that did me no good. So my list so far was: get untied, search the spare tire compartment for tools, and put the tools to use. A screwdriver would allow me to remove the covers to the taillights. If I could open the taillights, I could disconnect the wires and push the lights out. That would allow me some ventilation, which was sorely needed. It would also improve the chances of being pulled over for a ticket. If I found a lug wrench I could knock out the covers and the lights, messier but still an option. If the lug wrench had a pry bar on it to take off hubcaps, I could pry the trunk lid up, again for ventilation. The air in the trunk was hot. If there was no screwdriver or lung wrench in the space there might be a jack and jack handle which could be of use to me. I wondered what jacking up the lid of the trunk would do. Punch a hole in it? Pop it open? I was willing to try anything, but first I had to get untied.

You know, when you're counting minutes, even laying in a trunk working ropes can be living, really living. Every little positive sign is a reason to celebrate. A loosening. A waft of cooler air. A reason to celebrate.

It took me over an hour working those ropes to get my ankles free and then with my feet free I didn't have to worry about the ropes tightening around my hands so much. However, the ropes around my wrists were much harder to get at. I had to use my teeth. I knew all the places this rope had been, dragged through the muck of the barn, thrown over the head of a horse, carried on a saddle for days at a time gathering trail dust and ranch dirt. I didn't let that bother me. This was no time to worry about dirt. I had bigger things to worry about, so I pulled on the one piece of the knot that looked like it might budge. Pulling and tugging and sweating, I listened to the outside world zipping by. We were on a freeway!

That was bad news and good news. On the bright side there were people around so I could attract attention. On the negative side it meant we were going somewhere very fast and that place was not close to the ranch.

Conditions were getting worse inside the trunk. I was getting a headache, perhaps from the heat, perhaps from the poor air. I wondered if fumes from the freeway were making their way in. I was getting nowhere on the ropes binding my hands. I began thinking ventilation was gaining in importance. Could I open some small airway with my hands bound? I tried again to feel around the spare tire compartment. I could maneuver a little better this time because my feet were not bound. First I discovered that the spare tire was held in place by a bracket held in place by a wing nut. After awkwardly unscrewing the wing nut I stuck it in my pocket. There was no telling what I could make use of later. I pulled off the bracket and hefted it. Would it work for a pry bar? I looked for a way to wedge it in the crack at the corner of the trunk. I jammed it in as far as it would go but when I pulled down on it, it just pulled out with a sudden jerk. I tried again but it was shaped wrong for the job. I considered trying to knock out the tail light covers but thought I'd end up cutting up my hands so I went back to the compartment. Under where the bracket had been was a fake leather tool pouch. Yes! Celebration time! Inside was… the dinkiest lug wrench I ever saw in my life. It was maybe seven inches long. How was anybody supposed to get lug nuts to budge with that? Or a trunk lid for that matter. I jammed it in the crack under the lid and shoved it as deep as it would go. I pulled down on it as much as I could. I could only pull on it with one hand because my hands were tied back to back. I felt a little give but when I pulled the pry bar out there was barely a dent. Still, I could feel a little waft of fresh air. I tried again, shoving the pry bar further in. Damn but I sure could use a longer handle! I could put all my weight on that little bar and it didn't budge. I wondered if the jack handle was longer. I felt around for it but it wasn't stout enough to pry with. Again I wondered what would happen if I tried to jack up the lid of the trunk. I centered the jack in front of the latch and stuck the jack handle in the little bracket. It was almost impossible to pump the handle inside the trunk laying on my side, both hands tied together. Slowly, slowly the jack rose until it hit the trunk lid, then I kept going one pump at a time. There was a creaking and a groaning and I thought I was going to break off the latch but then there was a loud *punch!* and the jack went right through the lid of the trunk. I pushed and pulled the jack to widen the hole and then pushed the protruding part of the jack up where it might catch the eye of a motorist behind us.

When my arms got tired of pushing the jack around I got to work on the tail light covers. I didn't have a screwdriver. I tried using the pry bar as a screwdriver but it was too thick and unwieldy. I tapped on the covers and decided they were just fiberboard or plastic. I tried hacking at them with the tip of the pry bar but, with my hands tied together, I couldn't get a good hit in. I tried kicking them. I was wearing cowboy boots since we were expecting folks to come talk horses. I was thankful for the boots. The toe didn't do much but the heel cracked it a bit and that encouraged me. I continued kicking until I busted a hole in the cover.

There was cursing from the front of the car when things got noisy in the trunk. "Silencio!" he yelled at me. I knew what that meant. I ignored him.

Working at the wires with my hands tied together didn't work very well. The wires cut at my hands. I had to slip the pry bar behind the wires and pull to get them to come loose. The lug wrench end had just enough of a lip to snag the wires and I yanked them loose one at a time. I felt each one give with a snap. I wondered how many wires it took for one taillight. Let's see, blinker, brake light, warning lights, anything else back here? After a couple of wires snapped I stomped at the light with my foot again. I hoped the plastic covers snapped on and off for easy replacement. Maybe the lights could be pushed out from behind. I braced myself against the back seat and pushed hard on the taillight. What was left of the cover was getting in the way so I kicked at that some more. More cursing from the front of the car. When most of the housing was broken away I tried again and this time I was rewarded as I felt the light give and pop right off the car. I was so surprised that my foot went through the hole. As the light crashed to the freeway I heard brakes screeching and cars swerving. Oh, man! I hope I didn't cause a wreck!

I heard an engine revving beside the car and then pulling forward.

"Hey!" a voice called out, "Pull over!"

More cursing from the front. I wondered what all the words meant. I had taken high school Spanish but I never learned how to cuss. I barely remembered the common words.

"I'm telling you… pull over!" a man yelled.

I felt the car change lanes. I was sure my captor had no plans to pull over and talk to this guy while he had a kidnap victim in the trunk, but maybe I'd created enough of a ruckus to arouse suspicion, and if señor bounty hunter made a run for it maybe somebody would call the police. One lane, two, a swerving and a curb jumping sent me skidding across the trunk on my back. I pulled myself over to the hole where the taillight was. There was city. What city? Big city. Not skyscraper big, but big enough to have a very busy, older, shabby part of town. I saw garages with signs in foreign languages and corner grocery stores, also with signs in foreign languages. Nothing was in English. Some ethnic part of LA?

We almost immediately hit traffic but mister bounty hunter didn't let that slow him down. He drove on the wrong side of the street. He sped down little, narrow residential streets. I couldn't watch out the tail light because I was sliding all over the trunk. Finally I found a way to spread eagle my legs and brace myself with my hands above my head. The car lurched and swerved and sped up and slowed down unexpectedly. I didn't hear sirens. I thought I would by now but perhaps this guy from the freeway didn't own a cell phone. I hoped he wasn't taking the bounty hunter on by himself.

Things smoothed out a bit so I made my way around to the taillight window and looked out. I saw a red Mustang grill. Yikes! I hoped that guy had brakes! He was driving so close to the Impala that he couldn't see that there was a person in the trunk. I tried pulling down the jack but the metal had sprung back just enough to trap the post of the jack. I was hoping to stick a hand out that opening so the guy behind would know I was back there. I stuck my fingers up through the hole, hoping to bend the metal a little more but as soon as I did the car bumped over something and the metal sliced my finger. Ouch! I looked out the hole and saw that he had jumped the curb and driven down the bank to pass cars waiting to merge onto the freeway. Oh great, so this was going to turn into a high-speed chase. I held onto my bleeding finger but there wasn't much I could do about it. I didn't even have my shirt to wrap around it. I put pressure on it but it bled profusely.

I watched out the hole as much as I could trying to figure out where I was, but the driving was so erratic I was tossed to and fro. We weaved in and out of traffic and I began wondering if I was going to die in a fiery crash or tortured and shot in Mexico. The next time I saw the grill of the red Mustang it wasn't the same shiny red it was before. It had met with a mishap or two. I hadn't planned on civilians getting involved. I thought any person who suspected something would call the police. Leave it to me to find the one person in California without a cell phone.

The city began thinning and I felt the car exit and turn onto a long road through the desert. The speed limit the other direction was fifty but we sure weren't doing fifty. The Impala flew and the Mustang fell behind. Maybe the driver of the Mustang was wising up and decided he had better things to do than get shot by an angry motorist. When the Mustang was no longer in sight, the bounty hunter pulled off the road. There was silence for a bit, then cursing. I imagined the cursing came when he saw the condition his car was in. We continued on the two lane road. We passed through a small town and turned onto another two lane road. It was right about then that I remembered the tracking device hidden on me. We traveled perhaps ten minutes when we arrived at another small town and we began making our way to our final destination. It was dusk and there were very few people on the streets. There weren't enough businesses in town to attract people. All I could see out the hole in the tail light was a worn out gas station, a 7/11, and a lonely bar that had seen better days. The area turned rural. Fields lined the road. Miles of perfectly flat fields. There would be little cover if I managed to escape. I heard the crunch of tires on gravel and then everything went dark as we pulled into a dim garage. The door was pulled shut and everything went black, then a light was turned on. I heard footsteps coming toward the car and then Spanish in what I interpreted to mean: "What the hell did you do to my car?"

Chapter 50

The trunk lid clanked open and got stuck on the jack. It slowly lifted and I looked up into the eyes of my captor.

"You better be worth all dis trouble," he said with a thick accent.

"I *am* trouble," I said and he laughed at the idea. "When you took me you took on a whole boat load of trouble."

"How you untie dose ropes?" he asked.

"Patiently," I said.

He motioned me out of the trunk then he stuck his head in.

"Who you murder in here?" he said when he saw the blood, then he looked at me and smiled, "Señor Morales not let chu keep that vest. Then wha'chu do?"

He seemed mighty calm, like he was used to turning people over to Señor Morales.

"I guess we'll just have to wait and see," I replied.

"Why Señor Morales wan'chu? What you do?"

"How do you know he wants me?"

He pulled a piece of paper out of his pocket. It showed a newspaper clipping of a search. Like most photos of searches, it showed a group of firemen and police officers with emergency vehicles, lights flashing in the background. Landon and I stood behind the officers. I was circled with a faulty ballpoint pen. And, like usual, Landon and I looked like campers who had invaded real police business, not the people who had actually done the search and found the person. The press went for glitz. They photographed what the readers wanted to see. What the readers wanted to see was not us. It grated on some of the search and rescue guys. Many of the officers had inflated egos. They liked the action, the uniform, and getting credit when it was due. I was very happy to let them have it. My ten sixty-five was found, if they would be all right I was happy. If they wouldn't, the search could haunt me for weeks. The photo I was looking at showed a search that did not end well. It was the Cranston search. I'd found my man, but I'd found him too late. I handed the photo back.

"And you're sure that is me?" I asked feeling just a tad more dismal than I had when I was just kidnapped bait.

"It's you."

He pulled out a cell phone and hit a number. He put the phone to his ear. Everything he said was in Spanish. With my limited knowledge of Spanish I caught fleeting words as they flew by: girl, here, good. He pointed me at the door. The rope trailed behind. He didn't want to mess with the rope so he untied me and pushed me toward the door again.

I was still gripping my bleeding finger as we crossed the gravel drive and followed a sidewalk to the front of a Spanish style mansion. A quick knock and the bounty hunter opened the door himself. He put a hand on my shoulder and directed me into the living room. The furniture was all Spanish style. Señor Morales stood next to a desk and I was guided to the middle of the room. We stood before the desk and Morales looked me up and down. He walked over and took a lock of my hair and ran it through his fingers, then he felt the vest.

"Is good to finally meet you, señor," he said. "You not so grande in person." He reached out to shake hands but my hand was still bleeding so he withdrew it. "I toll you not to hurt her," he said to the bounty hunter.

"That… she do herself," he said.

"Lucia!" he barked and a woman in a maid's uniform stepped into the room. The uniform was not the classic French maid uniform seen in movies. It was brown slacks and a white blouse and practical black nurse's shoes. Her hair was carefully pulled up into a ponytail. He spoke to her in Spanish and she led me down the hall to a bathroom where she gave me soap and water. I washed, then she looked at the cut and applied a salve to it and bandaged it with gauze and tape. It wasn't a deep cut but it was stubborn, probably because it was on me. She gave me the gauze and tape and led me back to the living room. This time Señor Morales extended his hand. I shook it hesitantly. I didn't like bad guys being nice to me. It felt… fake.

I counted the cut as worth the knowledge it was buying me. As I walked to the bathroom I memorized the layout of the house. The bathroom and two larger rooms were on the right side of the hall and three medium sized rooms were on the left side of the hall. They had open doors and I was wishing it was daytime so I could tell more about the window configuration in the rooms. If a room was well lit it either meant the room was well used or the drapes on the windows were open. Everything was noteworthy. The candlesticks on the mantle. The glass bowl on the coffee table. The statue that stood next to the entrance way to the hall. There was no telling what I might find useful if things turned ugly.

"Can I get you something to eat? To drink?" Señor Morales asked.

"I am a bit overdue for dinner," I said.

"Carmen!" he barked and a different woman appeared from the other side of the room. "Get miss… forgive me, you didn't tell me your name."

"You can just call me Trouble."

His eyes narrowed. I didn't want to give him any more information than I needed to.

"Get Miss Trouble something to eat," he said, a little cooler than before. "Now, while she is busy I tink we have some business to attend to. Sit down. First, I tink, this vest have to go."

"Give me my shirt back."

He looked to the bounty hunter who shrugged. I knew the shirt was in Tony Macaluso's vineyard.

"No matter. Take the vest off." When I didn't make a move he looked to the bounty hunter. "Omar…" I found the gun pointed at my head, not in a threatening way, just enough to make a point. I was to obey or I could make things difficult.

It wasn't that I was shy or overly modest. Any mom will tell you after having a baby there is very little modesty left. I was mad, because they weren't just being practical here. They were being degrading. Behind all their pleasantries they enjoyed the fact that I was degrading myself by handing over the vest. The vest would do me little good, now that they knew about it. They could just pick a different spot to shoot at. I knew from the moment the shirt came off they wouldn't let me keep the vest, so I peeled back the Velcro fasteners and took it off watching their reaction. Underneath I had on a light tank top and a bra. A very light tank top. Umm, just enough tank top to keep chaffing from the vest to a minimum. I don't exactly have a model's build. And I am not even close to being voluptuous. If anything they were reminded of teenage girl. Maybe a little more up top, but stacked I was not. I stood before the two men with my anger burning and they stood there with their dominant arrogance and then Morales snapped out of it and called Lucia back.

"Bring Miss Trouble something to wear," he said.

She turned and walked down the hall.

"Now… step one." He went to his desk and picked up the telephone receiver. He punched in a telephone number from a list on his desk. He smiled when he got an answer quickly. "Señor Chase? Somebody here would like to talk to you."

He handed me the phone. I wished I had more warning.

"Chase, do me a favor and take the first flight to Toronto and guard some other border," I said.

"Can't do that kiddo. I got you into this mess."

"No! Stay away."

"We can find you. Getting you back is the hard part. Are you okay?"

"Better off than their car."

He almost laughed. "I knew I could count on you. Are you okay?"

"Yeah."

"Which side of the border are you on?"

"You can't tell?"

"Quiet!" he snapped. I got the message. Don't say anything that would make them look for the tracking device.

"North," I said and Morales made a move to take the phone. I dodged him and ran around the couch. "Is Rusty there?"

"Babe, are you okay?" Rusty said.

"Yeah, but I only have a second. Don't come here. Don't let Chase come here."

Morales motioned for Omar to come around the other side of the couch. Lucia stood at the hallway with a garment in her hands totally unfazed by the men chasing me around the room.

"We at least have to contact the local authorities."

"They're going to take the phone. I love you. Be careful!" Hug the kids for me.

"Cassidy… please don't fight them. They ask you questions, just answer them. Do what you can to stay safe."

"I have to give the phone back. Don't worry. I'll think of something." And the phone was snatched away.

"Rusty." Señor Morales said, "You hear that, Rusty? She love you. If you love her, you stay away. No police. Only Chase," he hung up the phone.

Omar asked a question in Spanish the last of which I thought meant: Chase come here?

"No, not here," Señor Morales said for my benefit. "He bring his friends here. We take her to Colina."

Omar nodded understanding. I wondered why they were feeding me information. Lucia quietly handed me a blouse and I pulled it on and buttoned it. It was three sizes too big but beggars can't be choosers. I'd wear Omar's clothes if it would cover up the tracking device.

"A bite to eat and then we go," Señor Morales said.

The food was good. I had to give Carmen credit. I wished I could get the recipe. It was like Texas chili but it had hominy in it. There were plenty of chunks of pork and every now and then I found tiny pieces of vegetables. The tortillas were not quite round, which made me think she made them herself. It wasn't a fancy meal but much more than I expected under the circumstances. So far Señor Morales was giving his prisoner the royal treatment. I hoped the royal treatment didn't include a dungeon like Chase had led me to believe.

I didn't see much point in being rude, especially to the girls who had only done good things for me so I said in my broken Spanish, "Gracias, Carmen, la comida es deliciosa." I thought that was at least understandable. She just looked shyly at me.

"How much Spanish do you speak?"

"Muy poquito," I admitted. Very little. "Most Spanish goes by too quickly for me to understand and my speaking vocabulary is worse. I don't mind embarrassing myself by trying, though. If I insult you in Spanish it was accidental. If I mean to insult you, I'll do it in English, and you'll understand the words."

"We have a long way to go," he said. "You are the lucky one. You can sleep the whole way."

"I doubt that," I said.

"I'm afraid you must," he said.

I didn't like the implications behind that.

"We cannot risk you making noise as we cross the border. Lucia, if you will bring my bags to the car."

"Sí Señor," she said and went down the hall again. As she rolled a cart with two large suitcases on it out the front door Señor Morales took a syringe from his desk drawer.

"No!" I said.

"You have no choice. You will enjoy it. You will sleep better than all the rest of us."

But I wouldn't know where I was going! Wouldn't be able to think! I backed away from Señor Morales right into Omar. I felt a stick and a burning feeling. As the burning feeling faded so did my legs and Omar caught me as I slumped to the floor. I felt Omar pick me up and carry me to the car. I felt the car moving. The same car? It had to be a different car. The Impala would draw too much attention with its busted out tail light. I tried to be observant, tried to listen, tried to form a plan but I quickly faded.

I had to admit Morales was right. I slept well, but I woke up sick and I knew I was a very long way from home, in a very bad situation. I was in Mexico. Beyond Rusty's reach.

Chapter 51

I lay there miserably examining my situation. Bars on the small window. One door. Thick walls. Sound would not travel. Twin bed. Sparse furnishings. I tried getting up but I felt queasy and dizzy so I lay down again. I knew even if there was a glowing green exit sign I couldn't escape in the shape I was in. When I had a chance to escape I needed to be ready to give it my all. I quietly examined my surroundings. It wasn't as lavish as the mansion in California. The room was chilly. I looked around but there were no vents in the ceiling or floor. I knocked on the wall next to the bed lightly. It was as solid as could be. Adobe?

I dozed hoping the queasiness would go away and it did after I slept again. I woke up to gentle shaking.

"Señorita? Señorita?" *Shake, shake.*

I opened my eyes to find a little Mexican girl standing over me.

"Señor Morales want to see you."

"Que es su nombre?" I asked.

"Elena," she answered, "Y tu?"

"Mí llamo Trouble," I said.

"Es un nombre comico," Elena said.

"Yo estoy mucho trouble," I said. I was out of my element here.

"Sí, Señor Morales es mucho trouble, tambien." Was she mocking me? It didn't matter. I got the message. Even this kid thought I was in trouble with Señor Morales. "Come," she said.

I got up and smoothed out my hair. My loaner blouse was all wrinkled but there wasn't much I could do about it. Elena struggled a bit with the thick, wooden door. It was a wonder she could open it. We walked down a short hall and turned a corner into another hall. She led me into a small room where a rough wooden table stood with six chairs around it. This room had a small, barred window like the room I came from. On the table was a deep plate with a stew of sorts in it. A small stack of tortillas stood next to it. Señor Morales motioned for me to sit and eat. A woman came in and poured a glass of wine. Wine? I didn't want anything alcoholic. I wanted to keep my wits about me.

"Only wine or water here," he said.

I took a sip. I needed water but I wasn't sure what the water would do to my system. Guess I had a choice, my head or my stomach. I sipped slowly and made sure I ate something. I ate everything they gave me. I'd learned the hard way that meals were unpredictable in captivity.

"After you eat I want you to call Chase again," he explained.

"And what am I supposed to tell him?"

"Tell him to come alone to Colina."

"No."

"If you refuse, things could get painful for you."

"That's okay. I won't let him turn himself in for me."

"You know he will come. He cares for you. He will cooperate if he thinks you will go free."

"Will I?"

"I haven't decided. Much depends on the way this ends. If Chase comes to me, alone, arranges a trade, then possibly. If I have to hurt you I'm afraid the police won't look kindly on that."

When the bowl was empty he handed me a telephone.

"Call him."

I thought an update couldn't hurt. At least Rusty would get word I was okay. I punched the numbers and Señor Morales noted that I didn't ask for the number.

"Cassidy, what's up?" Chase asked.

"Señor Morales asked me to call. Did you fly to Toronto?"

"Toronto? I thought you said Tijuana."

"No! Go back."

"Can't. I don't have a passport on me."

"Chase this isn't funny. Go home."

"Are you okay?"

"Yeah, I was drugged so I have no idea where I am, but I'm fine."

He began speaking very fast and very quietly. I thought I better listen good and hard. "I know where you are. You're in Colina. It's Spanish for hill. If you manage to get away take off due east, after about a quarter mile turn north. Take it easy. The walk to the spring is long and hot. You'll be able to spot it because of the green around it. After that head north west. Go around the base of a ridge and there's a little spring at the base, if you're lucky. If you head due north from there you'll hit a highway. Watch for border patrol Jeeps. Ask for Taz. He knows you. Got it?"

"Yeah."

"The place you're in is not easy to escape from. It's like a compound."

"Chase, turn around and go home."

"Listen to me while you can. The house is square. In the middle is a little courtyard. That's the only place they will let you go outside. It's just dirt and stepping stones but ask to go outside. You're good at finding ways out. There's only one way into the house. You'll have to cross the main rooms of the house to the front door but the door into the courtyard goes out the back of the kitchen. You better say something."

"Okay, so I'm in Colina. I still say go back. Is Rusty there?"

"Could I keep him away?"

Morales pulled the phone out of my hand.

"I said Chase comes alone. If there is any trouble I shoot the girl." There was a short pause while he listened. His manner was changing rapidly. "No police, no family, no friend, no nada!" He began pacing agitatedly. He looked like he was ready to slug somebody.

"Rusty! Whatever you're saying, stop!" I called out.

Morales yanked me out of the chair.

"You tell him! Tell him Chase only!"

"What in the world did you say to him?" I asked. "He turned into Doctor Jekyll or something!"

"Talk! Tell him!" Morales said angrily.

"Rusty, you're going to have to stay away. If he sees anybody but Chase out there he's going to freak."

"Are you okay?"

"Yeah, but whatever you did, don't do it again."

Morales thought he'd teach Chase a lesson. He marched up to me and slugged me in the stomach. I'd been taught in the Marines how to take a blow. I tensed my abdominal muscles, twisted to the side and the blow hit hard, but glanced off with the twist. Even with that, I doubled over. When the pain subsided, I straightened up ready to get a blow in myself but I could hear Rusty on the phone.

"Cassidy! Don't push him. Back off, girl. Are you okay?"

I was staring up into Morales's face. If looks could kill, he'd be dead. But I didn't really want him dead. I wanted him to be set up in such a way that his own people would lock him up. How I was going to manage that, and still get out of this fix, I didn't know.

"Yeah, I'm okay," I snapped. I didn't want to snap at Rusty. I didn't want things to get tense where he could hear. That was what made me mad. I didn't want to cause him worry.

Morales took the telephone away and hung it up.

"Now, I want you to tell me everything you know about Chase Downing," he said.

"Nobody knows Chase."

"Wrong answer," he said, stabbing a knife into the table top.

"He's a tracker."

"And?"

"He's a retired police officer."

I was trying to only tell Morales things he already knew. The fact was nobody really knew Chase. I certainly didn't.

"Does he have family?"

"None that I know of."

"Where is he from?"

"Arizona."

"Arizona is a big place."

"He's only told me of a house in the desert. He has never mentioned a town."

"You lie."

"Quit giving me reasons to lie."

"When will he be here? How long do we have to prepare?"

"I don't know. I don't know where we are. If you could show me on a map, then maybe I could tell you."

"I show you, but you will not try to get away. I won' stop you gently."

The information was well worth a little cooperation. He led me through the living room to an office. He pointed me to a chair and kept his eyes on me while he went to a drawer and pulled out a road map.

"Colina, is here," he said pointing to a blank spot on the map. I quickly noted that if I walked the way Chase said to go I was going to be covering a lot of very dry desert. I couldn't see the landmarks on the road map but I could see the sheer bareness of the land.

"Colina isn't on the map?" I asked.

"Colina is a place, not a town."

"Then you should understand that the place Chase is from is a place, not a town. Is there a road to this place?"

"Sí, it is here, like so," he said drawing an imaginary line on the map.

I was glad to know that, too. It would help me navigate if I ever found a way out.

I checked the scale of miles and Tijuana seemed far away.

"You have no time," I told Morales. "Chase is in Mexico."

"How?"

"He drove here."

"How would he know where you were?"

"He knows you better than you think," I said quickly trying to cover my tracks. "You wanted him to find me. He knew you wanted him to come after me. So why are you surprised that he did it? He knows about Colina. He can find it. He's been here before."

"Tell me more about this man."

"What do you want to know?"

"What does he value?"

"Nothing. He has nothing of value."

"Every man values something."

"If there was one thing Chase really valued he hasn't mentioned it to me."

"His home."

"There's nothing in his home he couldn't live without."

"Who are his friends?"

"I haven't met his friends. Tell me, how does Chase know about Colina?"

"Chase is a hunter. I am the hunted. I ask the questions. I ask you again. Who are his friends?"

The whole San Diego police department, Rusty's family, Elan's family, my family, me.

"Chase has no close friends."

He walked around behind my chair and put the knife to my throat.

"Think of something, someone. What does Chase value?"

"Threats to my life won't work. You won't get Chase without me so put down the knife."

"So, you think he values you?"

"No. I don't."

"You lie again."

He dragged me out of my chair and pointed me out the door and down the hall. When we got to the crude kitchen he pointed me to the door. The courtyard! Yes!

Señor Morales didn't take me out there to do me a favor though. He took me out there to torment me. He grabbed my arm tightly and led me to a corner of the yard.

"The children stay away from this part of the patio," He explained. "They get fierce bites."

There were two tie downs like one would use to stake a dog in a yard. Each stake had a rope and a handcuff tied to it. He positioned me next to a stake and put a handcuff on one wrist. He took the other wrist and walked around the center to the other side. This was when I spotted the ants. Large, red ants. Oh hell. I jerked my hand free but my right hand was trapped already. When he came after me to try again for the left hand I kicked him in the side. He roared with anger, especially when our struggles brought him over the ant's nest. He started chasing me around and around the stake but I couldn't go far. I did what I could to not stir up the ants, but I couldn't control his movements. Finally in frustration he called in recruits.

"Omar! Ramón!"

The silliest things pop into my head at the strangest times. When he called out the names and Morales's goons came running to subdue me and chain me up to be ant food all I could think of was that Omar's name was almost Ramón's name backwards. And when they came running on the double they looked like opposites, too. I could see why Omar was the bounty hunter and

Ramón was in-house security. Omar moved gracefully. I could see him hunting, stealthily making his way undercover until he found his man. Omar was tall for a Mexican. I don't know where he worked out in the middle of nowhere but his muscles proved he managed it somehow. Ramón was a barrel of a man. He was strong and stocky. But he moved like a cement truck. When he grabbed hold of me I wasn't going anywhere. It was like trying to move a tree. He held me in place while Omar slapped the other cuff on me. Morales nodded and the men left.

"Now… tell me, what means more to Chase than anything in the world?"

"Nothing. He's a loner. He doesn't care for riches. He has no family. He owns nothing of worth."

"Every man holds one thing close to his heart. Even a hard man. Even a cruel man. There is always one thing. Think about it," he said then he turned on his heel and went in the house. I was glad to have some time to observe, though I could do it a lot easier without the ants. In the commotion of getting me cuffed the ants had been disturbed. I could feel them under my pants legs. So far there were not many of them but soon there would be more. I knew to stay calm. The more I fidgeted the more stirred up they would become. When they bit me I could not swat them. I could kick at them with my other foot but to move my feet would disturb the nest. I stood as still as possible and endured the bites.

I caught Morales watching me from one of the windows as I studied my surroundings. I would not allow him see me suffer, only persevere. The bites stung like fire, but I just stood there, mentally gritting my teeth, examining the courtyard for ways out.

The house had a low, flat roof. I had been taught how to scale a six foot wall in the Marines, then again at police academy. I didn't know if the same principal would carry me ten feet. I looked for footholds on the walls, windows. I looked for furniture that could be put to use. I noticed that the edges of the courtyard got very little sun. Only the wall facing south got a lot of sun and on that wall grew an old, weathered vine. The wall facing south was on the north side of the courtyard, so I had my directions fixed. If I got a chance to escape, I'd know how to get to the spring.

The ants drove me crazy. I hated the crawling feeling almost as much as the bites. It took all I had not to squash them, but my head won out. I stood still.

I was left to stand there for about an hour and had dozens of bites. Morales finally came back out to the courtyard. He stood there watching me.

"This is a first," he said.

"Thank you," I replied.

"Tell me…"

"Nothing. There is nothing Chase values."

"His life?"

"Sometimes. He didn't choose an easy life. I bet he never expected to grow old. Any man who cheats death like Chase learns to expect it."

He spat on the ground. He stepped on an ant when it got too close for comfort. I didn't.

"Where is he?"

"In Mexico."

"Where?"

"Only Chase knows that. I doubt you can call him now. He could be watching this house right now and you would never know it. He isn't stupid. He isn't going to come knocking on your door."

"Chase is also a careful man. Why don't you call him and tell him where you are right now."

"No."

"If you do, perhaps I would consider removing the handcuffs."

"I can't even hold the telephone to my ear."

He called Chase himself.

"Buenos dias, señor," Morales said into the phone. "Your friend here would like to say something. Tell him, señorita, tell him where you are."

"Hey, Chase!" I said as brightly as I could, "I'm making progress. I know the route from my room to the front door. I know how to get to the courtyard. I've got my directions fixed. The vine in the courtyard grows on the north wall because the sun comes from the south. If I ever get out of here I'll know which way to go."

"Tell him where you are."

"I'm in the courtyard, trying to figure out how to get out."

"Señor Chase, your little friend here is dealing with the ants very well. You would be proud of her. I wish you could see her standing here in the anthill. She doesn't talk much. You should advise her to talk more."

The stupid ants were still biting me fiercely and all I could do was stand there and smile. Morales finally unlocked the cuffs and handed me the phone.

"Find out where he is," Morales said.

"Hi! You know what he wants to know."

"I'm on a hill looking down on the house," the snake in the grass voice said.

"He's in Mexico," I reported to Señor Morales.

He took the phone back. "What should I try next? The scorpions? Women hate scorpions." He talked as he paced and at first I stood there rubbing my wrists. I refused to acknowledge the ants until I was alone in my room again. But as I stood there, I realized he wasn't paying much attention to me, and I fell into a kind of a reverse stalk. When he was inattentive I inched away from him. I didn't like the quickly growing list of things he had planned to do to me, so when I had a decent head start on him, I dashed for the vine and leaped into its branches. Up the vine I scrambled, and I thought it would tear it loose from the wall, but I flung an arm onto the roof. There were yells behind me, and I just managed to pull myself up onto the roof when Omar made a jump for me. I rolled to my feet and dashed across the roof. What I saw nearly stopped me in my tracks. Chase wasn't kidding about a compound. There was a fence with razor wire around the top. Still, there was a lot of activity. I saw a furniture truck parked near the house so I leaped off the roof and landed on the truck. I scrambled down onto the cab and then the hood of the truck. I slid to the ground and dove underneath. I beat at the ants but I felt an urgency to keep moving. I had to stay unpredictable. I crawled to the back of the truck thinking I could hide in a piece of furniture but when I looked into the back of the truck I saw… drugs. I was sure of it. I wasn't exactly drug savvy but I could tell a sack of white powder from a chest of drawers. They were sneaking drugs across the border disguised as furniture. They probably even had fake payload receipts, fake records. Okay, so I wasn't going to hide in a wardrobe or behind a load of mattresses.

Chapter 52

Spanish was flying all around the place at ninety miles an hour. There must have been twenty workers around the outbuildings. They all sprang to action.

I melted into the shadows. My heart hammered in my chest. I hadn't known the risk I was taking when I climbed that vine. I thought it would result in me leaping from the roof, fleeing into the desert, and walking in stealth mode to the border. I hadn't planned on landing in a war zone. I was in the enemy camp and they all knew it. I was the only white American woman within fifty miles. I couldn't blend in with the people, so all I could do was blend in with my surroundings. I took off the white blouse and rubbed it in the dust, trying to take away some of the startling whiteness of it. I slipped it back on smelling the earthiness of it. I watched the goings on trying to find a break to a new hiding place.

A large, charcoal gray mastiff prowled by. I waited for the dog to pass by, and then a couple of men hurried by obviously looking for something.

I searched the grounds from hiding, trying to find a gate. The fence was no problem but the razor wire on top could slice a person to ribbons. I made my way from hiding place to hiding place, each time waiting for just the right break, then shrinking into the shadows out of sight. I hated to admit it to myself, but I was scared. People ran by, searching. They ran right past me, looked right at me, didn't see me. How could they not see me, or at least hear me? My heartbeat was so loud it was distracting to me. I found a stack of empty crates and crawled inside one of them. How long would they keep looking? How long could I keep running?

When my heart rate was more normal I peeked out. I spotted a forklift sitting alone. It offered a visual barrier so I moved quietly through the shadows until I was close to it. As I hid, waiting for another break, I realized the forklift would make it through the fence, but it would cause a hell of a ruckus. I might get it through the fence but I'd have twenty armed Mexicans on my tail.

My hiding place felt too open so I searched for another, keeping the location of the forklift firm in my mind. I needed to find a place I could trust to keep me hidden for hours, but all I could locate were little temporary ones. I spotted a building that looked like a garage or a small warehouse. The area behind it seemed overlooked. There was only a foot or two between the back of the building and the perimeter fence. Maybe I could find a weak spot. Getting there would be a hell of a risk, though. There was a wide open area I would have to cross. Workers were all over the place. Too many things could go wrong. I decided I better wait until dark, if I was still alive by then.

In a way I regretted escaping. When I did, I lost all contact with Rusty and Chase.

A patrol went by leading another dog. I didn't know if it was good news or bad news that they were getting more organized.

I needed a safe, quiet place, dark, an ignored spot, to buy me some time. I decided the crates had been the safest place I'd found. It was about five hiding places behind me. I made my way from one spot to another only to find out that just because someplace looked safe from one direction didn't mean it would appear that way from the other. I had trouble spotting my former hiding spots. It took me close to an hour to find the crates again and when I did I made my way in to the very back, bottom of the stack. I curled up in the rough wooden box, tried to tune out the overwhelming feeling that was coming over me, fought off the homesickness that replaced it, and numbed myself to feeling. Instead, I tuned my ears. I caught every sound and analyzed it. Patrols went by several times. Señor Morales confronted the patrols a few times threatening them within an inch of their lives and offering, I think, some reward to the person who brought me in. When he ranted they shrunk back from his wrath but then their fear turned to more of a friendly competitiveness and a few actually cheered. I waited silently, hopefully invisibly. I could see through the slats in the crates. I had to experiment to find the right angles but once I did I could catch glimpses of the happenings nearby. As I listened and waited I talked silently to Rusty, Katie and Carson. Rusty would have left the kids at the ranch. I felt a stab of guilt thinking about Katie wanting to go home but being stuck at Grandma and Grandpa's house not really knowing why we were there. Now she was stuck at Grandma and Grandpa's house alone.

Lunchtime was long gone and I didn't know dinnertime had, too, until it began getting dark. I couldn't believe I'd made it this long without being found. I imagined Rusty and Chase out in the hills watching all the action. What would they do when darkness fell?

Gradually the workers thinned out. Patrols still went by but my chances looked better. Then the patrols stopped. The whole yard went quiet. There were a few lights on in the house but the yard was still. I was suspicious. I was afraid to move. It was a trap. They were giving me too big an opportunity. Instinct told me to wait.

The night grew cold and I curled up tighter. I tried to sleep but I thought if I did something would happen. I was dozing and listening when all of a sudden the yard was brightly illuminated and immediately after there was the click of a rifle. In the bright lights a rabbit froze, dazed by the sudden brightness. There was a shot and the rabbit jerked up into the air and fell with a soft thud. A man strode into the light and picked up the rabbit's limp form and walked into the darkness again. I thanked God for careless rabbits. That could easily have been me. Instinct saved my butt that time! Now what was I going to do? I was counting on the darkness to hide my movements. If I waited until morning to make my move all the workers and patrols would be back.

I worried about Rusty and Chase. I was glad Chase was holding off, but Señor Morales had lost his bargaining tool until he found me. There was no sense in Chase making a move until my fate was certain.

Chapter 53

I woke at the first hint of light. Nobody stirred. I didn't hear a sound. I waited until there was enough light to switch off the flood lights, or at least make them less noticeable. I examined my options. The forklift would draw too much attention. I decided the fence behind the garage was a better bet. Before the yard could fill up with people again, I made my way back to the shortest dash across the yard. I crouched in hiding. I couldn't take too long to do this. I needed fast feet, a bunch of luck, and all the workers to suddenly need to be someplace else. I looked both ways and didn't see anybody. All right Cass, this is your chance. I was scared stiff as I dashed across the yard. I slipped behind the garage and sat there catching my breath and listening. If a worm stirred under the earth I would have heard it. I expected yelling and running and a group of victorious Mexican laborers to surround me. But they didn't.

All I found behind the garage was a rake, large shovel, and a broken handle. I found the handle to be useful. I hacked at the ground, finding it surprisingly soft. I expected cement-hard, desert clay. Next to the foundation of the building the soil was soft but next to the fence it was hard. That was odd. I decided to dig a shallow foxhole and use that to work from to make a crawl space under the fence. Once I began digging the reason for the soft soil was all too obvious. Aw shit… literally! The smell wafted up into my face and I fought down a retching feeling. I'd wandered into the men's room again! Augh! But I was stuck. I couldn't go back. Workers were showing up and the place would be busy again. I shifted gears, needing to hide more than ever. There was no use being squeamish. I needed a hiding place in the men's room so I hacked at the earth as fast I could. Then I had to lay down in it. When I made a list of things never to do twice I'd add this to the list. Never dig a foxhole in a latrine.

I lay on my side in the foxhole and pulled the putrid dirt back over myself. This was worse than the ants. I gagged. And I slowly and patiently dug toward the fence. I listened carefully. Twice men came behind the garage to pee. I was lucky they chose the other end of the building. When I heard footsteps I froze, barely daring to breathe, not really wanting to anyway. People tend to see what they expect to see, so the men turned the corner pulled out their penis, let loose and went on their way, not even thinking about what the soil looked like back there.

A few hours passed and I patiently listened and dug. As I made progress I covered it up with loose dirt. The movement behind the garage was minimal and constant except for the few interruptions. My luck ran out when a man came around my side of the building. He stepped right on my head squishing my face into the dirt and muck. I had the presence of mind not to react. I lay still. I knew I was in trouble when he quietly backed out and slunk away, then sprinted for the house. Damn. I couldn't go anywhere. I was pinned behind the garage. My hole under the fence was not ready and even if it was I wasn't venturing out in broad daylight. Still, the fence was my only hope. I rolled out of the foxhole and grabbed the bottom of the fence and pulled up with all my might. It moved about three inches. I heard footsteps running. I climbed the fence until I could go no further. I threw myself to the roof of the garage and hauled myself up. I looked at the gap. Three feet to the razor wire and a ten foot drop. I had enough adrenaline going to make me shaky. I could get caught without a dramatic exit or I could do it with a dramatic exit. Okay, call me a drama queen. I sprinted across the garage roof, took a flying leap, cleared the razor wire by inches and landed on bent knees on the other side. I rolled into a crouch and saw the enemy closing in on the other side of the fence. I made it! But I didn't have time to celebrate. I took off running, knowing my chances were nil but needing to try. All I can say is I ran for my life. I didn't mean to, but I ran toward the road. I didn't even know that was the direction I was heading but they opened the gate to chase me down and before they could get out a truck came barreling through, scattering the posse. A strap hung down to allow them to open and close the roll-down door. If I was lucky I could catch that truck. I never ran so fast in my life. The truck was slow getting any speed up. I grabbed that handle and made ready to leap onto the bumper but I lost my footing and got dragged along. When the truck sped up I knew I had no chance of a quick escape and I had to let go. I half ran, half limped into the desert and the men quickly chased me down and subdued me. I had so much pent up energy I was ready to take them all on, but I knew it was useless. I'd just end up being beaten and then dragged back. Every time they prodded me toward the compound I challenged them, though. I was furious. I was upset that I'd gambled away my life. I was scared what my punishment was going to be. I was ashamed to talk to Rusty. I was defeated.

When, at last I stood before Señor Morales again he wrinkled his nose at me, barked an order in Spanish and one of the men dragged over a hose. He told everybody to stand back and then he hosed me down. The cold water hit and I braced myself but I couldn't brace myself for what he did when I was clean enough to approach.

"Open your mouth," he said.

I backed away.

"Open your mouth," he repeated.

"Over my dead body," I said.

I knew what was coming and he wasn't going to do it. He could beat me, before he'd get that hose into me. He signaled the men and they closed in behind me. He pulled a phone out of his pocket.

"Señor, you can stop this any time. Are you watching? I teach this girl what trouble really is. See?"

He came at me with the hose again and I charged him. I pushed him and his hose away and then I came at him with a left hook and a right jab. The men pulled me off. They were going to pin me to the ground but they had a wildcat on their hands. Nobody wanted to touch me because they knew where I'd been. Even after being hosed off, I reeked and I was still filthy. We stood there defiantly glaring at each other.

"Eduardo, show the señorita to her room," he growled.

Eduardo grinned broadly. Oh no, now what? He motioned to the house and that option seemed better than the one I was leaving behind so I went into the house and down the hall to the room I had woken up in. Eduardo followed me in and closed the door. Eduardo and I stared at each other awkwardly. I was furious. He was grim-faced and serious. Eduardo opened the door when we heard a quiet knock. Elena walked in with a basin of water and some worn towels.

"You give you clothes and I wash them," she said.

I looked at Eduardo and asked, "What about him?"

"Señor Morales say man who catches have you for night."

"What?"

"I sorry, señorita. I wash you clothes?"

"I'll wash them myself," I answered. "Does he speak English?"

"I not know, here we speak Español," Elena answered.

"Well, there's one word that is the same in every language," I muttered to myself.

Chapter 54

Eduardo sat down smugly on the end of the bed.

Elena backed out of the room.

"Do you speak English?" I asked.

He just grinned.

"I know you understand some."

His grin wavered. He was enjoying this.

"Look, let's get one thing straight, if you're expecting sex tonight you're mistaken. And if you push for it you'll be sorry. I'm not the kid I look like. I'm married. I have two children. If you push me you'll have a fight on your hands."

"An if I don't I be…be, what you say? Dey all laugh a mí."

"Laughter never killed anyone. It's good for you."

"Luke, I not cruel. I not hurt you."

"That's not the point. It's wrong. It's wrong for you to push and it's wrong for me to give in. Would you go into town and demand to have sex with the police chief's wife?"

"She… not so hot."

"If she was hot, then would you?"

"No, I be arrest."

"You'd be shot. Then arrested. If it's wrong to do that, it's just as wrong with me."

"I think… maybe I shange your mine."

"I'm going to wash. You stay right where you are. I'm warning you, you touch me and you'll have a fight on your hands."

I pulled off my boots and set them in the corner. I took off my socks and decided they were the least of my worries. I set them in a *clean enough* pile. I took off my pants and went to the far side of the room and shook them out. They went in the *dirty* pile. I took off the blouse and dropped it in the *dirty* pile. I looked over the tank top and the outside of my underwear. I was not going to strip for Eduardo. In the tank top and panties I was basically wearing a bathing suit. I started at the top of me and began a sponge bath. Eduardo came up behind me when I turned my back to him and ran his hands down my arms. I stomped his foot and ground my heel down. He retreated. When he tried again he got an elbow to the kidneys. He wanted me to turn on him. He wanted reason to get rough with me, but I kept my attack low key and made things just miserable enough that he thought twice before trying again. As I was washing out my pants he came up behind me. Nude, he brushed his penis against my backside. He found out there are disadvantages to being short. I jerked my heel up and caught him in the crotch. I continued washing my pants. The water was brown now, but I didn't want Elena to come back and walk in on something inappropriate. I washed out the blouse in the brown water and set the pants and blouse aside to let the filth settle to the bottom of the basin. I'd try again in a little while, then let them dry overnight.

Eduardo patted the bed.

"No," I said.

"I make it gude, you be nice. You not nice I get rough."

"Then it's going to be a very rough night."

I guess I had it easy. The guy didn't really want to rape me. He just wanted to have a good time. But he felt pressure from his buddies. He couldn't go to work the next day and say this little blonde woman busted his balls. I busted his foot. I busted his hand. I broke his nose. Since he had to wash up from the broken nose I didn't have water to wash with anymore so I put the half filthy clothes back on thinking the less he could see of me the less he'd try. Wrong. Then he wanted a strip show, *anything he could use to brag to the guys*. We went through the whole process with me clothed, which he didn't enjoy much at all. I didn't have to break his nose again but I stomped his foot and his hand again, with boots on, and he found out that you don't mess with a cowgirl. Boots hurt. Boots can do major damage in places you don't want major damage. So he ended up sleeping on the bed with is hands between his legs and I ended up sleeping on the floor in cold, damp clothes.

I woke up in the night and Eduardo was sleeping. Silently I made my way to his pile of clothes on the floor. He had three cigarettes, a little cash, a set of keys and a small box of Chiclets. Not much of a haul. I figured he needed the cash more than I did and I needed the keys more than he did, so I only took the keys. The hope was he would get dressed in the morning and go out and lie to the guys and notice the missing keys long after he had other opportunities to lose them. I imagined him going to work the next day, walking bowlegged, the guys jeering and him telling them, "Next time she gets away you catch her."

When Eduardo walked bowlegged out of my room the next morning Señor Morales gave him a bemused look and came into my room. He looked me over; he looked into the washbasin. Red swirled around in the murky water and the brown filth had settled to the bottom.

"I tire of your games," he said.

"My games! I'm not playing games. I'm trying to survive here. It's your game we are all playing. Is this a betting game? If it is, I bet you lose."

"I want you to call Chase one last time. I want you to tell him how this is going to end. He walks in here and gives himself up, or you die."

"No. I won't let him do that."

"You would die first?"

"I'll call him, but he already knows you plan to kill me. As soon as I am no longer a use to you, you're going to get rid of me. But I'll call him, just because I'd like to hear him again and maybe I can hear my husband, too."

"I'll bring you the phone. You must be hungry."

"It doesn't matter unless you want to fuel an escape plan."

"I have to admit, I was impressed by your attempt. Not many could hide so completely."

"If Eduardo had peed at the other end of the garage I would have gotten away."

"I don't doubt that. Chase chooses his friends well."

"So do I."

"Why you care so much for an old man?"

"Chase isn't an old man. He's me in thirty years or so."

"What do you mean?"

"He's a tracker, you knew that. I'm a tracker, too."

"You? A tracker? I don believe it."

"That's okay, most people are skeptical."

"Skeptical?"

"Most people don't believe I'm a tracker either, because I don't look like one. If I live through this, I will go home and continue my work with search and rescue. I find lost people by tracking them. Someday, maybe I'll even be as good at it as Chase is. Right now that seems doubtful, but we'll see. The day isn't over."

"No, it is not. Tell me what you know about Chase."

"No. You will only use it against him. You can do what you like to me, but I won't make things harder on him than they need to be."

"I can *make* you talk."

"No, you can't."

He took a box out of his pocket. I sure was tired of his games. Inside the box was the scorpion he had talked about earlier.

"Give me a break," I said. "I know what those do. I've been stung before. All it will do to me is sting like crazy and then make me go numb. I'll be useless for a day. You don't want a useless woman to doctor for a day."

He brought out pepper spray.

"Been there done that."

"What you mean?"

"I've been pepper sprayed before, too. Part of basic training. It'll sting like hell; I'll salivate like crazy. I'll call you every name in the book while I wait for it to wear off. I know to not rub my eyes, not to breathe it in. I know to ignore all the symptoms and wait."

"Where you learn all these things?"

"The Marines. Police academy."

Oh hell, I thought, if he thinks I'm a cop he'll kill me for sure.

But he laughed. "You? The Marines no take little blondee women. They make men into killers. They teach men to make war."

"And they teach little blondee women how to escape from drug cartels who kidnap them and hold them for hostage. Don't laugh yet. This day is not done."

He went away and when he came back he had two things: the telephone and a four foot long stick.

"You remember this?" He asked holding up the stick. "Maybe I teach you not to try escape. This was part of the vine. Now, tell me something. Tell me about Chase."

"How many times do we have to do this?" I said. "No."

Out came the stick and he gave me a sharp whack across my leg.

"Maybe we make it so you can't run, too. Tell me about Chase."

"No."

Whack!

"Are you sure?"

"Yes."

He began swinging the branch like a baseball bat. It was stiff enough to swing but supple enough to not break when I was struck and it left a good sized welt each time it hit. *Whack! Whack! Whack!* When he began working his way up my body I turned around and he went to work on my back.

"Are you ready?" he asked.

"No!"

"Call him."

"No! Not while he can hear me being hurt."

"Call him!" he yelled. "Call him so he can hear it. I want him to know what he's done. We shall see if he really cares for you. If he really cares he'll come."

"No, he won't. His goal is not to free me. His goal is the same as it's always been."

"And that is?"

"No," I said sadly knowing the sting that would follow.

"Call him."

Okay, I'd call him. But I wouldn't cry out when I was hit. I punched in the number.

"Cassidy! Are you okay kid?"

"Morales wants me to call. He says this is the last time, but don't count on it."

Whack! Whack!

"I'm glad you did."

"Tell me!" Bellowed Morales, *whack*, "tell me about Chase!"

There was a pause and I got the feeling Chase wasn't alone. Maybe it was just a reaction to what he pictured going on.

"Cassidy, listen up. Tell him, that I dare him to do that in the yard, in front of his men."

"No, Rusty would see."

"Trust me. Do what you can to get Morales to do anything in plain sight. Put him on the phone."

My hope was slipping. I thought I wanted to hear Chase, but as he spoke my will was breaking.

"Chase, I need to hear Rusty, more than I need to get out of here."

There was some talk before Rusty came on the line. I couldn't even say hi. I was fighting tears harder than I was bracing against the strikes.

"Don't listen, just talk," I finally managed to say.

"I love you," he said. Better get that in before he lost the chance.

"I love you, too."

Whack!

"I never thought I'd tell you this, but do what Chase says. Do anything you can to get Morales to do that in plain sight."

"Talk to me."

Whack!

"You can do this. We'll be waiting."

"Talk to me, please."

Whack!

"Babe, what has he done to you?"

"It's not so bad. There's not much he can do to me that hasn't been done before. I don't want to talk about this."

"When this is over we'll go get the kids. We'll go home, rest up, gather our wits. Babe, tell me we're going to get through this."

"Rus… I don't know."

"Get your focus back and tell me…" *whack* "we're going to get through this."

I had to grit my teeth but I said, "We're going to get through this." And I figured I had built up enough pent up emotion to lash out at Morales so I turned on him. With all my pent up sadness I slugged him and then I got in his face. "You… are a coward. Hitting women behind closed doors. I dare you to strike me like this in front of your men. I bet you wouldn't do it. They may be used to the idea of you hurting people in here, but I bet if they were to see it in person you would lose your men. That's why you didn't go through with the hose torture! Your men would get disgusted and walk out! I *dare* you to do this outside."

Whack! I grabbed the stick I twisted it in both hands. Twisted and twisted and his arm twisted until he had to do something or let go. When his grip eased up I jerked the stick and gave him a whack of his own.

He got a wild look to him and I feared I had pushed him over the edge.

"Give me the telephone," he said icily.

When I handed it over he grabbed my wrist and dragged me out the door. Into the phone he was talking in Spanish. From the little bit I could catch he was saying, "This is your last chance. This is final. I give you one last chance." He pushed me out the front door and I dropped the stick as I stumbled to my knees. He picked up the stick and brought it down on my shoulder, then the other.

"Chase! You see this? I dare you come stop it!" Two more whacks and Morales scanned the hills. A crowd was gathering. Morales stood me at the end of the walk that led to the front door. He stepped away and pulled a pistol out of his pocket. "Señor Chase," he said into the phone, "You have one minute to show yourself. One minute to save Señorita Trouble here." He stood there with the gun aimed at my chest. I sure wished I had that bulletproof vest. I wondered if he was wearing it. No. If he was he wouldn't have felt the switch when I hit him with it. I wasn't counting down the seconds. I could tell it was getting close when a smile crossed his face. Then a surge of fear lanced through me. I turned and Chase was walking calmly out of the hills. No!

"No! Chase, go back! Please go back. Don't tell me this was all for nothing!"

Chapter 55

He ignored my pleas and walked calmly up to the gate.

A worker unlocked it and Chase stepped through.

I didn't know what to do! I couldn't let him give himself up. Morales wasn't going to let me go anyway. I heard Morales cock the pistol and knew my life was down to seconds.

I didn't want to die looking into the barrel of a gun. I scanned the hills looking for Rusty.

There was a shot. I heard it, but I was still standing. I saw Chase running toward the action, gun drawn.

I swiveled around, counting my options.

Morales was on the ground.

His men were scattering.

I was so stupid. I stood there, numb. And then some reasoning broke through, a snippet from academy about the two most dangerous times in an abduction being the initial kidnapping and the rescue. We were told that bullets could be flying around and to use cover. Find cover. I looked at the many places I hid on my first attempt at escape but there were men everywhere. There was a clear path to the gate so I ran toward it and when I reached it I kept on going. I didn't know what was going on behind me. I only knew I had to get away; far, far away, so I ran and when I heard footsteps behind me I ran harder. I ran until my lungs burned and I had a stitch in my side.

Voices called out to me, "Stop! Stop!"

Spanish words, English words, they all jumbled up and it sounded like a mob was chasing me. When I dared to glance back, I saw little figures fighting. Was Chase in all that?

I heard footsteps and took off again. Chase… what if they had Chase. I'd never forgive myself for running off and leaving him there. I'd never forgive myself. I was doomed to wander through life knowing I abandoned a friend. A friend who had come to help. But no matter what I did my feet wouldn't turn around. I was scared. I was one big chicken. And I was so mad at myself all I could think of to do was run myself into the ground. So I ran. And ran. Until I fell and I lay there gasping for breath in the middle of the Mexican desert. I didn't hear footsteps anymore. I noticed a wash just ahead so I dragged myself to my feet and walked wearily to it, hopped into the bottom, lay in the shadow of the arroyo wall and pulled sand over myself to hide me from anybody out looking, and I cried. I was all run out. I was all madded out. Now

I just needed to get all cried out.

After a while I heard a faint noise and I froze. There was a movement and then an odd jingling. It went *jingle, scoot, scoot, scoot, jingle*. I looked out of my dusty hiding place and a set of keys was scooting slowly across the sand of the wash. I thought I was seeing things, though it's not something I was prone to do.

"Can I hold you while you cry?" Rusty said. "Don't run. Babe, it's just me. Okay?"

He knew once I got in flight mode I might do anything. He hopped down into the arroyo and squatted in front of me.

"Good hiding place. I never would have seen you if I wasn't following you."

"Rusty… I can't go back."

"We're not going back yet. We're only going right here," he said holding his arms out. "Come here. My arms have been aching. They need you."

I rolled out of my hidey hole and peeked over the wall of the arroyo.

"We're alone," he said. "The police were chasing you but I convinced them they better back off."

That explained the mob that was running after me. It wasn't Morales's men. It was the police. Relief jumbled up with sadness. I walked over to Rusty and he sat and pulled me into those wonderful arms and he held me while I cried.

"What happened to Chase? Rusty… I need to know and I'm scared to find out."

"I took off after you, but he wasn't alone. He had backup. And Morales was dead as soon as he cocked that gun. That's why we had you get him outside. The local police were not convinced anybody out here needed help. They had to see it with their own eyes."

"The furniture trucks have drugs in them."

"Hush, it's over. We made it through this. No looking back. By dinnertime we'll be at Mom and Dad's house. Tomorrow we'll be back at the ranch. The next day we'll go home. Our home, and I want you to myself."

"I can't. I can't go to your folk's house knowing I turned my back on Chase."

"Hush, we're not looking back."

"I'm such a big baby," I cried. "Why can't I stop?"

"Cry all you want as long as I'm here."

"What's with the keys?"

"I needed to get your attention without scaring you. I thought you'd remember the ground squirrel lure. I guess you could say I was fishing for Trouble."

"You caught the one that got away. I don't think fishing works quite like that."

"A trophy catch."

It felt like we sat there for hours. I'd fret and he'd talk me back to the present. I cried and he consoled me. I clung to him and he clung back. Then there came a time when we both seemed to know we'd run the gamut and we were ready to face something new, so I rose and I offered him a hand up. When we climbed out of the arroyo, I couldn't see the compound. How far had I run? I followed Rusty's tracks back. They were more readable than mine. After a short walk I noticed a slight line in the sand beside Rusty's tracks and I started looking for more of them and when I saw them I knew, Chase was okay. He'd come out to check on us and when he saw that Rusty had found me he went back. The tears threatened again.

I tracked us back until the compound came into view. People were everywhere. A full-scale investigation was going on. Chase was advising the Mexican police on where to look for incriminating evidence. When I caught sight of him I stopped. Rusty put his hands on my shoulders. Chase rattled off some Spanish and a couple of officers walked off to continue their work. He looked up and saw me. I wanted to run again. I was so ashamed of myself.

Rusty wrapped his arms around me and said, "Babe, it's okay. You didn't do anything wrong. Come on."

He turned me around. When Chase saw the hurt in my eyes he looked away.

"Chase… I'm sorry. I'm sorry I freaked. I wasn't thinking. I had to find cover and the only place I saw was the desert. I shouldn't have run."

It took him a moment to realize I was asking for his forgiveness.

"Hey, kid, calm down. That was the plan. I just didn't get a chance to tell you. I worried there for a bit you were going to take a bullet. You did the right thing to clear out."

"He could have killed you…"

"He was dead. As soon as he cocked the gun a sniper took him out."

He stuck out his hand like he wanted to shake but when I took it he pulled me into a hug.

"You scared me kiddo. I thought we'd lost you. I'm sorry we had to hold off. It drove Rusty nuts politicking. We took turns watching the compound and jumping through all their hoops. When you tried to get away we thought they would kill you right then."

"I thought so, too."

"Sunrise was the change of watch and so we were both watching but we couldn't do anything without the cops rescuing Morales's men from us. Rusty came out of his shoes when you jumped off the roof. How's your hand?"

"Shut up," Rusty said.

"I sent him to town to report the goings on. When Rusty gets mad people listen."

I could imagine.

"There's a couple of buildings I was hoping to get into but they're locked tight."

I felt the keys in my pocket.

"Maybe these will help."

"Where'd you get these?" Chase asked.

"Umm, how do I put this? The man who found me hiding behind the garage was rewarded for his work. Morales let him spend the night with me."

A storm cloud began building over Rusty, but Chase laughed.

"Was his name Eduardo Cordova?" Chase asked.

"I don't know what his last name was. How did you know?"

"He looked like he'd been bronco busting in the nude and lost."

"I didn't do anything except what they taught me in self-defense class."

"Atta girl."

"Did they arrest Omar? Ramón?"

"They arrested as many as they could. You're going to have to ID the men with the authorities."

I had to, if I wanted to leave the country. Between Chase and I we managed to paint a pretty clear picture of all we had been through over the past month. Chase told his side of it in Spanish and then he interpreted for me. It was interesting watching Chase deal with the conditions we were working under. Our testimony was recorded and Chase wanted to do the interpretations himself so a Mexican interpreter would not gloss over things the Mexicans found hard to admit were happening right under their noses. It sounded like he might be doing a little embellishing of my story but I didn't know enough Spanish to correct him.

I had to pick Eduardo, Omar and Ramón out of a lineup. Everybody knew which one Eduardo was. He was the one with the crooked nose who tried to hide.

And I had to identify Morales as the man who had beaten me. They took me into that cold room and pulled the shroud back. As a Marine I stood defiant. I didn't feel defiant, though.

When the police were satisfied that they had everything they needed they brought forth a folder and went through each document. There was a folder for Rusty, too.

"Why don't you get one?" I asked Chase.

"Okay, I lied. I did have my passport. All those documents are things we had to send back to the states for to get you back home. If you plan to do this again you might think about getting a passport of your own."

Chapter 56

"Rusty! Cassidy! Where are the kids?" Rusty's mom asked.

"It's a very long story. They are at the ranch. We'll drive up and get them in the morning," I said.

"They could have stayed with us!" she said.

"Next time I get kidnapped and hauled off to Mexico we'll do it from San Diego. Then you can keep the kids. I should call my mom and let her know I'm still alive."

"You certainly should," Bev said.

"She got updates," Rusty said. "Patrick started calling Chase's cell. We made him stop and started calling the ranch. He had a way of calling at the worst times and we didn't have any good news. We decided to call the ranch so we could plan our calls and give them just enough information to keep their hopes up."

"The first thing I need is a shower. Then I need new clothes. Rusty? Could you run down to the store?"

"You want me to choose your clothes for you?"

"Size 5 or 7 jeans, and shirts, 34 B for the bra, size 7 socks."

"You want me to shop for women's underwear?" he asked.

"I buy yours," I reminded him.

"That's different."

"Buy a sexy nighty and have then wrap it all up in birthday paper. That ought to help you save face. Or you can go in there and beg for help. Just tell them your wife got buried in shit and she needs new clothes pronto."

Bev was watching, wondering how her big, macho son was going to take his newest assignment. She decided to bail him out.

"I'll do it," she offered. "Help yourself to leftovers. What size are the kids now?"

"Three and ten months," I said, "but they really don't need anything."

"Need has nothing to do with it. I'm a grandma. I have to do these things."

"Then Katie wants an easy reader book, not clothes."

"A reading book? But she's only three!"

"She likes A's the best."

"O… kay."

Talking about the kids made me so homesick. When Bev left I went up to the attic and threw myself on the nearest mattress. Rusty followed me and sat down. He rubbed my back, then he went down stairs and got me a big heavy towel. I'd feel better once I was clean again. I knew I would, but I was just about as down in the dumps as a person can get.

I showered and Rusty heated up plates of leftovers. I sat at the dining room table wrapped up in the towel, trying to keep it up as I ate. Good old American food. The food I had in Mexico had been good but I hadn't eaten or drank anything while I was on the run. I drank more water that evening than I thought possible.

Cody came home and found me at the table pulling up the towel for the hundredth time.

"Well, well, every time I see you I'm surprised."

"Mom's out buying a new set of clothes so we can trash the ones she was wearing," Rusty explained.

"Rats, I was hoping it was going to be another one of those death-defying, cliff hanger stories you usually tell."

After a moment of silence, Cody got the point.

"Wait until we're all together. We only want to tell this once."

"Oh dear," Bev said as she came in the front door, "I'm sorry, Cassidy. You've been sitting around in a towel for hours while I read children's books at the bookstore. There are so many cute ones!"

"I hope you didn't get carried away."

"No! Not at all. Can she really read these?"

"Not yet but she is learning. I wonder if she has driven Mom nuts yet."

"Of course not. She's a darling girl. What could she possibly do that would bother your mom that much?"

"Ask her to sound out every word she spots. On signs, labels, clothing tags, names of appliances… she finds words where most adults forgot there were any. Then if the word doesn't look the way it sounds she asks for a detailed explanation as to why that word is different."

"Carson is getting so big! I can't believe these fit him already!"

Bev could talk about the kids for hours. She asked every imaginable question so she would be prepared for our next visit, *with kids*. Then after Bill got home we had extensive storytelling to do from two perspectives. Bill was interested in Rusty's telling because he was a retired cop. And Cody wanted to hear my version because he liked to figure out just how I managed the logic to get myself into the fixes I did. The whole family was also concerned about Chase. Chase was a family friend and when he didn't come by occasionally they began to worry. They had known why Chase wasn't around but uncertainty about his situation had overshadowed their lives for the past few months. We assured them that Chase would be knocking on their door for dinner again very soon.

Before I went to bed I needed to call the ranch. Martha answered the phone as usual.

"Hello?" she said uncertainly. I realized I was on Rusty's cell phone and they were unsure if this was going to be good news or the news they had been dreading.

"Hi Martha," I said.

"Cassidy? Is that really you?"

"It's really me. I'm safe and sound in San Diego."

"Betty! It's Cassidy!"

"Cassidy? Is that really you?"

"Yeah, Mom. I just thought you'd want to know that everything worked out okay. I'll be up there tomorrow."

"Leave it to you to go chasing after a wayward horse and end up in Mexico."

"Did the horses get home okay?"

"Yes, but Michelle's father wouldn't buy Sky. He said a horse that took off that easily was dangerous. Randy went through the motions of standing up for Sky. He said any young horse would startle at being shot at but he wouldn't listen. He said he'd have the other ranch come retrieve Sky and tell them he was no longer interested."

"So Dad's keeping her?"

"He bought her the next day."

"Is Michelle okay?"

"She was skinned up, and the paramedics took her to the hospital for x-rays. We thought her arm might have been broken, but she was lucky. She ended up with just bruises."

"Has Katie been driving you crazy?"

"No… but I'm not going to read any long books for a while. I swear she's making me cross eyed reading little tags and labels. She misses you terribly. I better not tell her you'll be here tomorrow or she won't go to bed."

"I was hoping to talk to her."

"Do you really want to?"

"Yeah, but I'll wait. I know how wound up she'd get."

"Wayne? It's Cassidy!"

Dad's deep voice, "Cassidy? Is that really you?"

"It was a rough one. But it's really me."

"You okay?"

"Dad… It was hard. This one hurt in a different way. I'm not injured. But I sure ache. I'd do it again. But… I didn't think I was going to make it this time."

"You did make it. It's what you do best, making the best of the lot given you."

"Just keep on keeping on."

"Yup. And every day you wake up is a day you get to live."

"Not necessarily, Dad. I'm beginning to wonder how many times I can do this."

"Just keep on keeping on."

"I'll try. I'll see you tomorrow."

"Love you kid."

"Love you, too, Dad."

"Take care."

I closed the phone and lay down beside Rusty on the mattress in the attic. Then I needed to be closer so I turned to face him and snuggled closer. The tears came again, quietly. I'd been scared so long. I had three days of fear to work off. When my mind had been watching for breaks my emotions had been stuffed away. Now that my emotions were free again they seemed to be taking over. I felt like a wimp.

"You're not a wimp. You're my girl. Sometimes you're too strong for your own good. When you scaled the fence and climbed to the roof of that building I wondered how you could manage it. Then when I watched you jump the fence I wanted to catch you. Chase told me we needed to see any escape attempts you made, that we needed to watch you to find a way in. There was no way to jump that fence in reverse, though. I had to watch as you were caught and dragged back. And I knew you'd be punished. Chase and I got into a scuffle. I couldn't just lie there and do nothing and Chase had to put me in my place. That's how I skinned up my hand. But he was right. I shouldn't. It would have made things worse. You don't know what it's like to have to watch and not be able to do anything. I'm just glad you're here. I'll never let you go again."

"Then hang on," I said. "I need you to hang on."

"I've got you."

He had me all right. I fell asleep still in his arms and in the night when I relived the escape and I struggled in my sleep, he was there, waking me gently, and taking the fear, and he understood. He knew what it felt like to have the day stalk him into sleep. He'd had nights of fear, too.

"I don't want to go back to sleep," I cried.

"Okay, then tell me about it. Maybe it'll help you work through it."

"My legs itch like crazy."

"From the ants?"

"Morales was somewhat disappointed when I just stood in the ants and let them crawl on me and bite me."

"That was torture."

"I've had worse. The only thing he did that really scared me was come at me with the hose. I knew what that would feel like. I..." The drowning feeling closed in and I mentally recoiled.

"It's okay," Rusty said. "Babe, if it hurts don't go there."

"I could deal with the ants, and the switching, and the interrogations."

"What's eating at you? There's some key issue you're dealing with... something that is making this hard for you. Can you pinpoint it?"

I burrowed deeper.

"Rusty, I guess I'm still running. Maybe I'll stop when I land."

"And when will that be?"

"I can't promise. I'll try not to run. I'll try to see the day for what it is. I'll try to ignore yesterday trying to take over my thoughts. Like your dad says, move forward, no looking back."

"I wish the pool was warm."

"Me, too." We would slip down into its watery caresses and swim and touch in the darkness until we felt a sudden need to be upstairs, in bed.

"Today we see the kids again."

"It's today already? Are you sure you want to drive it all in one day?"

"I'm sure. I can't wait."

"Now, these are for Katie," Bev said at breakfast. She was holding a stack of gift wrapped items. "I've had restless kids in the car before. I suggest saving these for the trip home and then letting Katie open one at a time. And this is for Carson. It attaches to his car seat. Does he like things that make noise? Maybe it'll keep him entertained for five minutes. And there's an outfit for each of them. Be sure and hug the kids for us. And bring them for a visit as soon as you can. They grow up so fast."

"How far are you driving today?" Bill asked.

"Six hours. But we have a couple of stops to break up the trip," Rusty said.

"Where do you stop?"

"We'll eat lunch at Rusty's restaurant," I answered, "well, it's not really *Rusty's* restaurant, but it's a favorite of ours. We discovered it because his name was on the sign. Then, we usually stop for an ice cream and a walk on the beach in Santa Barbara."

We arrived at the ranch late in the evening. Mom was watching for us. She was out on the porch before we could come to a stop, then she went back in and called Katie. Katie stood on the porch clapping her hands, jumping up and down in anticipation. Dad came out carrying Carson.

"Mommy! Daddy!" Katie yelled as she ran down the steps. She ran to the truck and held up her hands to be picked up. Rusty walked around to my side and opened the door and I slid out. Rusty picked up Katie.

"Look at you princess, you're so pretty," he said.

"Gramma painted my nails," she reported holding out her fingers for inspection.

"Just like a real princess," said Rusty.

My mom looked very uncertain. My dad nodded. His way of saying, "You made it, good job."

"Cassidy," my mom said. "I thought I might never see you again."

"I know, Mom, I thought the same thing there for a bit."

"This little guy missed you," said Dad holding out Carson.

"Mommy," Katie interrupted, "I stalked the rabbits every day. Ranny helped me ride the horse. Gramma took me shopping. Gramma is a good story reader. Grammpa showed me how to play a game."

Grandpa did? Now that was odd. I even thought it was odd that he was holding Carson.

"What game did you play?" I asked.

"We played *Go Fish.* He said I had to find all the same numbers and all the same letters and if I found four that were the same I got to make a stack. I got all the A's and all the Q's."

We all filed into the living room and when we did the familiarity of it all was, almost, too much. I slowly sank into the soft couch, with Rusty next to me, and Carson in my lap, and Katie chattering away next to me. Right next to me! Things I thought I might never see again. It could have been gone with the pull of a trigger, but it wasn't, it was here. *I* was here.

"Mommy? Why are you crying?" Katie asked.

"It's okay sweetheart. Sometimes mommies cry because they are happy. I'm just so happy to see you."

Chapter 57

The doe raised her head and I froze. I stood without moving, patiently waiting for her to relax and go back to her breakfast. Even stalking deer I was on guard. I expected trouble to come at me every moment of every day. I woke with a start in the night expecting to see a gun barrel. Stalking deer I was just as alert as the deer were. Any little sound would make me look, just like the doe I'd wait, watch and when everything was peaceful again I'd go back to whatever I was doing. This doe and I had something in common. I wanted to ask her if she ever felt at ease. The deer *looked* peaceful as they milled about the yard but every time they caught my movement they were instantly alert, instantly focused. I wanted to ask them how they cope living like that all the time. It seemed I was going to have to learn that way of life. The life of a deer. The herd grew uneasy but I wasn't ready to go inside. And then I realized their nervousness came from another direction. When the focus was drawn away I dropped to the ground and lay there watching them. What did they see that wasn't me? They were uncomfortable. They looked boxed in. Trapped, though they weren't. They had plenty of options. It would take a small army to surround this yard. I crawled in closer to get an idea of how they felt, but I couldn't see it. Then, like an order was given, all the deer stood and trotted off. The doe closest to me sidestepped around me to join the herd.

"Damn it, Mick, I told you to wait in the car," Chase said.

I still couldn't see him. He stepped out of the junipers and walked into the yard.

Slowly I rose to a sitting position. He sat down next to me on the ground. We sat in silence for a minute and Mick got embarrassed and went into the house.

"You okay, kid?"

It took me a while to come up with an honest answer.

"Most of the time."

"I didn't mean for this to all fall on you."

"I know."

"I would have taken your place in a heartbeat, but it wouldn't have worked."

"I know."

"You do?"

"It would have been worse, and he would have made you watch. The treatment would have been worse, the punishments harsher. You chose right."

"Did I?"

"I need to know one thing."

"Yeah?"

"Is it over? Is there a way to know if it's really over?"

"*It* will never be over. As long as there is big money in drugs, the trade will flourish. The danger to *you* is over. Morales is gone. His top men are arrested. The reward is either given out or tied up with enough legal red tape to be unattainable. We hit Morales with enough firepower to shut down a major distributor. I think it worked out well. I just wish it hadn't fallen on you."

"Seems like a lot for a little American housewife to take on."

"Nah, not Dangerous Tracker Woman."

He stood up and offered me a hand up. That was the signal that this conversation was ended. I had a rookie cop inside who was going to want to go tracking. Or ground squirrel fishing. It looked like I had my old life back.

I've had many a close call. You name it, it has happened to me. Every time I managed to come back, whether physically, or mentally, or emotionally. I'd made it back and I'd keep making it back, but I no longer looked forward to the next challenge. There was too much at stake now. To leave Katie and Carson to grow up without a mommy. To hurt Rusty that way. I had to find a way to keep trouble away. We began life anew, with a new hope and a new focus. I still answered my phone whenever Strict had a call. But I held my kids close and I felt their warmth and their presence every day. I made it a point to stay close to Rusty. I needed his presence.

I kept sounding out words for Katie, though she drove me to distraction. I knew she was just being me at three. Except her focus was words. Right now it was words. It would always be something, because she was driven. If something caught her attention it didn't just exist, it was something to explore. So at the moment she was exploring words and someday the focus would shift and she would drive me bananas in some other way, because she was me, at three. I kept reminding myself, it was my own fault. She would always be hyper curious and hyper alert. And I would always be on my toes keeping up with her. And I was glad. I really was. I couldn't wait to see what Carson would come up with. And so I lived… semi normally, until the next time trouble came knocking.